# Rogue
## Sons of Sangue

Patricia A. Rasey

Copyright © 2016 by Patricia A. Rasey.

All rights reserved. No part of this publication may be reproduced, distributed or transmitted in any form or by any means, including photocopying, recording, or other electronic or mechanical methods, without the prior written permission of the publisher, except in the case of brief quotations embodied in critical reviews and certain other noncommercial uses permitted by copyright law. For permission requests, write to the publisher, addressed "Attention: Permissions Coordinator," at the address below.

Patricia A. Rasey
patricia@patriciarasey.com
www.PatriciaRasey.com

Publisher's Note: This is a work of fiction. Names, characters, places, and incidents are a product of the author's imagination. Locales and public names are sometimes used for atmospheric purposes. Any resemblance to actual people, living or dead, or to businesses, companies, events, institutions, or locales is completely coincidental.

Book Layout ©2013 BookDesignTemplates.com

Ordering Information:
Quantity sales. Special discounts are available on quantity purchases by corporations, associations, and others. For details, contact the email address above.

Rogue: Sons of Sangue / Patricia A. Rasey – 1st ed.
ISBN-13: 978-0-9903325-5-8

# Praise for Sons of Sangue

"Every book from this author catches you hook line and sinker. Each one gets better and better and makes you fall in love with all the men...I cannot wait for the next book. It cannot get here fast enough. Once again Patricia Rasey blows you away with her writing skills. A must read!!!"
—*Rogue: Joey, GoodReads*

"Outlaw vampire bikers. The women who tame them. What's not to love? Patricia Rasey's new series Sons of Sangue is hot!"
—*Viper: Monette Michaels, author of Security Specialists International series*

"A lot of the arcs started in the first book have some closure in this one along with a surprise at the end. Ms Rasey again does a perfect job of blending the life of a MC club along with the life of vampires."
—*Hawk: Cindy 0, SnS Reviews*

"Intensity is an understatement for the hot mess that plagues the Sons of Sangue in GYPSY. Deceit is thick in the air. Brotherhood is tested. Revenge is a must. Sexual tension is taken to a new level. That's just the beginning. Patricia Rasey has the reader going full throttle into a wicked storm. Action from beginning to end, twists that hit you like a brass knuckled fist and lust building like a bomb waiting to go off..."
—*Gypsy: Deana, Coffee Books Life*

**Other Books by Patricia A. Rasey:**
Viper: Sons of Sangue (#1)
Hawk: Sons of Sangue (#2)
Gypsy: Sons of Sangue (#3)
Love You to Pieces
Deadly Obsession
The Hour Before Dawn
Kiss of Deceit
Eyes of Betrayal
Façade

**Novellas:**
Spirit Me Away
Heat Wave
Fear the Dark
Sanitarium

### *Dedication*

*To my readers, for without you
I would have no one to share my stories with.*

*Thank you for reading my work!*

## Acknowledgements

Thank you to my cover artist, Frauke Spanuth, from Croco Designs for creating the Sons of Sangue covers, and making Rogue one of my favorite covers to date.

To my editor, Catherine Snodgrass, for helping me see what I cannot and helping me make my story the best possible.

## CHAPTER ONE

*IMBECILES!*
Each and every one of them.

Anton "Rogue" Balan sat sideways on the black leather seat of his custom Harley Davidson Road King, his booted feet kicked out in front of him, crossed at the ankles. Sweat slipped down his spine and dampened his tank as well as his mood. Two of his current MC brothers stood bloodied and bruised in the center of the gravel parking lot as they continued to beat the shit out of one another. Anton couldn't recall what started the blood bath, though likely nothing more than a vulgar joke or insult aimed at someone's mother. The Devils were a savage bunch.

One year, one month, and six days.

Lord, he wasn't sure how much more time he'd have to spend in the company of these fucks. A day would be too much.

The scent of human blood wafted to his nose. He had to tamp down the rising lust for arteries or wind up sporting fangs and having to explain the unusual change in his appearance. It had been a little over three days since he last fed. Anton needed to make the trip north, and soon, to get communion. He couldn't chance the death chill — the translucent presentation of skin — making a sudden appearance due to his lack of feeding. For all pretenses and purposes, his life depended on his anonymity and ability to blend in.

Well, as much as a six-foot-five, two hundred and fifty pound vampire could.

He had left his old life behind. His once blond hair had been dyed black and cut short. The hair color went along with the moniker Blondy. Now, those around him knew him as Rogue. Anton had buried Blondy over a year ago when he had taken the job asked of him. The Devils had only been too happy to help rid him of everything that reminded them of his past life with the Sons of Sangue, their rival MC.

Following the little power play between the two low-ranking Devils, he'd make his excuses and get the hell out of Santa Barbara for a few days. He had about enough of his present company to last him a good long while. Maybe this trip he'd hide out at his farmhouse off the Oregon coast for a few days of downtime. He didn't give a rat's ass what Tank, the Devils' president, might think of his unplanned trip for a little R&R. He had been doing nothing more than playing babysitter to a bunch of younger Devils, keeping them out of as much trouble as he possibly could.

Apparently, it was rumored the La Paz Cartel had fallen under the DEA's radar and their kingpin, Raúl Trevino Caballero, had ordered the MC to lay low. To Anton's dismay, as well as that of Cara Brahnam and her mate Kane "Viper" Tepes, who had helped him infiltrate the rival gang, he had yet to seal a meet and greet with the feared leader of the Mexican cartel.

Tank, on the other hand, had begun to trust in Anton implicitly. The Devils put in his charge either toed the line or received a beat down Anton was only too willing to give. Tank had told him on numerous occasions his crew had rarely feared anyone — that was until Anton had turned rogue against his own MC.

Little did Tank know, Anton would rather cut off his right arm than actually betray the Sons.

The shorter Devil, whom Anton knew as Spike, rushed the taller, thicker brother nicknamed Boston. The latter received his moniker due to his heavy New England accent. Boston sidestepped Spike and sent him sprawling to the gravel, before pouncing on his back, gripping his spiked hair, and shoving his bloodied face into the dirt and stones.

With a heavy sigh, Anton pushed off his bike, having had enough of the mostly one-sided beating taking place. His large hand easily spanned Boston's thick neck as he pulled the man from his comrade. Rather than fight a losing battle with Anton, Boston thankfully went willing. Once Anton let go of his grip, Boston wiped off his bloodied hands on his grimy, navy-blue work Dickies. Spike took a considerable amount of time to crawl off the stone parking lot, ignoring Anton's outstretched hand. The spiked-haired Devil spit gravel as he did so, maybe even a tooth as well. Anton wasn't about to look too closely at the blood and spittle landing precariously close to his boot. Had the ass made the misfortune of actually hitting it, Anton would have given him a second beating.

He had little patience left. Hence his much needed R&R.

"I could've taken care of myself." Spike spat to the gravel again, his shoulders slightly hunched. "I was just about to give Boston a whoopin' like he ain't ever seen before."

Anton raised one brow. "Can it, Spike. Or maybe I'll let Boston finish what you started in the first place. Guys like you don't know when it's time to shut your trap. Let me clue you in, you stupid son of a bitch. That would be now."

Spike opened his mouth, then wisely closed it. He ran the back of his filthy hand across his lips and turned his glare on Anton. Dumb fuck knew better than to mess with him. All the boys standing in a semi-circle, watching the party, did. Anton had the patience of a saint, but push him beyond his limit, and these young punks put under his watch were lucky to remain vertical.

He winked at Spike, unable to help himself from further pissing off the scrawny bastard. "Keep it up and I'll make you boys kiss and make up."

The Devils standing to his left and right chuckled at his little quip. Boston, however, scowled as he slid onto his Low Rider. He turned the key and gave Anton his middle finger before hitting the gas and spraying gravel against the brick side of Hades' Nest, the Devils normal hangout. Apparently, he wasn't in the mood for make-up sex. Spike, on the other hand, just sneered a "fuck you," before turning and walking back into the bar.

A song from Morbid Angel spilled into the parking lot before the door once again closed and muffled the sound. Anton ran a hand through his shorn locks and finger-combed the overlong bangs from his eyes. He headed for his own Harley and grabbed his skull cap, hanging from the rubber handle grip.

Bobby "Preacher" Bourassa approached him. He got his nickname from the twin cross tattoos on his muscled shoulders. That and the fact he used to be a preacher some years ago, before joining the Devils. The man was built like a beast.

"Where you off to, Rogue? Use some company?"

Bobby happened to be the one Devil Anton could say he actually liked. He placed the cap on his head and buckled it beneath his chin. "Not today, Preacher. I'm going north for a few days. You tell Tank I'll be back in about a week. If he needs me, he can call. I'll be a day's ride out."

He scratched his whiskered chin. "I doubt he'll be too happy to hear you left these boys on their own."

"They aren't fucking kindergartners. You tell them boys if they give me cause, I'll give them a beat down when I return."

"What do you want me to tell Tank?"

"I don't give a fuck. For all I care, you can tell him I have a piece of ass I need to attend to." Which brought one woman to the forefront of his mind.

*Kimber James.*

All legs and tits large enough to make a grown man's mouth water.

He always had been a breast man, and Kimber certainly had more than her fare share. *Pillows from heaven.* Too bad she'd no doubt rather take on a pit of vipers than bed his sorry ass again.

He shook his head at the injustice.

Being Mr. Nice Guy had gotten him on the fast track to nowhere.

His former best friend hated him and had mated with the one woman Anton thought he could be happy spending the rest of his days with. Tamera Cantrell, though, wasn't meant for Anton as much as he might've envisioned at one time. She belonged with Grayson "Gypsy" Gabor, no matter how much Anton had hoped otherwise.

Which brought him back to Kimber James.

The last time Anton had seen her, he had all but run her cute little derriere out of his house, while she cursed the ground beneath his feet. The motorcycle cut he wore over his white tank weighed heavy, damning him for the very thing she detested.

Her parting words mocked him. *"Too bad. I really thought you might be one of the good guys."*

Yeah, well so did he. Anton turned the key to his motorcycle and gassed the engine. With a final nod to Bobby, he turned the big bike around in the parking lot and aimed it north. With any luck, he'd leave California behind in a few short hours and be back on familiar turf.

*First stop?* The Blood 'n' Rave. He could certainly use one of the blood donors the barkeep, Draven, had hand selected for the secret society that fed the Sons of Sangue. He'd have to use the back door to keep any of his fellow MC brothers from seeing him. Even though his entire life at the moment was a ruse, the rest of his brothers actually believed him to be a traitor.

Tightening his hands on the rubber grips of his sixteen inch ape hangers, he pulled back on the gas and buried the needle of his speedometer. The taller handlebars aided in a more comfortable ride for someone of his height. Comfort was certainly key with the long ride he had ahead of him. Anton planned to lay his head on his pillow at his farmhouse on the coast before the sun rose over the Pacific.

THE FAINT, FAMILIAR SOUND OF a motorcycle approaching caught Kimber James's attention as she watered her soft pink heirloom roses she had cultivated off her back porch. She couldn't help the ache sneaking up and taking a hold of her heart. At one time she had fashioned herself very much in like with the large blond mechanic. So much so, she had easily fallen into his arms. *Not to mention his king-sized bed.* In truth, it hadn't taken much effort on his part to seduce her.

Too bad she had been nothing more than one night's entertainment.

*Lord, she hated regrets.*

Anton Balan was a crude, foul-mouthed biker. She had no business entertaining fantasies with him as the major player. And a player he was. He had played her like a violin.

Kimber couldn't help the small smile from surfacing at the remembrance. Okay, so she had thoroughly enjoyed every moment spent in his bed. Anton had been a consummate lover. He had taken his time to make sure she had enjoyed the act, if not more so than he had. A blush warmed her cheeks. Not that she had a lot of experience with men. He certainly hadn't been her first, but he had been the only man to have ever given her the big O.

Too bad he turned out to be someone she was better off not associating with, because she wouldn't have minded a repeat performance. Anton Balan was a walking, talking sex machine who knew his way around the bedroom. Just thinking about his hands on her flesh sent a shiver down her spine and an ache to her groin.

Now all she had left were memories.

*But oh, what good memories they were.*

Following Anton's send-off a little over a year ago, she had tried dating again, slept with a couple of men, but neither had measured up to the sizzling hot blond biker, leaving her with more regrets.

Damn the man for giving her a night she couldn't wipe from her memory, no matter how she had tried. He'd become the world's biggest asshole. So instead of winding up with a long list of failed dates, she poured herself into her job as head librarian at the Florence Library. At twenty-eight, she had plenty of time to find a man … once she managed to purge her gorgeous neighbor from said fantasies. Envisioning his handsome face and gym-perfect body while he sat astride his Harley Davidson wasn't helping matters. Put simply, the man oozed sex from every pore.

Unable to curb her curiosity, she shut off the water and skirted her rose garden. Clearing the side of the house,

Kimber caught sight of the large man astride his bike just as he turned into his driveway. Even as far away as she stood, she didn't miss the slight turn of his head, as if he had felt her presence. Another shiver washed over her. Sun rays glinted off his aviator style sunglasses.

No sense hiding the fact she had been spying. Instead of waving, though, she gave him her back and returned to the garden. She couldn't help the quickening of her pulse, but she damn well could keep from doing anything about it.

Just as she reached for her watering hose, her phone rang.

Kimber jogged up the back porch steps and grabbed her cell lying on the table to her patio set. At a glance, she saw it was one of her coworkers, making her wonder if everything at work was okay. She certainly hoped Tena wasn't calling to ask her to take her shift. Even though Kimber would oblige, as usual, she had been looking forward to the long weekend.

"Hey, Tena." Kimber brushed her wet hand on her jeans. "What's up?"

"I have a huge favor to ask."

"Let me get dressed. I can be at the library within the half hour."

"What? Oh, no." She heard Tena chuckle. "I'm already here and just about to clock in. That's not why I called."

Kimber's brow creased. Tena didn't normally call her out of the blue unless it was work related. "What can I do for you then?"

"There's this guy I met. He's hot as hell."

"That's awesome, Tena." Kimber chuckled. Her younger colleague seemed to find a "hot as hell" guy monthly, though this was the first time she had called Kimber about it. "So what does this have to do with me?"

She heard the hesitation in Tena's voice and couldn't help thinking she wasn't going to like what the younger girl was about to ask. "The Blood 'n' Rave is the place to be on the weekends. And ... everyone's busy tonight..."

"Except for me," Kimber finished for her. Was she truly that much of an introvert?

"You have to admit, Kimber, you rarely go out in the evenings. It's not like us girls and Chad haven't invited you before, but you say no more than you say yes."

*Yep, she had definitely become an introvert.*

Kimber had gone only on a rare occasion to the nightclubs with her coworkers, and Chad, being in favor of the same sex, loved to hang with the girls from work. The Blood 'n' Rave, though, pushed the boundaries of where she was willing to go for a drink. Murphy's Tavern was more her style. From her knowledge, most of those hanging at the Blood 'n' Rave were either ravers or the local outlaws, Sons of Sangue. Which brought Anton back to the forefront of her thoughts. The Sons of Sangue were a rival gang of the Devils. At least she wouldn't have to worry about running into her sexy-as-sin neighbor while at the nightclub.

"Kimber?"

"Oh, I'm sorry, Tena. I don't know."

"Please? I don't want to go alone and I know he'll be there." Her sympathetic tone had Kimber already caving to the request.

*Damn.*

Kimber needed to learn the word *no*. Even when it came to work, everyone knew to ask her if they wanted to call off. Her coworkers took advantage of her regularly, not that she really minded. Kimber loved her job. There was nothing better than the smell and feel of books. They had kept her company many lonely nights. Took her places she couldn't otherwise afford to travel.

"Pretty please?" Tena broke into her reverie. "This might be the future mister to my missus. You wouldn't want to be the reason I missed meeting Mister Forever-and-Always, would you?"

Kimber took a deep breath before slowly releasing it, knowing she would no doubt regret — *damn them regrets* — her decision. Not wanting to stand in the way of what could be true love, unlikely as it was, she sighed. "What time?"

"Oh, Kimber, I could kiss you." Tena giggled. Kimber could easily imagine her dancing about the library's break room. "After work. I can meet you in the parking lot at nine."

"You best not leave me standing."

"I'll be there. Promise."

Kimber smiled in spite of her reluctance to go within a hundred yards of the place. "Now if I can figure out what to wear."

"Just don't wear white. You'll glow like a beacon under the black lights. Okay, got to get to work. See you at nine," Tena said and the cell went dead.

She laid the phone on the table and stared at it for long moments. Kimber stifled a groan. Those regrets were already settling in.

## CHAPTER TWO

The setting sun cast an orange glow over the horizon as Anton pulled his bike to a stop on the gravel lot located behind the Blood 'n' Rave and killed the engine. Being shortly after nine, ravers were starting to pour into the nightclub. The muffled sounds of industrial music spilled into the parking lot, the loud bass thumping against his chest. He used his boot heel to kick down the kickstand before disembarking.

A sense of nostalgia washed over him.

He missed coming here, hanging with his brothers and the camaraderie they shared. His heart weighed heavy. Pulling off his skull cap, he hung the helmet from one of the handle grips and finger-combed his still-damp hair. Anton looked across the lot and the many cars illuminated by the streetlights, wishing like hell he could turn back time. He couldn't help wonder if this job hadn't cost him far too much. He still would've agreed to help Cara, for that he held no contrition, but not to keep the secret from his brothers.

Had he been able to turn back the clock, he wouldn't agree to keep the MC in the dark. Their hate of him was almost too much to bear. Not to mention they actually thought him capable of such a betrayal.

Upon arrival to his home turf, Anton had headed straight for his farmhouse in much need of a shower, removing the grime and dust from his long ride up the coast, and for a fresh set of clothes. He had felt her presence the moment he hit his driveway as surely as if her fingers had tickled up his spine, raising the goose flesh on his arms. Kimber James had stood at the corner of her house, her gaze locking with his. Instead of acknowledging his return, she had simply given him her back and walked out of sight around the corner of her quaint little farmhouse. Not even so much as a wave.

Anton grimaced.

*Good.*

No matter what his libido might have to say about the little librarian, she was off-limits. He had a job to do and he'd see it through to the end. Anton wasn't about to put Kimber in danger with the cartel or the Devils because he desired to have her long legs wrapping his waist. If the men he now associated with even so much as got wind he was working with the cops, they wouldn't hesitate to go after someone he cared about.

Like it or not, Kimber definitely fell into that category.

Which was reason enough to keep his distance.

No way in hell could he travel down that road with someone who didn't know of vampires' existence, not to mention that according to Sons of Sangue law she was not mate material. Only donors could become mates. Using his key to unlock the back door of the Rave, Anton stepped into the dim interior of the storeroom, his eyes easily adjusting. Draven had thought it best if Anton used the rear entrance to steer clear of the Sons — the barkeep no more privy to his undercover work than the rest of his brethren. Cara had made it clear, for all those involved, the less who knew about his involvement, the safer everyone would be. Draven was the highest risk, since the Devils wouldn't think twice about taking him out. Being mortal, he wouldn't stand a chance should they decide he had outlived his usefulness.

Anton's keen senses kicked in the minute he cleared the door. He scented Alexander and Grigore just beyond the door leading to the bar. They no doubt lounged there, knocking back whiskeys, which meant they were well aware Anton had arrived. He needn't have to worry. They had been in the building at the same moment many times before. The Sons may not like him much at the moment, but they wouldn't be cruel enough to deny him communion.

Over the past year, Anton had to rely on Draven either bringing donors down the coast, or making the long trek back, which wasn't always the ideal situation. On occasion, he had used an outsider for nourishment, having to resort to hypnotism to wipe their memories clean of the intimate act. He much preferred using donors. Taking someone's blood without their permission didn't sit right with him. Though color it any way he like, survival was animalistic. One needed food to remain among the living and at times he had to resort to whatever means necessary. Anton had to make do with the situation presented to him, and traveling home to Oregon every three to four days would have raised suspicion with the Devils.

He glanced at the clock on the wall. Nine thirty five. He had told Draven he would arrive on the half hour, and the barkeep had yet to bring him a donor, putting a damper on his already sour mood. The sooner he fed, the quicker he was on his way and back off the Sons' radar. Anton was pretty sure the two brothers on the other side of the door probably felt much the same. He detested the fact his comrades despised him for defecting. He might as well suck it up. In the end, it wasn't Cara or Kane's fault for the situation he found himself in. He had been the one to agree to it. Plain and simple. Anton couldn't leave Draven hanging out to dry on his own. Someone needed to be on the inside to protect him. In the end, if Kane got his justice against the man who had caused the death of his son, Ion, then Anton would consider it time well spent, no matter the repercussions.

The door to the bar opened, spilling the loud club music into the room. India, a dark-skinned donor, closed the door behind her. The woman was gorgeous, with a pair of legs that seemed to go on forever. Any man would feel lucky to have them wrapping his waist.

If he was only looking to get laid...

He had fed from India before, but never once mixing his food with pleasure where she was concerned. He preferred to keep things platonic with most donors. Not saying he was a saint. Just less drama in the end. India's blood had a smooth smoky flavor. Each blood donor had their own unique taste, which is why some of the Sons preferred one donor over the other.

He found India's blood definitely pleasing to his palate, but he wasn't about to feed exclusively. The less they expected, the fewer feelings that got hurt along the way. For now, his life was in Santa Barbara. Coming to Oregon was purely about nourishment.

Anton stifled a chuckle.

Who the hell was he trying to fool? Oregon was his home … always would be. No matter how many days and weeks he spent south of the border, his heart remained north of it. Spending much time on his home turf in the last year hadn't been an option.

*Until now.*

Anton needed a little R&R, and he didn't give two shits what Tank had to say about the matter. He'd lay low for a week or two before heading back to his life with the Devils. Fuck Tank, or anyone else for that matter, if they didn't like it. He needed to get the hell away from the men who occupied his days. He feared losing his shit and taking a few of them out. Some of them were simply a waste of good oxygen.

"Hey there, handsome." India smiled, taking Anton's mind off the unpleasantness of his life.

His gums ached as his fangs filled his mouth and his eyes heated, telling him they had transformed to twin obsidian coals. Anton worked the tightness from his jaw as he watched India approach with a slight sway to her hips. Her pink tongue darted out to wet her lips, divulging her nerves. India never hid the fact she preferred being just a donor, not really wanting more from the Sons. She needn't worry. Anton wasn't looking for a piece of ass.

Out of all the Sons, Anton probably abstained the most. Truth of it, in the past couple of years, he had been preoccupied with a fucked up love triangle. One he had been destined to lose from the beginning, but was too damn enamored to see it. Tamera Cantrell had been an infatuation for him long before Grayson stepped up to the plate and finally took back what was rightfully his in the first place. Disappointment and heartache had followed for Anton. He'd never stood a chance. The knowledge hadn't made the sting of rejection any less.

His feisty neighbor came to mind.

She too had a way with twisting his guts with longing. Kimber had no idea vampires existed, making her more off-limits than Tamera had been. Vampires and humans didn't mix for risk of exposure. Rules were put into place to keep them safe from exposure. Draven kept a good supply of donors around for feeding and sexual release. Each donor brought in knew the consequences of telling their secret. Their lives depended on the ability to keep their mouths shut. Mates were to be found among them.

Anton could only imagine what Kimber might think should she look upon him as he stood before India, ready to feed. The one time he had seduced the librarian into his bed, he had hypnotized her into forgetting his vampiric features. Foolhardy? Most certainly, but he couldn't say he regretted a second of it.

Repeat performance slammed into his thoughts, causing an arrow of extreme hunger of another kind to shoot straight for his cock. Maybe he ought to quit being the good guy — *look where that had gotten him.* He certainly could use the release.

Every muscle in his body ached with the thought of getting Kimber back into his bed. Christ, he wanted to sink his cock deep into her, feel her surround him and make him forget the shitty hand he had been dealt. Anton hadn't been exactly celibate over the past year. He had slept with a few of the Devils' club bitches, but they held nothing on Kimber. Strip away the outer appearances and the little librarian turned into quite the fiery little nymph.

His biggest regret in this whole mess was letting her walk away when all he wanted to do was bed her again. Hell, he needed to fuck her from his thoughts. No good would come from his obsession. But even so, that didn't stop him from wanting her.

India held out her hand and led Anton to the sofa in the corner of the room. He skirted the ottoman and sat, pulling the black-haired woman between his spread knees. Her gaze dropped to the bulge in his jeans. Blood lust easily caused the effect, but this hard-on had nothing to do with his hunger, and everything to do with his thoughts of the librarian.

*Kimber was taboo.*

He needed to get that through his thick skull.

This trip to Oregon had been a bad idea from the start. All it had accomplished thus far was his desire for Kimber returning with the force of a locomotive. And just like that locomotive, even if the brakes were applied, there was no stopping it on a dime. He'd need to find a way to exorcise her from his mind, no matter how long it took.

India's gaze quickly darted away, no doubt misunderstanding the cause of his erection. He needed to ease her apprehension and get on with the communion. Not that India wasn't beautiful, and maybe under different circumstances he wouldn't have minded taking the feeding a step further.

But not today.

Only one woman would do.

With a growl of frustration, Anton cupped the back of India's skull and titled her head to the side. The smell of her blood teased his nostrils. Anton opened his mouth wide and sank his fangs into her artery. The soft pop of her flesh carried to his ears. Warm blood ran over his tongue and coated his throat, filling him with heat and soothing the ache of hunger in his stomach.

India groaned, her body going languid in his grip. His hands smoothed down her spine, anchoring her to him. Her blood had a slightly different tinge than he remembered; he couldn't quite put a finger on it. As he continued to take his fill, Anton missed India's rising apprehension until she fisted the front of his tee shirt. He released his fangs with a hiss.

Anton quickly sealed the twin holes with his tongue, the saliva having healing properties, and set her away from him.

His gaze took in India's. Moisture gathered in her eyes. Damn, he was an ass. Gripping her chin between his forefinger and thumb, Anton tilted her face to his.

"I'm sorry, India. I never meant to make you uneasy."

Her gaze dropped. "It's me."

"Has someone hurt you?"

"You don't need me to unload my troubles on you, Blondy." She took in a shaky breath before looking him in the eyes again. "You're a good man. All the donors know you're the Son with the biggest heart. Look at what you did for Tamera, holding her through her change when Gypsy had all but abandoned her."

Her reminder soured his gut. "That may have been, India, but I'm not the same man I was a year ago."

She snorted as if she didn't believe it were possible.

"You really should stop referring to me as Blondy." Even though she had fed him over the past year, knew he had deflected, she continued to treat him as if her were still a Son. "He's dead."

"Because of Gypsy and Tamera?"

"It would be easy enough to continue to blame them, but no. I've changed."

Her gaze held his for a long moment, then she said, "You can fool the rest of them, but you don't fool me. If you were the changed man you say you are — you would've tried to take advantage of the blood lust. You didn't."

She was astute. He'd give her that. To tell her he hungered for another woman and wouldn't be crass enough to fuck her while he continued to do so would only solidify her argument the old Blondy was still somewhere in there.

He turned his lips down. "I needed to feed. That's your reason for standing here. Fucking's not part of the deal, unless the donor says it is. That doesn't mean I didn't want to."

India smiled, despite the moisture still filling her gaze. "You can change your hair, hang with assholes, and try to fool everyone, Blondy—"

"It's Rogue."

"Rogue, whatever. You don't fool me." She placed a palm over his sternum. "I know inside here, there's a man with a big heart. He's still in there. What you did for Tamera, helping her through her change when Gypsy was being an ass, proved you're a good man. Whatever's going on with you, I hope you get it figured out. No matter what leaves your lips, I think there's still a Son somewhere in here." She tapped his chest.

His face heated. Anton couldn't afford for her to trip up his game. He gripped her wrists and leaned down, his nose just inches from hers. "No one gives a fuck what you think, India, least of all me. You did your job, now take your nosy ass back into the bar and away from me."

Tears slipped from her lashes. "Whatever, Rogue. Go back down the coast, if that's what makes you feel better. Until you decide to be true to yourself, next time you need to feed? Request someone else."

She yanked her wrists from his grip and headed for the door. Anton's breath damn near stopped him dead. It wasn't from India's parting words, but the scent wafting through the opened door.

*What the hell was Kimber James doing at the Rave?*

Anton strode to the door and all but pulled it from its hinges. Fire slid through his veins as he caught sight of Grigore "Wolf" Lupei with his big ass paw on the small of her back, offering to buy her drink. Her gaze landed on his, pulling at his groin. Anton gritted his teeth just as Grigore's angry glare found his.

"What the fuck, Rogue?" Alexander, the normally quiet Son, drew his attention briefly. Anton couldn't help but wonder just what the hell his problem was.

Grigore frowned and his face turned ugly. "What the fuck are you looking at, boy?"

## CHAPTER THREE

Kimber felt Anton's eyes the moment they landed on her, heating her from the inside and making an already warm night damn near unbearable. He was the last person she expected to encounter at the Blood 'n' Rave. Yet, he filled the doorway on the other side of the polished bar, looking like a wet dream.

Two-hundred-and-fifty pounds of lean muscle.

And ... black hair? Though the color and cut more than suited him, she couldn't help wonder the reason.

A shiver traveled down her spine as his icy blue gaze raked over her, staying on her breasts a bit longer than appropriate before stopping at her waist and the hand now residing there. Kimber had been about to remove it when the over-friendly man rose to his feet, puffing his chest out. Moments ago, Tena had all but skipped off to the dance floor with said hot guy she came to meet. Wanting a margarita and not relishing the idea of standing alone near all the ravers, Kimber had approached the bar. Before she could place her order, the guy to her left, wearing a Sons of Sangue vest, had placed his hand on her person as if it were his right.

Although she was thankful for Anton's sudden appearance, and being saved from having to remove the man's hand, she now worried about being faced with an all-out war.

The Sons of Sangue would not be happy to have a rival gang member standing on their turf. She had seen situations like these in documentaries. Guns, knives ... out-and-out blood battles all over OMC territories.

Unsure what to do, other than save Anton from a beating the two Sons seemed ready to hand out, she skirted the bar. "There you are, honey."

Anton's dark brows met over the bridge of his nose as he looked down on her. "What—"

Kimber placed two fingers on his full lips, remembering all too well how they felt smoothing over her flesh and tasting every inch of her. Shaking off the erotic image, she needed to keep him from spoiling her brilliantly crafted ruse. She'd deal with the ramifications of it once she got him away from the threat of the rival gang.

"What the fuck are you doing here, boy?" The man who had taken liberties with her person spoke up again. His tone told Kimber she had been correct in her assessment. He meant to physically remove Anton from the premises if need be. "Rule is you don't fucking come out here."

"I suggest you mind your manners when a lady is present."

"I think the lady is capable of speaking for herself." The large man took a step in their direction. "You want to take it outside, Rogue?"

Anton's taut cheek told Kimber he wasn't about to back down. Before he could reply, she stood on her tiptoes and nipped his chin with her teeth. "What took you so long, babe?"

"What the hell are you doing, Kimber?" His deep voice washed over her like a shot of warm whiskey.

"I didn't realize this wasn't exactly an appropriate place to meet." She winked at him, hoping he'd for once keep his mouth shut. "We can go someplace else."

Placing a hand in the center of his rock-hard chest, Kimber pushed him backward, through the doorway and into the room he had shared with the tall, dark-skinned woman who had exited moments ago. Never mind what they might have been doing. It was none of her business. Clearing the door, she quickly slammed it with her free hand, effectively shutting out the bar noise and the two Sons.

Anton gripped her wrists and quickly set her away from him. His gaze moved to the door, causing her to worry he might stalk right back into the bar. Instead, he turned his anger on her. "What the hell are you doing, Kimber? Following me?"

Kimber yanked her wrists free of his large hands. "You *would* think that, you arrogant ass."

He raised one brow and waited for her to answer. Damn, this close there was no denying his hotness. His sexual appeal was off the charts. He smelled of man and musk. She gave her head a brief shake as she tried to remember exactly what Anton had asked. Too bad he turned out to be such a bastard. She wouldn't have minded taking him home for another go around.

"Answer me." His irritation was clearly evident in his cool gaze and the stern set of his jaw. "Well?"

She rubbed her nape. "Ummm... What was the question?"

"What. Are. You. Doing. Here?"

"I'm not deaf, Anton. Just flustered. Forgive me for not expecting to see you tonight." Kimber jammed her fists onto her hips. "As if it's any of your damn business, I came here at the invitation of a friend."

"A male friend?"

"What?" He had been the one to chase her off, not the other way around. Not to mention, he seemed quite often in the company of the opposite sex. He had no right at all to question anything she did. "As if you would care."

"You shouldn't come here, Kimber. Ever. Do I make myself clear?"

With a roll of her eyes, she snorted. "This isn't exactly my scene, Anton. Murphy's Tavern is more my speed."

"Good, then I'll escort you over to *that* bar."

Anton reached for her, but she took a step back. Lord, she didn't need the extra stimulation his touch caused. Just being in the same room with him had her naughty parts humming with unrequited desire. Even angry he was all sorts of sexy. Kimber shifted her stance, trying to alleviate the ache centered in the V of her thighs.

"I'm with a friend."

"Wolf or Xander?" he all but growled.

"Who?" Her voice rose, having had about enough of his surly attitude. He should be thanking her from stopping the beating he was about to receive from those two buffoons.

"The two idiots at the bar you were cozying up to."

"Lord, you're either blind or stupid." She ran a hand through her hair in frustration. What the hell did she see in him? *Plenty*, her overactive brain reminded her. "I'm here with a coworker. She was on the dance floor and I was about to order a drink."

"You in the habit of letting strange men paw you?"

Oh, he so overstepped his boundaries. Her ire shot to the metal roof. "Not since you. I guess I should thank you for curing me."

Kimber thought she heard a slight chuckle, but the look on his face didn't give way to any traces of humor. "Just in case you might be wondering, I'm a much better fuck than Wolf."

"The guy with the roaming hands? And you would know this because..." She let it hang in hopes he'd elaborate. *This ought to be good.* She'd be damned before she'd feed his ego, even if he no doubt was better in bed.

"You see any women hanging around Wolf before you arrived at the bar?"

"No, but that doesn't mean anything. The night is early. He has plenty of time to pick up a date."

"Looked to me like he was heading in that direction before I opened the door."

"What about the woman you had in here with you?" Her forefinger indicated the orange sofa in the corner. "I suppose you were offering her *your* services on that ugly couch."

"As I recall, you didn't complain about my servicing you."

Her face heated, no sense in pretending he was wrong. The regret was that he'd turned into an Grade A ass afterward and she hadn't gotten a second sampling. "I had no complaints."

A slight grin edged up his lips. "I don't suppose."

"You have sex with her?"

The smile left his face as quickly as it appeared. "I'm not about to deny what's obviously none of your business, Kimber."

Why the hell she allowed the thought of him screwing some other woman in the back room of a bar bother her, she refused to examine. It wasn't as if they had dated. They slept together … once. No strings attached. Anton had never led her to believe it had been anything more.

"You're right." She nodded. "Who you sleep with isn't my business, any more than who I do. Wolf? He's all kinds of sexy, if you ask me."

Anton swiftly gripped her wrist. In the blink of an eye, he pulled her flush against his rock-hard sternum. Her breath left her chest. His steely erection lay hot between them. Either that answered her question whether he had sex with the dark haired woman, or he was ready for round two already.

"Don't fucking think about it," he growled. "Every one of the Sons are off-limits to you."

"Why?"

"Trust me, they're not known to be nice."

"And you are?"

"I never claimed to be, *tesoro*. As a matter of fact, I'm the last person you should ever be alone with. Being nice to you isn't exactly what I have in mind."

Anton's gaze fell to her lips as if he meant to kiss her, and damn if she didn't want him to. It had been well over a year since she had slept with him, but the memory of it was still fresh in her thoughts. Every second of it, as if each moment of it was stuck on repeat. Just the thought of Anton filling her completely had her damn near crossing her legs in a pathetic attempt to quell the ache. She took a shaky breath, glad for the fact he'd have no idea how much he affected her. He was correct about one thing, Anton Balan was the last person she should ever be alone with. The man was temptation in the flesh. As if Satan himself stood on her shoulder, whispering for her to take her own turn on the ugly plaid sofa.

His nostrils flared and his eyes darkened. "You need to leave now. Go home, Kimber."

"I can't leave my friend—"

"And I can't allow you to go back through that door."

Kimber's gaze took in his dark shorn locks. "What's with the hair anyway?"

He paused. She supposed her question had thrown him off. "I needed a change."

"You were fine before."

"And I'm not now?"

She couldn't deny he was more than fine, regardless of the hair color, though it did add a darker edge. "What in the world has gotten into you?"

Anton's full lips thinned as his gaze dropped to her mouth again. "If you stay here, *tesoro*, make no mistake, I will fuck you."

Kimber gasped, unsure if she wanted to smack him or take him up on it. The latter would no doubt be a huge enjoyable mistake she'd regret the minute he walked out the door. And he would. Kimber held no illusions where he was concerned. Anton seemed to enjoy women far too much to saddle himself with one.

"If I let you walk through the door, there are two bikers by the bar guaranteed to scent your desire. They aren't exactly fans of mine. They'd try to get in your pants just to piss me off."

"You cannot be serious." Kimber harrumphed. "You think I desire you?"

He raised a brow. "I'd be willing to prove my point. If I place my hand between your thighs, I'm betting I'll find your panties wet."

*The arrogant son of a bitch!* He had no possible way of knowing how close to the truth he had hit. She all but squirmed. Regardless of what she thought of his attitude, Anton was sex on a stick ... ready to be licked. She refused to give way to the fantasies that evoked.

Time to put distance between them. "Let go of me."

"Not unless you promise to stay the hell away from Wolf and Xander."

"I gave them reason to believe you and I are together. They wouldn't dare try to pick me up now."

A muscle ticked in his cheek as his gaze held hers. Part of her wished he'd just kiss her and step over the line they danced around. His heart beat heavily against her palm, letting her know he felt much the same way. Anton's look was pure predator ... as though he was about a hairsbreadth of taking what he wanted. The fact a man like him desired her stoked a fire deep inside. The flames of which demanded release.

Anton grumbled beneath his breath in a language she didn't understand. He nudged her chin up with the knuckle of his forefinger. "Trust me, *tesoro*, they would go after you because of me. If you won't let me escort you from here, then when you go back through that door, you walk to the dance floor and find your friend. You tell her you're leaving, then don't come back to the Rave. This isn't the place for you."

Desire aside, he certainly had a way of pissing her off. "You know what, Anton? Screw you. I'll do what I want when I want, and with whom I want. You've made it perfectly clear you don't want me—"

"On the contrary, *tesoro*, I think the erection in my pants speaks otherwise."

Kimber backed from his touch. "You didn't let me finish. *In your life.* You don't want me in your life. I'm not about to be your passing — excuse my language — fuck buddy. I think you have plenty of women willing to step up to the plate. I'm not one of them."

"I believe it was you who put me in the friends' zone. Not the other way around."

She fisted the neck of his tee and hauled him close again, forcing him to bend down. Their noses were mere inches apart. "Your turn to answer my question, Anton. Do you want me in your life or do you just want a friend with benefits?"

Anton's jaw tightened. His nostrils flared as his icy blue gaze stayed focused on hers. "I only want to fuck you, *tesoro*. I don't recall saying I wanted your friendship too."

She released him. His admission stung. She had no one but herself to blame for her silly fantasies. He had all but said the same thing over a year ago. Kimber had been foolish enough to hope he might have changed his feelings. Apparently, not.

"We have nothing more to say to each other, Anton. I won't be a part-time plaything. Keep your nose out of my business and my life … and who I decide to date."

Without another word, she turned and swung open the door and headed past the two Sons. Kimber knew better than to toy with either of them. Where Anton respected the word no, she doubted the likes of those two did. Stalking the dance floor, she grabbed the hand of the first lonely man she saw and pulled him into the middle of the ravers. This might not be her scene, but she'd be damned before she'd allow Anton the right to dictate her choice of entertainment.

Taking the young man's hands, she placed them on her hips. She moved from side to side. He easily fell into step, his fingers digging into the soft flesh of her hips. Kimber turned in his hold, raised her arms, and shimmied her hips against him. Anton needed to see what he had turned away. One last look proved she had a struck a chord. His icy blue gaze had damn near turned black as he scowled in their direction. Anton turned and walked back into the storeroom, the slamming door going unheard over the loud bass music.

## CHAPTER FOUR

Anton shut the door of his green and white 1968 Ford F-100 Ranger, the other love of his life, the first being his Road King. He had left his bike at his farmhouse and opted to drive the old, restored Ford up the coast. Restless, he was unable to sit still. He had left the Rave the night before and headed home. The vision of Kimber grinding on some punk had started a fire in his gut he had no hope of extinguishing. It took the restraint of a saint to keep from giving the young man a beating for daring to touch what he denied himself.

Hell, his hard-on had demanded he act. He had scented her desire, knew it wouldn't take much coaxing to get between her long, lean legs.

Instead, knowing his eyes had transformed and his vampire self wasn't far off, he had hightailed it to the backroom. Taunts from Grigore had followed him, telling Anton he was nowhere near ready to forgive him for defecting to the enemy. Alexander, on the other hand, hadn't said a word. He had always been a man of few words. The look he leveled on Anton, just before the door closed though, was enough to tell Anton what the man thought about him.

Christ, these were his brothers. Brothers who now considered him the enemy. Anton's heart weighed heavy, his reason for the trek to the coast among other things. The ocean had a way of soothing him and letting his troubles melt away. He'd survive his undercover work and the censure of his brothers. When his own personal hell came to completion, he'd set his world right again.

Kimber slammed back to the forefront of his thoughts. Since arriving back in Oregon, and seeing her standing there watching him, he had trouble thinking of little else. Somehow, she had sneaked in and grabbed a hold of his balls with both hands. All the women he had fucked in the past year ceased to matter. The question that plagued him was, what the hell he planned to do about it?

He was a fucking monster. A vampire.

Something Kimber would never understand. Should she ever see his features and not have them masked by hypnotism, she'd be repulsed. Since their beginning, vampires hid from the scrutiny and judgment of humans, stayed under their radar. If humans found out about their existence, they'd be no doubt hunted down and eliminated. Not that Anton could blame them. He drank their blood, for fuck's sake. The world wasn't ready to live in peace with someone who considered them nourishment.

Walking to the viewing area overlooking a private beach, Anton sat on a grassy knoll, the ocean breeze feathering over him. He breathed in deep, taking in the salty air. Even if he had a choice, he wouldn't want to live anywhere else in the world. The coast of Oregon would always call him home. It wasn't as if Santa Barbara wasn't a nice area, but even after a year of being there, it wasn't home. He wondered how long he could stay in Oregon before Tank demanded his return.

Control freak didn't begin to describe the man.

The fact Anton hadn't asked permission to take a few days off to ride up the coast wasn't likely to sit well with him, though he didn't give a rat's ass. He'd head back when he was good and ready. Cara and the DEA be damned as well. It wasn't as if he hadn't already given up a year of his life. They could damn well wait for him to get a little R&R. Besides, the Devils weren't moving anything at the moment. Not with the cartel catching rumors about being under the DEA's microscope.

Every day they sat on their asses was lost money.

Anton would bet they wouldn't be lying low for long. With damn near every law enforcement in Mexico deep within the various cartels' pockets, Raúl Trevino Caballero would find a way to get his operation back up and running, no matter who he had to pay off to do it.

*The sooner, the better.*

He wanted nothing more than to get this show on the road so they could find a way to take the kingpin down. Anton would take him out personally if it come to that. He'd stop at nothing to get his life back and that of Draven's, even if the barkeep had gotten himself into the huge fucking mess. The dumb shit thought he could run drugs from his establishment with no repercussions. Now Anton was left with protecting him. Good thing he had a soft spot for the barkeep, or he might have just as easily turned the job down.

Movement below caught his attention. He was far enough away that he'd be hard to detect up on the hill. A woman exited through the rear door of the house, carrying a small bundle in her arms. The sun's rays reflected off her long red hair, reminding him of the fiery woman beneath it. *Tamera Cantrell.* What would she be doing here? Anton sniffed the air, trying to detect her scent, but with the ocean breeze he couldn't catch anything other than the salty air. Shortly thereafter, a man with dark brown hair reaching his shoulder blades, followed her onto the sand.

*Couldn't be.*

What the hell were they doing this far up the coast?

Grayson turned his head and looked in Anton's direction, causing him to scoot a few inches back from his perch. After a few seconds, the vampire turned his attention back to his mate, then took the squirming bundle from her arms. *Jesus!* Grayson Gabor was a father. His heart clenched. He watched the loving scene before him. He had made Cara and Kane promise to keep club business to themselves. Anton thought it might be painful to hear updates of his brothers and not share in their lives, just such proof below. Having missed the birth of Grayson's firstborn stung. He had given up too much.

They walked to the water's edge, too far for Anton to detect their conversation. Whatever Grayson said, a large smile appeared on Tamera's lips before she laughed and ran into the surf. Grayson chuckled in return, all the while cuddling the small infant in his arms. From Anton's view point, Grayson never looked happier as he watched his mate play in the ocean. She reached down and splashed water in his direction. Not enough to soak the babe in his arms, but enough to wet his shins. Grayson nodded at her, his lips moved, and Tamera laughed.

The two portrayed the picture of the perfect family.

Although Anton was certainly happy for his brother and one-time best friend, jealousy ate at his gut. He wasn't sure if he were more envious at Grayson for having won the woman he had one time wanted, or more so of the fact Grayson had the life he at one time envisioned for himself. Either way, he didn't begrudge Grayson. Tamera had taken Grayson's blood without his permission, thus securing herself as his mate. At the time, not a soul, him included, knew Tamera had been duped and used by Rosalee. Grayson had one hell of a chip on his shoulder and a lot of hurt to overcome.

Seeing him happy now, regardless of Anton's envy, his heart warmed with the knowledge Grayson and Tamera had found their peace. Rosalee, Kane's bitch of an ex-mate, had thankfully found her end by the hands of Kane and Kaleb Tepes's grandfather, Vlad. Rosalee had almost wrecked the love Gypsy and Tamera now obviously share. The man deserved nothing short of a medal for taking the woman's head. She deserved death and nothing less for all her deceit and misdeeds against the Sons.

*Good riddance.*

Not a single soul would miss the likes of the witch, other than maybe her stepdaddy, Mircea. Anton was sure Vlad would effectively handle his brother. He had done nothing more than take care of the problem Mircea should have months earlier. Rosalee had been living on borrowed time. Mircea's stepdaughter had been the cause of Kane and her son's death. The woman was evil and vindictive. Yet he allowed her to run roughshod over him. Talk about a spoiled brat.

Rosalee had written the book.

Movement below caught his attention again, and Tamera emerged from the surf, her tiny bikini hugging her curves. Anton had the urge to look away, feeling as if he had no right to see her. It occurred to him, as little as she wore and as she gorgeous as she was, he didn't feel even an inkling of lust ... not the way he had with Kimber the night before.

Christ, if he spotted Kimber wearing the tiny scraps of material barely covering Tamera, he'd be using his body to shield her from view. Who the fuck was he kidding? He'd be stripping her of it and burying his cock to the hilt. Just the thought had his cock semi erect, when moments ago Tamera had hardly gained his interest.

A smile crossed his face.

He was no longer jealous of Grayson for having won Tamera. He might be jealous of the family he had created, but no longer the woman. Tamera walked to where Grayson stood, holding the baby. They shared a laugh, just before Grayson lowered his head and kissed his mate. Anyone could see the love the pair shared for each other. He never thought he'd see the day Grayson would be happy with just one woman. And yet the smile he saw upon his friend's face as he looked at Tamera spoke volumes.

Grayson tucked the baby to his side, placed one arm across Tamera's shoulders, and led her back to the beach house. Just before they disappeared from site, Grayson reached down and playfully swatted his mate's ass.

Tamera Cantrell had chosen the right man.

Now if he could just figure out what to do about his little librarian. Oh, he knew what he wanted to do with her. No doubt about it. But anything more was forbidden. Without the consent of the Sons, human relationships were off-limits. Since he technically wasn't a Son at the moment, he wouldn't be petitioning them any time soon. Not that Kimber would want anything to do with his vampire self. Anton sighed heavily. Not to mention he was still neck deep in with the Devils and the cartel.

He stood, brushed off the seat of his jeans, and headed for his truck. He still had a few days of R&R left. Now to figure out what the hell to do with them since entertaining Kimber wasn't an option.

THE WARM SUMMER BREEZE ruffled her hair and tickled her flesh. Kimber sat on the whitewashed front porch of her country style home, enjoying the early Sunday afternoon. Twin white rockers she had restored from her grandmother's estate, flanked an oval, glass-topped, wicker table. The chairs were all Kimber had left of the gentle woman who had passed away nearly two years ago. Her grandmother had lived a pretty simple life. Some of Kimber's fondest memories were of her sitting in one of the rockers while knitting scarves. She could remember rocking in them as a kid, eating homemade treats from her grandmother's kitchen. When her mother had asked her what she wanted from the estate, it was a no-brainer for Kimber.

The floorboards creaked as she slowly rocked, a glass of unsweetened tea in her hand. She couldn't have asked for a better day to sit on her veranda and enjoy the quietude. Sundays had always been her favorite day of the week. Not only was it her one given day off from work, but it also meant dinner with her parents. Kimber hadn't missed one of those meals since buying a place of her own.

She had always been close to them, trying her best to fill the void left by her brother. Nick had left Oregon behind at the age of eighteen when he attended college in Ohio. Having gotten a job in Cleveland, he and his family made their home in Lakewood. He visited at Christmas time and, if they were lucky, a few days out of the summer. Kimber was a couple of years his senior, but he was already married with one child and another one on the way. Kimber was certain her mother wondered if they'd ever get grandchildren from her, but at twenty-eight, she had plenty of time to do the whole family thing.

At least that's what she had told herself. Daily in fact. Every time she looked in the mirror and found a new wrinkle had sprouted in the corner of her eyes or the laugh lines by her mouth seemed somehow deeper. She'd prefer to think she got them from having a happy life. Kimber tried to focus on the positives, rather than the negatives. To her, the glass was always half full. Her coworkers made her days go by quickly and never failed to make her laugh, and her job provided her with plenty of books to read. She had parents who loved her, and a house to call her own. Kimber had managed to make a good life for herself.

Who was she to complain?

Taking a pull from her tea glass, the liquid cooled her. There wasn't much she lacked for in life. She worried her lower lip. *Except for someone to share it with.* She wanted the kind of relationship her parents had shared the last thirty-five years. Her father still opened doors for her mother, waited on her hand and foot. Having a man like her father would definitely be a welcomed addition. Not that she needed a man. No, she had done quite well without one. Although having one to come home to would certainly be nice, someone who could fill the second porch rocker.

A year ago she had allowed herself to envision Anton filling that role. *Wishful thinking.* Kimber took another sip from her tea. A man like Anton would never settle for someone like her. Women no doubt clamored for his attention. Women with a lot more experience between the sheets and a hell of a lot more exciting than her.

A frown turned down her lips.

She hoped she hadn't embarrassed herself the one night she foolishly allowed the notion he might be interested in someone like her. She was a librarian, for heaven's sakes. *Head librarian*, she reminded herself. How much more lame could she get in his eyes?

Apparently, not as lame as she might think. She hadn't mistaken his erection last night at the club. The impressive bulge in his jeans had been a bit hard to miss. Kimber sighed heavily. She needn't flatter herself. After all, he had just been entertaining a dark-haired, attractive woman moments before.

No matter how hot or sexy as hell he might be didn't change the fact he was all kinds of wrong for her. He ran with murderers, drug runners, and thugs. She had watched the Discovery Channel documentaries on outlaw motorcycle gangs. Most hid under the guise of good deeds, when in reality they were nothing more than organized criminals. The federal government had repeatedly prosecuted various outlaw biker club members under the RICO, Racketeer Influenced and Corrupt Organizations, Act. These men lived under the scrutiny of the law.

Kimber gazed into the distance, wondering if she had known Anton wore colors before she had slept with him, if that would have mattered at the time. She hadn't exactly been thinking straight. The fact a man like Anton was interested in her had a heady effect on her libido.

An engine rumbled in the distance. She caught sight of a pale green and white truck making its way down the one-lane county road. Her heart tripped. Though Anton road his motorcycle most days, she knew he also owned the older style pickup. The Ford slowed as the vehicle approached her drive.

Her breath caught in her throat. She willed Anton to keep moving on down the road, not wanting to exchange words with him yet again. *No such luck.* The truck shifted gears and pulled into her drive, much to her discontent. His piercing blue gaze landed on her from behind the windshield as the truck rolled to a stop and he killed the engine. Alighting from the cab, his long legs closed the distance. He took the stairs with ease, coming within inches of her.

Kimber used her hand to shield her eyes from the bright afternoon sun. She looked up at her impossibly tall and arrogant neighbor, still trying to get accustomed to the new look. It didn't detract from him by any means, just added a dangerous edge. Her tongue stuck to her mouth, leaving her at a loss for words. Damn if he didn't look somehow sexier in the full light of day. His blue gaze rimmed black, bearing down on her. Kimber didn't miss the blatant interest she saw in their depths.

She cleared her throat and raised her glass of tea. "I'd offer you some tea, but you aren't staying if you're just here to lecture me on my choice of bars again."

"Not funny, Kimber." His deep voice warmed her from the tip of her toes to the top of her head. And she thought the afternoon was warm before Anton arrived. The temperature rose about ten degrees as he stepped onto her porch. "I was serious when I told you to stay away from the Rave."

"I didn't need your permission last night any more than I do today."

Anton crossed the white wood planks and took the rocker on the far side of the table, where he sat and looked across her well-manicured lawn. "I was a bit of an ass last night."

She nodded, finding humor in his need to apologize. She bet he didn't eat crow often. Kimber hid her smile. "You were."

"Seeing Wolf's big paw on you brought out my bad side."

"Why would you care?"

He bowed his dark head and looked to the porch at his feet, clasping his hands between his knees. "Because I know my brothers. *Shit*. I meant that in the past tense."

"Brothers?"

"I was a member of the Sons of Sangue before I became a Devil."

"Are they any worse than you?" She placed her tea glass on the table separating them to keep from beaning him with it. "You both wear motorcycle colors. What makes you a better choice?"

"I never said I was. As I recall, I told you that you should stay away from me."

"You did. And yet, here you sit on my porch," she pointed out. "I didn't invite you. Maybe I need to tell you to stay away from me."

He shrugged his large shoulders, stretching his white tee across his broad back. "You should."

"So then what brings you by, Anton? A social call?"

Anton glanced up, his gaze holding hers momentarily before looking back into the distance. Kimber detected a bit of sadness within the blue depths before he turned away. She couldn't help wonder who put it there.

"You want to talk about it?"

She had always been good at reading people and knew something troubled him. Kimber wondered how much she should pry, or if she should chalk it up as none of her business.

"There's nothing to talk about, *tesoro*." Anton cleared his throat, before giving her his gaze again. "Wolf is not the type of person you should spend time with."

"I wasn't. As you recall, I chose a different dance partner."

His full lips thinned. "I don't believe the young punk grinding on you last night was much better."

"What do you want from me, Anton? I'm not yours to order around. You can't come here and think you can tell me what to do or who I can see."

He took in a deep breath. "No, you aren't mine."

"This conversation is over. You want a friend? Fine. Stop by anytime. I always have fresh brewed tea. You want coffee? I'll stock it. We can sit across the table and we can talk about the weather, if that's what you want. But my personal life?" She leveled him with a glare. "That's off-limits. If I choose to date Wolf, or the other guy at the bar for that matter, then as my friend you need to learn to support my decision."

"Like hell I do."

"Not up for discussion, Anton. Take it or leave it."

"You aren't giving me another choice?"

Kimber shook her head and chuckled. "Exactly what other option do you want? I refuse to be your part-time stop when you need to get laid. I don't do friends with benefits well. Call me old-fashioned."

One brow raised. "And you think Wolf or Xander would offer you more?"

"Out of context. I was only using them as an example. Honestly, I don't think you or the other two are worth my time."

Anton snorted, but didn't bother disputing her. "What about the other punk at the bar?"

"If it makes you feel better, he's not my type either."

He braced his elbows on his knees and leaned forward. "Who is your type, *tesoro*?"

Kimber bit her tongue to keep from saying *you*. The look in his eyes seemed almost hopeful. Surely, just wishful thinking on her part. "When I find him, I'll let you know."

His answering smile reached his gaze. "You be sure to do that."

She held up her glass again. "Tea?"

"No thanks. But maybe I'll be back for that chitchat with my *friend* soon."

"I'll look forward to it."

As she watched his truck back down the driveway and head in the direction of his house, Kimber couldn't help but wonder what had she been thinking. Having Anton around as a friend was akin to putting a diabetic in a room full of candy. Why was it the things that were bad for you were always the things you wanted most?

She blew out a stream of air through pursed lips. Yep, she was about to regret inviting him back into the friend zone.

## CHAPTER FIVE

THE DAY TURNED OUT TO BE AN UNSEASONABLY WARM ONE. Hell, even on the back of his Fat Bob, he wasn't getting much release from the heat of the midday sun as sweat trickled down his spine. Kane parked his bike to the left side of the door, cut the engine, and stepped over the back of it. He quickly unsnapped his helmet and placed it on the brown leather seat. Using his forearm, he swiped the sweat from his brow and headed for the clubhouse. Irritation clawed up his spine for having been called for an impromptu meeting. He supposed his sour mood might have had something to do with being awaken and forced to leave Cara's side in their darkened, air-conditioned bedroom.

He would have much preferred to stay in bed and take advantage of his mate, who had the day off. Instead he had received a phone call from his twin. Kane couldn't help wonder what Kaleb "Hawk" Tepes wanted so last-minute. Kaleb, president of the Sons, had told him to come alone and that it wasn't an open meeting, meaning his brother wanted a one-on-one. He hoped that didn't mean he had found out about Anton's undercover work. No doubt he'd be mad as hell for being left out of the loop, but Cara was adamant the fewer who knew about their involvement and helping the DEA, the safer Anton and Draven would be.

Kane hadn't agreed about keeping Kaleb out of the loop, but Kane wasn't the one calling the shots. The police work was better left to his wife and her partner, Joe Hernandez. He didn't always see eye-to-eye with her partner, but Kane couldn't keep her in his sights 24/7 and he knew Hernandez had Cara's back. Joe seemed to care a great deal for Cara, despite their differences where Kane came into the picture.

He opened the door to the clubhouse, spotting Ryder and Alexander lounging on the sofas, a six-pack of long necks half gone on the scarred wooden center table. Ryder had taken over Kane and Cara's old room when they had moved out a little over a year ago. Alexander had claimed Grayson and Tamera's old room, when the two had moved to the beach house following the birth of their son. The house had been owned by one of Grayson's friends, who had moved farther south along the coast, selling the place to Grayson. Kaleb and Suzi still resided in the clubhouse, but Kane bet it wouldn't be long before they looked for a place of their own. Baby Stefan was growing like a weed. Kane figured Suzi and Kaleb would want to keep Stefan away from the MC dealings often going down in the clubhouse. It wasn't exactly an ideal place to bring up a child.

The door to the meeting room remained closed, probably why Kane couldn't scent his twin. The room had been soundproofed for private meetings such as the one called today. It also kept them from being able to scent who was in attendance.

Kane nodded at Alexander and Ryder, who acknowledged his arrival with a tip of their chins. Alexander pointed at the meeting room with his long neck. "Hawk said to tell you to go on in. They're waiting on you."

His brow creased. "They?"

A hint of a smile crossed Alexander's lips. "Your grandfather's here. He arrived about an hour ago."

"Shit," Kane replied. He doubted whatever Vlad Tepes had to say or what brought him back to Pleasant, Oregon was going to be good. The old ruler didn't leave his island off Belize unless he had a damn good reason.

Kane didn't bother knocking. He pushed down the handle and swung the heavy wooden door open. Both Kaleb and Vlad looked up as he entered the space, closing the door behind him. Neither seemed to be in a good mood. Awesome. It was bad enough having to deal with a surly Kaleb on his own. Add in one pissed off primordial and it no doubt spelled trouble.

Pulling out his chair, he sat and clasped his hands on the tabletop, his gaze taking in the half empty bottle of Gentleman Jack. "Do I at least get to knock one back before you two decide to rake me over the coals?"

One of Kaleb's brows rose. "Guilty much?"

"Why else would I get called here for a last-minute meeting and be told to come alone?"

Kaleb lifted the bottle of Jack, grabbed one of the empty rocks glasses, and filled it. He slid the tumbler across the table to Kane. Kane took it to his lips and downed the contents.

"Now that's more like it." He glanced at Vlad. "To what do I owe the pleasure, Grandfather?"

Kane couldn't get a read on Vlad's black gaze, but the set line of his mouth told Kane the old ruler wasn't pleased about whatever brought him here. "Mircea's gone missing."

No beating around the bush. "What do you mean missing? Don't you keep regular tabs on your brother?"

"Of course. Someone has to. The man is a danger to himself." Vlad glowered. "And since I took his stepdaughter's head, he hasn't been his same docile self. I put one of my men on him, to report back to me should Mircea do something stupid, like leave Italy."

"You forbid him to leave?" Kane grabbed the whiskey bottle from Kaleb and poured himself another couple of fingers. He quickly downed it, feeling the answering warmth. "I'm sure you giving him orders went over about as well as you taking Rosalee's head. By the way, thank you for that."

"You're welcome. I should've ended her ungrateful life years ago. But out of reverence for my brother, I allowed her to live. I see now that was a mistake." His expression hardened. "To say Mircea is not pleased with me is an understatement. I figured as much. His animosity toward me is nothing new. Mircea and my father left my brother Radu and me imprisoned by the Turks. I forgave him of his treachery when I turned him, but the fool feels Rosalee's demise was my way of getting even."

Kaleb shook his head. "Talk about turning a blind eye. The idiot refused to see his stepdaughter was a deceitful bitch who needed to die. So what does Mircea missing have to do with us exactly?"

Vlad's lips drew back in a snarl. "I don't think I have to tell you that Mircea will likely want an eye for and eye, which means he will stop at nothing less than seeing to one of your deaths. I'm not about to allow that happen."

"Good to know." One side of Kaleb's lips inched up. "But I don't intend to allow him the satisfaction. I took Alec Funar's head. I'll take his. It matters to me none."

"Which could give him reason to make you his target, Kaleb." Vlad's brow raised. "He allowed the killing of a primordial to pass because you were my grandson, and because Alec deserved his execution. However, now that I have taken Rosalee's head, he'll come gunning for yours or Kane's. I wanted to warn you both to keep on the lookout. If he so much as tries to hurt either of you, he will rue the day I gave him immortal life."

Kaleb easily shrugged off the threat. Kane, on the other hand, knew Mircea would be damn near impossible to defeat on their own. He was older, and therefore much stronger than him or his brother put together. If they were to defeat the man, they'd have to come up with a good plan — that or completely blindside him.

"So what do you want us to do?" Kane leveled his gaze on his grandfather. "Surely, you don't expect us to do nothing."

"On the contrary," Vlad said, one black brow arching. "If he so much as steps out of line, I expect you to kill the son of a bitch. He's my last sibling, and I'd rather talk sense into his damn head. But if he tries to kill one of you, then I came to give you my blessing to take the arrogant ass out. I've given him more than enough chances over the past few centuries. He hasn't learned a damn thing."

Kaleb sat back in his chair and laced his fingers over his chest. A genuine smile crossed his face. "Best damn news I've heard all day. It would be my pleasure to end the bastard's life."

"He won't be easy to defeat," Vlad reminded them. "This is no time to be cocky, Kaleb. Arrogance will get you killed. Mircea may have been sitting on his ass for the last few centuries, but trust me, he holds the power of many men."

"Duly noted, Grandfather. I will make sure my brother doesn't do anything stupid." Kane turned his gaze on Kaleb. "Club P or not, you need to include me on anything that has to do with Mircea."

"I'm confident, not stupid," Kaleb returned. "The three of us will keep an open line of communication. If any one of us suspect Mircea is near, then we need to make sure we all know. If we are to defeat this bastard, then we shall do it as a united front."

"That goes without saying, Hawk," Kane said. "You will need to keep a very close eye on Stefan. He may skip us entirely and try to take out your son. I don't think it's safe for you to stay at the clubhouse. We can move Wolf into your room. You and Suzi can move into the second bedroom of our house."

Kaleb shook his head. "I'd prefer a place of our own, if you don't mind. Cara's not exactly enamored with me."

"We're safer if we stay together for now. We have our mates to think of as well."

"And with your plan, we're also putting all our eggs into one basket," Kaleb argued. "I'll find a place that only the Sons, you, and grandfather will know about. I'll begin looking immediately."

"Good." Vlad stood. "See that you make the move soon. I'll be in touch. Hopefully, I will find Mircea before he makes it to Pleasant."

"You'll be the first person we notify if we get word of his whereabouts." Kaleb stood, shoving his hands into his jeans pockets. "I'll begin looking for a safe place for my son and mate."

"Make sure you tell no one other than those you trust."

"I'll be careful, Grandfather."

Vlad tipped his head. "Stay safe. I pray I find the bastard first. I'd prefer to keep this less messy… Well, less messy for my family. As for Mircea, on the other hand, I'll make no such promise. He either goes back to Italy, or I'll make sure he doesn't live to see another day."

"His death will be plenty messy if I have anything to say about it," Kaleb added. "This meeting is adjourned."

BEING BACK IN PLEASANT HAD been much harder than Anton had anticipated. Maybe he should call it a day, pack his shit, and head south. Having left Kimber's little farmhouse earlier in the day, he couldn't help the anger, and yes, jealousy from working its way beneath his skin. Needing to see Grigore and Alexander again, he headed for the Rave. The image of Grigore's hand on the small of Kimber's back played about his head, steaming him.

*Hadn't he already lost one woman to a brother?*

Tamera Cantrell never really belonged to him, and he knew it, but it didn't mean the hurt wasn't still there. Maybe it always would be. Anton let himself in the backroom of the nightclub, walked around the haphazard furniture, and headed straight for the bar. He wasn't playing by the rules tonight. Draven might not be happy with him entering the club, but he had a few things that needed to be said. Should it cause a fight between him and his former brothers, so be it. He wasn't about to allow either of them to put their hands on Kimber. She wasn't only off-limits to him, but all Sons. She was a human, for crying out loud. If he wasn't the one dicking her, then no one was.

He caught the scent of not only Grigore, Alexander, and Draven, but also Joseph "Kinky" Sala. *Great.* Now Joseph would be a witness to his meltdown as well. He could still save face, get the hell out of town, and no one would be the wiser of his feelings for the librarian. He may not admit as much out loud, but he couldn't deny the longing in his chest. He wanted one day what the twins had, what Grayson had. The idea Grigore might try to put more than his hand on Kimber again, if nothing more than to further piss off Anton, kept him moving forward.

He swung the door open, seeing his brothers at the bar, none too happy. No doubt they had already detected his presence the minute he hit the back door. None of them greeted him, nor did he expect them to, but the looks leveled on him wished him dead, cutting him deep. Damn Cara for making him deceive his comrades — his closest friends and allies. Not that he didn't understand her reasoning, but it still sucked ass.

He stepped beside Draven, who looked ready to bolt at a moment's provocation. He had no idea Anton worked undercover to keep his sorry ass safe either. For all Draven knew, World War III was about to break out in his bar, three vampires to one. The music blared, keeping most bar patrons oblivious to the turmoil brewing.

"Rogue..." Draven let the warning hang.

He ignored it. "Keep your hands off Kimber James, Wolf. That is if you want to keep that big paw of yours attached."

One brow raised in challenge, but Anton knew Grigore wasn't in the least distressed over the threat. "Who the fuck is that and why would I want to fuck her?"

Grigore had that rugged look chicks dug. He wasn't handsome by any means, but women seemed to like his shoulder-length, unkempt hair and beard. A long scar cut across his forehead and into his eyebrow, one he had received before his turning. His vampire genes would have kept a wound from leaving even the faintest of marks. Grigore would never be accused of being a pretty boy. Alexander on the other hand...

"You seemed to know who she was last night. You had your hands all over her."

A lopsided smile tipped up the corner of his beard. "The leggy brunette you chased off last night."

"Yes, that one."

"It's probably that new fucking hairdo that chased her off. You were much more comely as a blond."

"Fuck you, Wolf."

Heat rose up his spine and he clenched his fists at his sides. It wouldn't take much to leap over the bar and hand Grigore's ass to him, but then he knew he'd be fighting off two other brothers as well. Anton stayed put.

"I don't recall seeing a dog tag around her neck with your name on it, Rogue," Grigore challenged him. "Nor do I recall a donor necklace. So last I knew, she was off-limits to you as well."

"She doesn't belong to me."

"Then why the fuck come out here and act as if I was hitting on your old lady. You got something you want to tell us?" His hand did a sweeping motion of the two brothers at his side. Joseph and Alexander said nothing, true to form. Though they rarely chimed in, that didn't make either of them less of a threat.

"Last I recall, you need our vote in order to take on a mate. And unless she's a donor, not about to happen. Besides the fact, I'm not in a charitable enough mood to offer you anything. I'm thinking a vote for you wouldn't go favorably ... not as a *Devil*," he spat the last word with contempt.

"I don't believe I asked your permission to fuck her, Wolf." He braced his hands on the bar and leaned forward. "I'm not looking for a woman at the moment, since I'm still pretty miffed my last mate was taken from me."

Alexander sat back and crossed his muscled arms over his chest. He may be pretty, but he definitely had the body to back up his mouth. Where Anton thought he could take on Grigore and easily win, Alexander would give him a workout.

"You said yourself you never fucked Tamera," Alexander pointed out. "So I don't think, technically, she was ever your mate, Blondy."

"Rogue."

"What the fuck ever." Alexander bared his fangs, showing he had been anything but docile as he sat there watching the exchange between Anton and Grigore. "You will always be Blondy to me, regardless of how you change your appearance. One day I hope you come to your fucking senses and realize you're a Son, not a Devil. Everyone else here may have given up on you, but I haven't. You're hurting. I get that."

Alexander's faith in him warmed his cold chest. At least one brother believed he wasn't capable of defecting. Unfortunately, he had to do his best to prove Alexander wrong.

"Sorry to disappoint, Xander. I'm a Devil right down to the cut I wear. Tamera was mine to keep. Grayson had made his decision to not take her as a mate when he dumped her on my doorstep, then rescinded. Not part of the original deal with Vlad. Not a single one of you ever considered the fact I might be in love with her."

"And just like that," Alexander said with a slight nod, "you let her go."

Anton growled. "Vlad gave me no choice."

Alexander shook his head. "Whatever, dude. If it were me, I would've fought Vlad for her. Say what you want, you didn't love her. Not like Gypsy. He would've given his life up to fight for his woman. Not you, you turned tail and headed for California. But now? You're willing to take on all three of us for this new woman. Interesting."

Anton couldn't believe how very close to the truth Alexander had come. Hell, he wasn't willing to fight Grayson for Tamera, and yet, here he stood ready to take out any vampire who dared to touch Kimber. Too bad the woman he felt worth fighting for was off-fucking-limits.

"Doesn't matter." Anton pushed off the bar and stood straight, squaring his shoulders. "Regardless of what I might think about her, she doesn't know about vampires. I couldn't take her as a mate if I wanted to."

"Unless I bring her into the donor society," Draven spoke up.

His words damn near froze Anton's blood. *No one* would put their fangs into Kimber's arteries. "Don't fucking think about it, Draven. She doesn't donate her blood here. Not up for discussion. And if you value your puny little ass, you best listen to my directive. Kimber James is not donor material."

Anton leveled his gaze back on his former brothers. "Stay the fuck away from her."

Grigore's chuckle followed him when Anton turned and left the bar, slamming the door. He could hear the moving of bar stools as the three got up to leave. *Good.* They might not like him much at the moment, but he doubted any of them would go after what they thought another brother might want. And Anton definitely wanted Kimber, even if there wasn't a damn thing he could do about it.

Taking in a deep breath, he headed for the exit and stepped into the twilight. Anton stepped over the leather seat of his bike, turned the key, and gassed the engine. After donning his helmet, he pointed the bike for the front of the club. Grigore, Alexander, and Joseph exited the front entrance and headed for their Harleys parked near the door. He slowed his Road King as he approached them. Just before reaching them, something whizzed past his ear and slammed into Joseph Sala's forehead, knocking him back a few feet. Brain matter and blood spattered the bricks. It had been a clean shot, meant to stop his brain and heart simultaneously. A shot meant to kill... One meant to take out a vampire.

A roar left his lips as he kicked down the stand, threw his helmet to the ground, and hit the ground running for his fallen brother. Moisture filled his eyes.

*What the fuck?*

By the time Anton reached Joseph's side, Alexander had cradled his body against his side. What was left of Joseph's head rolled back across Alexander's arm. Grigore blocked Anton from reaching out. His beefy palms checked his chest and pushed him backward.

"If you had anything to do with this..."

Anton batted his hands away. "Are you fucking serious?"

"One of your brothers..." Grigore let the accusation hang.

"If one of my brothers took Kinky's life, I promise you that I will take his."

Grigore swallowed, his Adam's apple bobbing in his throat as his eyes glassed over with tears. "Son of a bitch. You find out, Blondy. I want to know who did this."

Anton rubbed a hand down his jaw, attempting to hold his own grief at bay. "If it was a Devil responsible, Wolf, the son of a bitch won't live to draw another breath. I promise you that."

With one last look at Joseph lying prone in Alexander's arms, Anton swiped at the lone tear running down his cheek, turned, and headed for his bike. *Christ, Joseph was one of the good guys.* If he found out anyone in the Devils ordered the hit on Joseph, he'd take out the whole fucking club with his bare hands, undercover work be damned.

## CHAPTER SIX

"What the fuck is he doing here?" Kaleb's tone spoke of obvious contempt. Apparently, a year did little to abate his opinion. "Only Sons are allowed in the clubhouse."

"I invited him." Grigore squared his shoulders, standing just inches from the club president. He never had been one to back down from authority. Respect, yes, but if Grigore didn't agree with a decision, he wasn't one to go along with it just because the hierarchy made a ruling. "I think he needs to be here, P."

"Says who?" Kaleb looked ready to put a beating on someone. His gaze trained on Grigore. "I don't recall taking a vote on allowing a piece of shit Devil anywhere near here."

Anton's gaze heated, barely keeping his vampire DNA in check. "I'm standing right here, Hawk. You got something to say, aim it at me. Wolf's not your target."

Kaleb took a step in Anton's direction, but Kane's hand on his biceps stopped his twin. The meeting room of the clubhouse crawled with Sons of Sangue members. Even though the only one aware of his situation was Kane, Anton wasn't worried. Kane would keep his twin in line. And as long as Kaleb didn't give the order to physically remove Anton, the others would stand down. Anton didn't want to go to battle with his brothers. Hell, he didn't stand a chance against all those in attendance should they decide to hand him his ass. Keeping them from the truth sucked major ass. Hell, he couldn't even mourn the loss of Joseph. Not the way he wished, standing around a pyre with his brothers while they ashed the remains. Instead, his grieving would have to be done alone in private.

Kaleb bared his fangs. "Why the fuck are you here, Rogue?"

"Because I want justice for Kinky, just as much as you."

"I doubt that."

Anton braced his hands on the large wooden table and leaned forward. "I may have joined the Devils for reasons you will never understand, Hawk, but that doesn't mean I stopped caring for every one of you. I wouldn't wish any of you dead."

"Sorry, Rogue, but I can't say the say the same thing."

Anton righted himself, feeling the blow physically. It was one thing to be angry because of his choice to defect, but to wish him dead? His respect for Kaleb dropped a notch. "Why don't you tell me how you really feel, asshole?"

Kane stepped around his twin and blocked Anton's path. Probably a good thing, because Anton suddenly felt like beating some sense into Kaleb. And since Kaleb technically wasn't his superior at the moment, he could do so without receiving a beat down.

Kaleb jabbed his finger at Anton. "You're the one who changed ... walked away, Rogue. So you don't get to care. Get the fuck out of my clubhouse."

Kane turned, slammed his palms against Kaleb's chest, pushing him back a foot. "Calm down, bro. We could use Blondy's help."

"How the fuck is that?"

"If any of the Devils are involved in Kinky's death, then Blondy can find that out."

"Rogue," Grayson corrected Kane as he walked around the table and stopped a few feet from Anton. He crossed his arms over his chest. "Given his hair color, the nickname doesn't suit him. Blondy died a year ago. You at the cliff this morning?"

Anton nodded. "I was."

"I thought I scented you." One dark brow rose. "You spying on my old lady?"

"I was there to clear my head. How the fuck was I to know you'd be there?"

Grayson seemed to mull over Anton's response. "I don't suppose you would unless you've been keeping tabs."

"I've been in Santa Barbara, Gypsy. I had little reason to return unless it was to feed."

He nodded slowly, seemingly turning the admission over in his mind. Apparently satisfied with Anton's response, he said, "I bought the place from a buddy. We made our home on the coast. Stay the fuck away from Tamera. She's my old lady."

"You happy, man?"

A quick nod was Grayson's answer.

"Then I have no reason to go near her." Anton stuck his hand out. For a minute, he thought Grayson might ignore the gesture. Instead he shook it. "Congrats on the son. What's his name?"

The tiniest of smiles itched the corner of Grayson's short beard. "Lucian. We call him Luke."

"I'm happy for you, bro."

The smile disappeared from the VP's face. "I wish I could say the same for you. You know you aren't welcome in Pleasant, let alone the clubhouse. Hawk has every right to want to kick your ass."

Anton's gaze left Grayson and took in the men surrounding the table. There wasn't a man in the bunch who looked happy to see him. Anton couldn't fault them. If the roles were reversed, he supposed he'd feel much the same. The Sons of Sangue were his brothers. No one or nothing came between them. They stood as one, fought side-by-side, and trusted each other explicitly. Anton had broken that trust.

"Look, I get it. I'm from a rival MC. Worse yet, I left you to join them. Mark my word, though, if any one of my new brothers ordered the hit on Kinky, I will see they pay with their lives." Anton cleared the emotion from his voice. "Their death will be a slow and torturous one. I know I am not welcome at tonight's sendoff of my fallen brother, but that doesn't mean I'm not mourning his loss with the rest of you. Kinky didn't deserve this."

"Your word is no good here." Kaleb paced away from Kane, anger evident in his stride. "I find the Devils had anything to do with this, I will take out every last one of them."

Kaleb's nostrils flared as he stopped in front of Anton and bared his fangs. "You included."

"Hawk," Kane warned, sidling between them once again.

"He doesn't need you fighting his battles, Viper."

Anton nudged Kane aside and advanced on Kaleb. He fisted his black K&K Motorcycle tee and shoved him against the wood siding. Kane held up his hand, staying the rest of the Sons. Anton's vampire DNA took over. He hissed at the man in his grip, his toes barely scraping the wood flooring.

"You're lucky I still like you, Hawk. I understand your asshole behavior. I'm only going to say this once. Not everything is as it seems. Why not curb your hate for what I am for just a second and realize we want the same thing — Kinky's murderer found and dealt with." Anton released his grip on Kaleb and shoved him back into the wall. "I'm walking out of here. And when I do, I'm going to leave behind your censure and forgive you for being an ass. I'd rather focus on the fuck responsible. You can either concentrate on your hate for me, or you can direct that at the person who killed our brother. Let's face it, you need me. I'm your only inside to the Devils."

Kaleb brushed the front of his tee with his palms, his murderous glare trained on Anton. "As much as I hate to admit it, you have a point. Not like those dirt bags will agree to help any of us. You find the person responsible, Rogue, and you bring him here. Retribution belongs to the Sons."

Anton gave Kaleb a short nod. "I'll bring the man responsible to you. You will get your retribution. I only ask that I am allowed to be here. I loved Kinky as much as the rest of you."

"Then why join the Devils?" Alexander asked. "Seems to me if you cared for us at all, you wouldn't have spit on us by joining ranks with our rival."

Anton couldn't allow himself to look at Kane for fear his brothers might realize the past P knew more than he let on. Instead, Anton widened his stance, focusing his attention on Alexander.

"I believe I already stated my reasons. Every one of you sided with one of my brothers, without taking me into account." He looked briefly at Grayson. "I felt you turned your back on me. I joined the Devils for reasons of my own and it's complicated. I'm not about to answer for that at the moment. There are more important matters than my grievances."

Kaleb closed the gap between him and Anton. "On this, I agree. Let's focus on finding this murderous bastard. We owe that much to Kinky."

"Deal?" Kaleb held out his hand, which Anton shook. "But that doesn't mean you're welcome here. You have every one of our phone numbers. You keep in touch via the cell. When you find the bastard responsible, you bring him here. Don't fuck with me, Rogue. I won't hesitate to take you out if I think you're double-crossing us."

"Fair enough. I'll be heading back to Santa Barbara soon. If I hear anything, you'll be the first to know." Anton looked at Kane. "My information will go to Viper. Not negotiable."

"Find yourself another donor, Rogue."

Alexander caught Anton off guard. "Excuse me?"

"India." His gaze blackened. "Keep your fucking fangs out of her."

"Duly noted." Anton was taken aback by Alexander's sudden possessiveness over the dark beauty, but kept his observation to himself. He turned to leave, but just before he quit the room, he turned and looked at Grigore and bared his fangs. "Stay the fuck away from the librarian."

Grigore's answering chuckle followed him from the clubhouse, further rankling his ire. The son of a bitch might just pursue Kimber if he thought he had a chance. Since Anton was no longer a member of the Sons, Grigore may feel the librarian was fair game. Anton needed to make sure that didn't happen. Even if it meant sleeping with her again to keep Grigore at bay. No way would he want to be Anton's sloppy seconds.

Anton might not be free to mate with her, but that didn't mean he couldn't fuck her just as long as she never found out about his vampire DNA.

## CHAPTER SEVEN

WET RAG IN HAND, DRAVEN POLISHED THE BAR SURFACE to a dull sheen. His hands shook and his limbs still trembled. He had relieved the bartender about an hour earlier due to the sparse crowd mingling about the Rave. Not to mention, he'd desired the solitude. He wasn't ready to answer questions about what went down outside of his club.

Christ, he couldn't begin to process it.

The hour grew late and he'd be closing up soon anyway. Following the murder of Joseph Sala, the patrons had begun to clear out, most oblivious to the evil that had played out on his doorstep. Hell, he couldn't stop shaking at the reminder. Murder. It was an out-and-out execution. Other than Detective Cara Brahnam showing up at the scene, the sheriff's office hadn't been called.

*The Sons of Sangue took care of their own.*

Calling in a coroner was definitely out of the question. They couldn't risk an autopsy. Joseph Sala would become a missing person, never to be found again, just another number. No doubt the Sons were sending off Joseph into the afterlife about right now, drinking and celebrating his life. Tomorrow they would want answers. Draven couldn't help but wonder if Anton Balan knew anything about it.

The execution style killing had cartel written all over it.

Draven tossed the rag behind the bar and leaned forward on his elbows, clasping his fingers and staring across the empty dance floor. Those who remained quietly finished their drinks at the tables, the normal Rave high energy gone. His bouncer, Rhett, who stood six-foot-two and easily weighed two-hundred and fifty pounds, had begun making the rounds and informing everyone the doors would be closing in about fifteen minutes. If they wanted to finish their drinks, then they needed to do so. State law would not allow the alcoholic beverages to be taken from the premises.

Several more party gatherers headed for the exit. Draven sighed in relief. Fifteen more minutes and he could lock the door and freak out. How he had kept it together this long, he had no idea. The blood and brain matter had been washed from the building using a garden hose, soap, and scrub brush. He had barely kept from losing his supper. Several times he had bitten back the rising bile and urge to puke.

Even though the Sons had promised to come by later to clean up the mess, Draven hadn't wanted to wait. The less that saw the gruesome mess, the fewer questions he had to thwart or rumors he'd have to squash surrounding the Blood 'n' Rave. Draven prayed like hell whoever the murdering bastard was hadn't stuck around.

*What the hell had he gotten himself into?*

Joseph's death could have been a warning to him. After all, it was outside his club they chose to execute the biker. Had the Devils found out about him working with the DEA?

Worse yet, the Cartel. He jammed a hand into his over long, black hair and pushed it from his face.

Fear clogged his throat.

He was way in over his head and there wasn't a damn thing he could do about it. He supposed if he approached Cara with the idea he wanted out, she'd tell him it was too damn late. He couldn't blame them. They had invested well over a year and a lot of money going after the La Paz Cartel. Like a wrecking ball set in motion, there was no stopping it until it came crashing to a conclusion. Cara and Kane wanted their retribution on Raúl Trevino Caballero. The DEA wanted the cartel cut off at the knees.

Draven watched his last patron down his draft and set the empty glass on the table before heading for the door. The bouncer followed the man, prepared to lock the door behind him, finally giving Draven the isolation he desired. He reached for a bottle of Gentleman Jack and meant to drink the whole damn bottle. He wouldn't need a glass, just a couch to fall onto. Parting the curtains, he started up the stairs when he thought he heard his name.

He couldn't be sure he heard anything at all, the feminine sound so tiny and frail. Draven stepped back down the few steps and found a woman no taller than five-foot-two standing in front of the bar. She couldn't weigh but a hundred pounds soaking wet. Her light brown hair, highlighted blonde, had been shaved damn near to null on one side, the top and left side left long, hanging just past chin level. She had a tiny diamond on her left nostril and the bluest eyes he had ever seen, swimming in tears. Her black mascara spiked from gathering moisture.

She repeated his name. "You are him, correct?"

Draven walked and set the bottle of Jack on the bar. Just over the top of her head, he saw Rhett's questioning look. Draven knew, should he give the bouncer the signal to remove her, the big guy would do his bidding without question.

More curious what she wanted from him, he waved the bouncer on. "It's fine, Rhett. Lock up. I'll see her out."

"Have a good night, boss," he said, then left them alone in the club.

Draven returned his attention to the woman in front of him. He towered over her with his six-foot-one-inch height, not to mention the platform boots he wore. Reaching down, he quickly unzipped them and kicked them to the side so it brought him slightly closer to her level. Draven had no idea what she wanted with him, though her reasoning wasn't what kept him from sending her on her way. The woman was a stunner. She had never been in the club before, he would've remembered. His sixth sense kicked in, putting him on high alert.

After all, it was only a few short hours ago Joseph Sala slid down the wall in a pool of blood and brain matter just outside the Blood 'n' Rave's entrance. Another part of him hoped she might be single and looking to hook up. For certain, he could use the release and distraction, not to mention she had his cock standing up and taking notice.

"What can I do for you…" Draven left the question hang, hoping she'd supply her name. Sweetheart would definitely work, for she was most certainly sweet.

"I was wondering if you could help me."

"What's your name, sweetheart?"

"Brea, sir."

Draven chuckled. "Stop. You're ruining the fantasy. No one has ever accused me of being a gentleman. Call me Draven. Or, for that matter, you can call me whatever you want, other than sir. Got a last name?"

She looked away briefly. For a minute he thought she preferred to keep that part from him. *Anonymity.* He got it. After all, most didn't know his last name.

"Gotti."

"As in *the* John Gotti?" He found himself chuckling for the second time since she appeared before him. "Related to the late mobster, are you?"

She didn't hide from the accusation meant as a joke. Instead, she looked him in the eye, her icy gaze holding his captive and answering his question.

*Seriously?*

Ah hell, what did he really care who her relatives were as long as she followed him up the stairs. Damn, he wanted to fuck this one in the worst way.

"My father's father was a brother. They were in the family business together. My father took over when my great Uncle John died. I was never a part of it, if that's what you're wondering."

What the hell. He only lived once. Why not live dangerously? After all, he was already in bed with the cartel. Add to that, fucking a mobster's daughter. How much more trouble could he possibly get into? Draven noted the five stainless rings piercing each of her ears, three in the lower lobes and two higher up in the cartilage, making him ponder over the possibility she might have hidden ones. The pressure on the front of his already tight jeans increased. He couldn't help wonder what she might think of his *Prince Albert*, the ring piercing his penis.

"What can I do for you, doll?" Her blue eyes rimmed black. His term of endearment apparently didn't set well. "You'd prefer sweetheart?"

"Neither, if you must know. Look ... Draven, I'm not here looking to get laid."

"My loss." Blunt and to the point. He liked that about her. Draven leaned back against the counter behind the bar and crossed his arms over his chest. "Want to tell me why you're here at closing and why I shouldn't just see you to the door?"

She blew out an unsteady breath. Something bothered her. He hadn't noticed the trembling of her hands until now. Her arrival had actually taken the edge off his own case of nerves.

"I'm looking for someone. He didn't come home tonight when he said he'd be early."

Draven shrugged. "Guys lie all the time."

"Not this one ... not to me."

"What makes you so sure?"

Brea worried her lip. He could tell she harbored secrets and warred with how much to reveal.

Leaning forward again, he braced his hands on the bar. "Look, Brea, I can't help you if you don't tell me who you're looking for. You're the one who sought me out, so obviously you think I can help."

"Joseph Sala." Moisture gathered in her eyes. "People call him Kinky."

Her admission damn near knocked the breath right out of him. "How do you know Kinky?"

"You're the one who provides donors for the vampires, correct?"

Damn, she knew more than she should for someone not a part of the society of women he recruited. "You want to tell me how you know about them?"

"Joseph told me if I were ever to get into trouble, I needed to come find you. That you would take care of me. He trusted you."

"I'm not anyone's babysitter. Not even someone as smokin' hot as you, sweetheart."

"I don't need a babysitter."

Her gaze narrowed and her irises turned black. Shit! An illusion due to the low lighting to be sure. Only vampire's eyes became obsidian in appearance. "So what do you want from me?"

"Tell me where I can find Joseph and I'll be on my way. He told me he was coming here. Did he go to the clubhouse?"

Draven grimaced. "You could say that."

"What do you mean? He's either there or he's not." She narrowed her gaze. "Something's wrong. I can feel it. What's happened, Draven?"

"You might want to take a seat first."

"Tell me." Her voice shook.

"Sweetheart, before I tell you anything, I need to know how you knew Joseph."

"You can't tell anyone." Her slender legs had appeared ready to give out. She pulled out a stool and sat. When Draven nodded, she continued, "Joseph Sala is my mate."

"You're a vampire." It wasn't a question but a statement. Her eyes had given her away, even if he had at first refused to see it.

She leaned forward, placing her chin onto her palms, her elbows atop the bar. He could tell she was damn close to becoming a sobbing mess. "You can't tell anyone, especially the Sons. Joseph would get into all kinds of trouble."

"They don't know?" Which explained why he had never seen her before and why Joseph frequently requested donors in pairs. Here he had thought the vampire liked his women in multiples, much like Grayson Gabor had before his mate came along and turned him into a family man.

She shook her head. "Joseph never told them. He was sure he'd never get the Sons' permission to turn me, nor their approval of him and I being together."

"Why?"

Draven was pretty sure if Joseph Sala had wanted a mate, the Sons would've approved unless they feared the woman would out them. After all, they had accepted Cara Brahnam, who wasn't a part of the donor society and she was a detective for the sheriff's office.

"I was pretty young when we met."

"How young?"

"Seventeen. And before you jump to conclusions, Joseph never touched me until five years later. And even then, I had to seduce him."

"You were twenty-two and Joseph was…"

"Ninety-five."

"Only a couple of years difference." Draven shook his head at the absurdity. Only a vampire would get so lucky at that age. "How did you become mated?"

"You already know Joseph was a pretty private man." She toyed with the chipped black polish on her fingers, keeping her gaze from his. "He hung with the Sons, but they never came to our house. That's because of me."

"There would've been repercussions to be sure."

"It's my fault." She glanced back up. "I loved him and I couldn't bear to be without him. I begged him to turn me. I wanted to be with him the rest of our lives."

"So why not go to the Sons? Ask for permission?"

Brea took in a deep breath. "I'm a Gotti."

Draven rubbed his chin between his thumb and forefinger. A sense of foreboding washed over him. He was pretty sure at this point, anything more she had to say wasn't going to be good. After all, her secret was big enough that Joseph chose to keep her and their mating from his brethren, the men he trusted with his life. Apparently not entrusting them with Brea's.

"And?"

"My father and grandfather got into business with the La Paz Cartel after my Uncle John passed away."

Draven stepped back, every curse word he had ever learned tumbled from his lips. "Your grandfather knows Raúl Trevino Caballero?"

She nodded. "He's been a guest at my family home many times over the years."

"You've met him?"

Tears fell from her lashes. "He's my godfather."

He wiped a hand down his mouth and chin. "Fuck me."

"Excuse me?"

"It's a phrase." Draven grasped the bottle of Jack and poured them each a tumbler. "I think we could both use this."

Brea took the offered glass to her lips and quickly downed the amber liquid. She slid the emptied tumbler toward him. "Can I please have another?"

Draven quickly obliged. "Kinky knew all about this?"

Again, she nodded before downing another glass full. "That's why he never introduced me to the Sons. They wouldn't have given us permission to mate. That or he worried they would use my connection to bring down my godfather."

"How long were the two of you mated?"

"Three years." Her lips turned down, no doubt detecting his slip for the second time in referring to Joseph and their mating in the past tense.

"What's happened, Draven? I can feel it in my bones. Something is not sitting right in here." She tapped her sternum with his fingers.

"Kinky was gunned down tonight, Brea." He gripped her hand on top of the bar. "I'm sorry. Whoever did it knew what they were doing. He didn't stand a chance. It was a kill shot."

Brea's lower lip trembled and more tears fell. "No. No…" She shook her head. Shaking fingers covered her lips. Her nose leaked. As he reached for a bar napkin she wailed, the sound cutting straight to his heart.

Draven knew, at that moment, he would do anything to protect the slight woman. No one could know of her existence. If the Sons found out, they would no doubt mate her to one of the single vampires or prospects. Women vampires were revered. Only through them were new male vampires born into population. They were to be protected at all costs and mated. Why Draven refused to let another mate with her, he wasn't sure. But he'd be damned if he'd allow them to use her family connections to get close to her godfather. They wanted Raúl Trevino Caballero, then they could damn well do it on their own.

*Or with his help.*

His job with the Devils and the cartel was far from over. Adding Brea into his already complicated life probably wasn't the wisest of decisions. If Cara found out he harbored her, she'd be livid. If the Sons found out, they'd likely want his balls. If Brea found out he was working with the DEA to bring down her godfather, she'd no doubt take her chances on her own, leaving him and his fucked up mess in the dust.

Draven would be damned before he'd leave Brea Gotti to face this on her own or allow the Sons to use her in their desire to seek revenge. Joseph Sala entrusted her care to him for a reason. He wasn't about to let the fallen vampire down.

No one would find out about Brea, even if he had to turn his back on the entire sting that had been set into motion over a year ago and disappear, taking her with him. Draven wasn't about to allow harm to come to the sobbing mess before him. Walking around the bar, he pulled Brea from the stool and into his arms, smoothing a hand down her back.

"I'm so sorry about Joseph, sweetheart, but everything will be all right," he whispered, placing a tender kiss atop her head. "I'll make sure of it. You and your secrets will be safe with me."

## CHAPTER EIGHT

THE COOL NIGHT BREEZE RUFFLED KIMBER'S CRUSHED voile sheers, causing goose flesh to pop out along the flesh of her forearms. The fresh scent of salt air tickled her nose, the rocky Pacific coast not much more than a stone's throw away. This far from town, she needn't worry about leaving her windows open. Rarely did anyone travel down the one-lane road. She headed for the stairs, ready to call it a night. A late one at that. Following her mother's regular Sunday fried chicken and twice-baked potatoes dinner, she had returned home and grabbed the latest novel of one of her favorite authors. Hours later, she found herself dozing in her recliner by the opened porch window, only to be awakened by the living room clock striking three. Four hours had passed and she now had a bit of kink in her neck as a result.

Thank goodness she worked the afternoon shift the following day and didn't have to worry about crawling out of bed at the crack of dawn. She'd pull down her room-darkening shades and sleep until noon if she pleased. Kimber had been glad for the few hours of peace and quiet, after the last couple of days she had spent in the company of her neighbor.

She stepped onto the landing of the stairs, pulled back the curtains and glanced out the window facing Anton's home. This late at night only blackness yawned back at her. The biker's house sat a short distance away, completely dark. Either Anton had called it a night himself and gone to bed some time ago, or maybe he had already headed back down the coast to California.

The latter made her heart pang.

The thought of not seeing him for possibly months again shouldn't bother her, but it did. More than she'd like to admit. He had looked damn fine sitting on her porch, conversing with her as if it were an everyday occurrence. She certainly wouldn't mind his visits becoming more regular. The company had been nice, the view even better. Kimber thought maybe come morning, if Anton were still in Oregon, she'd invite him over for a little home cooking and a glass of wine or two one night this week … just as friends, of course.

The ache settling low in her abdomen and between her thighs called her a liar. She might fool Anton, but she wasn't kidding herself. Her brain said friend. The rest of her, though, wanted more. Kimber might not like the idea of him packing his satchels and heading south, but she couldn't be trusted around him either. Wicked thoughts took over her fantasies. In truth, it wouldn't take much persuasion on his part to get her naked again.

Letting the drapes fall back into place, she headed for her master bedroom down the short hall. Knowing, for whatever reason, he also desired her wasn't helping matters. Kimber walked through her bedroom door and flipped on the light in the en suite bathroom. The sudden illumination momentarily blinded her.

She turned, heading for her wardrobe to fetch a pair of her silky, shorty-pajamas when she ran into a solid wall. Not dry wall, mind you, but the warm solid wall of a chest, causing her to squeal like a little schoolgirl. Her heart damn near jumped from her chest.

Glancing up, she found Anton standing in her doorway, all six-feet-plus of him illuminated by the bathroom light. He glared down on her as if she had done something wrong when it was he who stood uninvited in her house.

"What the heck are you doing?" Kimber placed a palm over her pounding heart. "You scared the bejesus out of me. You could've given me a heart attack."

His black gaze bore down on her. His normal vivid blue damn near nonexistent. "Do you have any idea how easy it was for me to walk in here?"

"Break-in." She slapped a palm against his unmovable chest. "I locked my doors, you big oaf. Please tell me I don't have to replace a busted lock or door because you felt the need to prove a point."

"I wasn't trying to prove a point."

"Then what in God's name are you doing?" Kimber harrumphed. "I don't recall extending you an invite."

*Even though she had been entertaining the idea mere moments ago.*

"I wanted to talk." Anton shifted in his stance, the only indication she had that he might feel a bit sheepish for entering her home.

"So you broke in ... at three in the morning."

His gaze narrowed. "I didn't break anything. Your door may have been locked but your windows were open. The screens easily lift out from the outside. I'd say that's a serious security issue."

"I'll have you know, it's never been an issue until now." She crossed her arms beneath her chest, drawing his gaze downward. "Eyes up here, big guy."

Anton chuckled. "Can I help it you have great breasts?"

She rolled her eyes. "You certainly don't beat around the bush."

"Honesty is always best."

Not that she could argue with him. "So what brings you by for a talk at three in the morning?"

"I drove by and your lights were on."

"One light." She corrected. "And my bathroom light, to boot."

His blue gaze twinkled in merriment. "It still indicated you were up."

Kimber's gaze flitted from his to the made bed behind him. Her heartbeat picked up again. Maybe it would be best to take him back downstairs for that chat. Her libido couldn't be trusted standing so close to Mr. I'm-A-Ten and her waiting bed only a hop, skip and a jump away. All thoughts of a good night's sleep were now gone, replaced with the desire to spend it heating up her cool cotton sheets with the Greek god standing uninvited before her. Yeah, she had it bad for the man.

*Hopeless.*

She didn't have a prayer in the world against his sexual prowess. The man was sex on a stick and looked good enough to lick, every delectable inch.

"If you don't quit that, I'm not going to be responsible for my actions," his deep voice rumbled from somewhere within his impossibly thick chest.

Kimber knew for a fact she could not wrap her arms completely around him. "Quit what?"

"Looking at me like I might be your next meal."

She chuckled, her cheeks quickly heating. Thankful for the darkened room, he wouldn't see how embarrassed she was for having been caught ogling his magnificent form. "I didn't realize I was."

"You were."

Though she knew better than to ask, she couldn't help herself. "And what actions wouldn't you be responsible for?"

His white teeth flashed against his tanned skin, appearing darker in the low lighting. He raised one brow. "Would you like to know? I could easily oblige."

Her own merriment kicked up, maybe a result of feeling giddy that he wanted the same release she did. It was obvious in the way his gaze bore down on her. Had she any hope it would be more than just another one-night stand with him, she would've dragged him to the waiting bed herself. Knowing it wasn't to be anything more, had her nudging his immovable form toward the stairs.

"We can *talk* downstairs."

Her first indication of the stairwell met with his immovable form. Her second had him glancing at her in what might have been disappointment, then turning and heading back down the stairs. Kimber followed, her own regret nipping at her heels.

Once they hit the living room, she blew out a steady stream of frustration. Anton turned, his gaze traveling her body, down to her bare legs and back up, momentarily stopping on her breasts again. Anton didn't even bother hiding his interest. He was no doubt a man used to getting his way.

Kimber cleared her throat and earned the attention from his eyes, along with a cocky grin on his handsome face.

"What?" He laughed. "Tell me you aren't thinking about it."

Her lips turned up. "I wouldn't even pretend to deny it. But that doesn't mean it's going to happen. Why are you here, Anton?"

"I need to head back down the coast."

Her gaiety fled. "So you came to say good-bye? Or did you think you might get a farewell piece of ass?"

"If you're offering…"

"Seriously?" Of all the damn nerve. "Get the hell out, Anton."

He chuckled again. "Relax. It was a joke, sweetheart. Although I wouldn't be opposed to it, it's not why I'm here. I wanted to let you know I was leaving."

"You would've left anyway."

"Yes, but I had planned to stay a bit longer. I really wanted to get to know you … as a friend."

Kimber toyed with the hem of her T-shirt, if nothing else than to still her trembling fingers. "You're really not what I expected, you know."

"I'm not sure I'm following. What did you expect, Kimber?"

She looked to her bare feet. "You're a biker. A gang member."

"I belong to a club, *tesoro*. Big difference."

"I would've thought that you would have taken what you desired. I mean, you're standing in my house. It's late."

Anton's lush lips became a straight line. "So you think I would come in here and what? Take what I wanted, whether you asked for it or not?"

She shrugged.

Stepping forward, he gripped her chin firmly and tilted her gaze to meet his. The dim light coming in from the windows highlighted the seriousness of his expression. "I think you have a misconception of motorcycle clubs. Yes, some are made up of very bad men. But I'm not one of them. I would never take what's not offered. I don't need to. If getting laid is what I want, there are several who are willing to fill that position. You're not like them. I know I've said I don't need you in my life and that can't change."

He stepped back, pacing away several feet as if he no longer trusted himself. He stuffed his large hands into his jeans' pockets, testifying further to the desire he held in check. "My life is really complicated at the moment. The last thing I need is a good girl complicating matters."

*He thought of her as a good girl?* The admission warmed her heart and oddly pleased her, given the number of women he likely took to his bed.

"And yet, here I stand when I should be heading down the coast."

"Will you be gone long?"

"I don't know." He pulled one hand from his pocket and ran it through his mussed black hair. His action made her jealous of his hand, desiring to run her own fingers through his shorn locks. "In truth, I have no idea what my future holds."

"Other than proving my house is easy to break into." Kimber laughed nervously, but she needed an answer. "Why are you here, Anton?"

If he was here just to get laid, then the angel in her wanted to send his ass packing. The devil side reminded her they had already had sex, so what would it really hurt? After all, no one would know. It was as elemental as two people coveting the same end, mutual gratification. She definitely craved him, the wetness between her thighs a good indication. And she was pretty sure Anton desired her.

Maybe, instead of worrying about what people might think, maybe she'd leave him with a reason to return to Oregon.

"You're right. It was unfair of me to come." He shook his head. "I can't even be dishonest about it. I came here to show you why you should stay away from Wolf."

Kimber took a few steps toward him, putting herself within touching distance. "Why should I stay away from Wolf, Anton?"

He rocked back on his heels, stuffing his hands back into his pockets. "He's not your type."

"And you would know this because…?"

His nostrils flared. "I think it's best if I got the hell out of here before I do something you'll regret."

She took another step and placed her palm over his pounding heart. "Why don't you let me worry about my regrets, Anton."

"You have no idea what you're asking."

"I do. I'm a grown woman." Wrapping her hands about his nape, she pulled him down so their lips were but a hairsbreadth away. "I'm giving you permission."

"Permission?"

"To take what you and I know we both want."

THE IMPACT OF HER WORDS HIT Anton like a sledge hammer to his chest. He had shown up on her doorstep with the idea of fucking any other man from her thoughts, specifically Grigore. After coming to his senses, he realized Kimber wasn't a piece of property he could stake his claim on, or slake his need with either. If she wanted Grigore, there was truly nothing he could do about it. So Anton had convinced himself that seeing her one last time before heading out of town would at least leave a lasting impression.

What he hadn't counted on was Kimber's proposition.

*How the hell was he now to keep her at arm's length?*

His dick hardened. One part of him certainly wanted to partake. And it was getting more and more difficult to think with the head on his shoulders, when the one in his pants was starting to do the talking.

He wasn't built to turn down sex.

Every part of his vampire DNA warred with his desire to do the right thing and get the hell out before he did something he'd later regret. And he would. Anton couldn't think to keep her safe from the load of shit his life had become if he gave into his baser needs. He needed to make his excuses, get on his bike, and head for Santa Barbara.

He had a job to do.

Fucking Kimber was not part of that.

As a matter of fact, giving into his dick's desires was completely against his need to protect her. Decision made, albeit not happily, he took a few steps back. If she continued to touch him, he wouldn't have the willpower to walk away. Anton needed to do what was right.

"I have to go, Kimber."

Her pretty little lips rounded, making him envision them wrapped about his cock. He shook the vision from his head.

"Are you turning me down?"

Anton rubbed his nape, trying to alleviate the muscles while his gaze began to heat. Much more and his vampire self would take over. "Not exactly."

"Then tell me? I need to understand why I get the vibe you might want this, and yet I all but throw myself at you and you turn me down." Kimber's expression closed. He couldn't tell if she were hurt or pissed. "Is it the pretty, dark-skinned woman from the club?"

"India?" His brow crinkled. "Hell, no."

"You slept with her."

"What? No." Anton stepped forward and gripped her chin again, forcing her to look at him. "Am I saint? No. But I have never slept with India."

"What were the two of you doing in the backroom of the bar? Am I'm supposed to believe you were talking over drinks?"

Yes, Anton, what were the two of you doing? *Not drinking … feeding*. The truth would freak her out. The desire he now scented on her would no doubt turn to revulsion.

"India's a friend. Nothing more."

Her gaze called him a liar.

"What do I have to do to prove India is not who I want?"

Her pink tongue darted out, wetting her very tempting lower lip.

His nostrils flared. The scent of her desire kicked up, wrapping about him tighter than a moth's cocoon.

"Show me," she said so softly even his keen vampire hearing barely picked it up.

Damn, just like that his willpower flew out the opened window. He could no more be blamed than the moth drawn to fire. Kimber had him by the balls. Even if his common sense waged a campaign against his hunger to have her, he was no longer listening. Anton cupped the back of her head and growled. He slanted his lips over her soft, pliant ones and took what he had wanted since stepping foot back into Oregon a day and a half ago.

If he were being truthful, though, way before then.

Kimber tangled her fingers in the short hair at his nape. His longish bangs fell forward, brushing his forehead. Pushing his tongue past her lips and into the silky cavern of her mouth, the answering sound of her moan fueled his desire. She met him thrust for thrust. His dick hardened, his balls tightened, and his gums ached. For the love of all that's holy, he was a hairsbreadth away from the monster in him unleashing. No way in hell she wouldn't detect the large, razor-sharp fangs about to fill his mouth.

Anton stepped back, his heated gaze falling on her wide, brown eyes. "Kimber…"

"Don't stop now, Anton. For once don't look a gift horse in the mouth. I'm not asking for forever, just one night. Then you can go back to your Devils."

"*I* need more, Kimber." The deep tone of his voice belied how close he was to becoming a vampire. Hell, even he was having a hard time believing he was asking for more than the one-night stand she offered. What happened to his man card? "I don't want just a casual fuck."

"You want… What? A relationship?"

"No." He shook his head. "I can't."

"Then what do you want?"

"Fuck if I know." He took in a deep breath and released it. "I can't give you anything other than tonight, but I also can't leave knowing you might be fucking someone else."

Kimber worried her lower lip, trying to hide the smile itching up one corner. "Then you have no worries, Anton. It's not like I have men knocking down my door."

"For the life of me, I don't understand why not." He tipped her face so she had little choice other than to lock gazes with him. Lord, he hated what he was about to do. "Kimber, look me in the eyes and *don't* look away."

She nodded, doing as asked.

"Hear me now. You will not remember all of what you are about to see. You will feel everything, know that it is me, but my face will remain in shadows. Do you understand?"

Her answering nod and glassy gaze told him the hypnotism had taken hold. She would remember everything about the night, and all the things they were about to do. His face, though, would be indiscernible, hidden in the shadows of her mind. Any time her memories of the night returned, his face would remain hazy, like looking at him through pebbled glass.

"I need to know you're okay with this." Anton had to have her clear affirmation. "I won't take what you aren't offering, Kimber."

"I've never stopped wanting you, Anton. I may not have liked you much over the past year, and the jury's still out on that one." Her eyes turned up with her smile. "But desiring you has never been a problem. Now how about you stop second-guessing the gift horse before I change my mind."

Anton worked his jaw. He could feel the muscles of his face tighten as his brow became more prominent and his cheekbones set higher on his face. Fangs punched through his gums and filled his mouth. The window of opportunity to do the right thing was swiftly closing. The hard ridge in his pants wanted appeasement.

Fisting her long, silky brown hair at her nape, he tilted her face back. His obsidian gaze reflected back at him in her dilated pupils. That line they had both been dancing around was about to be crossed. Pressing his lips to hers, he drew her plump, lower lip into his mouth, nipping the soft flesh and sampling her blood welling to the surface. She tasted sweeter than the finest of wines. Only extreme self-control kept him from sinking his fangs into her flesh and drawing more of the liquid ambrosia, knowing full well it was against club rules. Communion came from donors only, except under extreme circumstances. This wasn't one. Especially since it wasn't that long ago he had fed from India. Anton had thought India's blood pleasing. Christ, her life's fluid was like a generic version to Kimber's, not near as delectable.

Anton deepened the kiss, thrusting his tongue into her mouth and teasing hers into a response. It wasn't a chaste kiss by any means. No, it was filled with carnal promise. If Kimber were smart, she'd walk away. He couldn't give her any more than one night, for fear of the Devils or cartel using her against him. He'd have to keep anyone from finding out about the little librarian or how much she truly meant to him until the case could be put behind him. Then and only then, he'd figure out what the hell he was going to do about her.

Anton didn't want to let her go, but he wasn't sure she could handle the truth. Continuing to hypnotize her wasn't an option either. Whoever he decided to share his life with had to know him for the man he was, vampire and all.

Anton couldn't change, nor would he want to.

Kimber flattened her palm against his abdomen and slid her hand over the taut muscles, sliding past the sparse hair arrowing to his crotch and cupped his jean-clad groin. His breath caught on a growl. His mind went blank, rendering him stupid. Other than sliding his stiff cock balls-deep, he could think of little else. Damn his earlier decision to head for the living room. Her antique furniture wasn't exactly the type of furnishing one got busy on. And if he were to allow this one night, he planned to take his fill, on every damn surface that would hold them.

Kimber deserved better.

She should be cherished.

Anton didn't know if he was capable of offering that kind of nurturing. Tamera Cantrell came to mind. He had held her through her change, comforted her, took in her pain, but he had never fucked her. His hunger had always bordered on frenzied, and he desired Kimber more than he had any woman in his past ... even Tamera. Now was not the time to analyze what he was capable of, not while Kimber stood before him, offering herself.

Gripping the hem of her tank, he pulled it up and over her head, tossing it to the wooden flooring. His gaze fell upon her large breasts, barely contained by a demi bra. The dusky rose areolas peeking above the lacy white fabric had him licking his lips. His mouth salivated. Her snowy white lingerie was a huge fucking turn-on. Black had always been his preferred color, but the pristine white lace had quickly become his favorite. His blood heated. His pulse pounded in his ears.

"Fuck," he hissed, cupping the under sides of her breasts and cradling the weight.

Whoever coined the phrase *more than a mouthful was a waste* couldn't be much of a breast man. Without another word, using the pads of his thumbs to slip the lace past her nipples, he lowered his head and sucked one of the hardened peaks into his mouth. Anton nipped it before soothing it with his tongue, keeping his fangs to himself.

Kimber's fingers fisted his hair. A husky moan left her lips, fueling his hunger. Anton knew he wasn't going to last. Hell, he had dreamed of this moment over the past year anytime he thought about returning to Oregon. Using the pad of his forefinger and thumb to roll the other nipple, he continued to suckle the taut bud. He snaked his free arm about her lower back, anchoring her.

She trembled in his hold. "Please."

He released her breasts, placed his large hands on her tiny hips, and backed her toward the kitchen table. When her backside hit the wooden surface, he lifted her onto it. The swift rise and fall of her chest drew his gaze back to her breasts, where her white brassiere still rode beneath them. His smile turned feral.

With one brow raised, he took in her hooded gaze. "No foreplay?"

Her answering grin nearly made him chuckled. "Not that I don't like foreplay, but right now" — her gaze dropped to his bulge — "I need to feel that inside me."

*Fuck.*

Her admission had his cock ready to explode. Gripping the hem of her pencil skirt, he shoved it up her thighs to her waist, revealing a matching set of white lace, boy panties. So much more erotic in his eyes than a pair of thongs. He slipped his fingers beneath the band and eased them from her hips and down her legs, leaving her bare and perfectly groomed before him. He bit down, tasting his own blood as his fangs pierced the flesh of his lips. Kissing her at the moment was out of the question. Not until his vampire blood had dissipated and the tiny pierced wounds healed. Hell, turning her into a vampire wouldn't be the best way to reveal their existence.

Anton slipped the button free on his jeans, having worn no briefs, and pulled his cock free, running his hand the length of it. Kimber raised her head, watching the path his hand took. Her gaze widened as his stroke increased the size of his erection, causing him to bite back a chuckle. It wasn't the first time she had seen him, so maybe the catch in her breath was more from appreciation.

Dropping his hold, he gripped her behind the knees, slid her ass across the smooth surface of the table, and brought her forward. His bulbous head rested against her wet center. Extreme willpower kept him from pulling her farther and entering her swiftly. He grit his teeth. If she now told him no, he'd damn well finish the job himself. No way in hell he'd get his erection back into his jeans.

"Last chance, *tesoro*. Tell me no now and I leave."

"And if I say yes?"

"I'm going to fuck you until the sun comes up."

He loved the way her gaze twinkled in merriment. "Then it's yes, Rogue."

"To you, *tesoro*, it's Anton."

"Tony?"

He chuckled. "No one has called me Tony since I was a little boy. No, *tesoro*. I want you crying out my given name when I make you come."

"Once?"

Damn, she was sassy. "Until you cry mercy."

Tightening his grip on her legs, Anton pulled her forward and slid into her. Kimber's breath hitched. Fuck, she was a tight fit. Her sheath fisted his cock. He dare not move, for fear of embarrassing himself. He had wanted this for so long, fantasized about being inside her again. The reality nearly had him coming prematurely.

*Shit.*

His breath sawed out of him as he waited for her body to adjust to his size. Her thighs widened and her ass slid toward him. Anton smoothed his hands up her soft supple flesh to her hips. Her long-fingered hands gripped his as she arched from the table. Her pulse beat heavily at the base of her throat, drawing his gaze. His fangs ached with the scent of her blood. He wanted, needed to sink his fangs into her skin and draw out her first orgasm. Instead, he started moving slowly, testing her readiness.

She rose up on her elbows, her gaze trained on his face as he picked up the pace. The table creaked beneath them with each forward thrust. Her moan filled the room, sending his own blood racing through his veins. He wasn't far from his release, but he'd be damned if he would be selfish enough to take his before giving her hers. Releasing one side of her hip, he used the pad of his thumb to circle her tight nub of nerves nestled between her thighs. Her breathing quickened and again she moaned.

He slid his thumb down her slick slit to where his dick entered her and back up. As he slammed into her with more force, the slap of flesh hitting flesh filled the silent space. She arched from the table. Her knuckles whitened where she gripped the table. Her thighs trembled.

"Come for me, Kimber."

He leaned forward, capturing one of her nipples between his teeth and tugged. Using the slightest scrape of his fangs, he drew forth a minute amount of blood, damn near making him break his promise to hold off until she came. His balls tightened, his dick ached.

"Now, Kimber. Christ, now!"

She tilted her head, cried out his name and her silky sheath tightened about him.

*Sweet, Mother of God.*

Her pretty little backside tilted off the table, allowing him to go deeper. Anton grit his teeth. His ass tightened, and he held his breath as his cock pulsed, ejaculating all he had to give.

*Fuck, he was a goner.*

How the hell was he ever to head back down the coast, knowing what he was leaving behind? Anton looked down upon the incredible gift, and she was most certainly a gift, spread before him on the oak table, bra askew and black skirt still wrapping her waist. He released the breath he had held. This woman had gotten beneath his skin, and fucking her hadn't helped matters.

One glance at the clock told him they had a few hours before the sun rose, and damned if he didn't plan on taking advantage of each and every one of them.

## CHAPTER NINE

KALEB WALKED INTO THE CLUBHOUSE, GLAD FOR THE BURST of air-conditioning. The day was unseasonably warm and humid. A storm brewed just off the coast. There was no relief in sight, according to the weather man.

Alexander and Ryder weren't in residence, though they still had a half hour before the church meeting began. Most likely they were at K&K Motorcycles with the rest of the Sons, seeing to the day-to-day operations. He was sure they'd return at any moment. His men knew better than to be late. And those two, since they lived at the clubhouse, would have no excuse for being tardy.

Suzi and he had been out shopping for new digs, knowing soon they'd need to distance Stefan from club business. Tamera Cantrell had offered up her previous residence, the townhouse her parents owned since she and Grayson now lived at the beach house. Having just returned from speaking to the elder Cantrells, and liking the place well enough, Kaleb was thinking for now it might be the perfect arrangement.

Nothing long-term.

Kaleb liked being transient.

Suzi and Stefan had dropped him off and headed for Tamera and Grayson's. She hadn't seen baby Luke for a few days. Kaleb was only too glad to have her get baby time in with Grayson's little squirt. Better that than Suzi wanting to try for Baby Tepes Two.

*Hell. To. The. No.*

One baby kept him busy enough. Not that he didn't love Stefan. The kid had his heart and soul, just like his momma. But ready to add another child into the mix? He'd rather get a dog. It'd be a while before he was ready for round two. If Suzi had her way, though, they'd already be trying.

Entering the meeting room, he figured he'd be the first one to arrive since their trip to Florence hadn't taken long. Instead, Kane's scent wafted to his nose just before he entered the room and spotted him lounging in his chair, feet kicked up on the long oak table. His twin glanced out the double-paned window overlooking the river, seemingly deep in thought.

"What's got you all pensive?" Kaleb said as he skirted the chair Kane was in and took his seat at the head of the table. "You look like you have something weighing on your mind, bro."

Kane slid his feet from the table. The soft thud of his boots hitting the scarred wooden flooring carried through the room. He crossed his arms on the table and gave Kaleb his full attention.

*Always the serious one.*

"We need to increase our numbers, if you haven't noticed. As we stood around sending Kinky off last night, I looked about the semi-circle at our brothers. We're dwindling, Hawk. We lost two Sons and a prospect."

Kaleb nodded. He certainly couldn't disagree. "Count Rogue and that's three. I don't like it any better than you, Viper."

"Maybe we ought to think about calling Red?"

"You can't be serious?" Whatever he expected Kane to say, that wasn't it. "The Knights President hates me."

Kane chuckled. "Not exactly hates you. More like a lack of respect."

"Same difference," Kaleb grumbled. "I'm not about to bring them back as a puppet club if he can't respect me as club P."

"I was talking about patching them over."

He slid his chair back, stood, placed his hands on the table surface and glared at Kane. "No fucking way. I'm not about to turn his club into a bunch of vamps when he can't respect authority."

"You never gave him a chance."

Kaleb rolled his eyes. "Fucker never gave me a chance. He answered to you."

"Let him answer to me again."

"You talking about being President of another chapter of the Sons, Viper?"

"Not at all. I like past P just fine. Besides, I think it's better if Red stays Pres over his boys. They respect him. You bring in someone new to reside over them, and you'll have what you have now. Except it will be a lack of respect for their own president and not just you."

Kaleb shook his head and sat back down. "Out of the question, Viper. You want to bring Red and the Knights back into the picture, then do it as a puppet club. Red can answer to you because I don't like the fuck. I have to admit, though, we could use him having our back since someone might be gunning for us."

"So what do you suggest we do about increasing our size then?"

"We have prospects. They've been doing their time for over a year now. I say we bring them in, patch them over. We have Lightning, Xander's prospect; Rocker, Wolf's prospect; and Ryder, Gypsy's prospect. That makes three new Sons. Evens the numbers back out."

"We never replaced Ion." Kane couldn't help stating the obvious since it was his son's seat he occupied.

"Stefan will one day fill his place. Give him another twenty years."

Viper leaned back in his chair, the wood creaking with the shift of weight. "What's your problem with bringing in another chapter, Hawk? I really think expanding into Washington would be good for us."

"I'll think about it. For now, the Knights can be our puppet club, nothing more."

"You know if I bring back Red into the fold, he's going to want to run guns through our state again."

Kaleb toyed with the wooden mallet laying in front of him. He supposed they could use the added income. "He gives us the same forty percent. We'll give him the same protection.

Kane nodded. "I'll tell him."

"This is your deal, Viper. It goes sour, it's on your shoulders. I'll add this to today's agenda. As long as everyone is in agreement, then the Knights can come back under our protection."

"Red won't let us down, Hawk. Despite your differences, he's a good man."

Kaleb didn't know Red well enough to disagree, other than the fact he rubbed Kaleb the wrong way. Alexander and Ryder's scent wafted to him just before they walked into the room, followed closely by Wolf, Gypsy, and the rest of the Sons. The fourteen chairs surrounding the table quickly filled up, save for Anton's, Thomas's, and Joseph's seats. After today, those seats would be filled by the prospects standing at the back of the room.

Constantine "Lightning" Dalca, Alexander's prospect, was smaller in size, about five-foot-ten, and all lean muscle. Not to mention, the man was pretty damn fast for a human, earning him his nickname early on. The fucker had no fear and had worked side-by-side with Alexander at the motorcycle shop the last year. He knew his way around bike engines. And since Anton had gone rogue, they had needed the extra pair of hands around the shop. He'd make a good asset to the team.

Grigore's prospect, Peter "Rocker" Vasile, had dabbled at playing the acoustic guitar, earning him his nickname. He wasn't too bad at it either, though he lacked the confidence to play with the big boys. Instead, he had hung around the

Rave, played a few open mic nights, and came to Grigore's defense when it looked like he was outnumbered one night by some ecstasy junkies. They had become friends following the skirmish. Kaleb liked a man who was quick to jump in and help where needed. He hadn't known squat about motorcycles, but in the past year he had proven himself great with numbers and working the books. His long, dirty-blond hair and hazel eyes, made him a favorite of the ladies at the Rave.

Ryder Kelley, the latest prospect and sponsored by Grayson, had been a member of their rival MC, the Devils. Kaleb's heart went out to the man, having watched his girlfriend burned alive by the cartel. He had just as much reason to hate kingpin Raúl Trevino Caballero as his twin, Kane. The man had guts. He'd give him that. Ryder had tried to save his girlfriend by tackling her to the ground while fully engulfed. He had a nasty chest and shoulder scars to prove it. He'd already been turned vampire when his fellow Devils tried taking him out after finding out he was an informant for the Sons. Grayson took it personally and had been given the Sons his blessing to turn him.

Out of the three, Ryder was the most deserving of wearing the Sons of Sangue patch. Even though he had come from their rival MC, he had more than proven himself the past year. Ryder was definitely ready to be patched over. The next order of business for him would be to ink over the Devil tattoo in the center of his back. Because of it, he had been forbidden to go shirtless when leaving the clubhouse.

Murmurs filtered about the now full room as the members talked among themselves. Kaleb picked up the gavel and struck the wooded plate, gaining their attention. Silence fell about the room as all eyes trained on him. He was pretty sure he'd get no arguments where the prospects were concerned. Red was another story. The president of the Knights had always been Kane's project.

"Let's call this meeting to order. Before we get started, we could use some Jack." He looked at Ryder and indicated the door. The prospects couldn't be present while they discussed their fate within the Sons. Should any of them get a nay vote, they'd be cast out and not invited back. "Ryder, could you see to the whiskey? Make sure you return with enough for all of the members. Take Lightning and Rocker with you. Shut the door on your way out. You'll be summoned when the Sons' business is at its end."

Ryder stepped from his position against the wall. With a quick nod, he headed for the living area, the other two prospects following him without question. The heavy doors closed, sufficiently shutting all sound in. Kaleb returned his attention to his men.

"We lost another member," he said, his tone somber. "Our numbers are dropping. It pains me to say this, but we need to fill the empty seats if we're to remain strong. No disrespect meant to Kinky. I know we are still feeling his loss."

Kaleb glanced around the table, meeting the eyes of his brothers. Sober faces greeted him. "Wolf, I'll need you to take notes while Ryder attends to the whiskey."

A quick nod was his affirmation. Kaleb slid the iPad toward the gray-bearded Son. Ryder had been acting secretary in Anton's absence. After today, Kaleb planned to make that permanent.

"I would like to put it to a vote that Ryder Kelley should be patched over. I'd also like to add his position as secretary, in Blondy's absence, be made a permanent one. Do I get a second?"

Grayson raised a hand. "I second the motion."

"Thank you, Gypsy." Kaleb glanced back around the circle of men. "All those in favor of Ryder becoming a patched member of the Sons and club secretary?"

"Aye," traveled about the room, until it fell upon Kane who remained silent.

"You have an issue with Ryder, Viper?"

"Not at all." He cleared his throat. "I'm more opposed that he would be made secretary. Out of respect for the man Blondy once was, we ought to give him time to change his mind and realize his error."

"He's been given a year. How much time to you think he deserves?"

"Hell, Viper," Gypsy spoke up, "no one knows Blondy the way I did. He was my friend. Even I think he made his bed. Ryder deserves this. Blondy was the one to walk away."

Kane glanced about the room, meeting every man's gaze. He sighed heavily. "Aye."

Kaleb struck the gavel to the plate. "Let it be known Ryder Kelley is now a full-fledged member of the Sons of Sangue and club secretary."

Walking over to a locked cabinet in the corner of the room, Kaleb produced a ring of keys and unlocked the door. The metal door rattled as he pulled it open. Grabbing a vampire death skull center patch, along with the Sons of Sangue rockers and a secretary patch, Kaleb placed them on the table by Anton Balan's vacated seat. Ryder Kelley would now fill the one-time beloved vampire's seat.

The slapping sound of hands hitting the table filled the room, accompanied by several whoops and cheers. Following the motion to also patch over Constantine and Peter, the Sons of Sangue welcomed two more members into the MC. Kaleb laid out patches in front of the late members' chairs.

"Before we bring the prospects back in and give them the news, I have a couple more items of business to table. First, with the loss of Kinky, we lost our sergeant at arms. I would like to make a motion that Wolf be promoted to the position. Do I get a second?"

Kane gave a quick nod. "I second the motion."

A quick round of, "Ayes," and Grigore was promoted to club sergeant at arms. So far, the meeting was going well. Kaleb wasn't so sure with the mention of Red and the Knights the good hospitality would continue.

The talk among his brothers began again. He had to strike the mallet against the table to regain their focus. "We have one more item up for discussion."

The conversation died down. Kaleb felt Kane had a better chance at pleading his case than he would, since it certainly was no secret Kaleb wasn't a fan of Red and the Knights. If push came to shove though, he'd back his twin. If Kane felt bringing the Knights back into the fold was a good decision, Kaleb would give him his blessing.

Patching the rival MC was another story.

He looked at Kane. "The table is yours, bro."

Kane looked at his brothers in silence for a moment. Kaleb figured it was likely due to being put on the spot. This was his project. He damn well could present it to the MC. Kane slid back his chair, the legs screeching across the wooden flooring. He stood, leaned in, and braced his hands on the table.

"We have filled the seats of our fallen brothers. Let me be the first to say, I think the men filling their chairs will be good additions to the MC."

A round of applause made him pause. When the noise died down, he righted himself to his full six-foot-four height. His long, black hair framed his high cheek bones. Kane paced a few steps, then gave the table his attention again.

"I've made past mistakes, done things that weren't exactly by the book. I made club decisions without a vote. Please know, I've always had the clubs' best interest at heart. Any decision I made, I felt was a worthy one and good for the growth of the Sons."

He ran a hand down the few days' growth of whiskers littering his strong jaw. "The Knights ran guns through our state. We walked away from that lucrative deal when Kaleb took over as president. I would like to propose we start up with the Knights again."

Grigore shifted in his chair, the motion causing the wood to creak. "What the fuck, Viper? Why not patch them over while you are at it?"

A muscle in Kane's cheek ticked. He may no longer be club president, but as past P, Grigore should have shown him more respect. Kaleb allowed Grigore's disrespect to go unnoted this one time.

"If not for Hawk, Wolf, I would've asked that very thing. Hawk disagrees with my vision. He's club P and has ultimate say. He's given me his blessing, though, to ask that we bring them back as a puppet club. To do so would mean allowing them to run their guns again through our state and port. We go back to the original deal. We get forty percent of the take. They get our protection."

"Why?" Alexander asked, his brow furrowing. "Can you give us a good reason for bringing them back? Or why we should even trust them?"

"Someone may be gunning for us, Xander. We lost Wheezer and Red Dot to Rosalee. Kinky's assassination came out of nowhere. And we don't have a clue who wanted him dead or why." Kane began pacing again. "We increased our numbers tonight. That puts us back where we were before Wheezer was taken out."

He stopped and turned, his gaze sweeping over the men sitting around the table. "We aren't growing, boys. We need growth if we're to go up against clubs like the Devils."

Grigore chuckled. "We could take every one of those son of a bitches out if we wanted. The Devils aren't a match to our vampire strength."

"No," Kane agreed. "But someone found our weakness. By accident? Or did someone instruct them? We may be stronger, but we can't stop a kill shot. We ashed Kinky last night as proof to that."

Low murmurs started circling the table as the men slowly began to come to Kane's way of thinking. It was the exact reason Kaleb wanted Kane to bring it up to the MC. Kane had always been the more levelheaded one.

"I say we bring Red and the Knights back as our puppet club. They will answer to us and provide us income. In turn, they will have our backs, keep their ears open for who would profit by killing one of our men." Kane slapped his palms back on the table. "Christ, we don't even have a motive. Who the fuck would even want Kinky dead? I propose we vote on bringing back the Knights. Red will answer to me. I have Hawk's blessing. Should we take a vote?"

Gypsy scratched his beard, then shook his head with a chuckle. "Fuck, Viper … when you're right, you're right. I'll second the motion."

Kaleb placed a hand on Kane's shoulder. "Let's vote. I say aye."

The vote traveled the room easily earning approval, followed by a single disgruntled "Aye" from Grigore. In the end, the Knights were voted to be brought back in. Kaleb wasn't exactly thrilled with having to be cordial to the Knights, but he knew Kane had a point. They could certainly use the backing.

"This meeting is adjourned. Let's bring the prospects in and deliver the good news."

Kane walked to the door, opened it, and said, "Get your asses in here and you best have the Gentleman Jack with you."

Moments later, the prospects were welcomed as new Sons of Sangue members. Kaleb knocked back two fingers of Jack, feeling the burn and watching the celebration. He was certainly happy with the new editions, and truth be told, would be glad to have the Knights allegiance. So why the hell did the hair at his nape raise? Something still felt off and he couldn't put his fucking finger on it. Whoever took Kinky's life, Kaleb feared wasn't done by a long shot.

Vlad's confession that Mircea was missing came to mind. Could the primordial vampire be behind Kinky's murder? The fuck better pray not, because if Kaleb found out he was the one who carried it out, Kaleb would personally remove his fucking head.

VLAD LOUNGED IN A KING-SIZED bed, his back resting against the fabric headboard in a hotel just off the coast in Florence. He stared at the three naked women lying crosswise atop the white cotton sheets, making the bed feel three sizes too small. He preferred sleeping alone and rarely allowed women to dally for long following their sexual escapades. He hated sharing his space, and this was definitely too much sharing.

While on his island in Belize, any woman living there knew damn well when it was time to exit his room. Spending any time in his bed beyond sex was by invite only, which was on a very limited basis just to keep any one woman from getting too close. Not that he didn't like women. On the contrary, he enjoyed them, all shapes and sizes. So much so, he'd never again consider going down the same path as his grandsons. He had mated once. A fiery redhead who had been the love of his life and irreplaceable. She had given him three sons, one of which fathered the lineage to Kane and Kaleb.

Two of his sons never made it beyond their teens. While he and his eldest were seeing to his troops one day, his castle had suffered a great fire, destroying an entire wing. His mate and sons had not survived. To this day, Vlad continued to suspect someone had deliberately set the fire that claimed his family, though he had never been able to prove his theory.

His oldest son had mated and continued his genealogy. Unfortunately, the witch had not embraced the lifestyle and chose to drive a pike through his heart as he slept. Vlad took great pleasure in impaling her, then seen to the needs his of grandsons. Life had not been an easy road, with Kane and Kaleb being the last of his surviving family.

After his mate had died in the fire, Vlad had lost the desire to love again. He had sequestered himself away in a self-imposed exile since it seemed those around him too often died. Thankfully, Kane and Kaleb had survived over the years, and did a damn good job at making him proud. They had turned out to be true leaders without any help or direction from him.

Now, Vlad lived a cushy life on Belize. He had left behind his life as a feared ruler long ago. Too damn much work. Not to mention it left idiots gunning for him. Nope, after he did his disappearing act, leaving his tomb empty, he opted for a life of comfort and peace. That wasn't to say he had gotten soft. Hell, no. He was nothing like his lazy brother. On the contrary, he kept staff and the equipment on his island to keep him fit. He prided himself on working hard.

Some might call him arrogant, and they'd be right, but it wasn't without merit. No man or vampire alive could take him in battle. Even without the added fitness and grueling schedule he kept to say fit, his vampire genes were the original, which meant no one could match his strength or stamina.

One of the women at his feet, a cute little ginger haired woman, stretched. She rolled to her backside, then righted herself, a saucy smile pasted on her face. She teased one of his toes. Her gaze traveled up his thighs to his flaccid cock. Her tongue darted out, wetting her lower lip, as she caught his gaze.

Vlad frowned, making her full lips dip.

Her forefinger indicated his penis. "Somebody needs a little loving."

Raising a brow, Vlad shook his head. "What I need is you to be on your way and to take them with you."

Her hand smoothed up his shin, over his knee, and to his inner thigh. Her movement stirred the other two women. Unfortunately, his hunger had been filled … both hungers. The twin puncture wounds healing on her neck, soon to be invisible. He was no longer in the mood to entertain.

"Surely, you don't mean—"

"Oh, but I do. Time to take your friends and be on your way."

The blonde crawled up his legs, apparently not very good at listening, and fisted his penis, stroking it. It didn't take much for his cock to stand up and take notice of the three women now crawling all over him.

Rather than achieving their desired effect, Vlad was more annoyed at the disregard to his command to get their clothes, and get the fuck out. He had never allowed his penis to rule his desires, and he wasn't about to start now.

Before he had time to remove the women from his bed, his cell phone rang. Taking a quick peek at the lit face, he saw one name that sent his blood boiling.

*Mircea.*

*Son of a bitch.*

He disentangled himself from the bevy of beauties. Why the hell would his brother be calling him? The thought alone raised his irritation.

"Sorry, ladies, but I need to take this." He grabbed his phone and headed for the bathroom, hitting *SEND*. "I trust you know your way out."

Vlad shut the door behind him, before acknowledging his brother. "Mircea, to what do I owe the pleasure?"

"Surprised to hear from me?"

"Cut the bullshit, Mircea. Where the fuck are you?"

"Worried much?"

"What I am is damn annoyed." The sound of the outside closing door told him the women had finally abided by his wishes. Still nude, he returned to his now empty bed and climbed aboard, reclining against the headboard once again. "I suggest you tell me where you are. If I have to come find you, I promise you I won't be polite or accommodating."

"Why worry about what I am up to? Maybe I got tired of the scenery."

"And maybe you disobeyed my orders."

"You're not my boss, Vlad."

"No, but I gave you immortality. Try my patience and I'll take it away."

"You already took Rosalee. I'd say you've taken quite enough with your petty vengeance."

"Vengeance?" Vlad's ire rose. "It was Rosalee who was hell-bent on vengeance, dear brother. She needed to be stopped."

"And so you made yourself executioner."

"Don't make me take you out as well."

He heard Mircea's tsk. Vlad wished he could reach through the phone and cut the son of a bitch's breath off.

"Why did you call, Mircea?"

"To tell you the next time, I'll go after the kid."

Heat rose up his neck. "You threaten a child?"

"You think you can protect your grandsons and their family. And yet I was close enough to take out one of their own."

"You killed Joseph Sala?"

"Was that his name? Poor sap. But no."

"No one detected you?"

"I was careful enough to stand downwind. Once the poor boy's scent of his blood filled the air, it only aided in masking my presence. That's why I am calling. Pay attention. If I wanted to take out one of the Sons, I wouldn't bother with one of the lackeys. I would take out either Kane or Kaleb. Or the child if I so choose. The fact is, I have no desire to kill someone like the little fuck with curly hair. Where would the fun be in that?"

"What are you saying?"

"I'm doing you a favor. I'm letting you know there is another threat. I wasn't the one with the rifle outside of the Rave. I was close enough to do so, but it wasn't me. I was hoping maybe one of your grandsons would've made an appearance. No such luck. Let your grandsons know that I have no desire to take any of their band of brothers. And while you're at it, tell Kane it's his choice. Either him, Kaleb, or the baby who dies."

"You go near them and I'll personally rip off your balls."

"You have to find me first."

"Oh, I intend to."

"Good." Mircea chuckled. "I love a good chase. Have a great night, brother."

The phone went silent in his palm. The son of a bitch had issued him a challenge. He'd need to keep a close eye on Kane and Kaleb, make sure Mircea never got close enough to cause harm to them or baby Stefan.

Vlad let out his breath. It appeared he'd be spending more time in Pleasant. He wasn't about to leave with the threat of his grandsons' lives hanging over his head. If Mircea so much as touched his kin, he would impale his sorry ass and watch him die slowly. He'd beg Vlad for mercy before his life bled from him. No one threatened him or his family without repercussions. Not even his own brother.

## CHAPTER TEN

Anton removed his skull cap and hung it on the rubber hand grip of his Road King. The cloudless day and hot afternoon sun sent a trail of perspiration slipping down his spine. Running both hands through his sweat-dampened hair, he pushed the stray strands from his face and sighed. The morning weighed heavy on his conscience. He had crawled out of Kimber's bed at the ass crack of dawn and had planned on heading down the coast. Plain and simple. He was anxious to get back to the Devils. If any of those fucks were responsible for what happened to his MC brother, there would be hell to pay.

He supposed it was the same reason for the impromptu meeting called by Cara Brahnam and her partner Detective Hernandez. Cara no doubt feared he'd be pissed enough to blow the whole case. On the contrary, he was now more determined than ever to see it through. Someone had singled out Joseph Sala and he wouldn't put it past one of the Devils to have put out the hit. The fucker better pray Anton didn't find out who, because he'd drain the asswipe of every last drop of his blood.

Kimber played about his thoughts as he waited at the predetermined meeting place. His dick semihardened just at the thought of how incredibly hot she had been, meeting his sexual hunger and then some. He had fucked her to the point of exhaustion and she had fallen asleep in his arms. Once the sun crested, he had slipped from the bed, trying his best not to disturb her. Last thing he needed was a whiney female begging him to stay when he'd had a job to do. To his surprise, she had barely stirred, mumbling something about hoping he didn't mind if she got a few more hours of sleep. Kimber promptly rolled over and gave him her slender, bare back.

*How the hell could a spine be so damn sexy?*

The sheet had rested along the curve of her waist, stopping just above the cleft of her delectable ass. For the first time in his life, he found himself wanting to beg her to allow him to stay. Instead, he had pulled on his jeans, slipped into his boots, grabbed his vest and T-shirt, and exited the house. He had broken in far too easily the previous evening, which meant he needed to do something about her security before leaving town. Anton couldn't chance someone with an axe to grind finding out about her, and using her in any way to get to him.

Like it or not, he cared for the little librarian more than he wanted to admit. Anyone wanting to hurt Kimber James would have to go through him first. She may not want his protection, let alone the intrusion, but she'd damn well get it.

The sound of an approaching vehicle brought his focus back to business. Cara's black Charger kicked up a cloud of dust as she followed the curves of the dirt road, followed closely by a second vehicle. First he thought maybe her partner had driven separately, but he doubted the black Range Rover came with the job. So who the hell was invited in on the meet and greet and why wasn't he told?

As the vehicles neared, red hair secured into a messy bun caught his attention.

*What the…?*

Tamera Cantrell pulled her fancy new SUV alongside Cara's Charger as they came to a stop some twenty feet away. Cara alighted from the car, followed by her mate, Kane, and Detective Hernandez. Tamera was last to jump from her vehicle, a look of unease crossing her face. Why she was here, Anton had no clue. He supposed he was about to find out.

"You want to tell me why the fuck she's here," Anton all but growled. "She used to be a journalist, for crying out loud. You have a death wish for me?"

"I'm still a journalist, Blondy. What the hell did you do to your hair?"

He ran a hand through his dark, shorter hair, not really answering her. "I'm assuming you know about the cover."

"Yeah, well, you looked better as a blond." Tamera leaned against the front of her SUV, her booted foot propped on the bumper. "Cara can tell you why I'm here."

"I think she might be of help, Blondy," Cara said.

"So she knows?"

Cara nodded. "Joe and I decided having a journalist on our side might come in handy. She can do things, and get in places where we might otherwise draw suspicion. And you would draw too much attention if you asked the wrong questions."

"Gypsy know?"

Tamera shook her head. "For all he knows, at the moment, is that I decided to take my job back at *Florence Times*. I'm not sure keeping him in the dark is the wisest decision. He'll want to kick my ass when he finds out I knew."

"She's abiding by our wishes," Cara continued. "I told her if things get too heated, she can bring Gypsy in. But for now, it's only us."

Anton scratched his nape, still unsure if bringing in a journalist was the wisest move. "It's your call, Brahnam. Is that why you called this meeting? To tell me Tamera will be working the case?"

"Journalists have ways of getting informants to talk, people that are otherwise untrusting. We figure she could go in with the guise of wanting to do a piece on MCs, question some of the Devils."

"And you don't think they won't know her relationship with Gypsy?"

Cara shrugged. "I don't think so. I don't think the Devils care who their rival MC members bed. Besides, I think their arrogance will demand their voice be heard. Why the hell would they care who she sleeps with? They may want her to know the Devils' side of things so she doesn't slant the article in the Sons favor."

"They'll care if they think she's spying on them." Anton jammed a hand through his short hair. He raised his voice, his ire rising. "Christ, now I'll be responsible for keeping her ass out of trouble too. You think of that, Brahnam?"

Kane took a couple of steps so he now stood beside his mate, leaving Joe leaning against the Charger. "Cara knows what she's doing, Blondy. Anywhere Tamera goes, I'll be close behind. You keep an eye on Draven and your own ass. You let me worry about Tamera. I'm sure Gypsy wouldn't take kindly to you keeping an eye out for his mate anyway."

"Hello ... I'm right here. You boys act like I'm not in the room, or on this gravel road," Tamera added with a wink. "Before Gypsy goes all caveman on either of you, I'll make sure he knows what's going on. That was my deal with Cara. I'm not about to make the rift between Blondy and Gypsy any bigger. Whether you believe it or not, he loves you. You're his brother. He just can't figure out why the hell you would've gone rogue, and it burns his ass. He feels betrayed. Let's get this solved and bring you home."

"Amen," Joe spoke up. "I'm all for getting the DEA and Robbie Fucking Melchor off our backs. The DEA has 500k invested in this. They certainly don't want to lose their money."

Anton knew the DEA were fronting Draven the money, but as of now Raúl wasn't moving blow. There was little they could do about it. The more Draven pressed them, the more they'd think he was involved with the cops.

"No one knows more than me what's on the line, Detective Hernandez." He pointed at the man. "You can tell Captain Melchor to kiss my ass if he has a problem with the timeline. Draven pushes too hard too fast, his life's on the line, not Melchor's. Draven's already called me, trying to get me to go to Tank, the Devils P, to get him a meet and greet with Raúl. I won't do that until the heat dies down a bit. When he gets his meeting, I'll make sure you all know about it."

"Good. Sometimes Draven doesn't use his damn head. Pushing too hard could get you all killed." Cara looked at Kane. "You think you can keep a good eye on Tamera without being seen?"

"You know it. We'll get her down there, and she can begin questioning some of the Devils. We can come up with some ideas collectively, get their arrogance to talk, get them bragging. Being a reporter, they'll expect the questions she asks. Blondy can't get those kinds of answers without raising suspicion."

"I was doing fine."

Kane chuckled. "No one said you weren't, big guy. But the DEA is starting to lean on Cara and Joe. We need more. That's why we thought it best to bring in Tamera. Besides, it will do her good to get the hell away from Gypsy now and then."

Tamera smiled. "Oh, what fun he'll have being daddy without me."

Anton shook his head. "When he finds out he's been kept out of the loop, and forced into part-time single parenthood so you could go back to work, where your first case involves me, he's liable to light up all our asses."

"Give me your burner phone." Cara held out her hand.

Anton reached into his jeans pocket and pulled out the flip phone. Cara keyed in a number, then handed it back. "BABE is Tamera. If you need to warn her about anything coming up, you call her and get her the hell out of there."

Anton shoved the cell back into his pocket. "That goes without saying."

Cara heaved a sigh. "You get to act like your sweet on the little reporter, Blondy, giving her even more reason to hang around the Devils."

Lord help him if Grayson found out he was hanging all over his mate. He'd hand Anton his ass, DEA sting or not. Anton turned and headed for his bike. Straddling it, he grabbed the helmet and snapped beneath his chin.

He looked at Tamera. "You better fucking call me anytime you are in the Devils' territory. If Gypsy's going to be kicking my tail, it will be for breathing down your neck, not for any harm coming to you. Those boys are as mean as they come and they wouldn't think twice about trying to take you out if they think you're getting too nosy. You may be stronger than they are, but they have guns. You're not invincible."

"Just let me do my job, Blondy. I'm good at it."

"That's what I'm afraid of," he grumbled. "Now don't fucking forget… It's Rogue. I haven't been called Blondy since I burned my Sons' vest. You come in there calling me Blondy, they'll associate you with me and the Sons for sure, putting us both in danger."

Hitting the electric start, the bike roared to life. He had one more job before heading back down the coast, getting Kimber one mean ass dog for protection.

KIMBER PUSHED A DUST BROOM across the wood floor in her living room. She had a couple of hours before she needed to be at work, so she had decided to busy herself. Her mind traveled back to the night before, wanting much more of the same. Put her in a room with her hot-as-sin neighbor and she turned into a first class nympho. Kimber was sure Anton wouldn't mind a repeat performance, nor would she for that matter, but the last thing he seemed to want was a woman on his arm or in his bed. She refused to become the needy person he'd want to run fast and far from.

Waking around a quarter after ten, Kimber had stretched the aches from her muscles before slipping from her bed and heading for the en suite. She turned on the hot water, stepped in and allowed the heat to ease the soreness. One thing Anton had going for him ... well, other than moving up to an eleven on a scale from one-to-ten ... was being stellar in the sack. When no other man had managed to give her an orgasm, Anton had no problem finding her sweet spots.

Now, a few hours later, a silly smile crossed her face. She had loved every single reason for her aches and only hoped she could persuade him into spending another night once her shift at the library was over. The problem was that Kimber had no clue how soon he'd be heading down the coast and back to his MC. She certainly hoped he'd come see her before he left. Months could pass for she'd see him again.

At least she hoped it wasn't longer.

The last time an entire year had passed before she had set eyes on him. Oh, he had probably come home, checked on things and been gone without her ever knowing he had been at his farmhouse. After all, she had tried damn hard to forget the man for the way he had treated her before heading south last summer.

This time would be different. Anton had made it pretty clear he wasn't one to share. Kimber hoped he realized that went two ways. If he was keeping his libido in check while in Santa Barbara in order to keep her from seeing others, then she prayed his sexual appetite drove him north. Anton didn't seem like a man who would go long without.

Last night he had been insatiable.

Placing her hands on the broom handle, she braced her chin atop them, and stared out her picture window, memories of the night before making her wistful. Anton sure knew how to use his hands, not to mention more intimate parts of his hard body. Just the thought of how very talented he was left a pleasing ache between her thighs. A fully dressed Anton was striking. A fully naked one was spectacular. Sculpted in all the right places as though he spent hours in the gym. Kimber doubted he sported an ounce of fat.

Her mind recalled each sharp line, each ridge of muscle, tracing them all with her fingers and her tongue. Kimber recollected the Devil tattoo on his left shoulder, and the inked over tattoo of the Sons of Sangue skull, turning it into some sort of large tribal art, between his shoulder blade. Other than the two, the rest of Anton's flesh had been tattoo free. She preferred the look of clean skin. Not that she was opposed to tattoos, but for her personal tastes Kimber appreciated the fact Anton hadn't followed the trend of covering his body with them.

Now that she thought about it, she could recall every inch of him from the neck down, his smooth flesh, the light dusting of hair, the mouthwatering happy trail and so much more. But when she tried to recall anything north of his shoulders, recollect the ecstasy on his face, the indigo coloring of his eyes, it all came back foggy.

*Very odd.*

As a matter of fact, the year before had been much the same. It was as if somehow in the throes of passion her mind's eye somehow shutdown when it came to recalling his handsomely rugged face. She could recall the scratch of his beard against her breasts and between her thighs, but she couldn't for the life of her recollect the five o'clock shadow on his cheeks. Had it been so dark? Of course not. The moon had cast its light across her bed. No blinds had been drawn, and the curtains had been left open. This far out and on the second floor, there was no one to see in anyway. Next time, she'd be tempted to leave on the bedside lamp.

The rattle of the older Ford truck caught her attention. Kimber leaned her dust broom against the nearest wall, then walked out onto the porch. The wooden screen slapped shut behind her. Anton's dark head and bright smile greeted her from behind the steering wheel as he pulled into her driveway. A smile crossed her face and her heart kicked up a beat. Just before he slipped the truck into park, a gray dog poked his head up from Anton's lap and stuck its black nose out the window. She wasn't aware Anton had a dog. At least she had never seen one running in his yard, nor had she remembered him ever talking about one.

Taking the steps down from her porch, she met Anton as he exited the vehicle, the dog jumping down behind him. The impressive canine stood by his side. The animal had a large head, massive chest, and a wide stance, making him appear quite fearsome. He had a soft gray coat and a white marking running from between his eyes to the tip of his black nose. Each of his large paws appeared as though they had been dipped in white paint. But it was the dog's vivid blue eyes that made her fall in love.

"He's beautiful." Kimber grinned, looking back at Anton. "Is he yours?"

"Beautiful?" One of his brows arched. "A pit bull is not supposed to be beautiful. Fierce maybe, or even ferocious."

Kimber slowly lowered the back of her hand, which the dog tentatively sniffed. Once he decided she was okay, he pushed his large head into her palm, and Kimber promptly awarded him with a scratch behind the ear.

"Good boy," she cooed. "What's your name?"

"Diesel."

"Well then, Diesel, you're an impressive big boy." She patted his head and glanced back at Anton. "Better?"

He chuckled. "Slightly. More like dangerous ... mean, vicious."

"He's just a big baby." Kimber scratched beneath his white chin. "Aren't you, Diesel?"

As if on cue, the dog rolled over and gave her his belly. Anton shook his head and laughed. "Some watchdog I got you. No one told me a Blue Nose Pit could be such a big baby."

Kimber knelt down and gave his massive chest a good scratching. "Well, I for one, am glad he's a big baby. I think he likes me."

"I suppose that's a good thing since he's yours."

She stopped Diesel's belly rub and stood. "What in the world am I supposed to do with a dog? I don't have time for a dog. Not with my hours at the library. What will he do while I'm at work?"

"He's your protection, Kimber. He'll keep an eye on things while you're gone."

It was Kimber's turn to laugh. "Some protection. Give him a good belly rub and he's putty."

"Let's hope intruders won't get close enough for him to roll over."

"You expecting I might have visitors?"

Anton's grin turned grim. "Let's hope not. Your involvement with me could bring you trouble. And since I found out how secure your screens were, I thought maybe Diesel could watch over you while I'm not here."

"You heading out already?" She tried hard to keep the anxiety from her tone, but failed miserably.

He gave her a quick nod. "As much as I'd like to stay, I have to head back to Santa Barbara in a few hours."

Her heart ached. It shouldn't hurt. She knew she hadn't been promised more, but it stung regardless. "When will you return? You are coming back, aren't you?"

Anton stepped closer, fisted the hair at her nape and lowered his head, sealing his lips to hers. Kimber gripped his black T-shirt, holding him flush against her. His drug-inducing kiss had a way of making her want it to go on forever. Unfortunately, it ended just as quickly. Her gaze locked with his. Kimber swore his pupils were about to swallow his irises whole.

Kimber drew her lower lip between her teeth, before asking, "You're sure you have to go?"

"I wish I didn't have to." He winked at her as he cupped his jean-covered erection. "Trust me, me and my cock would much rather stay."

His lips thinned as his expression sobered. He ran a knuckle down her cheek. "It can't be helped, *tesoro*. I promise to return when I can."

"Can I call?"

He shook his head. "It's best that you don't. I'd rather my MC brothers didn't know about you. I'll call you."

A slice of ugly green jealousy sluiced through her. She really didn't want to be *that* girl. The idea of Anton sleeping with someone else, though, had her feeling a bit possessive. If he intended on coming back to her bed, then he best keep his pants on.

"Another woman?"

A grin tipped his lips. He gripped her chin and raised her gaze. "No, *tesoro*. Just you. I'll be back when I can. Until then, Diesel will keep you company."

Patting the dog's big head, he said, "You scare off anyone who doesn't belong, Diesel. You hear?"

The dog nudged his hand with his muzzle, then walked over and sat at her feet, looking into the distance as if he actually meant to do Anton's bidding.

Kimber smiled briefly at the dog. "I really do like him, Anton. Thank you. Where did you find him?"

"I rescued him from the Florence Humane Society. They said he had been abused and needed a good home. He was due to be euthanized in a couple of days. I couldn't help but save his life after I looked into his big blue eyes." A sheepish look crossed his face. Apparently, he didn't feel comfortable showing his sweet side. "He's housebroke, so he should be fine while you're gone. I wouldn't let him run loose, though, not until he gets used to your boundaries. Otherwise, you might come home from work to find him gone."

He pointed a thumb behind him. "I have food, toys, a couple of bones, and a bed in the back of the truck. Everything you should need."

"I love the dog and that you thought of me."

"I hear a *but* in there."

The dog trotted off to her nearest bush, raised its leg, and proceeded to mark her nearest azalea. Once finished, he bounded up the stairs and laid on the decking, placing his chin between his large paws, looking as if he had belonged there all along.

Kimber looked back at Anton. "Why do you continue running with men you obviously feel can be very bad?"

"It's complicated, *tesoro*."

"No, it's not. Stay."

"And do what?"

"You're a motorcycle mechanic. You can get a job around here."

Anton released a sigh. "I can't change who I am."

"You can if you want to."

"Fuck." He scratched his nape, mumbling something about getting involved with someone who didn't deserve him and his baggage. "Kimber, if you want this, I'll be back. I promise. If you want to cut your ties, and I advise that you do, tell me now. I'll walk away."

"I just wish—"

"Don't." He cupped her cheek. "Neither of us can change who we are. I'm not asking you to put on leathers and crawl on the back of my Harley, any more than you're asking me to put on penny loafers and pullovers. We come from two different worlds."

She nodded, not sure what to even say. They were from separate sides of the track, and knew the chances of this going any further than what they could do for each other in the sack were pretty slim.

"Look," Anton continued, "how about we don't try and figure this thing out. There's plenty of time for that down the road. For now, we'll just say it's two people enjoying the fuck out of each other's company."

"And while we're enjoying each other's company, you won't be keeping any other women company, right?" she couldn't help but ask. Kimber not only didn't want him entertaining others, she certainly didn't want him bringing back diseases either. As it was, they had taken a heck of a chance the other night. She added quickly, so she didn't sound like a jealous twit, "We didn't use protection."

"I don't have any diseases."

"I was tested after my last—"

"Boyfriend? Past tense?"

"I was going to say sexual encounter. The last guy wasn't boyfriend material." Her cheeks heated, hating the fact she was embarrassed for having casual sex when Anton probably did it with regularity. "I'm on the pill."

"Good to know." He smiled, though he hadn't seemed overly concerned at having forgotten to use a condom. "Look, to ease your mind, I won't be entertaining while I'm gone."

"I know I said I didn't do friends with benefits, but..."

Anton chuckled. "If that's what you want to call it."

"No expectations." Kimber thought she saw something akin to possession cross his gaze. Surely, she had merely imagined it. "Something you want to add?"

"No." He knelt down and whistled to the dog. Diesel jumped up and trotted to Anton, earning him a scratch to his head. Anton stood back up. "Other than the fact I wish I could stick around for a bit longer."

"That makes two of us."

Anton stood, cupped her cheeks, then placed a quick kiss upon her lips. "Do not let anyone you don't know into your house, *tesoro*. I'll be back as soon as I can."

He turned and headed for the old Ford, his ass looking damn fine in a pair of jeans. Anton pulled the cage filled with the dog supplies from the bed of the truck and walked them to her porch. When he returned to the cab, he winked at her before climbing behind the wheel.

*Regret.*

Damn, them regrets.

Kimber let out a sigh and headed for the porch, patting her thigh. "Come on, Diesel. Let's get you something to eat."

## CHAPTER ELEVEN

A VERY FIERCE LOOKING TANK BURST INTO THE BACKROOM of Hades' Nest, an obvious mission in mind. Everything about him spoke determination, from the square set of his shoulders to the thinned line of his lips. Anton doubted the man did little without purpose. Relax was not part of his vocabulary. Maybe that was why he seemed to be the perfect fit for the head of an MC like the Devils. They needed a relentless leader. One who could handle the vulgar bunch of miscreants.

The crude conversation quickly came to a rest. Tank's men not only respected his rank, they feared him. There was no doubt about it as Anton took in the room full of disreputable thugs. All eyes fell on Tank's feral presence.

Spider, club VP, followed Tank through the door, winding his dirty blond hair into a messy top knot. It certainly didn't do anything to help his looks. His long beard had seen cleaner days, making Anton wonder when the man's last shower had been. Grease dirtied his nails and darkened his cuticles. Black smudged his forearms and elbows. His holey, stonewashed jeans looked as if he disrobed, they'd stand in the corner by themselves. Anton positioned himself to stand upwind from him during the day's congregation.

A text had been sent out about an hour ago, calling the church meeting to a select few of the Devils. Not everyone in the MC was in attendance. Anton couldn't help but wonder what Tank had in mind that the rest of the club could not be privy to. Even more curious, Draven sat toward the back of the room, making small talk with Stitch. The barkeep wasn't a member of the MC, and most days, Tank acted as if he couldn't stand the man.

*So why invite him to a private club meeting?*

Stitch chuckled under his breath at something Draven had said, rubbing his salt-and-pepper beard, unaware of the barkeep's nervous ticks. Since Anton's arrival, Draven had trouble looking him in the eye. Something definitely nettled him.

*What the fuck had Draven so fidgety?*

Anton made a mental note to ask the barkeep what had him so bugged following the meeting. Last thing Anton needed was the fool blowing his cover because he'd gotten a sudden case of the nerves. Anton prayed none of the other men noticed Draven's jitters, especially Tank and Spider.

The fool needed to get his shit together before he got them both shot or killed. For sure as the day was long, if someone moved to take out Draven, Anton would be forced to save his dumb ass, thus blowing his own cover and the whole damn case.

Tank walked over to the bar, looked at Stitch and requested a whiskey, a very tall one. The club P jammed his hand through his black hair, clearly agitated by whatever had brought today's call to arms. Not skittish in the way Draven was. No, Tank was more ill-tempered and they were all about to be on the receiving end of whatever had him exasperated enough to spit nails. While Stitch poured the amber booze, Tank took a quick glance around the room, no doubt assessing those in attendance. Once the glass was set at his right, Tank grabbed the nearly full tumbler and downed it. He wiped the back of his hand across his mouth, then slid the glass back to Stitch for a refill.

He cleared his throat in an attempt to gain attention. The action had been unneeded. Everyone in the room had given him the consideration the minute he cleared the door. "Bet you fucks are wondering why I called this meeting."

Murmurs filled the room, but quickly quieted down when the man raised his beefy arm. "Raúl and I had a long conversation over the weekend. As some of you may know, I had made a little side trip to La Paz, Mexico. Raúl's getting restless. Every day we don't move his drugs, he loses money. Lots of it."

*Good. Let the bastard squirm.* Anton crossed his arms over his chest and leaned against the wall, one booted foot jacked up on the paneling. He doubted the kingpin made many mistakes, but a man desperate to get his operation back on track and income rolling in might. At least that was Anton's hope. Finally, after over a year spent with these fucks, they were about to get a little action.

Draven shifted in his chair, his eyes briefly darting to Anton before locking gazes with Tank. Anton wanted to pummel the bonehead. He'd get them both at the end of a very sharp blade if he didn't stop with whatever the hell had him so damn jumpy.

"As you all know, Raúl got a little nervous over the DEA's unwanted attention we were getting last summer. His sources within the Mexican federal police have informed him it looks as if the DEA has lost interest. So, we're to start moving some bonita. We'll start by targeting high schools and college dorms."

Anton grit his teeth. He'd rather they went after an older crowd. *Kids, for fuck sake.* He had a feeling he'd get vetoed on this one, but he needed to put it out there anyway. "I say we move it through the bars and raves. I'd rather stay away from the heat we'd get from selling to minors."

Tank turned on Anton. His lips thinned. "You have a problem with the way I do business, Rogue?"

"Not at all. I just think those attending raves, like Draven's, are more likely to buy the smack. Besides, Draven mentioned he already had distributors waiting. Why change the game plan now? I would think it would be safer to run the smack with those we already trust. Schools? We will no doubt piss off the feds and have them all up in our business again."

"I understand what you are getting at, Rogue, but no one questions Raúl." Tank's jaw set, dismissing Anton. His gaze landed on Draven. "You have the kind of money I need to run the bonita through your bar and distributors?"

Draven nodded. And to his credit, he leaned back, squared his shoulders, and didn't cower to Tank's scrutiny.

"My men have been waiting for my call, ready to hit the streets. I have about five-hundred K I can part with."

"You make that kind of money in your club? Fuck me. I'm in the wrong goddamned business."

"I'm a good business man," Draven continued. "I made a good deal off the X I ran through my bar before the Sons stepped in and forced me out of business."

One of Tank's dark brows arched. "How do you plan to keep their noses out of your affairs this time?"

Draven cleared his throat. *Showtime.* If he didn't convince Tank here and now, there would be no sting, the DEA would have to get another man, and his job protecting Draven would be over. No way in hell would they trust Anton with their smack if they didn't trust Draven. They both had too close of ties with the Sons of Sangue. Either Tank decided to trust them both, or the case was over.

"Unlike what Rogue was saying earlier, I don't plan to run the— What did you call the heroin? Bonita? —from my club. The Sons still hang there on a regular basis. They believe all is kosher between us." Draven rolled his shoulders, no doubt to alleviate some of the tension settling in. "As long as I play that role to a tee, then they'll have no reason to mistrust what I do outside of the club. My distributors have been instructed to steer far from the MC. May I ask a question of my own? Why heroin and not coke? I was under the impression we'd be running nose candy."

"I know we originally agreed to run blow. Truth of it, we're seeing bigger profits from the bonita." Tank took a pull from his glass of whiskey. "The La Paz cartel haven't risen to their position without being smart. Raúl is one of the richest men in Mexico. We want some of those profits. Raúl wants to target through the schools and there ain't a damn thing we can do about it. The teens seem to be buying the stuff up like candy. As long as there is a demand, we'll supply it."

He glanced at Anton, no doubt waiting for another argument about selling smack to kids. *Jesus.* Hell, yes, he had a shit load of reasons. Now, more than ever, they needed to stop the son of a bitch.

"I think we can make a profitable compromise. We can still sell heroin on the streets, but I also need some of your men targeting the University of Oregon. You and your men are only about an hour and a half out from one of Oregon's biggest schools. The student population is damn near twenty-five thousand. Those are some fucking big numbers."

Draven nodded. "I'll talk to my men."

"You will do more than that, Draven. You either get a foothold on that university or the deals off. Raúl is ready to cut us all off at the kneecaps unless we comply."

Tank grit his teeth and glanced back to Anton. "I wasn't excited about taking our operation into the schools any more than you guys. I know your hesitation. Unfortunately, this isn't negotiable. Raúl wants to make up for the past year in a big way. Kids are going crazy for heroin. It's becoming an epidemic. Schools are stocking antidotes, for fuck's sake. Raúl wants a piece of that pie. So, you are either in or out."

He glanced back at Draven. "You, Preacher and Rogue are in charge of Oregon. I figure no one knows the Sons better than Rogue. He can help keep the heat off. The rest of our crew will concentrate on the universities here. We will start with USC, UCLA, and Berkeley. He wants to move this stuff up the coast. The Siuslaw River is perfect for getting you the heroin. The University of Oregon is damn near a straight shot through Pleasant to Eugene down 126. There will be plenty of opportunities along the Siuslaw River to get that shit on land under the cover of night."

Tank was using Anton's position as an ex-Sons member to keep a close eye on his old MC. Smart move. Regardless of the reason, he thanked his lucky stars for being sent back to Oregon. Being positioned back in Oregon allowed him easier communications with Kane, who could keep the heat off.

Having Bobby "Preacher" Bourassa tag along might pose a problem. Not that Anton didn't like the man. Hell, no. Had he the choice, Bobby would've been his first pick to accompany him. Anton would need to get creative in shaking the man when meeting up with Cara and Kane. Any other day, he'd be thrilled about being given the opportunity to spend time with Kimber, but he couldn't afford to put her on Bobby's radar. If Bobby found out about his neighbor and the fact Anton had it bad for her, he could use that knowledge against him. No way in hell would he allow Kimber to get caught up in the mess, which meant he'd be back to keeping her at a distance.

"We got a deal?" Tank asked as he glanced between Draven and Anton. "I need to know we're full throttle."

Anton looked at Draven. "You cool?"

Draven nodded. "Are you cool with it? Last I knew, the Sons weren't exactly singing your praises."

"You let me worry about the Sons." He looked at Bobby. "You okay with heading for Oregon? I can put you up in the farmhouse I still own. It's off the beaten path, where we can lie low."

"I'm in." He pushed his overlong dark bangs from his face. The man's piercing gaze could put the fear of God in any man. "You'll barely know I'm there, man. I won't be a nuisance."

"Good." Tank regained the control of the meeting. "You'll leave in the morning. Scout out the schools. Once Raúl feels comfortable, I'll be in touch. You best be ready with the fucking money, Draven. You jerk my chain and I'll take you out. We cool?"

Draven nodded. "We're cool, man."

"You boys ride out at dawn."

"What about Raúl?" Anton wanted a meet and greet, but couldn't afford to be obvious. "We meet with him when it's time to pick up the smack?"

"No need. The only one who meets with Raúl is me. His preference."

Anton bit back a retort. He need to come up with a damn good reason to meet with the kingpin.

"Let's go drink some fucking whiskey." Anton strode from the church meeting and into the main bar to keep Tank from seeing his answering scowl.

Tank walked up behind Anton and clasped his shoulder. "I like you, man. You have some balls. This deal is going to make us very rich."

Anton picked up the full glass placed in front of him by the bartender and downed the two fingers. He couldn't leave Santa Barbara behind quick enough or the man standing to his right.

K<small>IMBER CARRIED A SILVER SERVING</small> tray of crystal tumblers, each filled with ice, and a pitcher of brewed tea onto the porch, and set it upon the glass oval stand between the twin wicker rockers. She poured Tena and Chad each a glass full of the unsweetened tea, handing them one.

"Sugar?" she asked, setting the glass pitcher back on the tray before taking her own seat. Kimber had brought out an extra folding chair to accommodate the three of them. The slight breeze made the day a pleasant one and it would be a shame to visit within the confines of her house.

"I'm sweet enough." Chad chuckled at his own joke before taking a sip from the freshly steeped, black tea leaves. "So what's the occasion, boss? I don't recall you ever extending an invitation to us before. You have a nice spread."

"Thanks." Kimber was warmly pleased by the compliment. "I don't know why I hadn't. I suppose it's because we've always met at coffee shops."

Tena covered a chuckle with her hand. "I can count on one hand how many times you've hung with any of us at non-work related events, Kimber."

Chad, looking sheepish, ran a hand over his closely shaved head. His natural good looks, blond hair and blue eyes, made him quite a catch. She had spied Tena's attention on him several times over the past year of his employment with the library. Too bad for her the man batted for the other team, which left Tena hooking up far too often with losers from nightclubs who usually only wanted one thing. Tena was pretty enough, but her low self-esteem had her overlooking men who would treat her with more respect.

"Okay, so you might be correct. Call this a new start." Kimber's face heated. She needed to learn to be a better friend. Having Anton down the coast for who knew how long, she wouldn't mind having a few friends to pass the time with. Reaching down and scratching Diesel's head, she asked, "How did your date go with the man you met at the Rave the other night, Tena?"

"Not well." Tena pointed the tip of her thumb toward the porch floor. "He followed me home, which was a good start. He was in and out of my bed so fast, though, I'm not sure I even had an orgasm. Haven't heard from him since."

"You little slut." Chad winked, earning a slug to his biceps from Tena. Obviously, the two were used to poking fun at each other. "You need to keep those legs closed, girlfriend. Don't be giving away the dessert so quickly. Make them work for it."

"Listen to you." Tena's smile widened. "Coming from the king of one-night stands."

"I haven't found a man worthy of all this hotness yet." His hand did an air sweep of his body. "You're just jealous I get more ass than you."

Tena rolled her eyes and Kimber laughed. Kimber was certainly enjoying being included in on a little fun between coworkers. She had to admit, she liked the camaraderie. Why she hadn't hung out with them more often, she couldn't answer. Kimber had been so used to holding everyone at bay, she supposed it had become the norm.

*Including Anton.*

Truthfully, his parting words last summer had cut her more deeply than she cared to admit. It was much easier to hide behind the novels she had been reading, than to face the possibility of being hurt again, which included the coworkers sitting on her front porch.

*What if they hadn't liked her?*

She would face yet another hurt. Now she saw how incredibly foolish she had been. Not to mention all the fun she had missed out on. It was time for a change. Anton had made it clear he didn't want to share her. Not that his declaration meant any kind of relationship, but it did mean she'd have him in her bed on occasion. It would be enough for now. In the meantime, she'd have friends to call upon to pass the time between his visits.

"You are such a male slut." Tena plucked an ice cube from her glass and threw it at Chad. "Such a double standard. You take off your pants and you're a stud—"

"Glad you noticed," Chad interrupted with a large smile.

His comment sent all three of them into a round of giggles. Kimber couldn't recall cutting loose and having so much fun. Her life had been about excelling at academics and being the all-around good girl. Had she truly become such a stick in the mud? Regardless of the answer, all that was about to change. The new, fun-loving Kimber had just emerged. She'd no longer govern her actions by what someone else might think of her.

"Don't get all full of yourself just yet, Chad. You ought to check out the hottie I spied Kimber talking to last weekend."

Chad turned and looked at Kimber, raising one brow. "Spill."

"We shared one dance." Kimber shivered at the reminder. Grabbing the man and pulling him onto the dance floor to make Anton jealous wasn't the smartest thing she had done. It had taken a bit to disentangle herself from him before escaping the club. "Trust me, he's not worth the mention."

"Not him, silly." Tena's eyes sparkled with interest. "Mr. Tall Dark and Dangerous you were hanging out with in the backroom of the Rave. Don't act as if you don't know whom I'm referring to. His gaze burned hot when you pulled the skinny twit onto the dance floor."

Kimber hadn't realized Tena had seen her speedy exit of the storeroom. "You mean my neighbor?"

"That man is your neighbor? Why the hell am I not getting an introduction?"

"No way." Kimber tried to hide the rise of the green-eyed monster behind a sip of tea.

"You're dating him?"

She quickly shook her head, busying herself with Diesel. "I'm not dating anyone."

"Then you won't mind getting me that introduction."

Raising her head, she looked at Tena, trying damn hard to school her reaction. *No. Way. In. Hell.* "He's hardly your type."

"How would you know? Unless..."

Pulling her bottom lip between her teeth, she went back to petting Diesel.

"You little slut," Chad chimed in. "You're sleeping with him."

Kimber giggled. "I might have."

Tena sat forward, wrapping her long fingers around her glass, forearms on her knees. "I'll repeat Chad's request. Spill."

"There is nothing to tell."

"Are you serious?" Tena darn near sprung from her seat. "The man oozes sex. Just once—"

"Forget it, Tena." Kimber wasn't about to let up. No matter that there wasn't a relationship. She wasn't about to share. "You aren't getting the intro."

"Damn it. Then I want details, sister."

Kimber laughed again, rising from her chair. "Who wants cake?"

"Nice change of topic." Chad gave her a thumbs-up. "I'll take a piece ... then we get the specifics."

Kimber walked into the dark interior of her house, her thoughts going to Mr. Tall, Dark and Dangerous as Tena had referred to him. He hadn't been gone but a few days and she already found herself missing him. Even a glance would do. Being a good day's ride down the coast, though, she knew it could be a month or longer before he made a trip back north. At least she hoped it wasn't longer. Too bad he had refused her his phone number. Being able to call him on occasion might have placated her desire to see him.

Cutting three pieces of her toffee streusel coffee cake, she balanced the three plates on her hand and forearm and headed back for the porch. Diesel's nose was plastered to the screen. She had yet to feed the dog even a morsel of people food, but it was obvious his previous owner already had. The vet had told her green beans and carrots wouldn't harm the dog, so she grabbed a carrot from the refrigerator.

Chad opened the door for her. Kimber tossed the carrot to her front yard and Diesel bounded down the steps after it, the cake she carried now forgotten. Handing off a plate to both Tena and Chad, she took her own seat again.

"Damn, girl," Chad piped up around a mouthful. "You are one mean baker. This cake is to die for."

Kimber grinned and her cheeks heated, pleased they both seemed to enjoy her baking. "Thanks. Maybe we should start having weekly potlucks at work."

"I agree." Tena took another bite of the cake, moaning. "I'm not the best baker, but I can make a mean casserole."

"Working with all women, I think I'd like that." Chad winked as he set his now empty plate on the tray. "I can always bring a bag of chips."

"I thought all gay guys were good cooks." Tena laid down her own plate. "You can't just bring chips. How about we get together and I teach you some tricks."

"I'm all for it, sweetheart. But what's the saying? You can't teach an old dog new tricks."

Diesel trotted up the stairs, stopped in front of Kimber's plate and barked. She laughed, knowing Diesel wanted her last bite. Speaking of teaching an old dog new tricks. But instead of feeding the sugary bite to him, she patted his head, then ate the last bite herself. "Sorry, Diesel. Anton wouldn't be happy with me if I started to spoil you after all the dog food he purchased for you."

"Anton? You're neighbor?" Tena asked.

"Yes. Sorry, I guess I never mentioned his name."

"He bought your dog food?"

"And the dog." Kimber scratched his chin. "This far out he thought I needed a little protection."

One of Chad's brows arched. "And you're not dating?"

"Nope."

"Whatever, girlfriend. A man does not worry about your safety if you don't mean a thing to him."

Kimber thought about that and certainly hoped Chad was correct. The idea of her meaning more to Anton than what they did in the sack brought a smile to her face, leaving her a bit giddy. She hoped he called soon, if for nothing else than to find out how Diesel and she were getting along. Truth of it, she was already falling in love with the big lug … the dog. *Of course, the dog.* She didn't know Anton well enough to have those type of feelings for him. Did she? Her mind refused to believe she might be falling for him, but her heart seemed to trip over itself every time she thought of him.

Kimber quickly closed the door on her current line of thinking. Feeling more for Anton, other than an occasional slip between the sheets, would bring her nothing but heartache. Loving him was not an option.

"We're good friends." She wondered at her declaration, not sure exactly what they were. "Who have slept together a couple of times. Just something to pass the time since neither of us were dating. I was quite surprised when he showed up with the dog. He was being neighborly—"

The sound of approaching motorcycles cut her off and kicked up the beat of her heart. She told herself it was just wishful thinking. Since it was more than one bike, she thought maybe it was a couple of the Sons of Sangue checking up on their rival's farmhouse. She supposed it wouldn't be out of the question for them to want to keep tabs on him.

The black motorcycle out front, sporting tall handlebars, was pretty hard to miss, though. Kimber stood and walked toward the steps as Diesel rushed down them and headed for the road. Both bikes slowed as they came near, but instead of stopping, they continued on their way. Anton barely acknowledged her with slightest tip of his chin. Thankfully, she had caught the small gesture or she might have wondered if he had paid her any mind at all.

*"I'd rather my MC brothers didn't know about you."*

Devils' patches were centered on the back of their black leather vests. The idea Anton would come to Sons of Sangue territory with another Devil spelled trouble, and Kimber didn't like it. If she got a chance to catch Anton alone, she meant to talk to him about it. He really shouldn't be bringing his MC brothers across state lines. The last thing she wanted to see happen was a brawl over territories with Anton caught in the middle. It was one thing for him to be in Oregon. He owned a farmhouse and was likely expected to check on it from time to time. Bringing another Devil here was borrowing trouble.

"Is that your man?" Chad asked, his voice near her ear.

Kimber turned her head and found him leaning over her shoulder, trying to get a better look at the men and their motorcycles.

"Girl, you are flirting with danger. But damn, I can't say I blame you. Did you get a glimpse of the guy with the tattoo crosses on his arms? That man is an absolute beast." Chad whistled. "Please tell me you can score me an introduction and that beautiful specimen is not yours."

Both bikes pulled into Anton's driveway and disappeared behind the house. "No, the other one is my neighbor. Getting an introduction to the second man probably isn't such a good idea, Chad."

"Why? You don't seem to mind Mr. Tall, Dark and Dangerous."

"He's my neighbor." Kimber turned and pushed Chad back toward the wicker chairs. "Whom I've slept with. Nothing more. Don't read more into it."

"If you say so." Chad looked at his watch, then grabbed his keys from the table. "Too bad, I'm due at the library in a half hour anyway."

Tena bounced to her feet. "I guess that means time for me to go as well. We're sharing the afternoon shift. Enjoy the rest of your day off, Kimber. If you happen to meet up with your neighbor again, we want details."

Kimber chuckled as she watched them head for their cars, then back out of the driveway. Diesel stepped up to the porch and sat by Kimber's feet. Her gaze traveled back to Anton's farmhouse. He appeared briefly, before he walked around the side of his house and let himself into the side door. The other man followed. Chad had been correct about one thing. That man was a beast, causing a sliver of apprehension to travel her spine.

Patting her thigh, she said, "Come on, Diesel. Dinner time."

Without a second glance, Kimber entered her house, Diesel trotting happily beside her and unaware of the possible danger entering their peaceful neck of the woods.

## CHAPTER TWELVE

Bobby Bourassa tossed his black duffle bag onto the wood floor with a thud, just inside the back door of Anton's farmhouse, and gave a cursory glance about the room. He ran a hand through his overlong bangs, pushing the nearly black hair off his forehead and out of his cerulean blue eyes. They were more vivid than Anton's own blue irises. Bobby wore his hair shaved on each side, but leaving the top lengthy, his bangs long enough to reach his bearded chin. The man could somehow pull off the style, only adding to his beastly look. He was built like a brick shit house. Anton had watched Bobby take on three men at once, not receiving a single punch. He'd gladly have Bobby watching his back in a fight any day of the week.

Anton walked over to the side lamp by the sectional sofa and turned the switch, lending the dim interior a little light. "This is it. My home away from home. Make yourself comfortable."

Anton headed into the kitchen, opened the refrigerator, and grabbed a couple of Buds. He twisted off the caps and tossed them into the trash can, positioned at the end of the counter before heading back into the living room. Bobby had already made himself at home. His black booted feet kicked up on the center coffee table. Pointing the remote at the television, he changed the channel, stopping on a preseason scrimmage of the Oregon Ducks.

Handing him a beer, Anton sat on the opposite side of the sofa. "You a football fan?"

Bobby shrugged. "Somewhat. I wouldn't go out of the way, but if one's on I'll watch it. You?"

"I grew up here, so I like to watch OU games. I guess you could say I'm a Ducks fan."

"Your parents still live around here?"

Anton shook his head. "Died years ago."

"Sorry, man."

"Don't be. It's life." Anton took a swig of his beer. "I suppose that's why I keep the farmhouse, though. It's my last tie to them. You?"

"My parents don't give a fuck about me. Kicked me out when I was fourteen." Bobby tipped back his bottle. "I don't know if they're still alive, nor do I care. I wouldn't walk across the street to visit them."

"That's tough, dude."

"I don't suppose I was easy to live with. I was a punk kid from early on. Once they kicked me out, I bounced around a lot. My friends took me in occasionally, other times I lived on the street. Shortly after I turned twenty-one, I found God. I got ordained online and followed my calling. Once I hit my early thirties, I began losing faith in humanity. I don't have to tell you there are a lot of hypocrites out there. I got tired of the moneymakers calling the shots, acting like they owned the church."

The crowd roared on the television, catching their attention briefly as the Ducks scored. "I met Tank around then." Bobby continued, "He was about the most honest man I knew. Didn't pull any punches. He said it like it was, even if at the time it wasn't what you wanted to hear. After getting to know him over a couple of years, he asked me to join his MC. I left the church and the hypocrites behind. Haven't looked back."

"You still believe in God, Preacher?"

Bobby rubbed his long beard. Damn thing was impressive. Full and long. "I've seen a lot of ugly in my life. It's mankind I've lost faith in. Not God."

Anton wasn't sure he believed in the afterlife. His parents had been believers. He hoped if there was a heaven, they had found it. Men like Tank, he was pretty sure wouldn't be meeting up with them. His parents were good people. No matter how honest Bobby thought the Devils' president to be, some sins you couldn't atone for.

"That scrawny little barkeep," Bobby shifted subjects, "you trust him?"

"Draven?" Anton picked at the label on his bottle. "Fucker's a weasel. He's all about making money. So yeah, I trust he'll do what's needed to get the job done. The faster he turns over the smack, the more money that's in it for him. He'll work hard to move it. But like him? No. I don't think that has any relevance on his trustworthiness, though. Just my personal preferences."

"You think he still might be in bed with the Sons?"

"I think the Sons cost him a lot of money. It's safe to say any relationship they may have had was severed along with his drug funds."

Bobby tipped back his beer, finishing it. "You're a standup guy, Rogue. You say Draven's on the up-and-up, then I'll take your word for it. I won't ask again. I could care less about your personal feelings. They don't count in business decisions. I'm not a fan of all the Devils either. But like them or not, they've become my brothers."

"That's where we agree, Preacher." Anton took the two empty bottles and headed for the kitchen, only to return with two fresh beers. "Just because I became a Devil doesn't mean I have to like all of the son of a bitches."

Bobby took the bottle and settled against the sofa to watch the game. Anton hoped, when the dust finally settled, he could save Bobby from the feds. He wouldn't mind bringing him on as a Son. The man seemed like he could use a good break in life.

Anton's gaze caught a glimpse of the house down the road through the adjacent window, making his pulse kick up a notch. Anton hoped she had noticed his slight acknowledgement as they rode past, small that it had been. He couldn't afford taking a chance of Bobby knowing about her. Though he believed the man on the up-and-up, he couldn't chance Bobby mentioning her to Tank.

She'd looked damn fine standing on her porch, dressed in black leggings and a long white top. He could see the hint of a black bra beneath her blouse, turning his blood hot. Diesel had definitely recognized him as he had bounded down the porch steps and headed toward the country lane. Anton was only too glad he had returned to Kimber's side and not tried to follow them to the farmhouse, saving Anton from explaining why the neighbor's dog had a soft spot for him.

The tall blond man on the porch hadn't escaped his notice either. Anton planned on asking her who the hell was keeping her company the past couple of days. Hell, her mattress had hardly cooled from them heating up the sheets a few nights ago. She best not be giving the young man false hopes because Anton had no plans of sharing. If the blond had any ideas at all of getting into her pants, Anton would make sure he knew Kimber's nights were already taken.

"What kind of action can we expect to find way out here in the middle of fucking nowhere?" Bobby asked, taking Anton's mind off his desire to head back down the road. "Not that I don't like your company, Rogue, but I don't think I can hang out here 24/7. There has to be somewhere we can go that ain't the Sons' territory."

"We could check out Murphy's Tavern. It's a country bar. It's close enough to the Rave, where we can keep a better eye on Draven. We'll leave the bikes and cuts here, take my Ford truck. The law hangs at Murphy's, so the Sons of Sangue steer clear of the joint."

Bobby looked at his nearly empty bottle and shook the small amount left. "How about we head over there once the sun sets and check out the action. You game?"

"I'm in. Don't forget we need to keep a low profile, Preacher. We don't need to attract the attention of the locals who hang there either."

"We're here to keep an eye on Draven and the Rave, make sure he's moving the heroin. He isn't doing his job, then Tank will have yours and my asses." Bobby ran a hand through his bangs again. "I'm not putting my ass on the line for that little drug dealer."

Anton, on the other hand, would. "Let me go shower and catch a few hours of sleep and I'll be ready to party. You're welcome to use the shower up the stairs and the bedroom to the right of it. We can head for Murphy's around ten."

"Sounds good, man. The only thing that would make my night better is to find some sweet young thing who would be into my ugly mug."

Anton laughed. "I'm sure there might be one little young thing willing to take pity on you."

Bobby stood, walked his bottle into the kitchen, and set the empty alongside the others. "I'll grab my bag, head upstairs, and see you back down here in a few hours. I could use a little shut-eye myself."

"Sounds like a plan, Preacher." He slapped him on the shoulder, then headed for his own room on the other side of the kitchen.

Anton needed to move smack ... a lot of smack if he were to catch the attention of Raúl Trevino Caballero to get him that much desired meeting. The sooner, the better.

Now that he knew Cara and Hernandez meant to send Grayson's old lady into the war zone, Anton was going to do everything he could to keep her out of it. No way in hell was he going to have Grayson kicking his ass for her involvement. Cara and Hernandez might have thought it a good idea, but they had yet to meet Tank and Spider.

TIM MCGRAW'S *LIVE LIKE YOU WERE DYING* filtered through the ceiling speakers. Kimber swayed in her chair, gently in time to the tune. It was one of her favorite country songs and sort of mimicked what she and Anton had been doing since his reappearance in Oregon. Living in the moment. A jukebox, pale blue and red lights circling the glass showcase, sat in the corner of Murphy's Tavern. If no one plunked quarters into the coin slot, then it had been set for auto play. Kimber had been the one to choose this song and the next three following.

Tena sipped from her glass of pink moscato, while Kimber opted for an ice cold beer. Occasionally, she enjoyed a beer on tap from a frosty mug, over her go to dry, red wine. Tonight had definitely been a beer night.

Murphy's was more her type of crowd, much more so than the Blood 'n' Rave. This crowd consisted of mid-twenty to thirty-somethings and up. A few off duty deputies, she recognized, sat at the next table over. The tavern had a safe, warm vibe. Quite the opposite from the Rave.

When Tena had called, following the evening shift at the library, and suggested they all meet up for a drink, she wouldn't take a no for an answer. Tena and Chad were bound and determined to get her out of the house. Kimber supposed a night out was better than sitting at home alone. After all, her night had consisted of her sitting in the recliner trying to read, occasionally watching out the side window, in hopes of catching a glimpse of Anton.

Unfortunately, she couldn't make the short trek to his house. Trouble had followed Anton home. Knowing he hadn't wanted to introduce her to that side of his life, he wouldn't be happy if she disregarded his warning.

Taking a sip of her ice cold beer, wiping away the foam from her upper lip with her bar napkin, Kimber had to admit she was glad her friends had called and talked her into leaving the house. No matter how much she wanted to spend time with Anton, it wasn't going to happen unless Anton managed to ditch his friend.

The bar's owner, Lyle Murphy, had bought them all a round of drinks. Apparently, Tena had gone to high school with his niece Tamera. Last Kimber knew, Tamera lived with one of the Sons of Sangue and had made Lyle a great uncle. Working at the library, Kimber heard all the latest gossip.

Chad took a sip from his frosty mug, while scouting the room for eye candy. "What about that one?" he nudged Tena with his elbow.

"Not my type." Tena shook her head. "He's more your type."

"I won't argue with you, girlfriend. I wouldn't mind getting a little rumpy-pumpy with that wolf."

"Wolf?" Kimber asked.

"A gay man who doesn't act like a queen," Chad supplied.

"Oh… How do you know he's gay?"

Chad gave Kimber a sideways glance. "You question my gaydar? Honey, did you not just watch his eyes as the man over there with the sweet little ass walked by? No straight man is going to ogle another man's backside the way he did. I'll be all over him before the night is over."

"I have no doubt." Tena laughed. "Sad, you pick up far more men than I do."

Not because Tena wasn't attractive. On the contrary, Tena was very cute. She might not be the next Victoria Secret model, being a bit curvier, but Kimber had always thought Tena cut herself short. She wore her blonde hair pixie style, complimenting her almond shaped, chocolate-colored eyes.

"Oh, my goodness." Tena gasped, catching Kimber's attention and drawing it toward the entrance. "Someone please tell me that's my next meal."

The large man walking through the door commanded attention just by making an appearance. He wore a pair of well-worn jeans low on his lean hips. A black leather jacket hugged his top half, with two tan stripes running the length of what looked to be very muscular arms. Beneath the jacket he sported a white T-shirt stretched across a massive chest. Kimber had a hard time looking away, even if he wasn't her type. He wore his beard long as well as the top of his hair, sporting a severe undercut. His bangs damn near reached his chin.

Tena all but salivated while Kimber's heart skipped a beat. She recognized the man as the same one following Anton home earlier in the day, which meant he might be trailing behind. Not that she didn't want to see him. Quite the opposite. She hoped he followed his friend through the door, even if just for the chance to ogle. Kimber couldn't help but worry what his reaction to her being there might be. Anton had no doubt planned a night out, and seeing her hadn't been part of it.

Thank goodness Kimber had arrived before him. Last thing she wanted was Anton thinking she followed him. Not that she didn't crave his company, but she'd be damned before she'd make a fool of herself, tripping all over him like a schoolgirl with a crush.

The large, bearded man walked over to the bar, pulled out a stool and sat, ordering a beer from Lyle. He paid little attention to the rest of the bar patrons, and instead focused on his beer. The tavern door opened a second time, producing Anton. His good looks never failed to catch her breath. By the once-overs he received from the rest of the patrons, half the women in the bar thought him damn hot as well.

Anton took a brief glance around, his gaze catching hers and holding. He tipped his chin in a barely-there nod before turning and joining his buddy at the bar, giving her his back. Kimber took another sip of her icy brew, hoping to cool her rising libido, knowing the night wouldn't end with her getting anywhere close to Anton. He had made his desire clear, to keep them a secret.

If all his brothers looked like the bear of a man who sat beside him, it was no wonder he didn't want them knowing about her. The large man didn't appear to be the least bit friendly. As a matter of fact, he looked scary as hell.

"Isn't that your neighbor?" Chad asked, bringing her attention back to her coworkers.

"It is."

"He's super yummy. Too bad he's a hetty."

"Maybe for you." Tena laughed. "We're quite happy with them being heterosexual. You keep your eye on the candy you found earlier. Leave Mr. Tall, Dark and Dangerous to Kimber. I'll take Mr. Bear-alicious for myself, thank you very much."

Kimber chuckled. "Somehow I doubt Anton's friend would be happy with the title you just gave him, Tena."

"You think?" She winked at Kimber, then stood. "Let's just see how he reacts."

Not giving Kimber a chance to stop her, Tena sauntered toward the bar, causing Kimber to groan. Not her fault. She hoped Anton realized she had nothing to do with her friend's actions or boldness.

Chad, oblivious to Kimber's distress, clapped his hands. "She is good."

Kimber's gaze widened. "Are you not worried?"

"Why should I be?"

"That man is an outlaw biker."

He shrugged. "Sweetie, Tena can take care of herself. Watch and learn."

Tena walked up to bar and stood to the man's right, the opposite side from Anton. Both men glanced Tena's way. Kimber could tell by Anton's expression he was more than a little curious. Instead of giving the men her attention, Tena motioned for Lyle. Leaning in, she whispered something to the owner, causing him to laugh. Anton briefly looked at Kimber, then turned his attention back to the curvy blonde and his buddy, who was now eyeing her from the feet up.

Tena grabbed her newly poured glass of wine, said something to the man beside her, who responded with a shake of his head and a large grin. Heading back to their table, she added a bit of extra sass in her sway. The big guy threw a ten on the counter, paying Lyle for her drink. Anton laughed, slapping his friend on the shoulder.

*What the heck had Tena said?*

She sat back down at their table, and smiled, seemingly quite pleased with herself. Whatever she had said, caught the man's attention enough, because he kept peering over his shoulder at her.

Chad smiled big as could be. "Spill it, girlfriend."

Tena took another sip of wine. "Give him a few minutes. He'll be making his way over."

Kimber leaned forward in her chair. "What did you say?"

"I asked Lyle for a glass of wine and whispered that the big guy would be buying. When the man looked my way, I simply gasped and said, 'Who let Mr. Bear-alicious in the door?' I asked if I could buy him a beer. He, instead, insisted on buying mine."

As if on cue, Anton's buddy stood, pushed back from the bar and headed toward their table. Chad quickly excused himself, heading for the wolf he had spotted earlier, leaving Kimber the odd woman out. Anton stayed in his position at the bar.

Not waiting to be asked to join them, the large man pulled out a chair, set his beer on the table and sat. "What's your name, doll?"

Tena toyed with the stem of her wineglass, telling Kimber she was far more nervous than she let on. "I don't believe you told me yours yet."

"Bobby. But most call me Preacher."

"I'm Tena." She held out her hand to shake Bobby's. He looked at her hand oddly for a moment, before taking it and giving it a quick shake. "Nice to meet you, Preacher. Thanks for the drink, by the way."

"My pleasure. You come here often?"

"Not really. But if you're going to be here, it might become my new favorite hangout."

Bobby laughed. "And they say men have all the pickup lines."

Tena shrugged. "Is it working?"

Bobby pushed his bangs back off his face, producing a pair of cerulean blue eyes. "Doll, you were working it the minute you walked up to the bar. You've got some killer curves."

Kimber almost groaned. She wasn't about to stick around and listen to their cheesy pick-up lines. She opted to risk upsetting Anton and approached the bar. He could always tell Bobby later he had no idea who she was. After all, she had been the one to approach him.

"Hey, handsome."

Anton turned his head. He greeted her with a grin. "What took you so long?"

"I thought you might be mad."

Lyle set a fresh icy mug in front of Kimber. Anton reached into his pocket and pulled out a five and handed it to Lyle.

"You didn't want your friends to know about me."

"I still don't." Anton took a sip of his whiskey. The strong scent tickled her senses. "If he asks, I'll tell him you were hitting on me. I'm not about to turn away a gorgeous brunette."

"You think I'm gorgeous?"

"If I could get you alone, I'd show you just how beautiful I think you are."

"Maybe they'll leave first." Kimber's thumb indicated Bobby and Tena behind her.

"Or we could make quick use of the bathrooms down the hall."

Her face heated and the sweet spot between her thighs dared her to be bold. Kimber glanced down the darkened hall and couldn't recall any woman using the bathroom in the last ten minutes or so. Was she actually thinking of doing as Anton suggested? Six months ago, she might have slapped him for such an outrageous suggestion.

Instead, Kimber stood and winked at him. "Let's see what you got."

Pushing away from the bar, Kimber headed down the hall for the ladies' room, praying it wasn't occupied and hoping Anton didn't keep her waiting.

## CHAPTER THIRTEEN

Draven paced his lavishly furnished apartment, more nervous than a cat in a dog pound. Brea sat cross-legged on his cream-colored leather, semicircular sofa. A large crystal chandelier cast little diamonds of light about the room, reminding Draven of the sparkle now missing in Brea's eyes. Most didn't know about his digs, the Sons of Sangue included. Today, he was certainly glad for not disclosing his home address.

He had returned home from California to find Brea in dire need of nourishment. Her pale, translucent flesh said as much. He had only been gone a few days, but her mate had been taken out five days ago and his dumb ass hadn't thought about bringing by a donor … until mere minutes ago when he walked through the door and found her curled into the corner of his sofa.

Her beautiful blue eyes were sunken, dark circles rimming her lower lashes. Her cheeks were hollow and her lips were a trembling thin line. Damn, he wanted to kick his own ass from here to the coast and back. Draven picked up the phone and dialed a number.

Brea lifted her tired gaze to his. "What are you doing?"

"Getting you communion. Something I should have done before I left. You need a donor like yesterday."

She gave a swift shake of her head. "No one knows about me. You can't."

"You've fed before, surely—"

"Kinky always brought the donors. He would feed from one, then drain enough from the other into a glass, telling them he was saving it for later."

Draven's brows drew together. "He could have hypnotized them into forgetting about you."

Brea took a shallow breath. "He didn't want to take the chance something might jog their memory about me."

"You expect me to cut one of them?" He shuddered. "Bring the blood to you?"

"You cannot heal their wounds." She paused, her blue eyes holding his. "You could feed me."

He chuckled, the sound belying his nerves. "Men can't be donors."

"Says who?"

"The Sons make the rules. I abide by them and enforce them."

"You're not a Son, nor am I."

"I'm not so sure I can, Brea." Another shiver passed through him. "I'm squeamish around blood."

She smiled, the sight so sweet that Draven was having trouble holding his ground. He wanted to see her nourished, give her blood, but he didn't want to lose his man card doing it. For damn sure he'd pass out at her feet. The only time he had given blood in his life, they had to scrape his sorry ass off the sterile flooring.

She beckoned him forward. Draven grimaced, rubbing his neck. Fuck. Not only was he squeamish, he truly was scared shitless of those fangs. For that reason, he had stayed away when the Sons fed, telling himself he was respecting their privacy. When in truth, vampires scared the bejesus out of him, far worse than any one of the Devils.

"Please, Draven." Brea's plea cut straight to his heart. She attempted to wet her overly dry lips with her tongue.

It was that one word, *"Please,"* that had him moving forward. He couldn't deny her. Draven forced his leaden feet to move in her direction. He kept his gaze to the floor, afraid to look upon her as she morphed into vampire form. He didn't want to taint the beautiful vision of her he kept stored in his mind. Brea had quickly become very special to him, and he wanted far more from her than he dare ask. She had belonged to Joseph, and one day another vampire would claim her. It was the way of their kind. Unmated females, due to the death of their mates, were to be claimed by another male. Without women vampires, there would be no male true bloods born. For that reason alone, the mates were to be cherished.

He slowly lowered to his knees just before the sofa. *Stop being a pussy.* Hell, he had faced guns, big ass guns, and men who weren't afraid to use them. Tipping his head, Draven pulled his black hair back so she'd have access to his carotid. His blood pumped through his veins, pounded in his ears. Surely, she could scent his fear.

How many times had he assured new donors how easy and painless it was to feed a vampire, when he had never done so himself?

"Draven." Her voice was thick with her fangs.

Brea whispered his name again, her fingers softly stroking the flesh of his neck, just beneath his ear. Damn, but it felt like a lover's caress. Not that he hadn't thought about it with her. Hell, no. He had dreamed about it in living color. He would've tried getting into her pants days ago, had she not been a vampire,

Had she not been a Gotti.

Had her godfather not been Raúl Trevino Caballero.

So much about her terrified him.

And yet her very essence called to him.

His name whispered from her lips again, before he finally had the courage to give her his gaze. Her blue eyes had transformed into twin black, glassy marbles, beautiful and mesmerizing. His reflection, full of wonder and terror, stared back at him. Her cheeks had become sunken, her brows more prominent. Though Draven had fully expected to be appalled by the transformation, he pleasantly found the exact opposite to be true.

He was enthralled, taken by her beauty.

His breath stuck in his throat when she opened her mouth and two long, razor sharp fangs jutted from her gums. Brea's fingers threaded through his hair, gently fisting it and holding his head steady. The inhuman-like strength he felt in her grasp told him he couldn't have made a mad dash for the door if he tried.

Her breath fanned his throat, causing a shiver to pass his spine and his groin to harden. The razor-sharp points of her fangs scraped his flesh mere seconds before the points punctured his skin and sank gums deep. A brief moment of pain quickly replaced with an ecstasy not found in any drug he had ever ingested. His dick ached with the need to rip her clothes from her body and bury himself deeply. Screw ethics and his promise not to touch her until her memory of Joseph had washed away. He desired her more than he had ever another human being.

*She isn't human,* he reminded himself.

She was a vampire, one capable of ripping out his heart in more ways than one.

Draven slipped his hands slowly up the inside of her thighs, needing to see if Brea also hungered for him. Surely, he wasn't alone in his desire. Just as he reached nirvana, cupping her sex through her leggings, she withdrew her fangs with a soft pop, licked the twin holes, then retreated from his touch.

Draven's face heated, embarrassed for his reaction and desire to take something not offered. "Fuck. I'm so sorry. I had no right."

Standing, he put distance between them. His erection still plagued the front of his now too tight jeans. The death chill he witnessed in her skin upon her arrival slowly left, replaced by a now warmer glow. Her fangs retreated into her gums and her features softened. Gone was the monster he once feared, only to realize her vampire form wasn't a horror at all. On the contrary, he found her more beautiful if that were possible.

Draven ground his teeth, disgusted with himself for trying to take advantage of Brea, realizing now how his donors must feel, especially those nourishing the mated ones. The sexual urges brought on by feeding them could never be satisfied. It was no wonder the Sons didn't want their mates feeding from male donors. The men would no doubt want to drain the males for taking such liberties, just as Draven had with Brea.

"Draven, there is no need to apologize."

He held her sky-blue gaze. "I damn near assaulted you, Brea. That deserves an apology."

"I felt it too, you know. We aren't immune."

"Then why—"

"Kinky was my whole life." Tears sprung to her eyes. "He held my heart. He still does. Having sex with you won't change that."

He ran a hand through his hair. Fuck, he felt like a heel. "I don't suppose."

"I feel the attraction too. But Kinky aside, you and I are never going to happen."

"Why?"

"Because I don't want to break your heart. And besides, you're human. Only vampires mate with vampires. Are you ready to make that transformation?"

His shock surely registered on his face.

"I didn't think so."

Draven took a shaky breath, knowing he had to deny his hunger for Brea and keep his dick to himself. She was correct about one thing. When she mated with another, it would break his heart. "What will you do?"

"When my family is no longer a threat, I'll present myself to Hawk. He'll choose a suitable mate for me."

"A man you don't love?"

She shrugged. "Who says I won't grow to love him? I'm tired of the secret. The Sons of Sangue need to know about me. I'll be a reminder of Kinky for them. His memory will stay alive through me. It's the least I can do for him."

"Until then?"

"You have a job to finish, Draven. You need to flush out my godfather."

"You're giving me permission?"

"You thought because he's my godfather I would want him protected?" Her gaze filled with anger. "I love my godfather. Make no mistake. But he's a very bad man, Draven. He needs to be taken down. I can't excuse his crimes. I may not stand in your way, but I won't help you find him either."

"Fair enough, angel."

Draven walked back over to the sofa and knelt before her. He palmed her cheeks and held her face so close her breath feathered his flesh. She smelled of white musk, a scent that would forever call to him, no matter who's mate she became. His gaze dropped to her lips. Not being able to help himself, he leaned forward and kissed her lips softly. Her answering moan told him what he had wanted to know. Even when he wasn't nourishing her, she desired him too. Brea may not ever be his, but before he gave her to another, he'd make damn sure she never forgot him.

A DIM, SINGLE BARE BULB, covered by a black wire cage, provided Anton shadows within which to shield his traipse down the hall. He took a quick glance over his shoulder to make sure no one spotted him entering the ladies' room. Not that he cared one iota what the hell people thought of him. Kimber's safety was at risk. Thankfully, Bobby had been preoccupied with the little blonde, who had been sitting with Kimber earlier.

Anton's gums ached with hunger. Blood rushed through his veins. His pulse thrummed in his ears. Having sex in a public restroom wasn't anything he hadn't done before. On the contrary, the Sons regularly looked for quick places to appease their need. The problem was, Kimber wasn't a seasoned donor used to a vampire's sexual appetites.

*Hell no.*

Protecting her at all costs should've been his first priority, not the erection demanding appeasement. Fucking her in a public place was high on his list of things not to do. And yet, he had been the one to make the outrageous suggestion. No way he could talk his dick out of heading for the restroom. Anton should be nursing a damn good whiskey and minding his own business. If anything happened to Kimber because he was unable to control his hormones, he'd have no one to blame but himself.

*Jesus, turn the fuck around.*

The idea Kimber had probably never fucked in public before, and was willing to do so with him, kept his feet planted to the floor just outside the door. He could hear her breathing, nearly feel her heart beat as if it were his own. He could scent her desire through the wood that separated them. His cock ached. His jeans were too damn tight. His little straight-laced librarian waited just beyond the door, and he'd be damned if he'd disappoint her.

Anton suppressed the growth of his fangs by gritting his teeth. The vampire wasn't far from the surface and taking over. He needed to put a leash on the little devil, at least until he could hypnotize Kimber. She wasn't ready for the truth. Nor did he think she would ever be.

Turning the rustic doorknob to the ladies' room, he pushed on the door. The creak of the aged hinges echoed down the empty hall. Even though anyone could easily bust through, locked or not, he flipped the bolt.

His heart skipped a beat. Kimber propped herself against a makeup vanity, her bare legs crossed at the ankles. Nothing but a flimsy white blouse hid her from his view. Damn, all he could think about was wrapping those legs around his waist while he pounded into her.

The lounge area suddenly felt as if it were two sizes too small.

The stalls must've been beyond the opened doorway to her right. Nothing more than a vanity and a well-used love seat graced the room — one he had no intention of using. The view from the mirror gracing the wall behind the vanity gave him a peak at her smooth, creamy white ass. Black pants dangled from her fingertips along with a pair of black lace panties.

Blood raced due south, robbing him of coherent thought.

His cock swelled all the more and Anton cursed beneath his breath.

The tail of her blouse hid what his nostrils detected. He'd bet if he slid his fingers between her thighs he'd find her wet. He didn't need the sense of touch to know. Hell, it tickled his nostrils. Her cheeks flushed. Anton sure hoped no one would be in need of the facilities, because no way in hell was he leaving without taking what she offered.

Kimber licked her lips.

He was hard enough to drive through a fucking concrete wall.

Anton reached down and ran a hand over the front of his jeans, hoping to alleviate some of the pressure. Her gaze heated, following the direction of his hand. Her breath hitched.

Cupping his erection, he asked, "This what you want, *tesoro*?"

Kimber smiled, then tossed her clothing to the floral love seat. An ugly painting hung on the wall above it, reminding him of an old cowboy rodeo. The bull rider hung on with one gloved hand to keep from being bucked off. Anton almost laughed at the parallel. He was about to give Kimber a ride to remember.

The crook of her finger had him moving in her direction. In two long strides, he gripped her waist and pulled her flush. His erection nestled hot between them, earning him a moan from her lips. He'd bet it wouldn't take her long to reach a climax. Christ, he was a fraction from coming himself.

"Kimber."

Her warm brown gaze hooded. Her pupils damn near swallowed her irises. He loved seeing the desire he caused in her expression. If she ever found out he had hypnotized her, forgiveness wouldn't be part of her vocabulary. Their short affair would surely come to an end and he wouldn't blame her for hating him.

"Hear me now. You will not remember all of what you're about to see. You'll feel everything, know that it is me, but my face will remain in shadows. Do you understand?"

Kimber acknowledged with a nod.

"Good." Razor sharp fangs filled his mouth. Thickening bones stretched his facial skin taut.

Kimber drew her lower lip between her teeth. She ran her hand down his sternum, dipping her fingers into the front of his jeans, and slipping the button free. Ah hell! Anton stepped back, giving her room to work the zipper before sliding her hand inside his briefs and encompassing him, her hand working his shaft from the root to the tip.

He hissed.

Kimber pushed down the front of his jeans and slipped his erection free from his briefs. The cool air-conditioning washed over his flesh, doing little to cool him. She had him damn close to going up in flames. Kimber's thumb brushed over the mushroom head, smoothing the drop of precum over the smooth tip.

*Damn, he'd never make it at this rate.*

Anton growled, wishing there was more time. He disentangled her hand, grabbed her by the waist and easily lifted her off the vanity. Her hands tangled in the hair at his nape and her thighs wrapped about him, her ankles locking at the small of his back. He needed to feel her wrapping his cock now.

He doubted it would take Bobby long to note his absence. Every second counted.

Anton slanted his lips over hers, pulling her lower lip between his teeth. His fangs nicked the soft flesh, allowing him to taste the sweet ambrosia of her blood, tempting the vampire in him. Damn him for wanting the forbidden fruit, to sink his fangs and drink his fill. Instead, he suckled the small cut, teasing his palate with the small offering. Her blood was off-limits. He may not be a part of the Sons at the moment, but his heart was still a full-fledged member. He'd continue to abide by their rules.

Her hands slipped beneath his tee and up his back, scoring the flesh with her nails. The delicious sting of the small scrapes had him growling as the last thread of his will snapped. Anton reached between them and gripped his cock.

The doorknob rattled, followed by a knock.

Anton's nostrils flared, the scent telling him Bobby wasn't on the other side. He didn't give a rat's ass who waited. He wasn't about to stop. Kimber's gaze flitted to exit, her cheeks flushing.

*Dear Lord, don't let her back out now.*

"Give me a moment." She placed her fingers over his lips, stopping him from telling whoever it was to take a fucking hike. "I'm not feeling well. I just need a minute or two of privacy."

Kimber stifled her giggle into the crook of his neck. Anton heard the woman's disgruntled response about not leaving a mess. Her footfalls thankfully retreated back down the hall, buying them a little more time.

Not willing to waste a second more, he kissed her deeply, fucking her mouth with his tongue. His cock ached as it nestled against her hot, wet folds. Kimber dug her heels against the cheeks of his ass, silently giving him permission to bury himself balls-deep.

Breaking the kiss, his breath sawed from his lungs. The pulse at the base of her throat hammered in his ears. His fangs lengthened, threatening to take the nourishment just scant inches from his lips. Anton kissed his way down her soft downy cheek to the hallow of her throat. Her blood pulsed just beneath his tongue as he tasted the salt from her skin. Kimber tipped back her head, unknowingly giving the vampire in him permission to sink his fangs. It took every ounce of willpower not to do so. Instead, he gripped his cock again and slid it along her slick folds, before positioning the head. Her answering moan had him shoving into her, burying himself to the hilt. He withdrew slowly, before sliding back in, loving the way her walls squeezed him in response.

Kimber tightened her hold on his hair.

"Hard," she whispered against his ear.

Digging his fingers into her ass, he withdrew, then trust back into her, unable to get the leverage for what she asked. Anton backed her to the neighboring wall, anchoring her. He pulled out and slammed back into her. Her back slid up the paneling. Kimber gasped, her gaze fixing his. With each thrust, she rode the wall, her breasts bouncing beneath her white blouse. It was then he realized she must have removed her bra as well. His mouth itched to draw her nipples between his lips, to suckle them deep. No time. The woman from earlier would likely be returning. Better that than Bobby getting curious.

Anton's jeans rode low on his ass, the front now cupping his balls. Kimber's breath quickened, telling him she wasn't far from reaching her climax. Anton released one delectable ass cheek, balancing her on his forearm. He ran his free hand between them, his thumb finding the tight knot of nerves, just above where they were joined. The sight of his cock sliding in and out of her, had him racing her to the finish line. He circled her clit, teasing the taut little bud.

Kimber tilted her head, the beautiful arch of her neck taunting him. He placed a kiss along the gentle curve, scenting her sweet blood just beneath the surface. The sound of her blood rushing through her veins traveled to his ears. It wouldn't take much to give into his hunger. Anton ran the sharp points over her silken flesh, just as her climax began milking him for all he was worth. Keeping his fangs in check, he slammed into her a few more times before his own climax let loose.

His ass cheeks tightened, every muscle in him going taut.

His forehead rested on her shoulder, his heart hammering against his chest.

They stayed locked together until both their breathing slowed. The soft knock to the door came again. Kimber chuckled as Anton groaned.

"Two minutes please."

The woman slapped the door, clearly disgruntled, before her footfalls could be heard retreating back down the corridor. Anton slowly lowered Kimber to her feet, the flush of her cheeks warming him.

"Gorgeous," he whispered before kissing her hard and quick.

He stepped back and tucked himself into his briefs and jeans. "I'll head out first. It will appear as if I'm leaving the men's. You wait a minute or so before following."

"How long are you in Pleasant?"

Her question surprised him. "As long as it takes. I can't discuss it, Kimber, but until it's done Preacher and I will be staying at the farmhouse."

Her well-kissed lips turned up. "I'll get to see you then?"

If he did what was best for her, he'd tell her no. "When I can."

She nodded. Anton hoped she would leave it at that. He wished things could be different, but until he finished his undercover work he was in it neck deep. Letting Kane down wasn't an option. Even if it meant putting his own desire on hold. Besides, when he wasn't trying to fool himself, he knew there was no possible way for this to end well. There was no way Kimber would see him for anything other than a monster once the truth came out.

Turning, he slid the deadbolt, peeked into the hallway, then slipped out of the room unseen. The sound of Kimber's slacks sliding over her silky flesh as she redressed, followed him down the hall. Sometimes his acute hearing was a damn curse. Jamming a hand through his hair, he bit back a string of curses. Anton walked over to the bar and ordered a whiskey — a very tall one. Instead of being replete, he wanted more. He wanted happy-ever-after, waking up at dawn and slowly making love. Hell, he wanted it all. Walking away for good one day was going to kill him.

Anton gripped his glass, turned and saw Preacher still talking to the blonde, paying him no mind at all. He downed the contents, then placed it back on the counter and headed for the exit. This close to the Rave, he might as well find the nourishment he denied himself moments ago. Bobby was a big boy. He could find his own way back to the farmhouse.

## CHAPTER FOURTEEN

"Y̲OU NEED TO KEEP TAMERA FROM HEADING DOWN THE coast." Anton leaned forward, bracing his forearms on the breakfast bar at Cara Brahnam's house, bringing him down to eye level with her. Anton had no clue where Kane had taken off to, but his scent wasn't in the house. "There's been a change of plans. Obviously, I'm no longer in Santa Barbara."

"You're running a little late with the information, Blondy." Cara's brows drew together, clearly perturbed. "Don't you think you should've told us about you coming back to the farmhouse after it was decided?"

Anton righted himself to his full height, bracing his hands on the granite. "I just found out Thursday. Not my fucking fault."

"Today is Saturday."

"Glad to hear you know what day of the week it is, Brahnam."

She ignored his jibe, turned, and grabbed a couple of mugs from the cupboard. Cara poured them each a hot cup of coffee from the pot in the corner, then slid a mug across the counter to him. Bringing the mug to his nose, he inhaled the smell of fresh brewed coffee. He still loved it, always would.

"She's probably already in Santa Barbara."

"Is that where Viper is?"

Cara nodded. "He's keeping an eye on her ... at a distance, of course. You were supposed to be her contact."

Anton steeled his jaw. Not his fault. He'd be damned if she'd make him feel as if it was. "Tank sent me and Preacher north. Couldn't be helped. He wanted us to keep an eye on Draven and their interest in Oregon. You should've called before sending her to Santa Barbara, Cara. Don't lay this shit on my doorstep. Besides, with Viper keeping an eye on her, he won't allow anything to happen to her."

Anton quickly brought Cara up to speed on Tank's order to run heroin through the colleges, more specific Oregon University. She hadn't been any happier about the plan than Anton. It was one thing to run drugs through the nightclubs, but taking it to the schools didn't sit well with him or Cara.

"Viper go alone?"

"Actually, no. He called in Red. It appears the Sons are bringing them back as a puppet club."

"Hawk agreed to that?"

"He wasn't thrilled, but he knew the Sons could use the numbers since someone seems hell-bent on taking out the members. Not to mention you going rogue."

"The P know where his twin went?"

"He only told Hawk he was heading to Washington to talk to Red. There's more." Cara placed the carafe back on hot plate. "Vlad told Viper that Mircea's in the States."

"You think Mircea might have had something to do with Kinky's death, or you still believe the Devils are guilty?"

Cara took in a deep breath. "You tell me. You're closer to the Devils than anyone else."

"I put out feelers, but no one's talking. Besides, what would the motive be?"

"I doubt they'd need one."

"Maybe not. But why Kinky? It doesn't make sense to come all the way here to take out one of the quieter Sons. Why not also Wolf or Xander? They were all there." Anton took a sip of his coffee, then set it back on the breakfast bar. "We already know Mircea has an axe to grind."

"I don't think Mircea's guilty. Neither does Kane. A gunshot to the forehead wouldn't be his style. If he wanted to come in and execute one of the Sons, he'd make sure every one of them knew he was judge, jury, and executioner. He wants retaliation for Rosalee. There's no doubt about that, but Kinky had nothing to do with Rosalee. I hate to say it, I think we might have two possible threats out there. Mircea gunning for Kane or Kaleb, and the Devils taking out one of the sons."

"What's your theory?"

"Turf war. Taking us out one-by-one, so they can take over our state. Running drugs here is only the beginning. They have no idea the Knights are now backing us, which is confidential, Blondy. I'd rather they didn't know about that."

"They won't hear it from me. And the big guy? What's he have to say about all of this?"

"Vlad says Mircea's on the run. Hasn't heard from him last we knew. I haven't heard from Vlad since our last meeting with him."

"So it's not out of the question he might be responsible. Maybe he's a chicken shit and hired the hit."

"He's definitely a coward. I still think he's far too arrogant not to let it be known he took out Kinky, for whatever his agenda might be." She took her mug to her lips and blew at the steam rising from the hot liquid before taking a sip. "Who's this Preacher you mentioned?"

"Bobby Bourassa. Have Hernandez check him out, but I don't think you'll find much other than a few minor arrests. He seems on the up-and-up. Good guy. He's staying with me at the farmhouse."

"He better be on the up-and-up. You brought him to Pleasant" — she jabbed her forefinger in his direction — "you keep him in line. He causes trouble in our state, it's your ass Hawk will be after."

Anton grinned. Kaleb already wanted his ass, so what was new? "I'll take responsibility for him. He causes problems, I'll take care of it. Something tells me I won't have to worry about him."

"I should probably call Kane, let him know the Devils went proactive and are back to running the drugs. Heroin? Damn." Cara worried her lower lip. "We don't get a handle on this, I don't have to tell you the ODs will rise. We're going to have a lot of strung out kids."

"Heroin is more profitable."

"It is. But that doesn't mean I have to like it."

"I wasn't a fan either when Tank laid it on us." Anton flattened his palms on the counter. "Tank wasn't budging when I posed an argument. His orders came straight from Raúl. The kingpin no doubt felt the economic crunch when he put things on hold because of the rumored DEA's interest. Raúl's going after bigger profits."

"Give me a few minutes, Blondy. I need to pass this along to Kane. Not sure I'm going to pull Tamera just yet. She might not get any leads on drugs, but maybe she can get one of those blowhards bragging about what happened to Kinky."

"Make sure you let Viper know, having Preacher along for the ride, I didn't have time to call and warn you I wasn't in Santa Barbara."

"You should've found time." Her gaze darkened. "Keeping Tamera safe is our number one priority. Thank goodness Kane and Red are trailing her or you would've left her ass hang out to dry down there."

"Fuck you, Cara." Heat rose up his neck. "I'm in this mess because you stuck me here. You don't like the job I'm doing, then fucking pull me."

"I don't have to tell you what Gypsy would have to say about this mess."

He chuckled and shook his head. "He'd no doubt blame me as well, giving him another reason to hate me."

Anton should've found a private moment and called, letting them know he was heading north. But how the hell was he to know they had already sent Tamera to Santa Barbara?

Cara was just as much at fault for putting her at risk and not calling him. Tamera was left to tackle the job on her own with a bunch of lowlifes who would think nothing of harming her. There was no doubt with Tamera's good looks and investigative skills, she might be able to help the case of Joseph's execution and get someone singing, that is if the Devils were guilty. But if she got too nosy ... it might just put her in a heap of trouble.

In which case, Grayson would hand him his ass.

THE SONS OF SANGUE WERE easy pickings. He could take out any one of them at any given moment he chose and they would be powerless to stop him. They weren't up to his caliber. The only thing keeping him from wiping them out was his brother. Vlad had already proved his feelings in the matter where they were concerned when he had taken his stepdaughter's head.

*Rosalee.*

Forgiving his brother for that deed wasn't going to happen.

No matter how long he lived.

Mircea stood in the forest, downwind, watching the Sons of Sangue's clubhouse from the rear of the building. The wind would work in his favor for masking his scent. One of the dark, short haired vampires arrived moments ago, took off his helmet and headed inside. A few other motorcycles sat in the parking lot, along with a box truck, telling Mircea the man wasn't alone.

Mircea had been in Pleasant for a short period of time, and he'd stay as long as need be. He was in no hurry. Hell, he had an eternity to obtain revenge. Being hasty wrought mistakes. When the curly haired vampire had been shot, execution style, he had been there. Not that Mircea gave a rat's ass who had fired the kill shot, but he took great pleasure in knowing he wasn't their only enemy.

Mircea couldn't take credit.

The dead biker wasn't on his short list of vampires he wanted executed.

No, Mircea gunned for Vlad's kin, Kane and Kaleb. He had told his brother it would be Kane's decision as to who he took out, knowing his ex-son-in-law would do the noble thing and choose himself. Since Kane had been the one to betray his stepdaughter in the first place, Mircea would be happy with his obvious choice. He'd take great pleasure in dealing out a slow, painful death. In truth, Mircea harbored no ill will toward Kaleb or his son. And since Kane would never allow harm to come to either, he'd sacrifice himself to save those he loved.

Kaleb's crime had been the taking of Alec Funar's head, a primordial, which should've earned the short-tempered fool a speedy trip to hell. Truth be told, Alec had been a pain in Mircea's ass from the get-go. The stupid shit considered himself superior, thinking he deserved a place in Mircea's household. Alec thought by fucking his stepdaughter it put him in good graces with Mircea.

He had thought wrong.

Mircea chuckled. When he heard Alec Funar had lost his head, Mircea had been elated. Rosalee used Alec to her gain, and he wasn't smart enough to see it. He wouldn't have allowed the fool to live much longer anyway. There was no way in hell he would've allowed Rosalee to mate with the idiot. So Mircea merely humored him, for he had an eternity in which to get what he desired most.

*Rosalee.*

His mate had not deserved the gift of eternal life he had given her. She had whined from the day she had been turned, not having the stomach to feed from mere mortals. Mircea was thrilled when Rosalee gave into her mother's wishes and took her immorality by ending her life and saving Mircea the trouble.

Who in their right mind would complain about being a vampire?

Little did Rosalee know she had played right into Mircea's hand. He had at one time loved his mate, but unfortunately he had grown bored with her. So he played the grieving widower to a T. No one knew he had wished to end her endless whining, to rip her beating heart from her chest. Since Rosalee wasn't of his lineage, and her mother's life had been cut short, he was free to pursue his stepdaughter. She was far more exotic looking than her mother, and far more calculating, which had been a huge fucking turn-on. Kane no longer stood in the way, since Mircea had gladly given him permission to mate with his little detective. Everything was falling into place.

Until Vlad ended her life.

Had Mircea convinced Rosalee that they should be mated, that they were perfectly suited, there would've been no stopping them.

Now Vlad must pay.

He wasn't fool enough to think he could ever best his brother. On the contrary, Vlad would separate his head from his shoulders with little effort, just as Vlad had Rosalee. Besides, ending his life wouldn't mete out the suffering he aimed for.

Instead, he'd take out the one thing dear to him.

*Kane.*

Mircea would be even with Vlad. He'd be free to find a mate and finally be able to live his life in peace. His family tree had all but died out. It was time he found someone to carry on his lineage.

To make sure Vlad wouldn't dare to retaliate, Mircea would threaten to take Kaleb's son. Oh, he wouldn't be so cruel as to kill a child, though he'd lead them to believe the child was dead. Mircea would raise him to be a mirror image, and make damn sure he never knew his real father and mother.

## CHAPTER FIFTEEN

"What's that smile on your face, Kimber?" Tena asked as she sauntered up to the main desk at the library where Kimber was checking in books.

Heat crawled up Kimber's neck and warmed her cheeks as she tried to suppress her smile. "I have no idea what you're talking about."

"You can't play coy with me. You may think I didn't notice you and your sexy, to-die-for neighbor doing a little disappearing act the other night at Murphy's, but I did."

Kimber raised her gaze. "Preacher didn't notice, did he?"

Tena's brows met over the bridge of her nose. "Why?"

"It's nothing, really." Kimber scanned a couple more books. "It's just Anton would rather his biker friends didn't know about us."

"So there is an us?" Her coworker clapped her hands and giggled. "I knew something was going on between the two of you. How is he in bed?"

"Tena!" Kimber did a quick sweep of the library with her gaze. Only two older ladies were on the second floor, and neither were within hearing distance. Still, she lowered her voice. "I'm not about to divulge details. Anton and I are just friends."

"So you went down the hall, occupied the bathroom for about fifteen minutes by yourself."

"Yes." Kimber went back to checking in new books, busying herself so she wouldn't have to look Tena in the eye. She was a horrible liar. "I wasn't feeling well."

"So said the woman who needed to use the restroom. She seemed a little put off." Tena chuckled, then leaned in. "I know different, because I happened to see Rogue leave the ladies' room about five minutes before you."

"Preacher didn't—"

"Relax." She chuckled. "His attention was on me. Besides, his back was to the hall. Lucky for you, I was the one facing it."

"I do hope you were careful with Preacher. You know literally nothing about the man."

"I'm betting you know very little about your neighbor, and yet you were holing up in the ladies' room together."

The heat returned to Kimber's cheeks. "I've known Anton for well over a year."

"So then tell me about him. Parents? Past girlfriends? What's his favorite food?"

Kimber took a seat on the counter-high stool behind the desk and sighed. "Okay. Point taken. I've known him for a while. I guess we've never shared anything really personal. Now that you mention it, I might've been a bit more forthcoming than he has been."

In fact, she really hadn't thought to question him at all about his life as their relationship had never gone beyond the physical. They were friends with benefits, whether she liked it or not. He had bought her a dog to insure her safely, which meant he had to care somewhat beyond the physical, didn't it? Something told her that if she started asking those kinds of questions, Anton would head for Santa Barbara as fast as his motorcycle could carry him.

Kimber frowned. "Okay, so I know very little about him. You know any more about Preacher?"

"His real name is Bobby Bourassa. How sexy is that?"

She chuckled. "I know Anton's full name too, smarty pants."

"I know he got his nickname because he used to be a preacher, that he grew up in foster care, then joined the Devils when he lost faith in humanity." She punctuated her knowledge with a wide smile. "Oh, and he has twin cross tats on his shoulders that I find super sexy. And may I just say, he looks like he's been working out for years. His arms are delish!"

Kimber placed another stack of books in front of Tena. One of her eyebrows raised. "You didn't take him home, did you?"

"No."

"Then how did you see his tattoos?"

"He had on a T-shirt under his leather. He raised his sleeve, Miss Gutter Mind." Tena gave her a toothy grin, telling Kimber she jested. "I tried getting him back to my place. He wasn't having it."

"Ooooh ... you little tart." Chad approached the two of them, his shift having just started. "The big guy turned you down flat? Say it isn't so."

Tena slapped Chad's shoulder. "I don't have to sleep with someone the moment I meet them."

"Could've fooled me, girlfriend."

"How about you?" Tena pushed a stack of books in Chad's direction. "You get the pants off the man you were chasing?"

"You know it." He grabbed the pile of books and headed for the bookshelves. Looking back over his shoulder, he said, "He was delicious with a capital D. I might even consider seeing him a second time."

Kimber laughed, enjoying the newly developed camaraderie. A few weeks ago, they wouldn't have thought to talk about their dating lives around her. To think she had missed out on all this fun because she had come across as a stick in the mud.

"So Preacher turned you down?" Kimber asked, truly surprised.

Tena's cheeks reddened. "It was worth a try. Couldn't let all that hotness go to waste, could I?"

"I thought he looked pretty interested."

"Oh, he's interested." Tena's gaze lit, her smile reaching her eyes. "He said he'd like to get to know me while he's in town. Said he wasn't into one-night stands. Wasn't his style."

"I suppose that's good. But how much can you really get to know him in a short amount of time? Hard telling how long they'll be in the area."

"Preacher said they would be around for a while, and that he and Rogue had a job to do. Until then, they'd be staying at Rogue's."

Anton had mentioned something about as long as it takes the other night. Kimber couldn't help wonder what job they spoke of. She liked having Anton back at the farmhouse. Spending more time with him made her pulse quicken. She hoped this job had nothing to do with the Sons of Sangue or put him in any kind of real danger.

Kimber thought about what Tena had said, that she didn't really know much about Anton. Maybe it was time to find out what made the man tick."

ALEXANDER WALKED FROM HIS room at the clubhouse, zipping up a pair of jeans. The material hung low on his hips, since he hadn't bothered with a shirt. His senses told him he was completely alone, not that he cared. He'd walk around nude if he so chose. Modesty wasn't a part of his vocabulary. Now that the baby was out of the house, no one would be there to care about his state of dress.

Kaleb and Suzi had taken the first load of their belongings to their new townhouse. He didn't expect them back for hours, no doubt wanting to break in every surface while baby Stefan took his naps. At least that's what the hell he'd be doing.

Ryder had gone to the Rave following work at K&K Motorcycles. The man seemed to have settled into his vampire lifestyle easily enough. The donors lined up when he graced the Rave with his presence. He had the whole dark and dangerous look about him that women seemed to love. With Grayson off the market, a good share of them had set their sights on Ryder. If they weren't looking to get into his pants, then it was Grigore's, big lovable oaf. Alexander chuckled.

He was more than happy to have the donors' sights set elsewhere. For now, he preferred an occasional fuck, but nothing long standing. Let his brothers fend them off. Alexander was not in the market for a woman, and word had gotten around quick enough, leaving his dance card pretty open.

Rolling his neck, a series of cracks traveled down his vertebrae as he worked the kinks out. Alexander hadn't arrived home until damn near dawn, partying well into the night with Ryder and Grigore, neither of whom came home. His skin had a rosy glow, having had fed the night before from Cathy. Ivy had offered, but something about the friendly, dark-blonde had drawn him. Cathy put him at ease. She was straight forward with no ulterior motives, such as trying to get into his pants or looking to land herself one of the Sons. She seemed more interested in the barkeep.

Alexander preferred his communion straight up, with no strings.

He didn't want to feel as if he had to fuck every donor or appease their egos. He wanted his nourishment without the addition of drama. No small talk, and no way in hell was he going to go down the same road as the twins, or Grayson. His brothers were family. Children were not a part of his vocabulary. Oh, he loved Stefan all right, even delivered the little bugger's ass, but he liked him best when he could spoil him, then send him home.

Dark hair and skin the color of melted chocolate came to mind, causing him to blaspheme. Not that he didn't like the exotic donor, India. Quite the opposite, in fact. The thought of her caused an ache in his groin, one he had no intention of appeasing. He had used her as a regular donor in the past, until his fucking emotions got caught up.

Alexander easily recalled the night Grigore had shown up at the Rave, looking for nourishment like it was yesterday. Fuck it had happened well over a year ago. India stood down the bar from Alexander, while he was busy chatting with a little redhead on X. He was trying his damnedest to disentangle himself when Grigore walked up and palmed India's delicious backside. Of course, he couldn't fault Grigore. His brother had no idea Alexander had any interest in the dark-skinned beauty, because he had never treated her as anything other than a donor, keeping his attraction to himself. Grigore leaned down and whispered something close to her ear, causing her to giggle and blush. Women naturally flocked to the big guy, and India hadn't seemed to be any different.

Christ, he had hoped for better from her.

Just thinking about Grigore's hand on her ass, even over a year later, brought his blood to a slow slimmer. Alexander had never made a claim on India, but he had thought his interest had been quite obvious. When Grigore took a handful of one side of her ass cheeks, he had wanted to deck his brother.

Alexander had seen red, his vampire self close to the surface.

India hadn't bothered to remove his brother's hand, which only added to the fire burning in his gut. When Alexander had finally managed to extricate himself from the pain in the ass, drugged out redhead, he left the Rave, and never once asked what had transpired between his MC brother and India.

No matter, Alexander had avoided India ever since.

*Like the plague.*

Alexander's father had doted on his mother for years, telling everyone who would listen to the drunken fool, she was the love of his life. The man had been fucking blind. While she was slipping out with the guys from the neighborhood pub, bringing home baubles his father could never afford, he sat home drinking himself into a stupor. And when his father was too drunk to take care of his only son, his mom would drag Alexander to the bar. He'd sit on a stool in the corner, watching the television, while the flavor of the month had his hand up his mother's skirt.

Which pretty much summed up his young life, until the night his mother and he had come home and found his father in a pool of his own vomit. The man had drowned in his own puke, leaving him with a woman who didn't deserve that kind of devotion, or the kid she had been saddled with.

Alexander walked around the bar and grabbed a bottle of Jack, noting they'd soon need to restock, especially with Grigore moving in. He peeled off the plastic wrap, then screwed off the plastic cap and took the bottle to his lips. After a long pull, he wiped the back of his hand across his mouth. The one thing he missed after his turning was the ability to get good and drunk. The warmth and momentary buzz was too damn short lived for his liking.

His recent thoughts of India had him wishing for the drunken stupor.

Maybe his father's thinking hadn't been so fucked up after all. Drowning himself in alcohol helped deaden the reality of a faithless wife. Alexander took another long pull, then slammed the bottle back on the counter, leaving it uncapped. As long as he kept women at bay, then there was no chance he'd wind up a fool like his father.

Walking to the clubhouse restroom, he stood in front of the commode and unzipped his pants, pulled out his cock and began to relieve himself.

"Oh…"

Alexander turned his head, just in time to see India's blush before she disappeared around the corner. He quickly finished, shoved his cock back into his pants, and zipped the jeans, not bothering with the button before turning to chase her down.

*What the hell was she doing here?*

Better yet, how had he missed the arrival of her scent?

Apparently, he had been too wrapped in his own thoughts and the bottle of Jack to detect he was no longer alone. He quickly washed his hands and grabbed the hand towel upon his exit. India had reached the front door when he called out to her. She stopped and turned her head, her hand still on the door handle, ready to bolt.

Her beauty was like a fucking wrecking ball, damn near knocking him from his feet.

"Looking for Wolf?" He raised one of his brows. "He doesn't live here ... yet anyway. You're early. He'll be moving in sometime next week if you want to come back."

"Wolf?" The warm vibrato of her voice smoothed over him and grabbed hold of his cock. She let go of the door handle and walked in his direction. "Why do you hate me so much, Xander?"

*Down boy.* "You give yourself too much credit."

"Excuse me?"

"Hating you is an emotion which requires me to first care."

"Wow." India crossed her arms beneath her breasts, looking extremely annoyed with him. "Was that supposed to hurt?"

"Cut the bullshit, India. I detest small talk. Why are you here?"

"I was looking for Suzi."

"Why?"

"Christ, Xander, you want my fucking itinerary while you're at it? I said I would babysit while they moved their shit. I was running late."

Alexander rubbed a hand over his chest, noting her gaze followed the trail, stopping on the unbuttoned area of his jeans. He had the insane urge to pull out his cock, to see if she'd continued to watch. Instead, he walked over to the bar, not inviting her to have a drink with him, or to tell her to get the fuck out, though the latter at the moment was the bigger temptation.

"Apparently, you're very late. They've already left and I doubt they'll be back today."

"Damn it." India placed her hands on her hips and looked to the floor.

"What's the big deal? So, they moved their shit without your help. Trust me, they won't hold it against you. What kept you anyway?'

India sniffed. "None of your business."

Alexander studied her. Had she been crying? Damn it, he hated to see a woman cry, even one he disliked. Already feeling his resolve softening, he asked, "Everything okay?"

Her lower lip trembled. Against his better judgment, Alexander skirted the bar and pulled the dark beauty into his embrace. He had always been a sucker for women's tears. Her sobs wet his bare shoulder. Smoothing a hand down her back, the sweet scent of her blood wafted to his nose and elongated his fangs. He ignored the hunger burning his gut. Even though he had recently fed, her blood had a way of calling to him like the finest of whiskeys.

Alexander would have to be a callous vampire to feed from her while she suffered from whatever had reduced her to tears. It would be a mistake to inquire further what had upset her. Alexander didn't want to know, didn't want to care … and yet, he was ready to put a hurt on who was the cause.

India stepped back from his hold and swiped her hands beneath her eyes, spreading the salty wetness across her flushed cheeks. "I'm sorry. I should go."

"You want to talk about it?"

A sob bubbled up. India covered her mouth with trembling fingers and shook her head. "I shouldn't have come."

Alexander grabbed the whiskey bottle from the bar and handed it to her. "Here. It will make you feel better."

She took the open bottle to her lips and took a small swig. Her answering grimace told him she wasn't a fan of the warm amber liquid. India opened her mouth and gasped. "No wonder I never drink that shit."

He chuckled and took the bottle back from her. "A few healthy swigs and you won't even notice the burn or the taste."

She grabbed the bottle back from him before he had a chance to set it back on the bar and took another tiny swig. Her shoulders shook in revulsion. "Yep. I'm pretty sure I don't like the stuff."

Alexander took the bottle and set it on the bar between him. "So what are you trying to drown away with the whiskey?"

India glanced back at the door, no doubt weighing her options of staying or getting the hell away from him. Decision made, she walked over to the bar and pulled out a stool and sat. Her forefinger indicated the Jack bottle. "You have anything else besides that to drink?"

Alexander opened the wine cooler door. "Looks like there's a couple bottles of red in here. Otherwise it's water or whiskey."

"Is it sweet?"

"How the hell would I know? I don't drink the stuff."

His response earned him a chuckle. "Whatever. It has to be better than the whiskey."

Alexander used a knife to cut the seal, then looked at the cork. He started rummaging through the drawers and finally came up with a corkscrew. Making short work of it, he pulled the cork with a pop, and set the dark bottle in front of her.

She gave him a crooked smile. "Do I have to drink it from the bottle?"

"No, smart ass. I suppose I could offer you a glass." Alexander reached overhead and pulled down a wineglass. "You want to talk about it?"

"Actually, I'd prefer to get good and drunk. I'd ask you to join me, but it's not possible for you."

"It's times like this I wish it were," he mumbled beneath his breath.

"What was that?"

He rubbed his nape. "I was just agreeing with you."

India picked up the bottle and half-filled the glass. She brought the glass to her lips and took a small sip. If she was looking to get soused, she wasn't going to get there anytime soon with her tiny ass little sips. Swirling the liquid in the glass, she watched the red wine as if it held the answers to whatever had upset her.

He covered her hand laying on the bar with his, not being able to stop himself from touching her. Hell, he wanted to touch her all over. It had been far too long since he had last gotten laid. The brief touch sent a bolt of desire sizzling up his skin and had him pulling his hand back. By the look on her face, she felt it as well. She toyed with the stem of the glass, suddenly unable to look him in the eye.

"Maybe I should go."

*Maybe she should.* "Something kept you from getting here on time, something that's upset you. If you want to talk about it, talk while I'm still willing to listen."

Yeah, he was pretty sure he needed his fucking head examined.

"I'm pregnant."

"What the hell?" *Fuck!* Whatever he expected, it wasn't that. "Then you definitely shouldn't be drinking."

He took away the wineglass and sat it on the counter behind him. He grabbed a bottle of water from the refrigerator and handed it to her. "What the hell were you thinking?"

"Seriously, Xander? I don't think I was thinking about babies when it happened."

"I meant the drinking."

Her beautiful brown gaze filled with tears again.

"Who is he?"

"No one."

Alexander leaned in, bracing his forearms on the bar and clasping his hands, when what he really felt like doing was wrapping his long fingers around the throat of baby daddy.

"You don't know?"

"I didn't say that." Tears slipped down her cheeks. "It wasn't supposed to happen."

"You know birth control usually prevents that."

Her jaw tightened, knowing he stepped over the line. He deserved the dressing down she'd no doubt give him. Something about knowing she carried another man's baby rubbed his ass raw.

"More like I should've been fucking a vampire, since vampires can't impregnate humans. At least then I wouldn't be in this predicament. And for your information," she looked back at him, holding his gaze, "he used a condom. It broke."

"What are you going to do?"

India's shoulders drooped, her gaze fell to her lap. "He wants me to abort it."

"And what do you want?"

His heart panged, not sure how he wanted her to answer. It was her body, her decision, no matter what he thought on the matter.

More tears fell and she swatted them away. Uncapping the water, India took a long pull. Putting the cap back on the bottle, she glanced back him. "I want to keep the baby."

Alexander reached for her small hand and encompassed it within his larger ones. "You don't need the sperm donor to help raise the child, India. You're strong enough to do this on your own. I'm sure Suzi and Tamera would be there for you."

"And you?"

He let go of her hand and stood, not sure what she was getting at. "What about me? You want me to beat his ass? Just say the word."

"That's not what I meant, Xander." Her pink tongue wet her lips. "How do you feel about me having a baby?"

"Why should what I think matter?"

India looked at the bottle in her hand, toying with the condensation gathering on the plastic. "Because you matter."

One of his brows rose. "Excuse me?"

She looked back at him, sucking in an uneven breath. "Christ, you've always mattered, Xander. If you haven't seen that, then you're blind. What I want to know is if I've blown any chance with you?'

"Whoa, India." He jammed a hand through his hair, panic clawed up his spine. Hell. To. The. No. He didn't want kids, let alone to raise someone else's, no matter how much he desired the woman before him. "There wasn't an us before you got knocked up."

"No, but I had hoped…"

Thoughts of Grigore and his hand on her ass came back to mind.

"Look, India, I'll be here for you … as a friend. I'm not boyfriend material. I never have been. You want a shoulder to lean on, I'll hold you up. You want someone to listen, I can be good at that. You want someone to be there when the baby is born, I'll hold your hand through it. You want someone to whisper *I love yous* and hold you through the dark of the night, promising you his every tomorrow, I'm not that guy. You being pregnant with some other guy's baby has nothing to do with that."

"I need a friend, Xander."

"Then as long as the fuck who got you pregnant doesn't come around, I'll take the job. He comes into the picture, I'll beat his ass first, and then I'm gone. Understand?"

India nodded, her dark brown eyes swimming in unshed tears. He was pretty sure he'd hand baby daddy his ass if he ever had the fortune of meeting him. The fuck did not deserve India.

And Him? He needed his head examined. Sticking by her side through the pregnancy and not touching her? Yeah, he was pretty sure he was going to regret his offer of friendship and sticking his nose where it sure in the hell did not belong.

## CHAPTER SIXTEEN

KIMBER AWOKE WITH A START. SHE GASPED FOR AIR, SITting up, and clutching her bedsheets to her chest. Her room swam into focus. Sweat dotted her brow and beaded her upper lip. Terror held her in its grip as the dream faded. Her gaze swept the room. The curtains billowed from the cool night breeze. Moonlight spilled through, lending a bit of illumination to her otherwise darkened room.

Aside from Diesel, who lay at the foot of her bed, she was completely alone. His head raised, cocking to one side. The dog emitted a soft growl, noting her unease, ready to pounce at first provocation.

The dream had been so vivid and real like.

A shiver passed down her spine.

Kicking her feet free of the white cotton sheets, she scooted to the side of her queen-sized bed and placed her feet on the carpeted floor. She stood and padded to the opened window, reassuring herself the dream was not reality. Diesel watched her from his spot on the corner of the bed, his chin now braced on his front paws. Kimber had never been one to chase shadows or fear the unknown, but something about the dream continued to unsettle her. Diesel's company was certainly welcome. If anyone were to enter her home, he'd alert her immediately.

Kimber's thoughts traveled back to Anton standing in her home a week ago. *"I'd say that's a serious security issue."* No way would an intruder get past Diesel. Although she was grateful for Anton gifting her the dog, before he entered her life there hadn't been much need for security.

What had she gotten herself into?

A remnant from the nightmare teased her subconscious.

White fangs standing out against blood-red lips.

*Vampire.*

Her vision of Anton with large, razor sharp fangs protruding from his gums and aimed at her neck seemed pretty damn real. His pupils enlarged, taking over his irises, swelling until nothing more was left of his eyes but the glassy black surface. Her reflection stared back at her from the endless black pools. Instead of terror, her gaze had been filled with raw hunger. Everything about Anton's appearance had screamed late-night horror flick, and yet Kimber had been drawn to the monster in her dreams.

Taking in a deep breath of the fresh air, she pushed aside the curtain and glanced down the road. The full moon lit a path clear to Anton's farmhouse, where a single light glowed in his bedroom window. A quick glance at her side table alarm told her it was just after midnight. Her heart skipped a beat at the thought of making the trek to his house. The burning light told her that he was most likely still awake.

Butterflies danced in her stomach.

Plan already forming in her head, she wouldn't be able to sleep now if she tried. She hadn't seen Anton since the quickie they had shared in the ladies' room at Murphy's. Not that it hadn't been fantastic, but he had left so quickly following their brief tryst.

Call it paranoia, but she had to know everything between them was still okay.

That and maybe a quick a first-hand look at his teeth.

Kimber opened the dresser and pulled out a pair of yoga pants and a pink sports bra. She'd sneak over, seek out Anton, and prove her dream was nothing more than fiction. Or maybe it was just a good excuse to see him. Either way, she was bound and determined to see him.

Two days had passed since their little bathroom get-together, and not a word. He had walked out and was gone from Murphy's by the time she had left the restroom. She couldn't very well ask Bobby where Anton had gone, so she was left with insecurities.

After pulling on a pair of socks and stepping into her running shoes, Kimber quickly descended the stairs. She grabbed a light jacket by the door and headed onto the porch. The screen door slapped shut, with Diesel now standing at the screen watching.

"Stay." Kimber shoved her arms into the jacket and zipped the nylon halfway up her abdomen. "You keep an eye on the house and be a good boy."

Kimber pulled her hood over her mussed hair, then loped down the few steps and headed for the road. Jogging the short distance between houses, she was at his back door within a matter of minutes. The night was silent other than the heavy sound of her breathing. She almost lost her nerve, turned around and hightailed it home. If his roommate caught her, Anton would be more than pissed for her disobeying his wishes.

She stepped back and looked up at his window. The light continued to glow. Her heart raced. Instead of knocking on the door, she opted to toss a stone at the pane of glass. The first stone missed the mark and bounced off the wood siding. Her second toss pinged against the window, sounding like a shot in the still of the night. Kimber stifled her giggle, waiting for Anton to peer out.

Seconds ticked by.

Maybe he wasn't in his room after all.

Bending down, she picked up a third stone and was about to toss it when a forearm snaked about her waist, stealing her breath. A large hand covered her mouth.

"What the fuck are you doing here?" The man's warm breath fanned her ear.

Panic seized her, keeping her from saying a word even if the big hand hadn't been placed tightly over her lips. The arm, banding her waist, tightened. Her nostrils flared as she tried to suck in oxygen. Her pulse beat heavily in her ears. Her heart leaped to her throat. Blackness edged her vision.

The back porch light blinked on and lit the area, just before Anton opened the door and stepped onto to porch. "Preacher, what the fuck?"

"I caught this little missy sneaking around your home."

"It's okay. I know her." Anton swore. "Let her go."

Kimber sucked in air when Anton's house guest released her. She had the notion to turn tail and run, not sticking around for the scolding no doubt forthcoming.

"I came outside for a little fresh air. Beautiful night." Bobby's hand indicated Kimber. "Then this cute little thing comes snooping around, tossing stones at your window. I recognized her from Murphy's a few nights ago. Can't be too careful since we're in Sons' territory. It would be just like those sons of a bitches to send a chick to do their poking around."

Kimber gaped. "You seriously don't mean I'd have anything to do with a barbaric motorcycle club?"

Bobby ignored her. "You want me to send her on her way?"

"No." Anton's tone dipped. Not to mention the pissed look on his face. "I'll take her from here."

"She one of your pieces of ass?"

"You, sir—"

"Kimber." Anton's warning had her quickly shutting her lips. She should've ignored her desire to see him and just stayed home with Diesel. Time to pay the piper. "She's my neighbor. I'll see her home, Preacher. She may be a pain in the ass, but she's no threat."

Bobby nodded, saying something sounding close to, "all yours," before entering the back of the house and closing the screen door behind him.

Anton crossed his arms over his perfectly sculptured chest. Damn, he had a drool worthy body. He wasn't wearing a shirt, her sudden favorite look for him, with a pair of nylon basketball shorts hanging low on his hips. Those muscles at his sides, love handles or whatever they were, definitely turned up the heat. She wouldn't have minded pushing him through the house and up the stairs to his bedroom. Damn his housemate anyway.

"Stop looking at me that way, *tesoro*."

Her gaze snapped up, feigning innocence. "What way?"

"Seriously? We're going down this road again?"

She tried her best to hide the smile itching at her lips. "Well..."

Anton shook his head, stepped off the porch, and gripped her right arm. He spun her around and headed in the direction of her house. "What are you doing here?" he hissed.

"I wanted to see you."

"We talked about this." His grip on her arm wasn't meant to cause pain, but it definitely spoke of Anton's temperament. "If Preacher didn't know about you before, he does now. What the hell were you thinking?"

Kimber jerked her arm from his grip. "Your bedroom light was the only one on. I thought Preacher had gone to bed. Forgive me for wanting to see you, you jerk."

"So you just invited yourself over." It wasn't a question but an accusation. "Have you not been listening to me?"

Her reasoning for making the jaunt now forgotten, her rising ire was starting to take over. "Just go home, Rogue. I can find my own way back."

"You aren't getting off that easily, *tesoro*. I want an answer to my question."

Kimber kept walking, shoulders back, not wanting to give him an answer. Regardless that she had disobeyed his wishes, he didn't need to be a dick about it.

"Kimber?"

She stopped in the middle of the road and spun on her heel. "What?" she damn near yelled.

Anton closed the gap between them and glared down on her. "Why were you at the house?"

"I think we already established that. I wanted to see you."

"Why?"

"Because ... oh, hell. Never mind." Kimber turned and began jogging the short distance, hoping he'd take the hint that it was meant to be and let her go. She had embarrassed herself enough for one night.

She hadn't gotten very far before Anton caught her. In fact, he had moved incredibly fast. His forearm wrapped her waist and snatched her up, leaving her legs dangling. "Answer me, *tesoro*."

"I wanted to see for myself you didn't have fangs."

Every muscle in Anton stilled. Not denying her accusations, nor making fun of her ridiculous notion. His arm slackened and her feet hit the ground. She stepped away, turned and looked up at him. His expression was unreadable. He probably thought her ready for a straightjacket.

His gaze narrowed. No smile, no humor at her asinine assumption. "Why in the hell would you think that?"

"I had a dream."

"A dream?"

She chuckled, knowing how foolish she must sound. Too late. She couldn't take it back. She pushed up his upper lip. No fangs there.

"Happy?"

"It was more like a nightmare. You had these long, white fangs. You dragged them down my throat. I could feel the points. They felt so real. You ... you were about to bite me. And your eyes ... they were glassy like big black marbles. Your face, I don't know, was different too."

"And this scared you?"

"Scared the hell out of me once I woke up and thought about it."

He looked at her queerly. "I'm not sure what you mean. Once you woke up?"

"In the dream..." Her face heated, not sure how much she wanted to confess. "I guess I was a little aroused, even if you did look like a monster. And the idea of you biting me was sort of a turn-on. Like I actually wanted you to."

"But then you woke up?"

She nodded, worrying her lower lip.

"And now?"

"I see how silly I was being." Kimber looked to the pink and blue jogging shoes she wore. "I suppose I was using the dream as a reason to see you."

He tipped her chin up with the pad of his thumb. "To disobey my order."

The word *order* rankled her as if she would just do as he told her to do. "I'm not yours to order around, Anton."

"No. But it's the deal we made. I cannot protect you from my brothers, if you won't listen to me."

"If you weren't running around with a bunch of miscreants, I wouldn't need protecting."

The sound of a ringing phone stopped Anton's retort. He reached into his pocket, looked at the screen, then slid the lock and put it to his ear. "Hello?"

Kimber couldn't help wondering who would call him in the middle of the night. Better yet, why he'd answer in the middle of their disagreement. She couldn't hear what was being said, but she could definitely tell the voice was female.

"Now?" Anton rubbed his nape. "I know I was supposed to be there. It couldn't be helped," he told the caller. "Where the hell is Viper?"

By the tone in the woman's voice, Kimber sensed the woman wasn't too happy with Anton, whoever she was.

"It's going straight to voice mail?" He took a deep breath and blew it out between pursed lips. "Fine."

The person on the other end sounded much like she was reading him the riot act.

"Look," he glanced at Kimber briefly, then dropped his gaze to the road where they stood, "I didn't ask for any of this... Shit! Yes, I'll be there by noon... I did promise to protect you... Pull up your big girl panties, Tam... See you as soon as I can get there... And Tam? I don't think I have to tell you to keep your fucking cool. They ask, you tell them you belong to me."

Anton hit the end and pocketed his phone. *You belong to me.* Hadn't he said the very same thing to her? No doubt, just so he'd have a piece of ass while he was in town, and she had played right into his hands.

He rubbed his hand over the shadow on his beard. The scratching sound of the whiskers against his flesh filled the silence between them. Anton grimaced. "I have to go."

Lord, she wanted to bust his balls, and yet all she could muster was, "You do."

"When I get back we'll talk." He reached out, meaning to touch her, but she jerked away from him. Anton shoved his hands into his pockets. "I have a job to do, *tesoro*."

"You do."

"Would you stop already?" His voice rose in his agitation. "I'll talk to you about all this when I get back."

"Don't bother, Rogue. I was fooling myself into thinking this might work." Kimber blinked back the tears, not wanting him to see how much he had hurt her. "I was wrong. Go save Tam or go fuck her for all I care."

"Kimber—"

She didn't wait for him to finish. Kimber turned and sprinted the rest of the way home, not stopping until she was secure in her home, with Diesel at her feet and her door firmly deadbolted. She slid down the back of the door, holding her emotions in until her backside hit the floor. Only then did she release the tears. Sobs shook her body. Of course, he would have a girlfriend in Santa Barbara. It wasn't like he would wait to get laid until he returned to Pleasant. She had been a fool to think otherwise.

*Friends with benefits.*

She had warned him she didn't do friends with benefits. Tam's phone call proved as much. For Kimber, it was all or nothing. She had to cut Anton loose. She'd never be able to trust him. She had been a fool to think she could.

Tam was her wake-up call.

Kimber supposed she should thank the woman before she had invested too much of her heart. Diesel came over, nuzzled her side, then laid down next to her. Covering her face with her palms, she allowed the sobs to take over. Who was she trying to fool? Anton had already claimed a good deal of her heart. Now, all she needed to do was learn how to ignore the big gaping hole left by his betrayal.

## CHAPTER SEVENTEEN

Anton watched Kimber and her delicious ass run in the opposite direction from him. Damn, she had looked smoking hot in those yoga pants. Not to mention the pink sports bra that barely contained her tits. It was all he could do to hold his ground. He jammed his fists onto his hips, his short nails biting into his palms. Had he taken chase, there would've been no stopping him. He would have carried her to her bed and fucked her senseless. His dick practically begged him to do so.

Unfortunately, there was no time to dally.

*Fuck!* Other than speak to Tamera, he wasn't even sure what the hell he did. Kimber had suddenly gotten a burr up her ass. Next thing he knew, she was telling him to go fuck Tam. What the hell? Thinking of the short call, he was pretty sure he hadn't mentioned anything about an intimate relationship with Tam. Why would he?

Her sobs carried to his keen hearing, cutting him to the heart. Damn, he hated the fact he was the reason for her sorrow.

Anton rubbed a hand down his jaw.

No matter what had upset her, he had a job to do and he couldn't do it from here. Grayson would kill him if anything happened to his mate because Anton wasn't there to protect her. Hell, he'd never forgive himself for not stopping Cara's asinine plan in the first place. He shouldn't have allowed her to talk him into giving Tamera the okay to stick her journalist nose into the Devils' business, even if Tamera wasn't supposed to be in the Devils' territory alone. When the plan had been hatched, they had no way of knowing Tank would send Anton back to his home state.

Christ, how had everything turned to shit so quickly?

Kimber rounding the corner of the bushes lining her property and disappearing from his sight, stuck in his mind. His heart fucking hurt. Not only had he lost Tamera to Grayson, he had potentially lost Kimber because of all his lies and omissions. The idea of her never speaking to him again damn near crippled him.

*Tell her or lose her.*

Anton wanted to confess everything, to come clean.

No more secrets.

He jammed a hand through his short hair, blowing out his breath in frustration. Having a twelve-hour ride straight south ahead of him, going after Kimber wasn't an option. Coming clean would have to wait. Not just about the Devils and his working undercover, but who he was. Who he really was. His heart was breaking wide open, telling him his feelings for Kimber went far beyond friends with benefits. If he cared for her, then he needed to be straight with her, including the truth about the fangs she had been looking for earlier. Her dream had no doubt been her subconscious recalling the truth.

*Vampire.*

Lord, she'd either run screaming or promise to get him help by checking him into the nearest mental institute. Freaking out, though, would be preferable to never wanting to see him again. At least then he might have a chance to prove to her vampirism wasn't the scary thing nightmares were built upon. He was human, living and breathing just as she was, only he needed blood to survive. Not to mention the fact they were extreme sexual beings. *Which she might come to like*, he thought with a wry smile. He'd already shown her as much. Add to that, the drinking of her blood, and he'd give her mind-blowing orgasms any woman would be reluctant to turn down.

A four letter word formed in his thoughts.

Hell, he wanted to shrug it off, dismiss it as nonsense. But as he stood there staring at her house, not knowing if she'd ever forgive him or allow him back into her life, it sure felt as if his heart was falling apart. The closest he had come to loving anyone was Tamera, and even losing her to Grayson hadn't felt nearly as distressing as the possibility of losing Kimber.

If it wasn't love, it was damn close to it.

Anton had always wanted what Grayson had found with Tamera. The family. The whole nine yards. Most ran away from the idea of loving one woman. Anton had always hoped to find that one special person, to live out his life with, to have little vampire true bloods. Just his damn dumb luck, Kimber had no idea vampires even existed.

The likelihood of her wanting him once she found out was nil. He'd be left with hypnotizing her into forgetting his confession, and walking out of her life forever, in love with a woman never to be his.

If she didn't find him crazy as a loon, he might consider petitioning Kaleb into letting him take a mate once this damn case was over. He could easily see himself in one of her white front porch rockers, cuddling a babe in his arms while she sat beside him, Diesel at her feet.

When the hell had he become such a sap?

Taking in a deep breath, he shook off his silly desires and headed for his house, reality staring him in the face. Bobby, the one man who had the ability to take him down by telling the Devils about Kimber. And Kimber, the one woman who, even if she forgave him, would never be able to love the vampire in him.

Anton jerked the screen door open and headed inside, calling out to his very temporary housemate. Not that he didn't like Bobby, he respected the man, but he despised the MC he stood with.

Bobby came around the corner from the kitchen, holding up a sandwich. "Want one, man?"

Anton shook his head.

"No wonder you don't have an ounce of fat on you. I swear you never eat. You even like food?"

"No time right now, Preacher." Anton ignored the question, because frankly, he did not like food, not since turning vampire. "I need to head back to Santa Barbara."

"Let me get my things." He took a large bite of the turkey sandwich, wiping the remaining mayo from his whiskers. "I can be ready in five."

"You're staying here, Preacher. Someone needs to keep an eye on Draven. That shipment is supposed to be here any day, and Tank would have our asses if that little shit took off with his smack." Anton grabbed his black T-shirt, draped over the arm of the sofa, and pulled it over his head. "We can't trust that two-bit dealer to pick up the heroin alone. You know as well as I do, there is way too much money involved to trust the barkeep."

"What will Tank think when you aren't here and you show up back in Santa Barbara?"

"Look, bro, it can't be helped. I have an issue with my old lady I need to deal with. If I run across Tank while I'm there, I'll make sure he knows this is on me. Not on you."

"You have an old lady?"

He shrugged. "Never mentioned her before. No reason to. I'd rather keep her out of club business, you know?"

One of Bobby's brows rose. "And the pretty little thing I detained a few moments ago? She wasn't here to see you?"

Anton winced, hoping Bobby bought it. "Yeah, let's not tell my old lady about her. She's my neighbor. I've fucked her a few times. Tam finds out, and she'll cut my dick clean off. Go all Lorena Bobbitt on me."

Bobby chuckled. "I can't seem to get one woman. And you've got one too many."

"You were doing all right the other night."

"Tena? She seemed to be nice enough, too nice to put up with my ornery ass." He took another large bite of his sandwich. Shifting the turkey and bread to one side of his mouth, he said, "I hope Tam's worth it, man. Your old lady doesn't cut that dick off because of your sassy little neighbor, Tank will have your balls for disobeying his orders."

"It can't be helped. I'll be back in two days tops. You'll cover for me?"

"Just get your ass back here before that shipment arrives. I don't want to have to excuse away your absence. I'd rather not be on Tank's bad side."

"You got it, bro."

Anton took the stairs two at a time. The sooner he got to Santa Barbara, the quicker he could get back, bringing Tamera with him. Pulling out his burner phone, he quickly dialed Kane's number, being sent straight to voice mail. *Shit!* Where the hell was Kane?

He entered his room, pulled off his basketball shorts and stepped into a pair of jeans. Sitting on the edge of his bed, he quickly slipped into his worn brown boots before heading to his wardrobe. Anton grabbed a couple of days' worth of clothes, stuffed them into his black duffle bag, then headed back down the stairs. Bobby sat, feet kicked up on the coffee table, remote in hand.

"Be safe, man," Bobby said. "Don't worry about Draven. I'll make sure he minds his manners, even if that means hanging out unseen at that bar of his."

Anton sure hoped it wouldn't come to that. He didn't want to risk Bobby being found out by the Sons. Hanging at the Rave would be risky at best. Something told Anton he could trust Bobby. If the man said he wasn't going to rat him out to Tank and that he'd have his back, then he believed him.

"Be back as soon as I can. I owe you, bro."

Anton trotted out the back of his house, heading for the barn where he had stored their bikes. He slid the door to the side and flipped the switch to the bare bulb. Taking his duffle bag off his shoulder, he strapped it to the back of his bike, then stepped over the seat and backed the motorcycle from the shed. Anton strapped the helmet onto his head, turned the key, and started the bike. The engine roared to life. Doing a wide arc, he drove the bike down his drive, stopping at the end, just shy of the road.

His gaze traveled to Kimber's house. He couldn't help wonder if she stood in one of the darkened windows and watched. If he did what was best for himself, he'd turn right, go make it up to her, kiss away all their troubles, fall into bed, and fuck the night away. Instead, too many lives depended on him doing the right thing for everyone else. So he picked up his feet, turned the bike left, and hit the gas.

He needed to get to Santa Barbara like yesterday.

Time was wasting.

Grayson's mate depended on him, maybe even her very life. He was supposed to have been her cover, and he hadn't been there for her. Not that it was his fault. He couldn't be blamed for what he didn't know. But he wasn't about to fail

Grayson, even if Anton had no idea Cara meant to send her so soon into Devil territory.

At the end of the country road, he flipped his turn signal, slowed at the stop sign, then turned onto the highway and buried the needle to his speedometer. Anton sure in the hell hoped he made it before Tamera got herself into too much trouble.

"What has you all down in the mouth this morning?" Tena grabbed her Styrofoam cup of coffee and took a long sip, wincing. "You made the coffee, didn't you?"

"Too black for your taste?" Kimber smiled weakly, about as much as she could offer at the moment.

Her heart had snapped in two last night when she heard Anton use the same phrase he had used on her, on some woman named Tam. *You belong to me.* How many women did he actually claim? Kimber swallowed, hoping to stay the tears. She had cried enough last night as she stood in the window and watched him pull out of his driveway. Part of her had hoped he would've headed in her direction, but he hadn't. Anton had turned his motorcycle toward the highway. She stood there watching the red taillight fade from sight.

"You could stand a spoon in it." Tena picked up a plastic spoon from the tray and stuck in the cup as if she actually expected it to stand. "Cream and sugar doesn't even help the taste."

"I needed the caffeine."

Chad walked into the break room, his eyes going to Tena's hand, spoon, and cup. "Let me guess. Kimber made the coffee."

Kimber actually chuckled. Chad had a way of making anyone smile, no matter their troubles. "If you guys want to make the coffee, feel free. Just get here before I do."

Chad shook his head and waved his hand, palm out, in front of him. "No way, girlfriend. That was Tena's complaint. I only made an observation. I'll gladly drink the dregs to get a few extra minutes of sleep."

"I thought so." Kimber grabbed her own cup and took a sip, her gaze going to the clock. "Ten minutes until opening. Aren't you early anyway?"

"I was up." Chad took a seat across the break room table from the two of them. "So what has you looking like you lost your best friend?'

Damn, she wasn't very good at hiding her feelings, even if she had just laughed at Chad's joke. "I'm fine. About time to get to work is all."

"Mmmm hmmmm. If you say so."

"I was just asking her the same thing before you walked in." Tena placed her cup on the table and shuddered. "I may have to go across the street and get me a latte."

"You guys don't know what good coffee is."

"Sure we do, it's called Coffee Haven and it's just across the street." Chad winked at Tena. "I'll buy if you fly."

"Hell, yes. Not too often you offer to buy."

Chad reached into his front pocket and pulled out a ten, handing it to Tena. "You want anything?" he asked Kimber.

She shook her head. "No, thank you. Unlike you two, I know good coffee. Not that sugared down weak stuff you get across the street."

Kimber took another sip from her cup. The hot java warmed her from the inside, though she doubted it heat the areas of her heart Anton made run cold with his words to Tam on the phone. What had she expected? She was the one who agreed to the whole stupid friends with benefits crap. Did that ever really work out for anyone? It seemed one party would always be more invested than the other, only to get hurt in the end.

Tena damn near skipped from the room, no doubt happy to get an extra-large coffee paid for by Chad. The man rarely offered to pay for anything. Kimber wondered about his motives, but didn't have to wait long. He looked at Kimber, his expression sobering.

"Spill, girlfriend. What did neighbor boy do? Do I need to kick his ass or toilet paper his house?"

That earned Chad a chuckle. She loved how he could so easily amuse her. Why she hadn't befriended these two earlier was beyond her. They had quickly become her closest friends.

"No kicking of his butt, Chad. I don't want to see you get hurt."

He wiped his forehead with the back of his hand in mock worry. "Whew. I was worried there for a minute. Not that I wouldn't have given it a try, but toilet paper is much more my style. I could egg his house too, if you want."

"You realize Preacher is staying at Rogue's, right?"

"Preacher? The big ass bear?" His gaze widened. "Sorry, girlfriend, you are on your own."

Kimber chuckled again, feeling better all ready. "No worries. No one needs their butt kicked but me."

"Stand up then." Chad rose from his chair. "Well?"

"What are you doing?"

"Getting ready to kick your butt." Chad laughed, then quickly retook his seat. "In all seriousness, what did Mr. Tall, Dark, and Dangerous do?"

This whole sharing thing was still new to her. Kimber wasn't used to talking about her life, let alone something as personal as this. Her heart felt stepped on, ran over, dragged, and ripped apart. Her feelings were still pretty raw, so she wasn't sure she was ready to talk about how deep Anton's betrayal cut. Chad seemed as if he truly cared, prompting her to spill the beans. Maybe having someone to listen would help her get it off her chest.

"Where to start is more like the question." Kimber picked at a cuticle on her finger. "I guess I was aiming a bit high."

"Don't be silly. Anyone would be lucky to have you. If I wasn't gay, I'd be trying to get in those pants. You may not see it, but for a girl, you're pretty smokin'."

Her cheeks heated. "You're such a charmer."

"Maybe. But I was being serious." He reached across the table and laced fingers with her. "Don't cut yourself short. If your neighbor doesn't want you, then he's not only blind but damn stupid. Now tell me what he did."

Kimber sighed heavily. Letting go of Chad's hand, she leaned back in the chair. "I wanted to see him last night. I think I should've stayed home. I thought I was special. Turns out I was wrong."

"Then he doesn't deserve you."

"No, he doesn't, but it hurts nonetheless."

"You need to turn this around. Show him what he's missing, girlfriend." Chad punctuated his statement with a wide smile. "Next time he comes around, you turn him away. Better yet, let's find you a hottie to make him j-e-a-l-o-u-s."

"Anton went to Santa Barbara and I have no idea how long he'll be gone. He went to see some woman called Tam, said in his phone conversation that she was to tell someone she belonged to him. So I doubt finding a hottie would work in my favor."

"Maybe, but men like your neighbor, they get all territorial when they see someone cutting in on what they want."

Kimber couldn't argue. After all, he had gotten pretty pissed when the biker from his rival MC had his hand on her person.

She shook her head. "I hate drama and I don't play games. If Anton wants to treat me that way, then I don't need him."

"That's the spirit. Make him regret his actions."

Tena walked in, carrying two tall paper cups with sleeves. She handed one to Chad. She looked between both Kimber and Chad. "Okay, what did I miss?"

Kimber looked at the clock and stood. "Time to open the doors."

"Really? Seriously?" She trailed Kimber out of the room, damn near on her heels. "You can't think to cut me out of your conversation. What did I miss? And don't tell me nothing."

"Ask Chad. He can tell you. I have a lot of work to do today."

Tena stomped her foot. "Not fair. Chad's a vault!"

Kimber chuckled, heading for the entrance. She turned the deadbolt, opened the steel and glass door covered by a large literacy poster, and squealed when someone jerked the door from her grip, making her heart jump from her chest.

Placing a hand over her sternum, she said, "Sorry, you scared me," before she looked up and into the eyes of Anton's roomy.

## CHAPTER EIGHTEEN

"What's up, P?" Grayson walked into the clubhouse meeting room where he found Kaleb sitting at the large wooden table, the other thirteen seats empty. His lips turned down and dark shadows rimmed his eyes. Kaleb scrubbed his palms down his face, then scratched at his beard. The rest of the house remained silent and free of any other vampire's scent, telling Grayson they were completely alone.

"Have a seat," Kaleb directed, followed by a yawn.

Grayson pulled out a chair and sat, unsure why Kaleb had called the meeting. "You getting much sleep, P?"

"Not lately."

Leaning back, he crossed his arms behind his head. "Where is everyone?"

"Just you and me, Gypsy. I sent Xander and Ryder over with the box truck to help Wolf pack his shit. Suzi and I finally got moved. It was time to get Stefan out of the clubhouse, safer for him."

"No doubt in that. Can't have everyone privy to your whereabouts."

"More specifically Mircea, the son of a bitch. Cara and Kane don't think he's responsible for Kinky. Me? I'm not so sure. I wouldn't put anything past the sneaky little bastard. And I'm certainly not going to give him access to my son."

"I couldn't agree more." Grayson tipped his chin. "So why did you want to see me privately?"

Kaleb leaned forward, clasping his hands in front of him on the table. "I need someone I can trust."

"You know I got your back, P."

"Tamera have Luke?"

Grayson's expression warmed at the mention of his son. "Actually, your mate is watching him. Tamera had an assignment out of town. Said she'd be back in a few days."

"How's it going having her back at the newspaper?"

"She loves being a journalist, and I love alone time with Lucian." Grayson smiled. "If Tamera's happy, bro, then I'm happy."

"I'll need to call Suzi, see if she wouldn't mind keeping an eye on Luke for a couple of days. I need you, Gypsy, can't trust anyone else with this."

"You want to fill me in?"

"Viper's MIA."

"I thought he was going north to recruit Red and the Knights, bringing them back into the fold."

"That's exactly where he's supposed to be. Unfortunately, Red's VP confirmed Viper had been there, but that he and Red went south."

"South? What in the hell for?"

Kaleb shrugged, leaned back, and toyed with the wooden mallet before laying it back on the table. "I have no fucking idea, and my brother isn't answering his phone. Cara assures me it's just a bonding trip between the boys. I'm not stupid. He either went fishing for Kinky's killer or something else is going on."

"Devil territory with just him and Red? Not the smartest thing to do."

"I agree." Kaleb leaned an elbow on the arm of his chair, his forefinger resting against his temple. "Viper isn't ignorant, so why head to Devil territory with Red? The man can't even help him, should he get into trouble. He's no vampire. Better yet, why keep me in the dark?"

"You think he's working with Blondy." Grayson rolled his eyes. "I'll never get used to calling him Rogue, even if he is a fucking traitor."

"I honestly don't know what the hell to think." Kaleb sighed, exhaustion clearly evident in his heavy lids. "You and I are going to Santa Barbara. Will Tamera be okay with Suzi watching the baby?"

"Tamera won't question club business. She trusts me and I know she trusts your mate." Gripping both arms of the chair, he rocked back on two legs. "Besides, we'll likely be back before she will."

"You may want to call her, just in case."

"She's on some assignment. Told me it's best I don't call." He rocked back forward, the front legs of the chair hitting the floor with a thud. "I don't want to blow that for her. If we don't make it back by tomorrow, I'll send her a text."

Kaleb grabbed his cell from the table and pointed it at Grayson. "I'll call Suzi. You go pack an overnight bag and meet me back here in an hour. I'd like to hit Santa Barbara before tomorrow."

"Any idea where we might find Viper and Red?"

He shook his head. "Not in the least, but I do know where to find Rogue. I was told by Prospect Lightning, that Rogue road out of town last night ... alone, said he followed him to the state line, which I believe means he headed back to Devils territory. Question is... Why the hell he didn't take that overgrown fuck with him? Lightning said the big guy was laying low at the farmhouse."

Grayson stood and grabbed the keys to his bike. "Well then, let's find out what the hell Past P is up to. If he's looking for Kinky's murderer, then I think we need to give him a hand. If he's not, then I want to know what the hell he's up to. See you in an hour."

KALEB WATCHED AS GRAYSON exited the room, leaving the clubhouse once again quiet. Something was up with Kane. He could feel it in every bone in his body. His twin might think he was pulling one over on him, but he and Kane had been born minutes apart. Kaleb could feel when something was off-kilter with his twin, and Kaleb planned on finding out what it was.

He stood and exited the meeting room, looking about the living area. He could hardly remember a time when it had been this quiet or this empty. It had always been a hub of activity, a constant flow of booze and women. There had been some damn good parties thrown here. He smiled. Now with him, Kane, and Grayson all mated, Rogue having defected, it gave the clubhouse a complete different feel.

Time to hand over the keys.

With Grigore moving in, the place would soon be overrun by bachelors again. The clubhouse would once again become what it was, something Stefan shouldn't be a part of. The torch had been passed with Kaleb having moved out. He'd miss the place, no doubt about it. Hell, he and Kane had lived under the same roof for years. There was a time when they shared everything, even an occasional woman.

Never had there been secrets.

He swiped his cell home screen, found Suzi's number and hit *SEND*. He needed to get Lucian taken care of so Grayson and he could get on the road. Time to find out what the fuck Kane was hiding. He sensed something was up with his twin, and he wasn't about to let up until he found out just what the fuck that was.

"Hey, babe." Her voice warmed him.

Damn, he loved his woman. "I need a favor, *piccolo diavolo*..."

"I DIDN'T MEAN TO startle you."

The man's deep voice raised the hairs on the back of her neck. Tena may trust Anton's houseguest, but Kimber couldn't say the same. There was a reason Anton meant to keep his MC brothers from knowing about her. She wasn't about to ignore the warning it was meant to be. She hadn't thought about it before, but maybe he was trying to keep Tam from knowing about her and there hadn't been any danger at all. Anton had seemed so sincere about keeping her safe and out of his motorcycle club business. She had easily bought into his reasoning.

Hell, he had even bought her a dog.

If this was nothing more than to keep his mystery woman from finding out about her, then Anton best keep his sorry ass in Santa Barbara. There would be no forgiveness for him this time around.

"I didn't expect anyone to be on the other side of the door so early this morning is all." Kimber stepped back and let the man enter. His presence filled the room as completely as his large frame had the doorway. "Is there something I can help you with?"

His ice blue gaze held hers, sending a shiver down her spine. "You do have books, I assume."

Heat rose up her cheeks. Of course. Why else would one come to the library? "Anything in particular?"

"Preacher?" Tena practically squealed as she skidded to a halt just short of running into the man. "What are you doing here?"

Kimber stifled a smile, waiting for another sarcastic retort sure to come.

"Is it that unusual you might find one such as myself in a public library?" His icy gaze warmed at the appearance of her coworker. No cold, unforgiving fixed stare. "I'm looking for books on spiritualism. If you could be so kind to point the way, Tena."

Tena grinned. "I got this, Kimber," she said, without once taking her eyes off the menacing man before them. "I'll be glad to help, Preacher."

"Do you have a last name, Preacher?" Kimber was unsure why she asked, other than the possibility of Tena becoming a missing person. It certainly shouldn't be ruled out. After all, this man didn't look as if he walked on the right side of the law.

"Bourassa, ma'am. Bobby Bourassa." He raised one of his dark brows. "Do you ask everyone who walks through the door their name?"

"If they're checking out books, I do."

His lips thinned, making them practically invisible behind his long whiskers. "I have yet to check any out."

"No." Kimber leveled her gaze, not about to back down from his scrutiny. "But you might."

He winked at Kimber and chuckled before turning and following Tena down one of the long aisles, between two of the eight-foot-tall book shelves.

"You do seem to be checking out one of my friends, though," she muttered beneath her breath.

"Are you that worried?" Chad asked over her shoulder, causing her to jump.

Kimber hadn't realized her other co-worked stood so close behind. She chuckled. "You heard that, huh?

"Mmmm hmmmm." Kimber turned, seeing Chad's gaze trained on the couple, now pulling books from the shelves. "I think the jury is still out on that one."

Heading to the front desk, Chad trotted quickly behind her. "Tena isn't really known for picking out upstanding guys."

"Really?" Chad chuckled, stopping on the front side of the check-in desk as Kimber skirted behind it. "Really?"

Kimber knew he insinuated her own recent choices. Anton wasn't exactly on the upstanding list himself. Especially after his fast retreat to Santa Barbara. Maybe she ought to be analyzing her preferences rather than criticizing someone else.

Pushing the power button, she started up the computer. "You're right, Chad. Point taken."

"I'm not saying I agree with her Bear-alicious hottie over there, even though I can certainly see the appeal. I got to say that man oozes sex."

Kimber smiled and shook her head. Her gaze went back to the keyboard as she signed in and typed in her password. "You're incorrigible."

"What I am is honest." Chad punctuated his statement with a wide smile. He walked over to the night drop box and started pulling out books that had been deposited. "Tell me you wouldn't want a piece of all that hotness."

"Not my type."

Carrying the stack of books needing to be checked back in, Chad shook his head. "I won't bother with a response, girlfriend."

"What? Anton is nothing like Mr. Bourassa."

"Which is why your neighbor also goes by the name of Rogue? Not to mention the fact he left you to go see someone else. Hmmmmm?"

Kimber winced. "Ouch. Point taken."

"You needed a reminder, girlfriend. Tena needs to make her own mistakes."

"You're right." Kimber looked up as she heard Tena's giggle. Tucking one side of her short blond hair behind her ear, Tena smiled at Bobby. It was clear in her actions she was smitten with the biker. "Maybe he's a better man than Anton."

"Maybe. Maybe not." Chad started scanning his stack of books back into the system. "But if you don't give her a chance to figure it out on her own, she'll resent you for sticking your nose where it doesn't belong."

Kimber couldn't argue with Chad's advice. She had no right trying to tell Tena who she should date, any more than anyone had the right to warn her about Anton. Though, in truth, someone probably should have. Fact, Anton had gone south to see Tam, a woman he clearly said belonged to him. Time to suck it up and move on, find someone who might actually be good for her, and not someone who considered friends with benefits a good arrangement.

She wasn't getting any younger. Someday she wanted to settle down, have the relationship her parents had, not to mention have kids. Her biological clock would soon start ticking. She needed to find someone who would make a good husband and daddy.

Anton Balan was a biker. Worse yet, he was an outlaw motorcycle club biker. She didn't know him well enough to make an assumption that he was one of the good guys. Not to mention, his lifestyle was not daddy material. She had lived beside him for a few years, but they hadn't exactly gotten to know each other outside of the sack. What did she really know about him other than he knew how to give a great orgasm?

"Maybe you're right, Chad."

"I'm always right." He looked up from his stack of books and smiled, a sparkle in his light brown gaze. "What am I right about?"

"You said I needed to find someone else, make Anton jealous."

"And as I recall, you said you hate drama and playing games."

"I do." Kimber nibbled on the tip of her nail. Anton needed to see her life did not revolve around what day he might next make an appearance. Time to move on with her life. "I think maybe we ought to see if Tena and Preacher want to make a trip to the Rave."

"You're going to try to make neighbor boy jealous?"

"Nope. But I don't want him thinking I'm going to fall to pieces because he has another woman either."

Chad picked up his stack of books, ready to place them back on the shelves. "So what's your plan?"

"I say we get Tena and Preacher, if he wants to tag along, and we all go out for a night of dancing."

"At the Blood 'n' Rave? You hate that place."

"Murphy's is definitely more my style, but right now I'd rather defy Anton and go where Anton forbid me to go."

He narrowed his gaze. "He said that?"

"He did. Preacher will surely tell him we were enjoying our evening."

"And that isn't playing games or trying to make him jealous?"

"I have no intention of trying to make him jealous. He can have Tam for all I care." She lifted her chin. She could go where she wanted and do as she pleased. "I want Anton to know I am my own woman and I'm not his to order around. I don't belong to him, and I sure in the hell am not going to wait around for his return. I say we go out for a night of fun, drinks, and dancing. You in?"

"You know it." Chad held up one hand not cradling the books and gave her a high-five. "I'll go shelve these. Why don't you see what Tena and her man candy are up to tonight?"

Kimber's gaze traveled to Tena and Bobby now making their way to the desk. To her surprise, Bobby actually had a few books in hand. He placed them on the desk. *The Secret* by Rhonda Bryne lay on top of the stack, surprising her at his choice of reading material. Maybe Bobby was deeper than she gave him credit for and she had unfairly misjudged him.

Pulling the books toward her, she handed him a sheet of paper. "I'll need you to fill this out, Mr. Bourassa."

"Call me Preacher." He dropped his gaze to the sheet of paper, picked up an ink pen, and started to fill it in. Finished, he slid it back across the desk. "You need anything else?"

"Driver's license ... and an agreement to accompany the three of us to the Rave tonight."

His brows knit over the bridge of his straight nose. "Why?"

"Because I need your license on file in case you forget to return our books."

"No. Why go to the Rave?"

"I could use a night out, a little fun between coworkers. I'm thinking Tena might like to have you along. You game?"

Bobby looked ready to refuse. He smoothed his beard as his gaze went from studying both her and Tena. His eyes twinkled, and he chuckled. "Sure. Why the hell not."

## CHAPTER NINETEEN

MIRCEA SAT IN THE COFFEE SHOP BY THE LARGE PICTURE window, watching traffic as he sipped his Italian roast espresso. Even though his gaze caught the cars and foot traffic passing by the quaint little corner shop, it never truly left the front of the townhouse on the adjacent side of the street. Kaleb may have thought he had hidden away his family, fooled whoever had taken out one of his club's members, but he hadn't deceived Mircea.

Nor had Kane.

The Tepes twins may no longer live at the clubhouse, preferring anonymity, but they hadn't pulled the wool over his eyes. Mircea kept close tabs without either being the wiser. He had even managed to keep one step ahead of his brother. The fool. Vlad stayed in Florence, at a posh hotel, thinking he could keep an eye out for Mircea. While his brother slept in comfort, Mircea had gone back to nature, sleeping only when necessary and staying very close at hand.

Ruffling Vlad's otherwise composed feathers gave Mircea enjoyment. He had yet to forgive Vlad for taking Rosalee, and probably never would. Not even after he exacted his revenge and Mircea called them even. Truth of the matter, Vlad had always been the spoiled ruler, the one who needed to be knocked from his pedestal.

Mircea would gladly be the one to finally do it.

The only peace he had gotten in life was when Vlad and his younger brother, Radu the Handsome, had been imprisoned in Adrianople, only to be released in 1448, following his father's assassination the year before. Supposedly, he had been taken out with his father. Not many knew Mircea had actually survived.

The only thing Vlad had truly ever given him was immortality.

He supposed he should thank his arrogant brother for sharing his DNA. He owed Vlad as much, though it pained Mircea to give him credit for anything. Which is why Mircea lived in Italy, away from Vlad and his offspring. Everything had been going as it should be, Mircea was the ruler of his household, king of the castle … until Rosalee had met Kane, spoiling all of his well laid out plans. Kane had taken Rosalee as mate, a mate who should have been his.

Mircea had given her immortal life. When his ungrateful mate was finally dead, Rosalee should've stepped up to take her place. She, too, had been spoiled rotten. His mistake had been allowing her the freedom to sow her wide oats, thinking once experiencing all there was to life, she'd return to the posh life he afforded her.

His mistake.

One he would forever regret.

Now Mircea needed to bide his time. Take what belonged to Vlad and aim high. The opportunity would present itself to take out Kane … and he would. He may have told Vlad he'd give Kane the choice as to whom would forfeit their life, but Mircea's mind had already been made up. He'd taunt his brother, make him wonder what Mircea's plans were, not knowing who of his offspring to protect. If he convinced Vlad into thinking he meant harm to Kaleb's offspring, he'd leave Kane unprotected. Kane's guard would be down, looking to protect those he loved, and Mircea would eventually be presented with his opportunity.

Kane was no match for his strength.

He'd be easy enough to take out.

The door to the townhouse opened and Kaleb's little mate stepped out, one baby in her arms, and young Stefan at her feet. The woman was pretty enough with her short, dark bob and exotic appearance. His nephew definitely had good taste. Which was more than he could say for Kane. The man had given up Rosalee for the blonde who could never compare. Cara had served her purpose, taking Kane away from Rosalee once and for all, so he had only been too happy to grant Kane the permission to mate again.

Life had been so fucking unfair.

Mircea picked up his phone and dialed Vlad's number. The cell began to ring. Kaleb's mate strapped the small baby into a stroller. Picking it up from the porch, she walked it down the brick steps and waited for Stefan. He giggled and trotted after his mother. She reached out and grabbed his hand, then used her free one to push the stroller, heading in the opposite direction from the little coffee shop.

A nice day for a stroll.

Time to taunt his brother.

"What the fuck do you want, Mircea?"

His eyes stayed trained on the trio, though he could care less what was on their agenda. Mircea smiled. Vlad was so easily rattled. "Is that any way to greet your brother?"

Vlad sighed, the sound traveling through the mic of the phone. "What do you want, Mircea? Please tell me it's to let me know you have returned to Italy."

"Not a chance."

"Then to what do I owe the displeasure?"

"Stefan is growing into a cute little boy. All that curly brown mop of hair. He'll no doubt be a lady killer like his daddy one day."

"What the hell are you saying, brother?"

Mircea chuckled. "His blue striped shirt and khaki shorts look adorable on him. And I have to say, Kaleb's little mate looks stunning in a pair of skinny jeans. Your grandson is one lucky man."

"You son of a bitch. You touch them—"

Mircea looked at his nails. He was in desperate need of a manicure. "You have no worries ... for today anyway."

Vlad growled. "You'll wish for death if you so much as harm a hair on their heads."

"You'll have to find me first, dear bother."

"Oh, you can count on that." Vlad's menacing growl spoke of Mircea getting beneath his skin. About damn time. "You best be saying your prayers to whatever god you believe in."

Mircea smiled. "Who needs a god when you have immortality?"

Vlad's curses traveled through the line, just as Mircea ended the call. Oh, he planned to take Kane's sorry excuse for a life, but first he'd enjoy a little game of cat and mouse with his younger brother.

Anton walked into Hade's Nest, his eyes taking the briefest of moments to adjust. He spotted Tamera the minute he cleared the door. The stifling heat had little to do with the atmosphere and everything to do with his rising ire. What the fuck did she actually think she was doing, coming into this bar alone? No wonder she had to call him to get his ass back to Santa Barbara pronto. She was playing with fire in a den full of lowlifes. Any one of them capable of trying to take advantage of her, or worse … rape her.

Though pity the fool who tried.

With her vampirism, not a single man in here would stand a chance against her. Put them altogether, though, and she wouldn't stand a fighting chance. Tamera was still new and she wasn't as strong as a vampire who had spent decades honing his skills.

He skirted the long black, painted bar, which was lined with several Devils sitting on the stools. Some wearily glanced his way, probably wondering what the hell he was doing back in Santa Barbara when Tank had ordered him north, while others ignored his presence. With any luck, he'd nab Tamera and get the hell out of town before running into the president. Oh, these little fuckers would certainly rat him out, but at least by the time Tank heard, he'd be back on the road to Oregon.

Tamera looked up, her slim smile broadened as he approached the booth she sat in with a couple of his MC brothers. Thankfully, she had chosen the less radical ones. And although she had basically called for his help, she looked completely at ease sitting there. Tamera was playing her role well.

"Hey, babe?" Tamera asked, already scooting out of the booth. She wrapped her long arms around his neck and planted a kiss on his lips. Granted it wasn't an open mouth one, but damn just the same. "What took you so long?"

Anton motioned for Stitch to get the hell out of the booth, then he allowed Tamera to slide in first, before he sat next to her. Stitch sat across from him with another one of the Devils.

"What the hell were you two doing hitting on my girl?" Anton asked, leveling his glare on the two men in front of him.

Stitch spit a stream of tobacco onto the floor, then smiled. Chew coated his yellowed teeth. "We weren't hitting on her, Rogue. We were keeping her safe from the other assholes in here. You should be thanking us."

Anton raised a brow. "I need to kick someone's ass?" Because he would if anyone had laid a hand on Grayson's mate.

"Spider was trying to work it—"

Stitch didn't get another word out before Anton rose and headed in the VP's direction. The man turned when Anton stopped a mere foot away. Spider gave him a once-over, then turned back to Boston and ignored the fact Anton had just invaded his space. Either too cowardly to tell Anton to back the fuck up, or too stupid thinking he didn't need to give Anton the time of day. Gripping Spider by the shoulder, he forcibly turned the man to face him again.

Spider sneered. "You got a fucking problem, Rogue?"

"You touch my girl?"

He rolled his bloodshot hazel eyes. Apparently he had been drinking for some time, which gave the man equal amounts of liquid courage and stupidity. "If I recall right, you're not even supposed to be in California. Club P sent you to Oregon with Preacher. You're supposed to be keeping an eye on that two-bit dealer."

"Doesn't answer my question, Spider." Anton stepped forward, looking down his nose at the man. "You think sending me north gives you rights to my woman?"

Spider squared his shoulders, his hands fisting at his sides. "I'm VP. I have the right to fuck your woman if I want."

Anton didn't give the man a chance to move. He drew his fist back and punched Spider in the nose. Bones cracked, blood splattered, tears pooled in the man's eyes. He covered his nose with both hands and swore up a blue streak. If Spider was smart, he'd back the fuck up and apologize. Anton counted on him not being.

He growled a, "You son of a bitch," before he rushed Anton, only knocking him back by a foot, and only because he hadn't set a good stance.

Anton fisted the neck of his grimy white T-shirt and lifted him easily off the floor. Even though the man was damn near as tall as him, he was all lean muscle, nowhere near a match for Anton even if he wasn't a vampire. Backing him to the wall, Anton slammed Spider against it hard enough to rattle some sense into him, as well as a few of the framed pictures on the wall.

Spider struggled in his grip, getting the man's blood on Anton's hands and shirt. His nostrils flared and his gums ached as his fangs threatened to make an appearance. Anton bit back the urge to rip out the fucker's throat. Releasing his right hand, he punched Spider in the face again. One of his eyes instantly swelled.

"You walk away and I'll release you. You threaten to touch my woman again, and I'll fuck you up, Spider, VP or not."

He struggled again, his feet kicking out but not finding purchase. Anton dropped his hold and the man dropped like a sack of potatoes, buckling at his feet. "Stay down, Spider. You won't win this."

True to his nature, Spider stumbled to his feet and rushed Anton again. Anton stepped to the right, sticking a booted foot out. Spider went sprawling to the filthy wooden flooring, his hands breaking his fall. He jumped back up and faced Anton. By this time, they had gathered quite the crowd circling them. Most were Devils. Taunts and snarky remarks were tossed about. Some telling Spider to be smart and stay down while others egged him on. Tamera stood in front of the crowd, arms crossed beneath her breasts, a smirk on her full red lips. Anton could tell she was enjoying the show.

The VP jumped to his feet. "I'm going to fucking kill you," and he rushed Anton again.

Anton growled as he grabbed Spider's wrist, turned him and yanked his arm behind his back. His forearm wrapped his neck, pulling him flush against his chest. "You give yet, asshole?" he said close to his ear.

Dumb ass shook his head. "You let me go and I'm taking you out."

Anton chuckled. "Wrong answer."

Putting pressure on his carotid arteries, Spider went limp in his arms within fifteen seconds. Anton sat him in the nearest booth before he glanced around at the rest of the MC. "Anyone want to be next?"

The men shook their heads, grumbling beneath their breaths, and went back to what they had been doing before the idiot VP took him on. Anton approached Tamera. Her smile widened. He led her back to their booth with his palm in the low of her spine. Stitch slid into the booth across from them again. Stretching his arm across the back of the booth, Anton's fingers lightly caressed her shoulder. He needed to come across as her beloved, hoping he wasn't overstepping her comfort level.

Last thing he wanted when this was over was Grayson kicking his ass for putting moves on Tamera, even if the job called for it. Hell, he should be kicking Kane's ass for putting her in the predicament in the first place. If his phone wasn't working, then he should have gotten her out of there.

Anton looked at the blood on his hands. He needed to clean up. The bartender must have caught Anton inspecting the filth on his hands, for he walked over with a wet bar towel and tossed it at him. He caught it, thanking the man. Quickly divesting himself of the blood, staving off his and no doubt Tamera's reaction to the scent, he then tossed the rag back to the bar.

He glanced at Tamera. "Spider hurt you?"

She shook her head. "Not that he hadn't insinuated what he wanted from me."

"Your reason for calling me home?" Anton hoped she understood his reference to Santa Barbara as his home.

"That and I missed you, babe." She gave him a dazzling smile.

"What were you doing here?" Anton's lips turned down. He didn't need to put on a face of displeasure, finding Tamera in Hade's Nest. Hell, no. It more than displeased him. This was no place for a woman. "This isn't the best place for my woman to hang out."

"I was working on a story for the paper."

His brow creased. "What story?

Tamera reached for his hand and intertwined her fingers with him. "The newspaper wanted an informational piece on MCs. I thought I might as well start with your MC."

He glared at Tamera. "You should have waited for me."

"You were gone. My story couldn't wait." Tamera feigned innocence. "Besides, you're here now."

Anton held her gaze for a moment before asking, "Get anything interesting?"

"I was just talking to Stitch. Obviously, my chat with Spider hadn't gone as well."

"And?" Anton was hoping she'd bring up Joseph's execution. He couldn't very well bring it up, not without raising suspicions.

She shrugged. "I was hoping to do a story on your rivalry with the Oregon MC, the Sons of Sangue."

"Seriously? You looking to start trouble?"

"Not really. I heard a Sons' member died about a week ago, execution style. It sounded like a scoop. But no one here seems to know anything about it. Although, Spider had an unusual reaction to my investigation. He pretty much told me to keep my pretty nose out of it if I wanted to live."

Heat rose up Anton's neck. "Did he?"

"That's why I called you." Tamera winced. "Thought I might be getting in over my head a bit."

"Did you?" Anton shook his head and grumbled beneath his breath. "I just wish I would've known he threatened you before I busted his nose. I would've been a lot harder on his ass. You know anything about the execution, Stitch? I haven't heard anything about us ordering a hit on any Sons of Sangue member."

Stitch scratched his neck, just beneath his ear. He looked around, as if making sure no one was listening. "No one's saying anything about it. Honestly, if a Devil ordered the hit, no one's claiming it."

"So either it came down from Tank or Spider and everyone's being tight-lipped, or someone else took out the Sons' member." He turned to Tamera, tightened his arm about her shoulders, and brought her closer. "How about we get the fuck out of here? I've been gone for a bit and I could use a little lovin'."

Tamera smiled. "Let's get your sexy ass out of here then."

Anton stood, extended his hand to Tamera, and helped her alight from the booth before heading for the exit. What he planned on doing was finding Kane and sending her cute little ass back to Grayson. Bottom line, he had to return to Oregon before Tank came looking for him, and Tamera wasn't safe here without him. She may be stronger than any one man here, but they also carried weapons and wouldn't hesitate using them. They wouldn't think twice about fighting dirty, woman or not.

Spider groaned from his bench as they passed him. Anton paused and kicked his booted foot. "You tell Tank I'm heading back to Oregon. If he wants to know why I left, tell him it was your dumb ass moves on my old lady that had me making the impromptu visit home. She's coming back with me, so don't get any wise ideas I might have to slit your dumb ass throat for."

Spider wisely said nothing, but his glare told Anton he wasn't too happy with Anton's blatant show of disrespect. Hitting the door, Anton pushed it open, his arm still tightly wrapped around Tamera. Once they got outside, Anton meant to drop his hold when Spider and a couple of the crew followed them through the exit.

Anton turned by his Road King, pulled Tamera in and kissed her, staking his claim so Spider wouldn't second-guess Anton's actions inside. Funny, even though he had kissed Tamera soundly, had even wished for as much a year ago, it didn't even register as a blip on his sexual radar. Not even close to the fire set in his loins when kissing Kimber. Maybe Tamera had never been the right woman for him to begin with. Even if at the time he had hoped she would've chosen him over Grayson. Releasing her, his chin tipped, indicating she should crawl onto the back of his bike. Thankfully, she complied without question.

He faced off with Spider and his lackeys. "You got something you want to say, asshole?"

"Don't think Tank won't hear about this."

Anton winked at him. "I'm counting on it. You tell Tank to give me a call."

Dismissing the idiots, he climbed onto his bike, kicked up the stand, and handed Tamera his helmet. She quickly strapped it on. He only needed to take her as far as her Range Rover. Then if he didn't get a hold of Kane, he'd follow her all the way to Pleasant to make sure she went home. Pulling out of the lot, they turned left. Tamera leaned forward, telling him to take a quick right. They came to the lot where she had parked her SUV.

To his misfortune, standing beside it was Kaleb and Grayson. *Great!* Grayson looked poised for murder. Anton took a quick look behind him, noting Hade's Nest's parking lot was probably visible from the corner of the lot. No doubt, Grayson had witnessed their kiss.

Anton cut the engine and stepped over his bike.

*Christ!* Anton held his hands out to his sides. "Let's get this over with."

Grayson stepped forward, drew his fist back, and punched Anton square in the mouth. Before Anton could throw one of his own, Tamera quickly jumped between them.

## CHAPTER TWENTY

Bright green neon lights illuminated the room, bathing the crowd in color. White LED stage lighting flashed about the room, reminding Kimber of glowing lightsabers straight out of *Star Wars*, creating a strobe like effect. She couldn't help but think maybe the Blood 'n' Rave should come with a warning for people who were prone to seizures.

The crowd jumped in time with the song, singing along with the well-liked tune, *Beautiful Now*, by a musician named Zedd. Kimber hadn't known much about electronic music, only knew the name of the song and artist because apparently Chad was a pretty big fan of the artist.

Upon arrival, they hadn't even secured a table before Chad grabbed a couple of glow sticks from a box by the door, snapped them to mix the two liquids to ignite the flare, and headed for the dance floor. Kimber smiled at his contagious enthusiasm. She found it hard to stand still herself, swaying in time to the tune.

Tena and Bobby made their way through the crowd, finding a table along the back wall and away from the masses. Probably safer to stay off the Sons' radar in case any of them recognized Bobby. Kimber had one of two choices, follow the two to the back of the room, or head for the dance floor with Chad. Surprising even herself, she opted for the latter. After all, Kimber didn't come here to hide. She could've done as much at home.

Tonight was about cutting loose.

Stepping outside her comfort zone.

Weaving through the throng of dancers, she found Chad smack-dab in the middle. It almost appeared as if he had a pogo stick, jumping as one with the crowd. Kimber laughed, absorbing the energy and rush. She took one of the offered glow sticks from Chad and began waving it in the air and moving to the beat of the sound.

The heavy bass beat thumped against her chest and pounded in her ears. Bodies knocked and bounced against her, throwing her occasionally off-kilter. Kimber couldn't help but laugh, enjoying the electricity of those around her. She was so far outside her norm, usually avoiding crowds like the plague. Nothing like throwing herself into the multitude. Chad leaned down, spoke loudly against her ear, something she couldn't begin to hear over the music. He laughed when Kimber shrugged, having no clue what he had tried to tell her. When the song came to its end, Kimber indicated to Chad she was going to head for the bar. He grinned and waved her on.

Dry pipes called for something wet.

She couldn't help the smile on her face, feeling much more lighthearted. *Just what the doctor had ordered.* Skirting the chairs and tables surrounding the tiled dance floor, she headed for the back of the club. Tena caught her gaze and waved at her, before holding up a glass of wine. Kimber could forgo a trip to the bar. Next round would be on her.

Taking a left between the tables, she bumped into a very solid chest. She stepped back to apologize when she glanced into the face of the very Sons' member Anton had warned her to stay away from. Out of jealousy? Possibly. Either way, she was a big girl and didn't need him coloring her opinion. She was capable of coming to her own conclusions.

"Pardon me." Kimber shouted to be heard over the music.

The man's hand slipped to her waist as he leaned down to her ear. "My pleasure, I assure you. Where's your bodyguard?"

"Bodyguard?" Her brow furrowed. "I'm not sure who you mean."

"Sure you do, sweetheart. If Rogue is here, you'll have to excuse me for kicking his sorry ass out."

"He's not, Wolf."

"You're alone?"

Kimber paused, unsure how she wanted to answer his question. She couldn't be positive about him not knowing Bobby. Best not to take a chance. Bobby had left his motorcycle vest at home, not wanting to draw attention. The same reason for he and Tena picking a table at the back of the room.

Kimber pointed to the dance floor. "I came with a friend. He's on the dance floor."

Wolf leaned down again, his breath tickling the shell of her ear. "Your boyfriend?"

She thought about lying, but should Wolf spot Chad, he'd no doubt see the truth. "Just a good friend. Coworker."

"Then he won't mind if I buy you a drink."

*Crap!* She couldn't very well refuse and draw attention to Bobby and Tena by heading back to their table. Wolf may not know him, but again, she didn't want to take the chance.

Detecting her hesitation, he said. "I won't bite ... not yet anyway," he added with a wink.

Kimber chuckled. Regardless of Anton's cautioning, she found Wolf quite the charmer. He may not be as classically handsome as Anton, but there was definitely sexual appeal radiating from him.

"You by yourself?"

He glanced at Kimber sideways, before understanding settled into his gaze. "You mean Xander? Please tell me your more enamored by a man such as myself, than one who looks as if they stepped off the cover of *GQ*. That boy probably spends more time in front of the mirror than most women."

Kimber smiled, patting his barrel chest. "No worries there, big guy. Xander's good-looking, but I prefer my men a bit more rustic."

Wolf's deep laughter grew. Kimber found she liked the sound and couldn't help but laugh with him.

"Come on, sweetheart." He placed a palm in the center of her back and began leading her to the bar. "Let me buy you a drink. I promise to keep my hands to myself. Just a little company is all I want. I hate drinking alone."

The bald bartender tossed aside his white towel and headed in their direction. The man Kimber knew to own the bar seemed to be absent, though she supposed he couldn't be present every night. Kimber side-stepped a stool and placed her hands on the bar's surface, hoping Tena understood her reasoning for not retrieving the wine she had already purchased.

"What's your poison?"

Kimber leaned closer to the bartender as to be heard. "I'll take a glass of zinfandel."

The man nodded, grabbed a wineglass from the rack overhead and used a clean bar towel to wipe it spotless. He then held it to the light. Satisfied, he opened the wine bottle with a slight pop, then poured her a glass of the pale pink wine. He slid it across the polished bar. Wolf reached into his pocket, pulled out a twenty, and laid it on the bar. Without asking Wolf, the bartender grabbed a rocks glass from the shelf, added a few cubes of ice, and poured two fingers of Jack Daniels into it. He handed it to Wolf.

He took the glass to his nose and inhaled before holding the glass up to her. "Salute."

Kimber clinked her wineglass to his. "Cheers."

He took a sip from the glass, then set it on the bar, his large hand nearly encircling it. True to his word, he did keep his hands on the bar and to himself. His gaze easily roamed over her before returning to her face. He smiled, not in the least apologetic for ogling her.

"I can see why Rogue is all territorial when it comes to you."

"He said that?" Kimber's brow creased, shocked Anton had spoken of her as if she were his property. "It's not as if we are dating."

"Maybe not." He arched one of his brows. "But he made it damn clear you were off-limits. Not that I give a flying fuck what he wants these days. I respected him at one time. Not anymore. The fucker's a traitor. You do know that?"

Kimber drew the corner of her lip between her teeth, uncomfortable with the direction of their conversation. She looked to her glass, toying with the stem. Anton and she may have parted on bad terms, but she wasn't ready to throw him under the bus either.

"Maybe there's a reason he's with the Devils."

Wolf chuckled. "I'm sure there is. Fucker doesn't take rejection well."

*Rejection?* "What do you mean?"

He smirked. "I take it the coward didn't tell you why he left the Sons. Who he thought of as his girl? She chose the wrong Sons' member according to him. He believes our supporting her decision was a betrayal to him."

Something tickled the hairs at her nape. "Who?"

"Gypsy's mate" — he cleared his throat — "woman."

"The redhead?"

His gaze narrowed. "You know her?"

"Met her briefly last year. I first met her at Anton's place. Later, she came by my home and told me to keep an eye on

Anton. I was a bit shocked since her and I didn't exactly hit it off."

He smiled, splitting his beard. "Sounds like Tamera. The woman always had a soft spot for Rogue, but her true love was Gypsy."

*Tam.* Tamera. Of course. Why hadn't she put two-and-two together? Kimber was an even bigger idiot. Anton had left her to go to Tamera. Her heart plummeted. At this point, she didn't even know for sure Anton had gone to Santa Barbara. All she had was his word.

"Anton left the Sons because she chose to be with Gypsy?"

"Long story, but Anton thought she belonged with him. She lived with him a short time. When she went back to Gypsy, he was hurt. I get that." He took a sip from his whiskey. "Anyone could see Tamera clearly loved Gypsy. Rogue couldn't handle the rejection, took the betrayal pretty hard and turned his back on all of us."

Something in Wolf's gaze told her there was more behind the story. He was holding back. "You think he still loves Tamera?"

"A few weeks ago, I might have said yes. Not anymore."

"What changed?"

"You, sweetheart." He reached out and ran a knuckle down her cheek. "I don't think I've ever seen Rogue go all territorial. Not even with Tamera. I think he knew, down deep, she belonged with Gypsy. He just didn't want to admit it. Watch your heart, baby girl. I think Rogue's out to steal it."

Kimber thought about what Wolf said, having a hard time believing it. Not that she didn't want to. But all it took from Tamera was one phone call to set Anton into motion. The very same woman she had caught in his house wearing nothing but a towel over a year ago. Whatever the truth, Anton had a lot to answer for when he returned. If she decided to give him the time of day.

Out of the corner of her gaze, she saw Bobby and Tena heading for the exit. Not that she could blame them. It wasn't their idea to come the Blood 'n' Rave, and yet they were left to sit alone in the back of the club. Instead of spending time with them, she passed away the night, keeping Wolf's attention off the fact a Devil was in their territory. Tena was probably dying to get Mr. Bear-alicious alone anyway. Time to make her own speedy exit. Wolf had certainly given her a lot to think about.

She took the glass to her lips and finished off her wine, then placed it back on the bar. Smiling up at Wolf, she gave his large hand a quick squeeze. "Thank you so much for the drink, Wolf. I think it's time I call it a night."

"It's nothing I said?"

Kimber leaned in and kissed his cheek. "Nope. I think down deep, you might be one of the good guys. Thank you for the conversation."

He winked at her again. "Thank you, sweetheart. You decide to give Rogue a chance, don't go easy on his ass. I may be still pretty damn pissed at him for being a complete shit, but I still love the bastard. Don't you dare tell him I said that."

Kimber laughed and bussed his cheek a second time. "I wouldn't think of it."

Turning, she headed for the dance floor to find Chad. She didn't want to leave without letting him know and seeing if he had a ride home. Tena and Bobby had arrived on his bike, while Chad had hitched a ride with her. He stood near the exit, chatting with a dark haired, good-looking man, who appeared to be a good ten years older than him. Kimber bet Chad wasn't about to leave, not with her anyway.

Chad saw her approach. "Hey, boss. Having a good time?"

"I was." She smiled, looking briefly to his friend. "I was about to head home. You need a ride?"

"I'll give him a lift." The way he looked at Chad told Kimber he was all about spending more time in Chad's company.

"I think I'll stay a bit longer." Chad's blue eyes spoke of his delight. "You okay to head home alone?"

"I am." Kimber pulled the car keys from her small handbag. "See you at work tomorrow."

The heavy glass and steel door closed behind her, muffling the sound of the music as she stepped outside. Pressing her key fob, her car horn honked, and the lights flashed once. Kimber walked between the row of cars until she reached hers.

Anton and Tamera came to mind. What the hell was going on? Kimber had been pretty sure Tamera was head over heels when it came to Grayson. Not that she didn't care about

Anton, that much was evident in her asking Kimber to befriend him. So why had she called Anton and why had he said she belonged to him?

When Anton came back to town, she definitely planned to ask him. Knowing now which Tam he referred to, she was more than ever determined to get to the bottom of whatever Anton was up to. Kimber was pretty sure if Anton stepped over the line where Tamera was concerned, Grayson would kill him. Whatever she thought she heard, Kimber didn't believe for a minute Anton would betray a friend, Devil or not.

ANTON'S HEAD SNAPPED BACK and blood streamed from his nose. Tamera screamed and all hell broke loose. He hadn't wanted it to come to blows, but Grayson wasn't about to listen to any explanations at the moment. His brother's eyes filled with black rage. Long fangs extended from his upper lip. Kaleb pulled Tamera clear, keeping her from getting into the fray. Bottom line, they needed to fight it out, even if Anton hadn't wronged Grayson.

Well, other than kissing his mate.

And though it was a pleasant kiss, there was nothing hot about it, not like locking lips with Kimber. Damn, he had a lot to make up for. The kiss between him and Tamera had been all for show. Too bad the act had also worked on Grayson. The man was out for blood.

*Anton's blood.*

Tamera tried to get her mate to see reason, but Grayson wasn't listening, and Kaleb found amusement in the entire scene, cackling like an idiot from the sidelines.

*What the hell?*

There wasn't a damn thing funny about the situation from where he stood. Anton ducked Grayson's right and delivered an uppercut to his jaw, sending him stumbling back. It didn't take long for him to right himself. He charged Anton, throwing a shoulder low and into his gut, sending him sprawling to the asphalt. His shirt ripped and the blacktop tore at his skin. Grayson leaned down and bit his shoulder.

*The motherfucker actually bit him.*

Anton growled, his own fangs lengthening, his anger getting the best of him. If he didn't stop the brawl soon, they'd both be bloody messes. He grabbed Grayson's shoulders and ripped his fangs from his skin. Anton bit back a roar as white lights flickered in his gaze. Red hot pain shot through his shoulder. He tossed Grayson like a rag doll. His one-time friend's backside skidded twenty-feet along the parking lot. Before Anton could pounce, Kaleb released Tamera. She moved with lightning speed to stand between them again, her hands held palms out.

"Enough."

Turning to Grayson, Tamera fisted his shirt and jerked his sorry ass off the ground, landing him on the hood of her Range Rover.

"Damn, you're sexy as hell when you use your vamp strength, doll." He grabbed hold of her shirt, stealing a quick kiss. "But right now, I have a score to settle."

Kaleb pointed a finger at Grayson, stopping him from leaping on Anton again. He stepped forward. "This true? You down here with Tamera?" he asked Anton.

Anton ran the back of his hand beneath his nose and swiped away the blood. "I'm not fucking Gypsy's mate, if that's what you're getting at."

The club P looked mighty pissed, more so than just being angry with him for possibly fucking Tamera. His glare told Anton his anger was much more personal. "Nope. Not what I'm getting at, asshole."

Kaleb looked back at Tamera, who had wrapped herself around Grayson from behind. Grayson now stood in front of her vehicle and she sat on the hood, watching Anton and Kaleb. Tamera looked ready to leap from the hood and jump between Kaleb and Anton if need be.

"While you two knuckleheads were going at it, Tamera told me you were working undercover. That true?"

Anton took a quick look behind him to the gateway of the alley. If they weren't careful, they'd blow the whole gig. He couldn't be sure they weren't followed. "Not here, P. Meet me at the pier, just north of town, in twenty minutes. For now, let me go. I need Tamera to follow in her Range Rover. Make sure you and Gypsy aren't seen when you leave. We'll talk there."

Twenty minutes later, Kaleb and Grayson pulled their Harleys onto the asphalt parking lot next to the pier. Anton and Tamera had parked their rides a half mile down the beach. The salt water hung heavy in the air, clinging to their skin and stinging the healing cuts on his flesh from his skirmish with Grayson. Now the foursome stood in the sand at the bottom of the wooden pier, out of sight.

"You want to start by telling me what the hell is going on, Rogue?" Kaleb leaned one shoulder against one of the support posts of the pier, legs crossed at the ankles. "If I'm guessing right, my brother and his mate most likely know about your involvement with the Devils."

"Why would you think that?" Anton glanced at Tamera, who merely shrugged. The last thing he wanted was to have the twins at odds because Cara thought it best to keep it between them.

"Because the son of a bitch was always coming to your rescue. Stepped between us at the club meeting you busted in on."

"It wasn't his idea, Hawk. Cara wanted it kept quiet."

"I'm club P. I had every fucking right to know. You guys had no right cutting me out. So, it's true then. You really didn't turn rogue."

Anton ran a hand through his short dark hair. He'd be so glad to get his old life back and his old look. "We had to make it believable, Hawk. I didn't like keeping you and Gypsy in the dark. Tamera swore she'd bring Gypsy up to speed first sign of trouble."

Grayson looked at his mate, one of his brows raising. "You knew about this?"

She shook her head. "Only within the last month. Cara thought after Kinky's death I might be able to find out which of the Devils might be involved. Anton was to be my cover. We were supposed to act as a couple."

"Did you find out who ordered the hit?"

Tamera shook her head and snuggled into his side. Grayson wrapped his arm about her and tucked her tightly against him. Anton was glad the case had not caused problems with his one-time best friend and his mate.

"It doesn't appear the Devils were involved." Tamera looked at Kaleb. "Not that I was able to ascertain. The Devils' VP was getting a little too friendly, regardless of me telling him I was with Rogue. I think it was more because he didn't trust me, reporter or not. He seemed pretty suspicious of me. That's why I called Rogue in."

Grayson glared at Anton. "If you were supposed to have her back, why the fuck weren't you there?"

"Not his fault, babe." Tamera gripped his chin gently, taking his gaze from Anton to hers. "Tank sent him north. Rogue had no way of knowing I had left for Santa Barbara. As soon as I called him, he headed south. Even at the risk of pissing off Tank for not following orders."

"Well, I want to speak with Viper," Kaleb grumbled, stepping away from the pier and straightening his spine. Anger rolled off him in waves. "The son of a bitch had no business keeping this from me. You" — he pointed a finger at him — "shouldn't have kept this from me."

"Cara thought it would be better the fewer people who knew." Anton squared his shoulders, tired of being everyone's punching bag. "She wanted your reaction to my defection real, Hawk."

Kaleb's jaw tightened. Waves slapped against the beach, cutting through the uncomfortable silence. The tension was thick. Cara and Viper were going to get a piece of Kaleb's mind, no matter what Anton had to say. Not to mention Joe Hernandez, Robbie Melchor, and the DEA knowing about Anton's undercover work. This was bigger than Kaleb's ego. He needed to learn it wasn't about keeping him from the know, but more about protecting Anton and Draven. This was Cara's sting and she'd have to answer for it.

For now, they needed to get the hell out of Santa Barbara before the entire mess came crashing down on their shoulders. Anton needed to get back to Bobby ... and Kimber, if she were still speaking to him. They couldn't close this case soon enough for his liking.

"Sorry, Rogue, but she isn't getting off the hook that easy," Kaleb said.

Anton took in a deep breath. "Whatever, man. You take it up with Viper and his mate. Honestly, I am getting a little tired of being everyone's kicking stone. You, Tamera, and Gypsy can sit here all fucking night and talk about it for all I care. You find Viper, kick his ass if it makes you feel better. Just keep me the fuck out of it."

He turned and started for the beach. Stopping just shy of stepping on the pier, he looked back. "I have a job I signed up to do and I need to finish it. I'd appreciate it if you two asswipes didn't get me killed in the process of your desire to soothe your egos."

Anton reached the top of the sand dune when Grayson called out. He stopped and turned back. Grayson's arm dangled over Tamera's shoulder, reminding Anton of what he wanted … had always wanted. *A family.*

"Glad to know you aren't a fucking traitor, man."

"I wouldn't have turned my back on the Sons for the Devils, bro. But for the sake of the case, I'm glad you bought it. Don't think it doesn't bother me, though."

He turned and jogged down the beach to where he had left his bike. He had to get back to Pleasant before the shipment of heroin came in. If he wasn't there, Tank would have his ass and the gig would be up.

If Anton were a betting man, he'd say his chances of securing a meeting with the cartel kingpin had become very slim odds. Once word got out he disobeyed, Anton wasn't exactly going to be getting favors from the Devils' P. Not to mention the condition he left Spider in. Yep, he wasn't going to be earning any brownie points over his beating the VP's ass.

Stepping over the seat of his bike, he started the engine and turned his Road King north, speeding off down the road. Anton gritted his teeth. Over one year of his life had been lost to this case, and they still were no closer to wrapping it up.

He wanted his life back. Hell, what he really wanted was a shot with Kimber.

*Fat chance.*

Should he come clean, she may forgive him over the Tamera incident and understand why he had kept her in the dark about his undercover work with the Devils. But Anton was pretty sure, should she find out about his desire to sink his fangs into her carotid artery, she'd freak the fuck out, which wasn't conducive with his desire to keeping her in his life.

## CHAPTER TWENTY-ONE

Anton hadn't gotten out of California before the cell in his pocket began to vibrate. He pulled his bike to the side of the road and cut the engine. One glance at the home screen had him rolling his eyes. Time to face the music with Tank. He took off his helmet, tapped the *SEND* button, and placed the phone next to his ear.

"Where the fuck are you, Rogue?" Tank's deep tone radiated with anger.

"Somewhere between Santa Barbara and Oregon."

"You want to explain why you aren't with Preacher?"

Anton chuckled, devoid of humor. "Cut the bullshit, Tank. You already know why I was in Santa Barbara. If your fucking VP would've kept his hands to himself, I wouldn't have had to leave Oregon. So instead of ragging on my ass, why not give your anger to someone who deserves it?"

"You fucked him up pretty good."

"Think I care? The piece of shit deserved it. He knew damn well Tam was my woman. Spider told me since he was VP, it gave him the right to fuck her."

"He said that?"

Anton smiled, happy to place Spider on Tank's bad side. The P was no doubt wondering if Spider ever put the moves on his own old lady. Spider had broken the unspoken code between brothers. A brother's old lady was strictly off-limits, no exceptions.

"He did."

Tank blasphemed. "You let me worry about Spider. I'll take care of his disrespect, make sure it doesn't happen again. I want you back in Florence. My shipment is coming in day after tomorrow. I need you and Preacher to accompany Draven to the delivery point."

"Which is?"

"I'll text you."

A car sped past Anton. The ass didn't bother slowing down. Thankfully, the berm where he sat wasn't particularly narrow on this stretch of the highway. "I'll be back to the farmhouse where Bobby and I are staying by morning."

"Good." Tank paused. Anton could hear a woman speaking in the background. He spoke rudely to her, telling her to mind her fucking business and get him something to eat before returning to their conversation. Anton grimaced, wanting to kick Tank's dumb ass just as he had Spider's. He couldn't imagine what woman would put up with the man. "Anton?"

"Yep."

"You want to tell me why your old lady was questioning my men?"

"She's a reporter. She gets paid to be nosy."

"Nosy gets you killed."

"I wouldn't fucking touch her if I were you." He left the part off about doing so would get Tank killed. For now, he had to keep the level of disrespect he felt for the man to a minimum.

He ignored Anton's threat. "Why would she be interested in our rivalry with the Sons of Sangue?"

Tank's accusation hung thick between them. His trust in Anton had wavered. He could hear it in the man's tone. Anton had Cara to thank for sending Tamera into the foray and fucking up all his hard work over the past year.

Anton crossed his arms over his helmet, which rest between his thighs, and looked out to the ocean. White caps hit the shore. "She's doing a piece for the newspaper she works for. Tam hadn't bothered to tell me about it, with good reason. I would've never allowed it. When I questioned her, she told me she was interested in the hit on Kinky Sala. He was the Sons of Sangue member executed over a week ago."

"I heard about that." Tank went quiet. Anton was about to ask if he was still there when he said, "The Devils didn't have anything to do with the slime's execution, if that's what you're getting at. Can't say I'm sorry if any of those bastards meet Death's door, though. You tell your old lady she needs to keep her nose to herself."

"I already sent her ass home." Something about the way Tank had answered, made Anton think he knew more than he was saying. The Devils may not have ordered the hit on Joseph, but Tank knew who did. "She won't be asking any more questions."

"Good. See that she doesn't."

"You know who took out Kinky." It wasn't a question.

Tank chuckled. "Nice try, Rogue. I'm not giving you the fucking information so you can let your little girlfriend write a piece about it. All I'm going to say is this goes deeper than gang rivalries. You want her to live, then I suggest you get her to drop the story about the bastard's death."

"I'll make sure she drops it."

"See that you do. Now, I need you in Florence like yesterday. I suggest you get that bike headed north and do the job I asked you to do. Make sure if you take off again, you take Preacher with you."

Tank's statement lay proof Tank no longer trusted him. He'd definitely let Cara and Kane know about the setback. Now that Tank's faith in him took a dive, getting private meetings with Cara, Kane, and her partner were going to be tricky. He'd have to get creative in shaking Bobby. No doubt, Tank already ordered him to stick to Anton like glue.

"I won't let you down."

"See that you don't," he hissed and the line went dead.

Anton pocketed his phone and jammed his helmet back on his head. Starting the engine, Anton pushed off the stone berm and sped down the highway. He wanted to tell Cara to shove her case. One serious misjudgment and it had seriously setback all he had worked for.

*Fuck!*

A full year's worth of work down the drain. When he had signed up for the assignment, he had no clue all it would cost him. At the time, he had nothing to lose. He wanted his life back. Anton wanted a chance to get to know Kimber better, without having to fear her getting caught up in this mess and putting her in danger.

Burying the odometer needle, his tires ate up the asphalt. Time to get home and get the show on the road. Once they picked up the heroin, they'd have evidence to turn over to the DEA. He may not have been able to tie it all back to the La Paz cartel, but at this point, he no longer cared. He'd be happy to put the Devils out of commission.

He wanted Tank's ass off the street.

Let Cara and Hernandez worry about the cartel. Anton's job was done. Time for him to cut his ties with the Devils.

KANE HEADED FOR HIS HOUSE, his bike taking the curves on the country road with ease. He pulled back on the throttle as he hit the straightaway. Most days, he appreciated being outside of town, not a neighbor in sight. Today wasn't one of those days. He hated knowing Cara was alone. Twenty minutes ago, Cara had informed him she thought she detected the scent of a primordial, possibly coming from the woods beyond their home. Having arrived at the house, following her day at the sheriff's office, she told him she had alighted from her Charger when the scent tickled her senses and raised the hair on the back of her neck. Cara didn't rattle easily, but the idea of Mircea gunning for them, had them all on high alert.

Kane's job of keeping his eye on Tamera was cut short with the arrival of his twin and Grayson in Santa Barbara. His phone's reception was shoddy at best, so he had no idea why the hell the two of them were outside of Hade's Nest. He was about to quiz Kaleb when Anton exited the bar with his arm wrapped around Tamera. Grayson had thrown the first punch. Kane figured he'd let the two fight it out. Kaleb could handle the aftermath and Tamera could catch everyone up to speed, hopefully before Anton and Grayson made a bigger mess of things.

*And a mess it was.*

He and Red had almost made it back from their trip to California when his mate had called. Red continued to Washington with promises to catch up, and Kane made a beeline for home. If Mircea even so much as touched his mate, he'd separate his head from his shoulders. Kaleb wouldn't be the only one guilty of taking a primordial's life. With Alec Funar and Rosalee both dead, the only primordials left were Vlad and his brother. If Cara detected the scent, then no doubt Mircea lurked in the woods. Vlad wouldn't have a reason to be there.

He had been against the idea of keeping his brother and the Sons in the dark about Anton being undercover. Especially Kaleb and Grayson, since they were the heart of the MC. Cara hadn't agreed. Kane consented since it was her case, and her ass on the line with the sheriff's office and the DEA, not to mention the prick, Robbie Melchor. Thankfully, Kane didn't have to deal with the self-important ass. Cara had made it clear, where Robbie was concerned, she could handle him. She had actually made him promise to steer clear when Captain Melchor came to town.

Which was probably for the best.

If Kane got word Robbie so much as stepped over the line, the man would be spitting dirt from about six feet under. Kane had a no tolerance rule for the little bastard.

Pulling into their gravel drive, Kane parked his Fat Bob and stepped over the seat. He took off his helmet and tucked it under his arm, heading for the back door. His gaze perused the surrounding area, while his nostrils flared in hopes to detect Mircea's scent. The humidity hung heavy in the air with the promise of oncoming storms, leaving him scenting nothing more than dirt and evergreens.

Hopefully, the idea of Mircea being in the States had spooked Cara into thinking she detected primordial blood and nothing more.

Cara opened the back door and jumped into his arms. He dropped the helmet to the grass with a thud and wrapped his arms about her as her legs circled his waist. Damn, it didn't take much from his mate to have his cock growing hard with hunger. He leaned down and kissed her soundly. He doubted he'd ever get tired of making out with his woman.

"Someone is happy to see me." Cara smiled, digging her heels into the cheeks of his ass. "Want to meet me upstairs?"

He laughed, his hands now palming her sweet ass. "How about we chat first? We need to talk about the case ... and the son of a bitch that is my great uncle."

Cara released her hold, then slid slowly down his length, tantalizing every inch of him, making him aware of every curve. He had been away far too long. She cupped his erection, earning her a groan. "Okay, seduction can wait."

Kane's fangs threatened to immerge. "You certainly know how to get a man's attention."

"Only yours." Just before she turned and headed back inside, Cara took a quick look around, her nostrils flaring slightly. Once inside, Cara turned and hopped onto the breakfast bar. "So let's talk about the case. What did you and Red discover?"

Kane set his helmet on the counter beside her and positioned himself between her spread legs. He tipped her chin with the pad of his thumb. "Not before I get to kiss you proper."

Lowering his head, he sealed his lips to hers. Cara opened to him, tempting him with her tongue. She tasted of peppermint candies and a unique flavor that was all her. Damn, he loved this woman. He deepened the kiss, taking full possession, letting her know just how much he missed her. Her hands tangled in the over long hair at his nape. The scent of her desire weaved about him like a satin ribbon, tethering him to her.

If they kept this up, there would be no talking until later. Much later. Kane released her and stepped back. Her gaze flashed black, her tongue smoothing over her upper lip. Okay, he'd make quick work of this conversation so he could slide between her lean thighs.

"You got problems, *mia bella*."

Her expression sobered. "What's going on?"

"Hawk and Gypsy were in Santa Barbara."

Cara's eyes widened. "What? Did you intercept them before they saw Tamera?"

He shook his head, tossing his cell on the counter. "This phone was about worthless. I couldn't get a good reception down there. By the time Red and I caught up with Kaleb and Grayson, it was too late. I left the four of them in the parking lot. Gypsy was about to kick Blondy's ass."

"Why the hell didn't you stop them?"

Kane chuckled. "They're big boy vamps. I figured Tamera could handle the motley crew better than I could. After all, Gypsy would listen to her before me. Besides, the Devils' hang out was just beyond the alley where they were congregating. I didn't want to draw more attention. Hawk will no doubt look us up once he gets back to Pleasant anyway. He's bound to be plenty pissed."

Her brow furrowed. "Is the gig up?"

Kane shrugged. "Sorry, *mia bella*, you'll have to ask Blondy. I'm betting he did everything he could to move along Hawk and Gypsy as not to bring attention." He tucked her pale blonde hair behind one ear. "Whatever happened, you need to be prepared for the outcome. Blondy may have gotten them out of there without notice, or he could've been found out. You'll have to wait and talk to him."

She picked her cell phone up from the counter. "I'll give him a quick call."

"Let it go for tonight." He laid his hand atop hers. "I'm not even sure he's headed back. Don't panic and make this worse for him."

"Wolf told me the Devil who was staying with him at the farmhouse, was still in town."

"What's Wolf know about him?"

"Not much. Just said he spotted him at the Blood 'n' Rave last night."

Kane rubbed the couple of days whisker growth on his chin. "Stepping into our territory. Pretty ballsy. What did Wolf do?"

"Let him go." Cara smoothed a hand down his T-shirt. He was having a damn hard time concentrating on their conversation. "He didn't want to make a scene in front of Kimber. He was pretty sure she was with them. She tried to hide the fact, but he caught her attention on them a time or two. Blondy's MC brother didn't cause any problems, so Wolf let him leave without incident."

"Call a meeting tomorrow with Blondy. I'll call Hawk, get him and Gypsy there. We need to see where your case sits, if Blondy is still onboard."

"I'll leave Hernandez out of this meeting. No sense worrying him yet. He's the one who's been handling the DEA and Robbie."

Kane chuckled. "Might be wise. A den of angry vampires wouldn't be the best place for your partner to be. Now about the primordial…"

Cara drew her lower lip between her teeth. Kane's gaze lowered, jealous of her mouth. He hoped to quickly dispel her fears of Mircea and get her upstairs posthaste.

"I caught just a hint of a primordial's scent outside."

"Mircea?"

She shrugged. "The weather wasn't exactly conducive of me getting a clear read on it. I can't even be sure what I smelled."

"Mircea's no longer in Italy, so we can't be too careful. If you think you caught his scent, we need to take that seriously. Vlad thinks he's looking to take one of us out. I can't help believe he wants me."

Worry filled her blue gaze. "Why you?"

"Because he's going to think Rosalee's demise started with me dumping her." He leaned in and lightly kissed her lips. "No worries, *mia bella*. I'll be careful. The son of a bitch won't catch me unaware."

"I can't lose you."

"You won't. We can't allow him to rule our lives either."

Her eyes filled with moisture. "I don't want to be too paranoid. I'll be smelling him everywhere, if I do."

"Don't let your guard down, *mia bella*." Kane palmed her cheek. "I can't lose you to a mad vamp. If it isn't me he wants, then he might go after you to get back at me. I'll get a hold of Vlad tomorrow, see if he's had any luck finding his brother."

Cara leaned into his palm, then turned and placed a tender kiss in the center of it. Kane growled. Threading his hands through her silky hair, he leaned down and took her lips again. Cara drew his lower lip between hers and suckled it. His dick hardened and he was done waiting. His fangs elongated. Kane wrapped one arm around her back and the other beneath her legs, picking her up with ease.

"How about I get a proper homecoming?"

Cara nipped his chin with her fangs. "You're the one who wanted to talk."

Kane pressed a kiss to her forehead. "I'm done talking."

## CHAPTER TWENTY-TWO

Every part of him ached, from the top of his head to the tip of his toes. Anton was soaking wet, having gotten caught in a short storm that had rolled in off the coast. He was chilled to the bone and could definitely use communion. Having left the night before for Santa Barbara to extricate Tamera, being spotted by Grayson at the worst time, and having Kaleb chew his ass out…

Yeah, he was pretty fucking tired of the whole ordeal.

Not to mention he hadn't slept in over two days. Anton had done a lot of soul searching in the last twelve hours. He was no longer sure all he chanced to lose was worth getting Kane his revenge. Hell, it could be another few years before he managed to get an audience with Raúl Trevino Caballero.

*If ever.*

The sun peaked over the horizon. Tank expected him and Bobby to accompany Draven to the pickup point tomorrow. Once he got the specifics, he and Bobby would retrieve Draven and head for the specified drop off.

The heroin best show the fuck up.

Anton was done.

He would hand the shit over to the feds and walk away. Time to hang up his undercover work. If he ever stepped foot back in Santa Barbara again it would be too soon. The loss of his previous year had never really bothered him until now. Once Kimber came crashing back into his screwed up life, everything changed. Anton realized what he was missing. His life was far too lonely without her in it.

*Vampire.*

*Fuck!*

How the hell did he broach the subject of the monster living just beneath his surface? Hypnotizing her the rest of her natural born life wasn't an option. Anton needed a plan — one that didn't result in her freaking out. If she couldn't handle the truth, he'd be left with wiping her mind of all knowledge of vampires from her and walking out of her life forever.

There would be no going back.

His heart felt as if an elephant sat on his sternum at the thought of losing her to his dark secret. She might despise the fact he was in a motorcycle club, but it would suddenly be preferable over the fact he had sported fangs and fed off the blood of humans. He was pretty sure that conversation wasn't going to go well.

*Double fuck!*

Kimber deserved better, but Anton was far too selfish to let her go unless he had exhausted all options. For once he was looking after his own needs. The sound of her parting sobs when he had left for Santa Barbara to rescue Tamera had just about killed him. He had a lot to make up for.

Bobby came to mind as he closed in on his farmhouse. A lone light glowed in the kitchen window. He assumed the man sat at the kitchen table, a cup of steaming java in his hand as he had every morning. Anton had gotten to know the ex-preacher pretty well over the past year. Bobby was an early riser, said he loved the solitude. The man was the only Devil he had come to trust and the only one he liked. If he were to be honest, Anton was going to miss him when he walked away.

He took in a deep breath and blew it out. Anton needed to keep Bobby from the fallout. He didn't deserve prison. Bobby had been against the selling of heroin in the schools just as much as Anton had. Tank had ordered Bobby into commission with Anton. Bobby had done nothing more than follow the president's directive without question.

Anton needed to talk to Cara soon. She might not be happy with his decision, but he had given her so much of his past year. He wanted out, but he also needed to protect Draven's ass. Even if the Devils didn't know there was a connection between him and the barkeep. Draven couldn't be left behind to work with the cartel without Anton to watch over his scrawny ass. He meant to tell Cara it was time to cut their losses.

After a year, other than Tank's say so, he had no evidence linking the La Paz cartel to the heroin. A sting this big would require more than another year of undercover work, and Anton wasn't willing to give more time. The DEA could arrest the major players within the Devils MC, specifically Tank and Spider, with the evidence Anton had on them. Kane's revenge against Raúl would have to wait for another day. Anton would gladly help the past P out, but he was done with the DEA.

Regardless, everything would have to wait until he spoke with Kimber, his number one priority at the moment. He slowed his bike as he came to her drive. Pulling in, Diesel's ears perked when he lifted his head and spotted Anton. He came trotting toward Anton as he slowed his bike to a stop and cut the engine. Lights illuminated the windows of the lower level of her house, telling Anton that Kimber was also an early riser.

Taking off his helmet, he stepped over the bike and set it upon the seat. Diesel stood on his hind legs, his front paws landing on his abdomen, his barks echoing in the early dawn. Anton scratched the dog's ears, leaning down and speaking to him, when the porch light went on. Kimber stepped onto the porch, the screen door slapping the wood frame behind her. Her gaze spoke of her annoyance and displeasure of finding him making friends with her dog.

"Too bad Diesel doesn't know the word attack." Kimber perched her fists on her hips. "What are you doing here, Anton? Tam tired of you already?"

"You going to enter a verdict of guilty without hearing my case?" Anton stopped petting the dog and headed in her direction. "Not fair, *tesoro*. I may have been an ass, but I should at least be given the chance to explain myself."

"Come on, Diesel," Kimber called to the dog and held open the screen door.

The dog trotted into the house without a backward glance. *Traitor.* Kimber accompanied the dog, not bothering to invite him in. No matter, she hadn't shut and locked the house door either. He'd take that as an invitation. Taking to the steps, Anton then crossed the porch, his boot heels striking the wood.

The door creaked as he opened it and stepped into the living area. Kimber sat in a straight-back chair, shoulders a stiff line, her lips turned down. Diesel lay at her feet. Pissed didn't begin to describe the look on her face. And yet, Anton thought she hadn't looked more beautiful. Just being near her again, his heart swelled. He hated he was the reason for her frown. One of her bare feet tapped the wooden floor, either out of nervousness or agitation. Which he wasn't sure.

"Well?" One brow arched.

Anton's gaze went from her sexy bare feet, with her adorable pink-painted toenails, up her stiff exterior, and landed back to her face. "Well what?"

She rolled her chocolate-colored eyes. "You wanted the chance to explain."

Anton approached her chair and sank to his knees. He encompassed her cold fingers gently within his much larger hands. "I'm sorry I made you cry, *tesoro.*"

"You said I belonged to you." Her voice wavered. "You made me feel special. Like I mattered."

"You do." He squeezed her fingers. "Christ, Kimber, I can't begin to make up for all I've done."

Her gaze rose from their joined fingers to his eyes. The mistrust he saw in her warm eyes cut him straight to the heart. Anton had run off to help another woman without so much as an explanation. He deserved her doubt and anger.

"How can I trust you, Anton? I know nothing about you."

"I adore you." He brought her knuckles to his lips and kissed them. "I don't want another woman. What more do you want to know?"

"For starters? Tell me the truth about the woman you were so anxious to leave me for."

Anton dropped his hold on her fingers and framed her thighs with his hands. "You remember Tamera?"

She nodded, her expression unreadable. "The woman wearing nothing but a towel at your house over a year ago. Not easy to forget. She had been quite rude, if I recall."

"She was very rude to you and I'm sorry about that. I allowed it and I shouldn't have. Tamera and Gypsy are" — okay, he couldn't say mated — "they live together. They have a child."

"Why didn't she call Gypsy then?"

"It's complicated."

Kimber briefly glanced at her wrist watch. "I have a few hours before I'm needed. I'm all ears."

"*Tesoro*, I promise I'll come clean after tomorrow. I need you to trust me one more day."

Her gaze narrowed, accusing him of being the bastard he was. "I can't live with the secrets and lies any longer, Anton.

Otherwise, you can walk right out that door and not come back."

Anton sat back on the wooden floor, jamming a hand through his short hair. "I can't, *tesoro*. I might be putting you in danger and I'm not willing to do that."

"And yet you don't worry about putting Tamera in danger."

"Tamera can take care of herself. Besides, she has Gypsy."

"And yet, it was you who went to her rescue." She sighed. "What aren't you telling me, Anton? Something is going on with this MC of yours. I get that. The motorcycle clubs are always into something illegal."

"Not always. But the Devils more so than most."

"Why ride with the Devils? Honestly, Anton, I'm not sure I can be with you as long as you continue to be a part of their gang."

"Club."

"Cut the crap, Anton. You and I both know their club is just a front for organized crime."

He had to know. "Do you feel the same about the Sons of Sangue?"

Kimber leaned forward and placed a hand on his knee. "If you want the truth, I really don't know. I've always known of their existence in Oregon but until you, I never really met any of them. I only know what I've read about these motorcycle gangs that hide behind their toy runs and charities."

"The Sons aren't at all like the Devils." Christ, he wanted to come clean. "Give me one day, *tesoro*. That's all I ask."

"No more secrets?"

*Only one.* And damn if he knew how to reveal the vampire side of him. "We'll talk."

"Anton…"

He stood and pulled Kimber to her feet. Uncertainty swam in her gaze. Before she could protest, he leaned down and sealed his lips to hers. Not a tender kiss. No, he wanted to possess her, show her how much he craved to be inside her. His erection plagued him, begged for appeasement. Even though he knew the right thing to do would be to come clean before making love to her again, he couldn't wait. He had already waited too damn long.

Kimber broke the kiss, stepped back, and placed a palm on his wet shirt. "You aren't getting away with everything that easy, mister. You hurt me. I still haven't forgiven you for leaving me to rescue another woman."

Anton growled. "I—"

She placed her fingers on his lips and stilled his words. "You will answer for that. If you want this — us — then no more friends with benefits. No more running off to other women."

Anton grinned. "I'm all yours, *tesoro.*"

"Promise?"

Anton crossed his chest with his forefinger before capturing her lips again and sealing out any more protests. His tongue swept the inside of her mouth, tasting her, savoring every second. He knew damn well this could be their last time. After today, he would no longer hypnotize her into forgetting. She would know him for who he was. All of him. If she ran from his vampire form, then he'd be forced to make her forget him forever.

For now, he wanted far less clothes between them.

Kimber slid her arms up his chest and threaded her fingers into the short hair at his nape. Giving in to mutual desire, she kissed him back. The scent of her hunger rose between them. There was certainly no doubt, his Kimber wanted him.

His damp shirt became increasingly uncomfortable. Breaking the kiss, he stepped back and stripped the shirt over his head. Her gaze dropped, lingering over his bare flesh before lowering to the bulge in the front of his jeans.

Kimber ran her fingers down his skin, her nails lightly scoring the flesh before reaching for the closure of his jeans. "Your pants? They look pretty wet too."

He covered her fingers with his hand. "Kimber? Don't start something you aren't prepared to finish. It's been too damn long. If you continue, make no mistake, I will fuck you."

"Such language."

"More like a promise"

A smile crept up her cheeks. "You aren't getting off scot-free. No matter what happens between us this morning, you still owe me the truth."

"And you'll get it."

"Then stop talking." She pushed the wet material down his hips and his cock sprung free. Her hand encompassed him, sliding from the crown to the base and back.

"Fuck," he hissed. He might just die from the sheer pleasure.

Her cute little pink tongue wet her lips. "Oh, I intend to."

He chuckled. "I was hoping you would."

A wicked twinkle filled her gaze. "Right now, I plan to show you how happy I am to have you back home. Tomorrow, though, we'll talk."

Her gaze dropped to her hand and his cock, just seconds before she sank to her knees. He couldn't stop her if he wanted. Who was he fooling? He was dying to see her lips wrapping his erection, dying to feel her take him into his mouth. One of her hands slipped to the cheeks of his ass. Her tongue darted out and captured the drop of precum on the mushroom tip.

Anton sucked in air just before Kimber took him fully into her mouth, damn near swallowing the entire length. Fighting back the urge to go vampire, he kept his gaze on her lush red lips surrounding him, her tongue licking the rigid vein beneath. Ah hell, he couldn't look away if he wanted to.

His gaze heated. His gums ached.

Anton bit back a string of curses, pulling her from his erection and ignoring her protests. He pulled up his pants and picked her up, heading for the stairs. "Sorry, *tesoro*. I want to be inside you when I come. No more waiting."

Kimber wrapped her arms about his neck and snuggled against his chest. Seconds later, he tossed her upon the bed and divested her of her clothes. An angel spread before him. Her hair fanned out across the pillow case. Hell no, he didn't deserve her, but he was damn glad to have her. He shucked his pants and joined her on the bed. The mattress dipped from his two-hundred-fifty pounds. Just before he slid inside, before his fangs punched through his gums, he framed her face within his palms and reluctantly hypnotized her.

Her gasp as he slid his cock between her legs and sank into her was the balm he needed for his soul, the music his ears had been missing. Even if she left him, he'd never forget the sound or the feel of being buried to the hilt in her.

*Home.*

Anton had come home.

VLAD'S SENSES KICKED UP, telling him he was getting closer to his brother. Mircea, the fool, thought he was an equal to Vlad, just as powerful in every way. Fat chance. Vlad could take his life with little effort. Mircea might be older in age, but he was younger in vampire years. No matter how much his big brother might wish it, he couldn't begin to best Vlad.

Mircea had issued him a challenge when he had called out Vlad. *As if he had a chance in hell at winning.* The one thing Mircea had accomplished with his phone call was pissing off the vampire in him. And he was furious.

Mircea tried to use Stefan to send him on a wild goose chase. Stefan meant nothing to Mircea, other than another annoying descendant of Vlad's. No, his true target would be Kane. Kane had been the one to take what Mircea considered his, not to mention he blamed him for Rosalee's death.

He might think to hurt Kane through his mate, to see him suffer, but his real issue had always been with Vlad's eldest descendant.

Arriving behind Kane's house, Vlad masked his scent with the coming storm, something Mircea had never bothered to learn. His brother much preferred instilling fear in other vampires, letting them know he was near. In truth, Mircea had gone soft, lazing about his stone fortress back in Italy, never really having a reason to leave. He preferred to be doted upon by his servants.

Mircea may have loved Rosalee, but his bitch of a stepdaughter never respected him. Had she listened to her maker, she might still have her head. Her obsession with Kane had gotten her killed.

Mircea stood a few hundred feet from him, watching the house. He squatted beneath a pine, his back against the bark, having no idea Vlad stood so close. Mircea was probably biding his time. If he didn't catch Kane unaware, Vlad would bank on his great grandson taking Mircea in a fight. Which meant his brother would want to take Kane after his mate left the house. Mircea would always take the path of least resistance.

"Brother."

Mircea damn near jumped out of his skin at the sound of Vlad's voice.

Vlad could have easily taken his head, ended his miserable existence, but his damn sentimental side in hoping his brother could yet be redeemed kept him from doing so. Mircea was, after all, his last living sibling.

Mircea turned on him, quickly schooling his expression. "I thought you'd be guarding Kaleb's baby. Foolish to leave him alone."

"Even more so to leave my eldest grandson unprotected." He arched one brow. The wind picked up, whipping his long black hair across his face. "You're a fool if you thought for a second I'd follow your shell game."

An evil smile crossed his lips. "So you now… What? Take my head?"

"Foolish as I may be, I had hoped I'd talk some sense into you."

"And what, dear brother, would you like from me?"

Vlad reached out, lightning quick, and gripped his brother by the throat, squeezing his windpipe. His hyoid bone snapped beneath the pressure. Good thing for his brother's vampire DNA. He'd heal soon enough.

"The States have nothing for you. Return to Italy."

"And do what?" Mircea wheezed. "You've taken my reason for returning."

"Rosalee was never to be yours. You were a fool to think so." Vlad tightened his grip, earning him a squeal from Mircea. "Find another reason. Quit sitting on your ass and find a new plaything."

"Why would I do that?" he croaked.

"To keep me from killing you, you ass. Threaten what's mine and I'll see you don't live to sire another descendant. I'm giving you a chance to carry on your lineage."

He released his hold and Mircea stumbled back. His hand went to his throat. "Why not end me now? Obviously, I came here to kill your beloved Kane."

Vlad clenched his teeth, biting back his anger. His fury would do him no good. "I don't doubt why you're here. But I do doubt your skill. You'll never get close enough to my grandson. I won't allow it. And even if you managed to get by me, you underestimate Kane's strength and skill. I'm offering you a last chance. Take it and live."

Mircea glanced at the back of the house. He rolled his neck, his hyoid bone probably already healing. "Even if I do as you ask, I'll return one day to kill him. You know that as sure as I'm standing here."

Vlad sighed. "And that is the day I will kill you."

With a wink, Mircea turned and sped through the forest, his answering cackle taunting him every step of the way. Why the hell he allowed Mircea to live, he didn't know. Vlad was sure he'd one day live to regret his decision. Glancing back at his great grandson's house, he knew for now they'd be safe. Tomorrow would be a new day. If he couldn't convince Mircea to return to Italy, then his broken hyoid bone would be the least of his brother's worries.

ANTON STRODE INTO THE clubhouse meeting room, the estranged year draining away. A feeling of peace and serenity washed over him as his gaze took in his brothers sitting around the big table. Contentment filled him now that the gig was almost up. He may not have completed the entire mission, but he hoped what he had to give would be enough.

Kaleb sat at the head of the table, Kane by his side. Cara leaned against the back wall beside Tamera, who sat on a bar stool, while Grayson sat opposite of Kane. Ryder, Grigore, and Alexander were also in attendance, their expressions unlike the last time he had seen them.

Anton had come home.

Pulling out a chair, the legs scraping the wooden floor, Anton took a seat. He laid his large hands atop the table and smiled. Damn, it had been too long since he last sat at the oak table. Too fucking long, if you asked him. He was ready to end this case once and for all, and get his life back.

Cara tucked her phone into her back pocket and leaned forward, bracing her hands on the table and glared at him. "How the hell did you fuck this up so badly, Blondy?"

"Are you fucking serious?" Anton growled. "Go to hell, Cara."

Kane cleared his throat. "Don't make me hand you your ass, Blondy."

"Sorry, Cara. No disrespect meant." Anton rubbed his nape. He might not be happy with her at the moment, but that didn't mean he didn't regard her position. "But you can't lay this on my doorstep. You sent Tamera to Santa Barbara without checking with me. She couldn't get a hold of Viper."

"Not my fault, man." Kane growled. "My cell's reception was crappy. I was near enough, but Tamera wouldn't have known that."

"No, she didn't." Anton returned his attention to Cara. "As soon as Tamera called I headed south, even though I knew it would piss off Tank."

Cara lips thinned. "You did, but the plan was for you to be there."

"Tank ordered me to Florence." Anton's ire rose, heating his vision. "You know I had to follow his order."

"You should've called me."

Which is where Anton went wrong. He should have found time. "We went over this. I was with Preacher."

Cara righted herself, crossing her arms beneath her breasts. "Tamera told me no one was talking about who took out Kinky?"

"Correct. Tank told me yesterday they had nothing to do with it." He glanced around the table at his MC brothers. Some of the members looked at him with indifference, while others seemed to sympathize with his position. "He told me it went deeper than club rivalries. That if I wanted to keep Tamera alive, I should make sure she drops it."

"*It* meaning who killed Kinky?" Kaleb sat forward in his chair. "You think Tank knows who ordered the hit?"

Anton nodded. "My gut tells me he knows."

"You think he'll talk?" Grayson asked.

"Not a chance in hell. I'm not exactly on his good side at the moment."

"And why would that be?" Kaleb stood and walked to the door, telling one of the prospects to bring them whiskey and glasses. When he returned, displeasure filled his gaze. Aimed at him or the whole situation, Anton wasn't sure. "One year and you couldn't manage to earn his trust?"

Anton shook his head and chuckled, the humor misplaced on him. "Oh, I had his respect all right. Right up until I handed his VP an ass beating before I left. I don't think Tamera playing nosy reporter helped my case any."

"Agreed," Tamera said. "I probably didn't. This isn't Blondy's fault."

Tamera had been there, seen the Devils at their finest. They were a crude bunch of law-breaking bikers who held little regard for human life.

Anton glanced back at Cara. "There's a shipment of heroin coming in tomorrow along the Siuslaw River. Tank's supposed to call me with the details. Preacher and I are to accompany Draven to the pickup point. I'll pass along the details to you as I get them. You can call in the DEA. After that I'm done. I suggest you get Draven the hell out as well. Without me, he won't be safe. The Devils may have respected me at one time, but they've never held Draven in high regard. He means nothing more to them than someone to move their drugs. Which is why Preacher and I have been ordered to accompany him."

Cara pulled out a chair at the table and sat, ignoring the rule about women not being allowed to sit at the meeting table. After all, she had called the meeting. "We haven't caught Raúl Trevino Caballero. That was part of the deal."

"It was, but you won't catch him through this case." Anton shifted in his seat. "After a year of being under, I'm no closer than when I started. I'll help you get your revenge on Raúl, just as everyone here will no doubt assist you and Kane. But it isn't going to happen with the Devils. I have enough evidence to take down most of them. It's going to have to be enough."

Cara looked at Kane. "It's okay, *mia bella*. We'll wait for another day."

Giving her attention back to Anton, she said, "You give us the location where the heroin is landing tomorrow and I'll turn it over to Captain Melchor and the DEA. Then we walk away. I can't say I'll be sad to see Robbie go."

"What about Preacher?" Anton had to know his friend would walk too.

"What about him?"

"You keep him out of this, Cara. The man doesn't deserve to go down with the rest of the Devils. He's one of the good guys."

"You get me the information. We'll come up with a plan to get Preacher out of there before the DEA gets there."

"You think he's Sons material, Blondy?" Kaleb asked.

"I do." Anton leaned back in his chair, lacing his fingers over his chest. "Not sure what he'd think about becoming a vampire, though."

"Your call, Blondy." Kaleb glanced around at the Sons ringing the table. "If you think he's worthy, we could use another good man. You bring him to the table, the Sons will vote on patching him over."

"Thanks, P. I appreciate that."

"It's the least we could do."

Kaleb stood as the prospects brought the whiskey to the table on a wooden tray, along with enough rocks tumblers. He passed out glasses, then handed the bottle of Gentleman Jack to Kane. They each poured a couple of fingers of the amber liquid and passed the bottle onto the next man.

"Let me first say," Kaleb stated, "that I'm still pretty furious at being kept in the dark about your undercover work. I think I speak for everyone here when I say I apologize for treating you like the shit-head traitor we all thought you to be."

Damn, but it felt good to hear the club P saying he screwed up, even if he couldn't be faulted. "I knew what I was getting into."

Kaleb glared at Cara. "This is on Cara for not trusting us to have your back."

"Hawk—"

Kaleb cut off Kane from defending her actions. "I'll have my say, Viper. From here on out, anything like this comes up again, you best bring it to the table. Viper and I will decide collectively if it needs to be kept from the club. Am I clear?"

"I did it for the good of the case, Hawk. It wasn't about your ego. It was about keeping Draven and Blondy alive."

One of Kaleb's brows rose. "Viper?"

"Let's hope a situation like this doesn't arise again." Kane reached over and squeezed Cara's thigh. "But if it does, I'll make sure you're included, Hawk. You're club P and as so, you had the right to know."

"Kane is correct. I owe you an apology. All of you. I should've trusted you to keep Blondy's secret. Instead, I caused hard feelings within the Sons. It won't happen again." Cara glanced around the room, making eye contact with them all before stopping on Kaleb. "Hawk, you get to know what's going on from here on out. Providing you don't keep anything from Kane either. You need to realize Kane's got your back and I'm not your enemy. Kane was against me not telling you about Blondy."

"Thank you, Cara." Kaleb, dropped the matter and obviously satisfied, picked up his glass and held it in front of him. "This matter is done. Let us toast to having Blondy back among us."

"Hear, hear," Grayson said, raising his glass, along with the rest of the Sons.

"Salute," Kane said, and the others followed suit.

Anton downed the amber liquid and set his glass back on the table. "Glad to be home. Now let's get this show on the road tomorrow and hand these son of a bitches over to the DEA."

"Glad to have you back," Alexander said, followed by the rest of the Sons at the table welcoming his return.

Damn, but it felt good to be home.

## CHAPTER TWENTY-THREE

Anton glanced at his watch as Bobby, Draven, and he pulled into the designated pickup point along the Siuslaw River. Tank hadn't given them a lot of notice when he'd called about an hour before the drop was to happen. He hoped his call to Cara bought the DEA enough time to set up around the perimeter. There would be no second chances. Once the money transferred hands and the drugs were given to Draven, the DEA would swoop in and all hell would break loose.

DEA special agents had also been sent south to Santa Barbara. Once the exchange was completed, the special agents would be given the green light. The major players from the Devils would be apprehended and taken into custody. First to go down? Spider and Tank. No two were more deserving.

Anton's job now was to get Bobby Bourassa out of the picture before the drugs traded hands. Better yet, before the boat ever docked. Cara promised to keep his name from the reports. He'd be given the opportunity to start over, a new life. Anton thought he'd be a great asset to the Sons of Sangue, but something told Anton he wasn't about to embrace the vampire lifestyle any more than Kimber might.

*Faith.*

The one thing Anton ran short on these days. The ugly truth that he preferred her artery over a thick juicy steak, might just have her packing her bags, selling her house, and leaving behind her blood-sucking neighbor. If she couldn't handle the truth, then Anton would have no choice but to let her go. He'd be forced to hypnotize her into forgetting everything they had done together. He wasn't cruel enough to leave her with regrets over a love that wasn't to be.

Anton took in a deep breath, then blew out a steady stream.

Time to get the show on the road.

The three alighted from their bikes, under his directive, and headed for the docks. Anton had purposely parked the motorcycles out of sight from the pickup point. He'd send Bobby back to the bikes on a fool's mission before the vessel ever arrived. With any luck, Bobby would be miles down the road before the DEA descended and arrested Anton, Draven, and the entire boat's crew. Once at the sheriff's office, and word came of Tank and Spider's arrest, then Draven and he would be free to go.

Following his release, he'd contact Bobby, hoping his MC brother might see reason. Anton was giving him a shot at a better life, whether that included the Sons of Sangue or not. Hopefully one free of the Devils, though.

Reaching the dock, Draven fidgeted like a mouse in a snake tank. His gaze continued to look toward the mouth of the river. The envelope with the DEA's cash was tucked into the inside pocket of Draven's black leather jacket, Anton having put it there himself. The barkeep's hand patted the breast pocket, no doubt making sure he hadn't dropped it on the ride.

Anton did a quick sweep with his gaze of the area, hoping the feds had yet to arrive. It was all in the timing. He needed Bobby free of the area.

Shoving his hands into his jean pockets, Anton cursed. "Fuck. Preacher, I need you to do me a favor."

"What's that?"

"I must've I dropped my phone back at the rest stop where we all met earlier. I made a phone call." Anton rubbed his nape and grimaced. "I don't answer when Tank calls, I'm dead. Can you make a quick trip back there and see if you can find it? I'll stay here with Draven, just in case the boat arrives."

Bobby raised a brow. "Why don't I watch him and you go back find your own damn cell?"

"Draven doesn't trust you, man. I've known him longer."

Bobby looked at Draven, who shrugged. "No offense. I'm not trusting all this money to someone I barely know. I've known Rogue for a few years. I'll take my chances with him."

Draven had been filled in earlier on Anton's undercover work and how the sting was to go down. He did his part perfectly. Bobby grumbled something about it being *a bad time for clumsiness* before heading for the motorcycles. Moments later, Anton heard the bike's engine, followed by the tires spinning gravel. He caught site of Bobby heading down the dirt path leading to the road. Mission accomplished.

"Let's hope the DEA gets here before the boat arrives. Preacher should still be gone. And if he's smart," Anton continued, "he'll see the place swarming with cops when he returns and hightail it the hell out of here."

"I doubt he'd be stupid enough to stick around." Draven pulled the envelope from his breast pocket and slapped it against his palm. A heavy sigh escaped his lips. "Too bad we have to hand all this cash over."

"Don't even think about it, Draven." The two fell into a moment of silence before Anton asked, "Everything okay with you?

"Why wouldn't it be?"

He shrugged. "Don't know. You tell me. Last couple of times I've been around you, you've been jumpy as hell, man."

His gaze stayed on the river. "Nothing to worry about here. Just want this damn case over with like you."

Anton clapped his shoulder. "Then let's get this over with."

Moments later, the boat's engine caught Anton's attention, long before the bow came into view. It made its slow trek around the bend. Anton glanced about, his keen sight picking up a couple of special agents moving into position. Luckily, no stray pedestrians lurked about. The gloomy day, with the threat of rain, likely kept most away. Bobby may have passed some of the special agents on his way out. He wasn't wearing colors, and since he wouldn't be here during the drop, they'd have no reason to suspect a man on a motorcycle. "Showtime."

"Let's do this." Thankfully Draven's case of the nerves seemed to have evaporated as he walked out onto the short pier and waited for the boat to dock.

Anton stepped up behind him. One crew member jumped from the boat to the dock and tethered it. The captain killed the engine and silence ensued. Taking the tan fisherman's cap from his head, the dark-skinned man steering the vessel headed in their direction. He stuck his hand out as he reached Draven, who shook it. Anton had never seen the man among the Devils before. He couldn't help wondering if he might be from the La Paz cartel.

"You have something for me?"

Draven nodded and handed the captain the white envelope.

He opened it, quickly counted the money inside, then looked back to one of the crew, giving a short nod. Two other men emerged from the stern, carrying a large shipping crate, one that might ordinarily be used to carry fish. A thin layer of ice spread across the top. The men set the crate at the captain's feet, then stood closely behind. Anton hadn't missed the guns stuck into the back waistband on their pants.

Draven crouched, fished through the ice, and pulled out a plastic bale of heroin. Reaching into his pocket, he pulled out a small switch blade, flipped it open, then cut a small hole into the plastic. He dipped his pinky into the cut, then took the brownish powder to his tongue.

Standing, Draven nodded at Anton, before looking back at the shorter, dark-skinned man. "We have a deal."

Anton turned and gave a short nod of his own. He and Draven bent to retrieve the shipping crate. Before the man on the dock could begin to untie the boat, the DEA agents swarmed the area, circling the docks, guns drawn. One of the crew standing behind the captain pulled the gun from his waistband and aimed at Draven. Anton dropped the heroin to the dock, moving lightning quick and grabbing the man's gun arm, twisting his wrist, feeling the snap of the bones. The man cried out about the same time Cara and Kane appeared. The normal eye wouldn't have picked up Kane's speed as he apprehended the second man, yanking his gun arm behind his back and dislocating his shoulder. The gun dropped from his hand and thudded to the dock near Kane's feet.

Moments later, all four men were in custody and Cara had put in the phone call to the special agents in Santa Barbara. The heroin and money were safely in the hands of the DEA. Robbie Melchor stood next to his vehicle, taking all the credit from the DEA special agent heading the case.

"The man's ego has no bounds. Maybe now he'll get the hell out of my state." Cara grumbled, disconnecting her call. She walked over to Anton. "Tank and Spider will be taken into custody soon, Blondy. Looks like your job is done. I can't thank you enough."

Detective Hernandez stepped forward and shook his hand. "I know the last year couldn't have been the easiest. I wanted to thank you before I head out. Someone needs to speak with Captain Melchor and send him on his way. I sure as the hell ain't letting Detective Brahnam anywhere near him. She's liable to castrate the idiot. Not that he doesn't deserve it."

Hernandez winked at Cara. "See you back at the office, Brahnam. Good work."

"Thanks, Joe." Cara smiled, obviously pleased with how things had gone down.

They may not have gotten the kingpin or shutdown his operation, but Kane would still one day get his revenge on Raúl Trevino Caballero, without the help and knowledge of the DEA. The Sons of Sangue would handle this one personally, without being under the scrutiny of the law.

"Get what you need from your rides, Anton." Cara walked with them toward the parking area. "Then I'll take you and Draven into custody. I'll have Xander come out with the box truck to pick up your motorcycles."

Anton couldn't be happier to have his job undercover finished. Once he left the sheriff's office, he'd get his life back. Hopefully, he'd talk Kimber into being a part of it. No more secrets. It was time to come clean.

Just as he and Draven reached their motorcycles, movement near the highway caught his notice. Bobby straddled his bike, arms crossed over his chest. From the distance, Anton couldn't judge his temperament. He no doubt watched the DEA take the boat crew into custody. Instead of waiting for an explanation, Bobby kicked up his bike stand, turned the bike and headed down the road.

"Fuck."

Anton fished his cell from his backpack he had left with his bike, having known it was there all along. He found the name Preacher and hit *SEND*. Bobby never picked up, not that Anton expected him to.

"Problems?" Cara asked.

"Nothing I can't take care of." Anton held his hands out for Cara to cuff. "Let's get this the fuck over with, Brahnam."

KIMBER FINISHED TIDYING UP the library, placing the final books on the shelves and clearing off the main counter. Chad had gone home a couple of hours ago, while Tena had the day off. She didn't mind closing. It gave her a few extra hours of reading time during the slow hours, once the night shift duties had been completed. Draping her purse handles over her forearm, she picked up the romance she had been enjoying and headed for the door.

A quick glance around proved everything was perfectly in its place, ensuring her an easy opening the next morning. She flipped the switch and doused the lights, before walking out the door. The heavy steel and glass door closed behind her. Sticking her key in the lock, she secured the deadbolt, listening as it clicked into place.

The parking light illuminated the lot, hers being the only car remaining. She had parked beneath a streetlamp toward the back of the lot, as she always did. Not that she ever had anything to worry about. Who would think to rob a library? Anton's words of warning came to mind and the fact he thought she needed protection. Had he not been a member of the Devils, she wouldn't need to worry about her safety. Kimber had no idea what was going on with him, but she intended on finding out. He had bought himself another day. If he didn't come clean, then she'd be forced to move on.

Kimber knew absolutely nothing about him, other than the fact he was phenomenal in bed, which might have been enough over the past few weeks, but no longer. He promised to remain faithful, no more running into the night to save women he didn't have a relationship with. She wanted to know more about him, get to know the man beneath the pretty exterior. Not that she expected a proposal or promises of forever.

But she was done sharing.

Either he opened up or they'd become neighbors in name only. Because quite honestly, after all they had done together, Kimber couldn't imagine going back to being just friends. No stopping by for coffee. No afternoon chitchats. If she couldn't know all of him, then she wanted none of him.

Kimber used the key fob to unlock the door to her vehicle. The lights blinked twice and the click of the door unlocking echoed in the empty parking lot. Just as she grabbed the handle, something cold and hard was shoved against her spine. She had been so caught up in her own thoughts, she hadn't bothered with paying attention to her surroundings.

"Give me the keys and get into the passenger side." Kimber sucked in her breath, recognizing the man's voice. "Don't make this more difficult than it already is, Kimber."

She glanced over her shoulder and into Bobby Bourassa's cold eyes. His mouth was set in a stern line, his mouth nearly disappearing beneath his whiskers. Running wasn't an option. He'd easily overpower her. Instead, she did as she was told and skirted the vehicle, hoping for another opportunity to get away. Bobby crawled behind the driver's seat and started the car.

"Where's Tena?"

She needed to get him talking, hopefully finding out what his plans were and where he was taking her. Maybe she'd be afforded a moment of time in which to text Anton.

Bobby kept his gaze trained in front of him. He shifted the car from park. "She's not my concern at the moment."

"Then who is? Me?"

"Not really." Bobby pulled the car to the stop sign, flipped on the left turn signal, then pulled from the lot.

"Where are you taking me, Preacher? If you just wanted the car, you could've asked."

"I needed you, not the car. We're headed for Santa Barbara, so buckle up. We got a long ride ahead of us."

His gun lay tucked between his thighs. If she could just reach...

"Don't think about it, doll." He no doubt detected her attention on his lap. "You'll never get to it before I do. Why not make this easy for us both? Just settle back and take a nap."

"Why are you doing this?"

His gaze stayed focused on the road, both hands on the steering wheel. "Because Rogue can't be trusted. Tank thinks the only way to get through to him is with you. If we have you, it's only a matter of time before Rogue comes to get you."

"Tank?"

"The Devils' president."

The car rolled to a stop at the final stoplight before heading out of Florence. If Kimber didn't act now, there would be few opportunities along Highway 101. She slowly moved her hand toward the unlock button.

"Don't think about it, Kimber." He glanced at her just before the light turned green. "If I have to tie you to the seat to get you there, then I will."

"What's Rogue done?"

His fingers tightened on the steering wheel, apparent by the whitening of his knuckles. "Not your concern."

"The hell it isn't." Kimber turned in her seat, tucking one foot beneath her other leg. "You've brought me along for the ride. That makes it my concern. What makes you think Rogue will come after me?"

Bobby chuckled. "That man is crazy about you. He finds out the Devils have you, he'll come to your rescue. It's only a matter of time."

"And then what?"

The car slowed, made a right and took the on ramp onto Highway 101. "Whatever Tank wants. This isn't my gig. I'm only following orders. Once my job here is done, I'm getting the hell out of here. I'm washing my hands of it. Tank can clean up his own fucking mess."

"So you'll just stand by and allow Tank to kill Anton? I thought he was your friend."

"You don't know what you're talking about."

"Don't I?"

Bobby shifted uneasily. "Rogue messed up. He needs to answer for his actions."

"Enough that it's worth killing him for?"

His whiskers moved as his jaw worked. Kimber hoped Bobby didn't want Anton harmed any more than she did. She'd need to appeal to his sense of guilt if she were to get him to let her go. If Anton was forced to come get her, Kimber knew he wouldn't leave Santa Barbara alive.

"I didn't think so. What did he do, Preacher?"

A heavy sigh escaped his lips. Bobby looked at her briefly, the ice now gone from his gaze. "He ratted out the club. Feds came in, arrested a lot of the Devils. Some of them will be going away for a good long time. Tank managed to give the feds the slip."

So that's what Anton had referred to about coming clean? No wonder he hadn't wanted to tell her. "They'll kill Anton. And you have to know they won't allow me to walk either. They can't afford to leave witnesses. Do you think for a minute you'll walk out alive? What's the saying? Three men can keep a secret if two are dead. Think about it, Preacher."

Silence filled the space. Kimber shifted in her seat and stared out the side window. If she could manage to text Anton sometime during the trip, she'd warn him to stay away. Coming after her would be a fool's errand. The best she could hope for was Bobby having a change of heart — that or the feds finding Tank before Bobby had the chance to hand her over.

Kimber leaned her head against the seat and watched the sun's rays cast an orange glow over the horizon. Bobby wasn't a bad guy. She could feel it in her heart and had seen it firsthand in the way he treated Tena. Somehow, she needed to convince him of that. Regardless of his loyalties to the bloody MC, turning Anton over into their murdering hands was a horrid idea with only one outcome.

Not one of them would walk away.

She had a good ten hours in which to get him to see reason. Whatever Anton's sins, they weren't worth dying over.

Brea ended a call on her cell and sank to the orange plaid sofa in the corner the storeroom of the Blood 'n' Rave. Something in her expression told Draven the call hadn't gone well. He wanted to ask who it was and why it had her so forlorn, but feared he didn't know her well enough to pry.

He and Anton had been released from the sheriff's office just shy of an hour ago. Cara Brahnam had told them to lie low until they received word from the DEA that Tank had been taken into custody. No sense tempting fate. Draven had first gone to his home and retrieved Brea, then immediately came to the club so he could find her a proper donor. Not that he was opposed to feeding her, but the whole idea still sort of creeped him out. He was used to providing donors, not being one.

His bartender was quite capable of running the place without him for a few days while he took Brea back to his place and stayed out of sight until the nasty business with the Devils blew over. The Devils MC weren't about to be too happy with him and Rogue, not to mention what the cartel might do in retaliation.

*Lord, what the hell had he gotten himself into?*

He wasn't even sure yet what to do with Brea. He couldn't keep her at the Rave. The Sons of Sangue would smell another vampire easily enough. Her scent wouldn't be familiar, which meant they'd no doubt seek her out. If Brea had wanted their protection, she would've gone to them in the first place. Instead, she came to him because Joseph trusted him. He missed the fun-loving biker. He might have been a man of few words most days, but he always wore a smile.

*Who the hell would want to end his life?*

Draven shook his head at the fact the son of a bitch had left Brea without her mate. Looking at the funky little sprite, he couldn't help but want to protect her from the ugliness her life had become. She appeared broken and defeated. First plan of action, get her a donor and speak to his bartender about handling things for a few days, then get her out of the club before any of the Sons stopped by.

He needed a solid plan. Hell, he couldn't hide her away forever. Draven wasn't a vampire and had no way of keeping her from harm. Joseph Sala may have entrusted his mate to him, but Draven would be damned if he knew what the hell to do with the gorgeous vampire.

Not to mention her connections to the mob and cartel.

That alone scared him spitless. Draven was pretty sure her godfather wouldn't be too happy with him hiding her away, let alone his failings with the Devils and the drug deal gone wrong just hours ago. They'd no doubt want restitution for their lost money and drugs.

Brea's bow-shaped lips turned down. "I need to leave, Draven. Go somewhere where no one else will get hurt."

His brow creased. "Where do you want me to take you?"

"You can't come. Lord knows you wouldn't be safe. You didn't ask for me in your life."

"And yet, here you are." Draven grabbed a rubber band from the corner desk, wound his hair into a messy knot, and secured it at the back of his head. "Who were you talking to earlier? Do they have something to do with your sudden need to flee?"

Brea took her forefinger to her lips and nibbled on her cuticle. "You're better off not knowing. Can you get me a car? One that can't be traced to me?"

Draven approached the sofa and sat beside her. "Does this have anything to do with your godfather?"

She looked to her hands folded in her lap. "Raúl called me."

Draven laid his larger hand over her smaller ones. "What did he want?"

When she lifted her gaze, her beautiful blue eyes swam with tears. "I think he's responsible for Kinky's death. That he's the one who put the hit out."

Draven's gaze widened. *Jesus.* "He told you this?"

A single tear dropped from her impossibly long lashes. "In so many words. He sounded so angry, Draven. He's never spoken to me with such animosity. He more or less asked me if I hadn't learned my lesson with Joseph."

"Meaning?" Draven's heart thudded in his ears.

The man was a monster. Did Raúl already know about his part in the earlier DEA sting? If so, he needed to disappear with Brea, whether she wanted him along or not. At least until things calmed down. He wouldn't be safe here with or without her.

"I'm not positive. He hinted at being careful about those I choose to befriend."

"Meaning me?"

She looked back to her lap. Tears fell to the back of his hand, making a wet track. "I'm sorry to have put you in danger. This is all my fault and why I need to get away ... without you. Raúl has eyes everywhere. I can't be responsible for something happening to you. Kinky's death is already on me. I don't know how I'll ever forgive myself."

He tipped her chin up, then used the pad of his thumb to brush away the tears. "You had nothing to do with Kinky's death. You can't blame yourself for the actions of a mad man."

"He's a bad man, Draven. Deep down, I knew that. But he's my godfather. He treated me like a princess. I thought maybe if his dark side never touched me, I could almost pretend it didn't exist."

"And now?"

Her blue gaze iced over. "I want to kill him myself."

"You can't think to kill Raúl Trevino Caballero."

"No?" One of her finely plucked brows raised. "You might not get close enough, but no one would question me wanting to see him. Besides, he's all but demanded my presence, so they'd be expecting me."

"Don't be foolish, Brea."

"I loved him. And now I want to kill him for what he did to Kinky. I'm not foolish enough to believe I'd get out of there alive if I did." She pulled her hands from his and scrubbed the tears from her face. "That's why I need to disappear for a while. If I'm alone, then there's no one for him to hurt for my defiance and disobedience."

"Maybe we should contact Kane and Kaleb from the Sons. They have their own reason for hating your godfather."

"Kinky told me about their desire for revenge. It was his reason for keeping them from knowing about me. He didn't want them to use me to get to Raúl."

Draven was pretty sure they would've exploited her relationship just to get closer to the man. "Kinky was probably correct."

"It no longer matters." Brea took a shaky breath. "If I'm awarded a chance, I'll take him out myself … for Kinky."

"I can't let you do this, not on your own."

"If I allow you to come with me, you cannot tell a soul. My godfather has eyes and ears everywhere. You will have to walk out of here, leave everything behind, and not say a word to anyone."

"I'll tell my bartender to keep an eye on things—"

She shook her head. "Not even him, Draven."

If they were to disappear, then they had to do so tonight, before anyone came looking for either of them. "Then let's get the hell out of here."

"Who will be my donor? You?"

He fought the urge to groan. "Yes, until we find you someone on the road you can hypnotize."

Brea's lips arched ever so slightly. "You hate feeding me that much?"

"Not when I'm wanting to fuck your brains out." He pulled her to her feet. A quick glance at the clock told him the sun had already set. No one would see their hasty exit. "Let's get on the road. We'll decide where to once we put a lot of miles between us and Pleasant."

"We can't leave a paper trail. How will we live?"

"No problem."

He walked over to a framed movie poster of Easy Rider and moved it. Quickly working the dial, he opened the safe. Draven grabbed several bands of hundreds, counting out a hundred thousand. He never little trust in banks. Opening a leather satchel, he deposited the money and closed the safe, replacing the movie poster back in its place.

Placing the strap over his shoulder, he turned to her and grabbed his keys from the desk. "Ready"

Brea took his offered hand and intertwined their fingers. "Kinky would thank you."

He smiled, leaned down, and kissed her temple. "Not if I caved to my desires, he wouldn't."

Opening the back door, Draven took a quick glance in both directions before pulling her through the exit after him. He opened the car door and she slid into the leather seat on the passenger side, fastening her seat belt. Draven quickly skirted the car, climbed in behind the driver's wheel, and started the engine. Putting the car into drive, they headed for the back drive on the lot. Good thing he filled his Camaro up with gas earlier, because he didn't plan to stop until Oregon was far behind.

Hopefully, they'd have a solid plan before Raúl ever caught up with them.

## CHAPTER TWENTY-FOUR

THE FARMHOUSE WAS COMPLETELY DARK WHEN ANTON ARrived home, not a single light glowed in any of the windows. He had noted the same as he drove by Kimber's place moments ago. After being released from the sheriff's office early in the afternoon, Anton had stopped by the clubhouse. Too damn much time had passed since he had been welcome and he had needed to unwind. Nothing like tossing back a few whiskeys with his brothers and letting the past year melt away. Kaleb had presented him with a new cut and patches.

Damn, but it felt good to be wearing Sons of Sangue colors again.

He noted his back door had been left unlocked, though not unusual this far out from town. Often times, Anton left it unsecured if he were making short trips. No one ever bothered the place. He couldn't help but wonder if Bobby had packed his stuff and headed out, without so much as a word.

He hadn't seen or heard from him since the early morning. Anton had trying calling his cell a few times, but the man was not answering his phone. Word had it the feds were still looking for Tank — the last Devil involved in the transportation and selling of the heroin to be apprehended. Cara had asked Anton and Draven to lie low until the Devils' president was taken into custody. Anton wasn't all that worried. Tank wouldn't think about crossing over into Oregon territory without his MC to back him up.

No, he was more than likely on the run and several states away.

Walking into the kitchen, Anton flipped the light switch when the cell in his pocket trilled. He pulled out the phone, seeing Bobby's name.

*About damn time.*

Anton hit *TALK*. "I've been worried about you, man. Talk to me."

"You sold out the Devils, dude. Not cool."

"They were going to sell those drugs to school kids. Tell me that didn't bother you, Preacher." Silence greeted his comment. Anton didn't need confirmation. He knew Bobby hated the idea. "Where the hell are you at?"

"Where you need to be apparently." Shuffling sounds greeted him before he heard Bobby say, "Talk."

The hairs at his nape rose.

"Anton, don't do what they say—" Kimber said before she was cut off. Anton picked up on the sound of a struggle. His heart climbed up his throat.

"You need to come rescue your girlfriend, Rogue."

"What the fuck are you doing with Kimber?" His fangs immediately punched through his gums. "You harm her—"

"You get your ass to the border, bring Tank his money or drugs, and he'll let her walk."

"You know fucking well I can't do that, Preacher. I don't have either. And unless you have some brilliant plan to get those things from the DEA, it isn't going to happen." Anton growled, his vampire self fully surfacing. "How about you bring her back here and I allow you and Tank to live?"

More shuffling could be heard, just before a loud crack, followed by Kimber crying out.

"What the—" *Jesus!* He was going to kill someone before the day was finished.

"Listen, man." Preacher gained his attention. "We're at the border. Little cafe off 101 called Last Stop Diner, just past Winchuck River."

"I know the one," Anton all but hissed, just before the line went dead.

He cursed a blue streak, attempting to reconnect the call to Bobby. No answer. Anton grit his teeth, feeling the ache all the way to his temples. It would take a miracle not to kill the lot of them when he got down there. He'd have to fight the urge with Kimber present. No good would come of him ripping the fuckers apart, limb from limb. If he gave into his desire for blood, it would only ensure he'd lose Kimber for good.

Just as he reached his bike, his cell vibrated in his hand. Anton answered the call. "This better be good, Preacher. Time's a wasting."

"Just get your ass down here, Rogue. I'll make sure she stays safe." The line went silent for a moment, then Bobby came back on. "I fucked up, man. I should've waited for you to be sprung and listened to your side. Instead, I followed Tank's orders. He's gone off the deep end."

"What's his plan?"

"I thought he just wanted to get his money back. After all it's his ass on the line with the La Paz cartel. I understand that. Fuck, Rogue, I'm sorry. He's planning on killing you and Kimber both. No survivors. And me too, for all I know."

"Where's he at now?"

"Sitting in a booth at the back of the diner. Cocksure. Look, I can't be gone too long before my absence raises questions. Just get here as soon as you can and I'll do what I can to get you and your woman out of here alive."

"How many?"

"Tank and three others. Two are guarding the entrance. The other one is with him in the cafe."

"Get back inside, Preacher. Don't let that fuck touch her again." Anton tasted his own blood as he bit down, his fangs puncturing the soft flesh of his inner lip. "I can be there in less than two hours if I don't pass any cops along the way. Make sure she stays safe."

"With my life," he heard, just before the cell went silent. Anton grabbed his helmet and shoved it onto his head. If Tank harmed one hair on Kimber's head, the piece of shit wouldn't live to see tomorrow. Fuck that. Tank wasn't about to see tomorrow regardless.

RAIN POURED FROM THE HEAVENS. Mud, pine, and the scent of fresh rain wafted to his nose. Cara had left fifteen minutes prior. Kane sure in the hell hoped she pulled over if she hadn't yet made it to the clubhouse. Visibility would be poor at best.

The downpour worked in his favor. He had sent Cara on an errand in hopes of flushing out Mircea. Had he told his mate about it, she never would've left him alone. Kane knew with the promise of heavy rains he'd be able to sneak up on Mircea before the jackass tried to blindside him.

If his distant relative gave him reason, Kane was prepared to take his ass down, regardless of what Vlad might think about it. He was not about to spend the next how many years looking over his shoulder and worrying about what Mircea might do to his mate. The primordial was just vindictive enough to take out Cara as a way of punishing Kane. And all because his crazy ass stepdaughter hadn't listened to the point she pissed off the granddaddy of them all.

Vlad Tepes took shit from no one.

Least of all his brother's stepdaughter.

He hadn't thought twice about removing her head from her body. Something told him Mircea would be an entirely different story. After all, he was Vlad's last living sibling. If Kane were to guess, he'd bet Vlad would do everything he could to spare the white belly's life.

*Not Kane.*

He'd just as soon wipe the earth of the bastard and not have to ever worry about his threat again. It was time for the man to pay the piper. Kane wasn't about to allow him to cause any more trouble with him, his mate, or his brothers a day longer.

Stepping around a large evergreen, he spotted Mircea standing beneath the protection of an overhang of one of the outer lying buildings behind his house, telling Kane he'd watched Cara leave. His sixth sense had told him Mircea had been out there watching, waiting, biding his time. And the hair raising at his nape had been correct. Kane had exited through the front and skirted the house through the surrounding woods. The rains easily masked his scent.

Ever since Cara had thought she scented a primordial behind the house, Kane had known the man watched and waited, biding his time. Kane hadn't taken it lightly, even though he led Cara to believe he had. He was no fool and wasn't about to take Mircea for one either.

Pulling a large hunting knife out of the sheath at the side of his pants, Kane waited for the perfect moment. His hair plastered to his head. Water collected on his lashes and dripped into his eyes. Mircea, the smug bastard, not once looked behind him. He was too focused on the back door in hopes Kane would exit. Mircea had no clue of the threat so close behind. In a matter of seconds, Kane would have his arm banding his chest and the knife at the old man's throat.

*Say your prayers, motherfucker. Better yet ... save them. They won't help you where you're going.*

Kane slipped into the clearing, careful not to alert Mircea with his footfalls. The rain pinged off the metal awning over his head. It wouldn't be likely, he'd hear Kane's approach even if he made a hell of a racket. The downpour definitely blessed him.

Just before he reached Mircea, the primordial turned his head. Too fucking late. Kane wrapped one arm about his chest, pinning his arms to his side, the other hand holding the razor sharp knife to the primordial's neck. Kane's fangs filled his mouth. Anger rolled off him in waves. He was a hairsbreadth away from slicing the elder's throat.

To hell with what Vlad thought.

"What the fuck are you doing here, Mircea?" he hissed, close to the old man's ear, increasing the pressure of the blade.

A trickle of blood skirted down his flesh before the wound quickly began healing itself. "Apparently, the same thing you're here to do."

"You lose, Mircea. You should've stayed in Italy."

The elder didn't bother testing Kane's strength. Maybe he was waiting for the right opportunity. Too bad. Kane wasn't about to give him one.

"You best do what you came out here to do, boy."

"Or what?"

"Or your little mate will come home to find you without a head. You don't act now, mark my words, I will."

Just as Kane was about to do as Mircea suggested, Vlad strolled out of the forest as if he had all the time in the world. His black gaze fixed on the knife and his fangs told Kane the ruler was anything but calm.

"Put down the knife, Kane."

It wasn't a request. Vlad had issued him an order. To disobey would most certainly earn him retribution, no matter how much Mircea deserved to have his head separated from his neck.

Kane released him with a curse and shoved Mircea in Vlad's direction. The rain continued to fall. Water ran from the woods and muddied the ground they stood on, making their footing precarious. Kane stayed beneath the awning, while Mircea and Vlad stood just beyond.

His grandfather fisted the back of Mircea's shirt, keeping him from fleeing as the coward no doubt was wont to do. "Mircea's my problem. And as such, I'll take care of him."

"To do what? Send him back to Italy?" Kane laughed, feeling none of the humor. "You know as well as I do that as soon as he's out of your sight, he'll be back. This little thing between him and me is far from over."

Vlad bared his teeth. Great Grandfather was not used to being challenged. "You'll take his life no more than I'll allow him to take yours. He's the last of my living siblings, Kane. He lives until I say otherwise. Have I made myself clear? Or do you dare challenge me again?"

Kane grit his teeth, hating that he had no other choice but abide by Vlad's wishes. Why the hell couldn't he go back to his damn island already? He growled his defeat. "I won't challenge you, Grandfather. Until he disobeys your orders again, that is. Then all bets are off."

"Vlad—" was all Mircea got out before Vlad turned, hit his sternum with the heel of his palm, and sent him flying across the yard. His back slammed against the trunk of a tree.

Mircea crumbled to the base, groaning from the impact and most likely broken bones.

Vlad didn't give Mircea a chance to right himself. He ran across the distance as if his feet had wings, gripping his brother by the throat and pulling him up. Mircea's feet dangled inches off the ground.

He bared his fangs and shook the primordial like a rag doll. "You son of a bitch, you did not heed my warning. I told you to go back to Italy and yet you defied me. I should crush you like a bug, you fool. I will personally see you get back to Italy. When we arrive, I will leave a couple of my men to guard you. If you slip by them, and so much as step foot outside of the country without my knowledge, I will impale your sorry ass outside my home near Belize. You'll serve as a reminder the next time I get soft. Do. Not. Test. Me. Dear brother. You won't get another chance."

Releasing his hold on Mircea, he dropped to the ground, barely standing on his own, his hands going to his neck and chest. He couldn't so much as croak and answer, so he nodded instead. Kane bet Vlad crushed his windpipe with his grip.

Vlad turned back to Kane. "You take care of your own, Kane, and I'll take care of mine. I'll personally escort Mircea to his home. Should he give you trouble again, you have my permission to kill him."

Not waiting for a response, Vlad grabbed his brother by the shirt and headed into the forest. In the blink of an eye, they were gone. Shaking his head at the injustice of not being able to take Mircea's life, he headed for the house. The rain pelted his back and cooled his ire. The bright side? Should Mircea ever show his face again, he had permission to take his head.

Kane smiled.

He looked forward to the day.

ANTON STRADDLED HIS BIKE just around the bend. Close enough he could see the metal and glass double doors to the diner, not close enough for the men to detect they were being watched. The sun had long since set and he doubted anyone else, other than those he targeted, was in the diner at this hour. Only four motorcycles, Kimber's car, and one other vehicle were present in the parking lot. Probably one worker who had no doubt been terrorized and dealt the hand of death by the Devils.

The two men playing guard dogs outside had no clue their life was about to be cut short.

Anton's clothes were damp. He had driven through some pretty heavy rains on his way south. Thankfully, the storm had passed through and the only remnant was the strong winds coming off the ocean. Waves crashed to the shore. Normally, the sound soothed him. Today, however, it did nothing to calm the storm brewing within.

Anton wasn't walking away until all four Devils met the Grim Reaper. Bobby would be free to go, and only because Anton respected him. He had protected Kimber. Stepping over his bike, he took off his helmet and laid it on the seat.

His fangs punched past his gums and his gaze heated. He rolled his neck as the rest of his vampire genes took over.

There was no saving the motherfuckers who dared to take his Kimber.

He walked down the highway with one purpose in mind. *Death*. The two by the door caught sight of him, heading in their direction. Anton recognized one of them as Boston. He'd take great pleasure in stomping his sorry ass into the ground.

So damn much had transpired in the past two weeks, since his returning to Oregon. He certainly hadn't planned on hooking back up with Kimber, let alone falling in love with her.

The knowledge of his true feelings for her hit him like a blow to his chest. Right now, though, he had no time to analyze just when the hell that happened. It simply was.

"Boys," Anton greeted.

Boston grinned, his teeth smeared with chew. "Boss is looking for your sorry ass inside, Rogue." His chuckle rankled Anton. "Someone's about to meet his maker."

Before the son of a bitch could issue another taunt, he was gurgling on his own blood. Anton used the knife he carried in his boot to slice cleanly through his throat. As fast as Anton moved, the son of a bitch hadn't seen it coming. The second man didn't stand a chance either. Anton palmed the sides of his head and twisted hard, snapping his neck and dropping him to the cement.

Neither had a chance to warn those inside.

Anton picked up his knife lying beside Boston, wiped the blood on his jeans, and ignored the pooling blood calling to him like a drug to a junkie.

*Two down, two to go.*

Anton yanked open one of the heavy doors, damn near pulling them off its hinges. Four sets of eyes looked at him. One set widened in fright, and the only damn one that meant anything at all to him. One body already lay dead on the floor. Anton had been correct, the Devils had taken out the worker so he wouldn't be able to give an account on what horrific deeds happened after the sun went down.

"Jesus," Tank mustered. "What the fuck are you?"

Spike, the scrawny ass biker by Tank's side, stood, gun pointed at Anton's chest. "Stay the fuck where you are, Rogue."

His gun hand trembled. Anton doubted at the moment he'd hit the broad side of the barn. Bobby gathered Kimber and pulled her away from the booth. He kept her behind him near the lunch counter. More brownie points for the ex-preacher. Anton moved quicker than Spike's trigger finger. The gun went off, striking the far wall. His aim had been kicked out of position by Anton's foot. One fist to the man's throat collapsed his windpipe. He wouldn't live to see the sun rise. He'd suffocate long before.

His attention landed on the Devils' P. For the first time, Anton saw fear in Tank's eyes. With everything Tank had done in his life, the horrible things he was guilty of, Anton was only too happy to be the one ending the miserable fuck's life.

Intent on administering death, Anton missed the gun aimed at him beneath the diner table until the bullet hit his gut. Pain seared his abdomen. Anton grunted. His hands covered the wound. Blood spilled through his fingers.

Kimber cried out and Bobby rushed Tank as he stood. The two went down and the gun fired a second time. Anton wasn't sure who got hit. That was until Tank rolled Bobby from him. A large gaping hole, just beneath his neck and likely hitting the aorta, spurted blood. Kimber grabbed a stack of towels from the counter and fell to her knees, putting pressure on the wound. Even so, Anton bet Bobby had minutes to live.

Thanks to Anton's vampire genes, his own wound had nearly healed already.

Grabbing Tank by the back of his collar, he hauled the man to his feet. Anton knocked the gun from his hand. The Ruger hit the tile and slid across the floor out of reach. Tank kicked at Anton's knees, doing no real damage. Anton, tired of Tank's wasted efforts as one might a gnat's, dropped his hold on his shirt, and punched him in the face.

Blood splattered from his broken nose. "I'll kill you, you son of a bitch."

"Not today, Tank." Anton advanced on him slowly. "Today, I watch you die."

He gripped his shoulders, hauled him upright, sank his fangs deep into his neck, and drank the man dry. Anton discarded his empty shell to the floor like yesterday's garbage.

His black gaze sought out Kimber and the blood soaked towels. Bobby gurgled on his blood, unable to say a word.

*Fuck!*

*No time to call the P.*

Knowing they had already discussed bringing the biker onboard, Anton took it as his okay to turn the man. He dropped to his knees beside Bobby. Kimber's wide-eyed gaze landed on him. He must look like a circus freak show.

No time to explain, Anton bit his wrist and tore open a vein, he held the dripping wound to Bobby's mouth and said, "Drink."

Without question, Bobby followed the directive, clamping onto Anton's wrist like the lifeline it was. Maybe it was instinct, maybe it was delirium. Either way, Anton was glad he hadn't gotten an argument out of him. Several seconds later, his wound began to heal and he released his hold on Anton. His eyelids flickered a time or two, then closed.

"What the hell did you just do?" Kimber squealed. When Anton reached out to her, she batted his bloodied hand away. "You killed him."

The fight fizzled out of Anton. Sitting back on the floor, his gaze took in the carnage. His vampire self receded. "I may be responsible for the rest of these miserable fucks, but Bobby will live to see another day. He's healing."

"What the hell are you?" she whispered, her gaze wide as she glanced about the bloody scene. "My God!"

"Kimber—"

She held out her hand, cutting him off.

"Oh my…" Kimber sucked in her breath. "What the hell did you do to me?"

"I'm not following."

"Why the hell did I think your fangs were part of a nightmare? They weren't, were they?"

Anton rubbed a hand down his cheek. Shit! The trauma of today must have triggered her recollections. She no doubt recalled his vampire form every time they had been together. This wasn't going to end well.

He reached for her again, but she scooted away. "Get the hell away from me. I don't even know what you are. You … you…"

Her eyes took in the dead men, then back to Bobby, who still wasn't moving, other than the rise and fall of his chest. The wound had damn near healed.

"How?"

Anton drew his knees to his chest and wrapped his forearms around them. "When he drank from me, he ingested some of my vampire DNA."

"Vampire?" The very word shook from her.

"My blood is healing him."

Kimber gasped. "He was dying. Now you're telling me he will be fine?"

Anton nodded. "Like me."

"You mean a vampire?"

Again he nodded.

"I have to be in some sort of alternate reality. Vampires don't exist. Wait..." Her brow creased. "Vampires rise from the dead."

"Fictional vampires, yes. I assure you I'm very much alive."

She grabbed a towel and tried to wipe her fingers free of Bobby's blood. "I need to get out of here."

Anton stood, holding out his hand to help her off the floor. Kimber rose on her own, as though she were afraid to touch him. She took another look around, tears slipping down her cheeks. Her breath hitched. Before he could stop her, Kimber grabbed her purse and keys from the diner counter and ran for the door. She let out a startled scream when she came across the other two men lying on the cement just beyond the entrance.

She turned and looked back at Anton, swiping a hand beneath her nose. "I need to wake up. This can't be real."

"Kimber, you shouldn't drive. I'll take you—"

"No." The scent of her fear drifted to him. "You need to stay away."

"I can't." And he knew it to be true, sure as his heart was breaking. He needed to convince her he wasn't the monster she witnessed moments ago. Now wasn't the time. "When you've calmed down, we'll talk."

She placed the back of her blood smeared hand over her lips. "What could we possibly have to talk about?"

"Seriously?" He raised a brow. His hand swept the diner. "This. You need to hear me out. Jesus, Kimber. What I'm trying to tell you is that I'm in love with you."

A sob escaped her. She turned, opened the door, and ran the short way to her car. Anton watched the car back from the parking lot and head up the highway. He hung his head. Hell, he should go after her, hypnotize her into forgetting the entire night, into forgetting everything that happened between them. But he couldn't. He wanted her to come to terms with everything, and part of him was the monster she saw moments ago wreaking havoc on the place.

He shoved a hand into his pocket and pulled out his phone. Alexander answered quickly. "We got a situation, man. Bring the box truck." He rattled off the address. "We need a quick clean up, and I need to get Bobby Bourassa back to the clubhouse before his change begins."

"What the fuck happened?"

"Too damn much to explain over the phone. Just round up the troops and get here STAT."

Anton ended the call. Another glance around told him it would take a miracle for Kimber to get beyond the horrific scene. This certainly wasn't how he envisioned telling her all his secrets.

The talk would have to wait. First, he needed to wipe the place clean. No one could know he or Bobby were here. He'd leave the others for the cops to find. A robbery gone wrong. No one would care about the bikers' deaths. Life was better without them in it.

## CHAPTER TWENTY-FIVE

TWO WEEKS HAD PASSED SINCE KIMBER HAD LAST SEEN ANton. Not so much as a glimpse. She wasn't any closer to accepting the fact he was something other than human, let alone what he could be capable of. Softening, maybe. Definitely not ready to fully embrace it. He hadn't stopped by or tried to contact her, other than one phone call to assure she hadn't gone off the deep end. The call had been awkward at best. She had politely told him she was fine, thanked him for saving her life, then they both fell into awkward silence.

*What exactly was she to say?*

A few weeks ago, she hadn't even known vampires existed outside of paranormal fiction novels and movies. What she had learned from them was nothing compared to reality. Anton wasn't the undead, he didn't sleep in coffins, and he didn't turn to ash in sunlight. No, he was definitely a hot-blooded, living and breathing, sexy as hell man. One she found herself still hopelessly attracted to, if not out and out in love with.

Her heart ached.

She missed him more than she'd care to admit. He may have kept his vampire side a secret from her, but what was he supposed say? *By the way, I need human blood to sur-*

*vive. Mind if I tap your artery?* Kimber was pretty sure however he tried to present it, she would have freaked out, nonetheless.

Tamera Cantrell had stopped by following the incident. Kimber preferred to refer to the night at the diner as "the incident" to prevent her from actually thinking about all the carnage and what Anton was actually capable of. He had taken four lives with ease, speaking of his unnatural strength as a vampire. Tamera had tried her best to explain about their existence, to assure her they weren't all that different or unusual. Well, except for Vlad Tepes, the eldest of the vampires and his appearance in Oregon.

Yep, the ancient Romanian ruler. The one who impaled people and instilled fear in his followers. Kimber knew little about him from history, other than his tomb had later been found to be empty. The fact he still walked the face of the earth and was Kane and Kaleb's great, many times over, grandfather was a little mind boggling.

*How the hell did someone live for centuries?*

Tamera made Kimber promise not to tell a soul about what she had learned. Their very lives depended on the anonymity. If humans were to learn about their secret, they might take to hunting them like animals.

Kimber wasn't about to tell anyone, even before Tamera had made her swear to keep to secrecy. Who would believe her anyway? Should something happen to Anton, or any of them for that matter, because of her loose lips, she wouldn't be able to live with herself.

Anton came back to the forefront of her mind as he often did in the past couple of weeks. Part of her wanted to see him, find out where this thing between them stood. The other part of her was petrified. Not that she feared Anton hurting her. No, she was scared to death of losing her heart to a vampire.

*A little late for that, missy.*

If she were truthful, then she knew she already had. Over the moon, so they say. Kimber was in love with Anton, though she had no clue what to do about it. Even though Tamera had given her insight, and she knew there wasn't much to fear from the Sons of Sangue, their lifestyle still left her panic-stricken, petrified her into non-action.

It wasn't exactly her fault. Kimber had been blindsided. Watching Anton kill the men with little effort had shaken her to her core. And yet, following the bloodshed, he had treated her with kid gloves, which Kimber rewarded him by fleeing into the night. Thank goodness for Diesel. Poor dog. Kimber had held onto him the entire night and into the dawning hours. Her dreams had been filled with bloodshed, fangs, and the daunting faces of the four men who had held her captive. She'd awake in a cold sweat, safe at home in her own bed, with Diesel still by her side. As the nightmares subsided, they were quickly replaced by visions of her and Anton naked and tangled in the sheets, his vampire features no longer hidden or frightening to her.

A car door slammed, bringing Kimber's focus to the present. *Anton?* She hurried to her large picture window facing the road. A teary-eyed Tena walked across her porch. Her doorbell rang, and even then it took a moment to get her leaden feet, from the disappointment of it not being Anton, moving to answer the call. Kimber opened the door and invited her in. With all the craziness her life had become, she had forgotten to check in on Tena.

From what Tamera had told her, Bobby had taken flight and abandoned those who had given him eternal life. Well, not exactly abandoned. He had given his word to one day return, once he had come to terms with what he had become. Kaleb had made him promise to check in once a week. To do otherwise, would be in violation of a direct order. Should that happen, he'd send Anton, Alexander, and Grigore after him. She couldn't help but wonder what the ex-preacher thought about being given immortality Sons' style, or how that might work out with his faith.

Kimber had taken a few weeks' leave from work to get her shit together. Lord, she had been self-centered. Not once had she considered what her friend might have been going through with Bobby's sudden decision to leave town.

"Please come in, Tena." Kimber held open the door for her. "I'd ask if everything was okay, but it obviously isn't."

Tena gave her a watery chuckle. "I just heard from Preacher."

Kimber's gaze widened, surprised the man had called. "Where did he say he's been?"

She couldn't imagine he had confided in Tena that he'd just been upgraded to vampire, and she wasn't about to supply that particular information.

"He said he left town, needed some time on his own to sort his life out."

Kimber couldn't imagine why he'd leave the MC he had been given carte blanche to. "Back to Santa Barbara?"

She shook her head. "I got the impression he might not return. He said he was done with the Devils and wasn't wearing colors."

"No colors?"

"Meaning he's done with the motorcycle clubs."

Kimber happened to be just as baffled. Tamera had said Bobby picked up and left following his change, but she hadn't said where to. Not to mention he had promised to return. Regardless, Kimber wasn't at liberty to say what she knew. "So he's not staying at the Sons' clubhouse?"

More tears fell. "From what he told me, he was only there for a little over a week. He packed up and headed out for the east coast ... on his own. Said he needed to reflect on the nightmare his life had become. When I asked him what he meant, he didn't elaborate. Told me I was better off not knowing."

"Woo hoo? Anyone home?" Chad's voice came through her screened door. "Tena told me she was headed out here. I hope you don't mind I extended myself an invite. You two can't think to be partying without me."

Kimber headed for the door and held it open. "We wouldn't think of it, handsome. Trouble is, there isn't anyone in the mood to party here."

Kimber beckoned for Tena and Chad to follow her into the kitchen. Might as well drown their sorrows in alcohol. She opened her wine cooler and pulled out a bottle of moscato. After pulling three stemmed glasses from the rack, Kimber poured them each half a glass.

Kimber toyed with the stem. "You really liked him, huh?"

"I'm being stupid." Tena picked up one of the glasses from the counter and headed for the breakfast nook in the corner of the kitchen. "I haven't known him very long, but there was just something about him."

Kimber and Chad followed, taking adjacent seats. "I don't suppose we can govern our hearts. If we could, I could stop thinking about Anton and move on."

Tena grabbed a tissue from the box on the table and blew her nose. "Aren't we just a couple of whiners."

Chad tsked. "I say we all stop being pissers and head for a nightclub."

"No," both Kimber and Tena said in unison.

"Oh, please." Chad waved his hand. "Party poopers. Well, then, should we drink to no more broken hearts?"

"Hear, hear." Kimber and Tena held up their glasses and clinked them against Chad's.

Tena quickly downed the sweet wine. Chad walked over to the counter and returned with the bottle, pouring her another glass. "Well, if we're to stay in, I say we might as well get drunk. *Men.* The bane of our existence."

Kimber passed him her glass for refill. "You having men troubles too, Chad?"

"Oh, honey, I'm always having men troubles. So what's got you all upset, Tena? What did Mr. Bear-alicious do?"

Tena shrugged, moisture gathering in her eyes. "I told myself I wouldn't do this. No man is worth it."

"Oh, honey, let me tell you. That bear of a man was worth it and then some. He was capital D-elicious—"

"He's leaving, Chad," she interrupted. "Said he was heading east."

"How far east?"

"I believe all the way to the coast." She blew her nose again. "It's not like I can drive there over the weekend to check on him. I fear he's never coming back."

"Maybe." Kimber patted Tena's hand. "How about some optimism. He did call you."

"He did, didn't he?"

"See, there is a bright side."

"The only bright side would be if he would've asked me to go with him." Tena plopped her chin onto her palm, her elbow braced on the table. "Instead, I'm left sitting here nursing my sorrows. I'm so pathetic."

"Honey, there is nothing wrong with giving your heart to a man." Chad poured her some more wine. "The sorrow is in him not taking it. We should drive across country and show him what he left behind. You're a prize. Any guy—"

"That's it!" Tena righted herself. "You're a genius, Chad. I'll go after him."

"I was speaking in jest, silly. You can't go traipsing halfway across the country after a man you barely know."

"I can, and I will." She nearly leaped from her seat. "Don't you see? It would be such a romantic gesture."

Kimber didn't know what to say, but following Bobby was probably not a good idea. To begin with, Tena had no idea what he had become. "I don't think…"

"He said good-bye, Tena," Chad chimed in at the same time. "I doubt showing up on his doorstep would make him think of roses and wine."

"Oh, come on. Where's your sense of adventure?" Tena swirled the wine in her glass, then drank what was left. "I say road trip. I have his number. I'll keep in touch with him along the way, tell him I just want to know that he's okay. Then when he finally stops, I'll get his address. Tell him I have a gift for him. Then I'll show up on his doorstep, wrapped in a big bow."

"Really, Tena?" Chad began before she cut him off once again.

"That's exactly what I'll do. It's not like once I'm there he'll throw me out, right?"

Kimber suppressed her groan, afraid that's exactly what Bobby just might do.

"You can't go alone," Chad said. "It wouldn't be safe."

"And what are you going to do, follow me?"

Chad groaned. "I'll no doubt regret this come morning. Hell, no. I'll drive the damn car."

Kimber watched the exchange, nibbling on her nail. This was not a good idea at all.

"Don't worry, Kimber. I'll keep her cute little ass out of trouble." Chad winked at her. "And you, missy, aren't about to change anything by sitting here wallowing in self-pity when your man is a hop, skip, and jump down the road. Stop worrying about all the crazy crap life throws you. You love that man. I can see it in the way you look at him."

When Kimber meant to argue, he held up a finger. "You can't deny what the heart wants. I know Mr. Tall, Dark and Dangerous is all crazy about you. Trust me, girlfriend, if nothing else, I'm an expert at reading men. Now, Tena and I are going to take our little butts right out that door and you're going to go after what you want. It's time you took charge and did something for yourself. Don't let your silly fears get in the way. Since Tena and I will be taking a leave of absence from work, you best call us with the juicy details."

Tena pushed Chad toward the door. Probably hoping to get Chad out of there before Kimber talked them out of their ridiculous notion to cross the country, looking for a man who no doubt didn't want to be found. Kimber couldn't be held responsible for what trouble those two might get into. Hell, she had her own life to sort out.

Just before they cleared the door, Chad looked back and said, "I'll take good care of Tena. You take care of you."

And she would. Starting with Anton.

Time to go after what her heart wanted. Kimber would figure the rest out later. So what if Anton was a vampire. It wasn't like he'd be biting her with his fangs ... right?

Then again, maybe she'd let him nibble just a little. Mind made up, Kimber took the stairs to her bedroom to pick out the perfect outfit. She had one seriously sexy vampire to seduce.

"So what's it going to be, Blondy? You coming back as club secretary?"

Kaleb had arrived at the farmhouse a short while ago and was just now getting to his reason for stopping by. Not that Anton didn't enjoy the club P's company. Hell no, he was damn glad to be back among the Sons of Sangue. He never wanted to leave behind his colors again. Getting the Devil tattoo inked over on his shoulder was definitely high up on the list of to dos. It was a constant reminder of the past he'd rather move forward from.

He ran his hand through his short hair. Going back to his natural dark blond was right up there too. Dying it was a pain in the ass. Not that he hadn't grown accustomed to his moniker Rogue. He was starting to prefer it over Blondy.

"If you don't mind, P, I think I'd like to keep the name Rogue."

Kaleb's eyes bored into him. "You want to give me one good reason why? It's bad enough half the fucking year I was left to believe you deserted us."

"The name is a reminder of the hell I went through, I'll give you that." Anton shrugged. "But just like scars, they become part of us. I'm not the same man I was a year ago. I left him behind, pining away for a woman that wasn't mine to begin with."

"And now?"

"I love another."

A line formed between Kaleb's brows. "You telling me you want to ask for a mate?"

Anton sat on the arm of his sectional and placed his hands on his knees. "I'm afraid I'm asking for an even bigger favor. I can't ask her to be my mate when she's just learned what I am, saw firsthand what I'm capable of."

"So what are you asking me for?"

"To allow her to know what I am." Anton sighed, his shoulders sagging beneath the weight of what felt like a two-ton bolder. "I don't want to hypnotize her into forgetting me. Please don't ask that of me."

"She could become a donor."

Anton's gaze jerked up. His eyes heated. "Hell no, Hawk. Kimber is no donor. Not now, not ever."

"What you're asking for has never been given, Rogue. Humans outside of donors aren't allowed to know we're vampires. Rules are in place to protect us. Why not take her as a mate?"

Anton rubbed his nape. He couldn't imagine asking her to become like him, not after all she had been through. *Oh, by the way, you're going to become a vampire.* He'd rather walk away and erase her memory of him. Kimber needed time to adjust to the lifestyle.

"She's not ready, Hawk. I need time to ease her into it."

"And you're sure she'll stay with you, that one day she'll be ready?"

"It's my hope, yes."

"Christ, Rogue. You're asking me to break our rules." Kaleb leaned back on the sofa and crossed his ankle over one knee. "If I table your request at the next church meeting, the outcome won't be in your favor. You have to know that."

Anton nodded. "Which is why I am asking you. And why I haven't answered your earlier question."

Kaleb chuckled. "Your answer hinges on my response to your request."

"It does."

"And if I say no."

"Then I'll hand back my vest, as much as it would pain me to do so."

He draped his left arm over the back of the sofa. "You love her that much?"

"I do." Anton leaned forward, clasping his hands between his knees. "I don't want to choose, Hawk. And after the last year I spent, I was hoping you could make a concession."

One of his brows crooked upward. "You realize that was Cara and Kane's party. Not mine."

"Getting rid of some of the Devils benefits all of the Sons."

"You going back to secretary?"

Anton held Kaleb's brown gaze. "If you say yes."

"What the hell." Kaleb chuckled. "Not like shit with the club ain't all messed up anyway. You have my blessing."

"Thank you, P." Anton stood and grabbed a couple of tumblers and a bottle of Gentleman Jack from the cupboard. "What's going on? I was hoping life would get back to normal. No such luck, huh?"

Kaleb took a glass and held it out so Anton could fill it. "Xander's lost his marbles, for one. Apparently, India's pregnant and he's agreed to see her through it … as a friend."

Anton chuckled. "Sure she doesn't want more?"

"There is no doubt in my eyes. She may be a donor to whomever needs her, but she never gives it up. Everyone knows she's been hung up on Xander for a while now."

"So who's the baby daddy?"

Kaleb shrugged. "Xander says she never told him. This ought to be interesting. My bet is on Xander not having a chance, baby or no. India's gorgeous. He spends that much time with her, there's no way he can remain unaffected. He should've told her he wasn't up for seeing her through delivering some other man's spawn. Then there's Preacher."

Anton had talked to Bobby before he left town. "He needs time, man. I'm sure the immortality he's been given is in direct opposition to his faith."

"You think he'll obey my directive while he's gone, that he'll be back one day?"

"I'll keep in touch. Make sure he's doing all right. He'll come around given time. I'll go see him personally if the need arises. He took Ivy with him so he'll have a donor. Is that everything?"

"I wish, bro." Kaleb shook his head. "I'm afraid Draven's gone missing."

"What the hell do you mean? We left the sheriff's office together."

"His bartender said he stopped by the Rave. Came in through the back door, stayed a short time, then left. Hasn't seen or heard from him since the day you two walked out of the S.O."

"You think the Devils?"

"Not many of them left, not after you took out four of them. The DEA took several others into custody. I wouldn't say it's out of the question, though. Let's hope it's them anyway and not the cartel."

"Fuck."

"Pretty much my feeling on the matter." Kaleb finished his whiskey and set the glass on the side table. He stood and headed for the door. Turning back, he said, "You take care of your shit and then get your ass back to the clubhouse next week, Rogue. Glad to have you back. And Rogue?"

"Yeah?"

"I didn't mean it when I wished you dead."

"Thanks, P."

Kaleb nodded, then shut the door, leaving Anton staring at the wall. What the hell had happened to Draven? Looks like they might have a manhunt on their hands. Anton stood, picked up Kaleb's glass, and headed for the kitchen. A knock sounded on his door. Setting the glasses and bottle of whiskey on the counter, Anton strode back into the living area, wondering what Kaleb might've forgotten.

When he opened the door, Kimber stood before him, dressed to take his breath away and hitting the mark, yet nervously wringing her hands. "Hi."

His tongue stuck to the roof of his mouth, making him incapable of speech. A pink halter dress hugged her chest, the neckline dipping well into her cleavage, and slipped softly over her hips, stopping just beneath the curve of her killer ass. A pair of strappy-style sandals wrapped her feet and ankles. Cute little pink-painted toe nails polished off the look. She teetered a bit on the five-inch heels, telling him she probably hadn't worn them much.

Anton smiled. Kimber had come with the intention of seducing him. Well hell, he wasn't about to turn away a gift. Grabbing her hand, he pulled her into the living room and shut the door behind her, firmly locking it. Her hands slipped up his T-shirt to his shoulder, no doubt to steady herself on those skyscraper heels she wore. Anton gripped her waist and pulled her forward.

Damn, he itched to taste her. His gums ached. He bit back the emergence of the vampire. Kimber wasn't ready yet. He'd need to ease her into it.

"Look, Kimber." He leaned his head against her forehead. "I'm so fucking sorry I kept everything from you. Most specifically what I become."

Her pink tongue wet her lips, causing his groin to tighten. "Can I ask how you did it? I'm curious."

Her warm chocolate gaze filled with nothing but curiosity. "We can hypnotize humans into forgetting what's necessary to keep our secret."

Her gaze studied his. "Will you hypnotize me again?"

"No."

The tiniest of smiles turned up her lips. "Good."

"Can you handle the truth?" He tipped her chin up with the pad of his thumb. "Desire makes me turn, for the vampire in me to come forth."

"I've spent two weeks thinking about what I saw. I have to be honest, Anton. It scared the living crap out of me. I'm a librarian. I live in a small town." Kimber paused, looking briefly toward the door. If she chose to bolt, he'd go after. Anton was done letting her run from him. Her warm gaze finally came back to his. "Two weeks of not knowing what to do. Could I handle all the violence that comes with you?"

"It's not always like that, *tesoro*."

"Maybe not. But you do drink blood to survive."

He nodded. "Human food does nothing for me. Without blood, I cannot survive."

Kimber searched his eyes, staring silently into his.

"What's it going to be, *tesoro*? Will there be an us?"

"The one thing I realized over the past two weeks is that I may not yet understand everything, but I don't want to live without you either. Vampire or not." One delicate brow rose. "Will you bite me?"

Anton ran a knuckle over her downy of her cheek. Damn, but he feared never being able to touch her again.

Anton couldn't help but smile. "Only if you want me to, *tesoro*."

"Will it hurt?" She drew her lower lip between her teeth.

"At first." Anton ran his fingers down her spine, causing her to shiver. "But I can promise, it will give you the best orgasm of your life."

His gaze was drawn to the quickening pulse at the base of her throat. "How about you let me be the judge of that?"

Kimber ran her palms down his shirt to the hem, shoving the material up his chest. He assisted her in yanking it over his head. Smoothing her hands across his flesh, she stopped at the waistband of his jeans.

"You have far too many clothes on, Anton."

Damn, if he didn't like this saucy side to her. "I'd say the same to you, but I'm kind of digging this outfit."

"You like?"

"Like? I fucking love it. Although, at the moment, how about you lose the dress and keep those killer heels on?"

Kimber smiled, pushed away from him, and unhooked the halter at her neck, letting the silky fabric fall to pool at her waist.

*Damn!*

His fangs punched through his gums and his dick hardened instantly. No more hiding. He had become a full-fledged vampire right before her eyes. To her credit, Kimber gave his face only a cursory glance, showing no fear. His black gaze watched as she shoved the soft material down her hips to collect at her feet.

*Fuck!*

She wore no undergarments. Anton was struck dumb and motionless at her perfection. If he moved, there wouldn't be any foreplay involved. He wanted to fuck her with the force of a hurricane.

Placing her fingers into the waistband of his jeans, she pulled him forward and released the button. She gripped the zipper pull and slid it down over his erection. His cock throbbed and his balls tightened. Fuck, but he wanted to slide into her heat. No one completed him as she did.

Kimber glanced back up, her gaze going to his lips. She ran her fingertip over the point of one of his fangs. "How about we test out your theory?"

"You want me to bite you?"

Instead of answering, she tilted her head to the side and pushed her thick mane over her shoulder. He could scarcely breath, let alone move, for fear he'd wake up from his dream. Anton scented her sweet blood, heard it pulse through her veins as if it pumped through his own heart.

"One day, I want you to be my mate, *tesoro*. When you're ready, of course. Do you think you can make the change and stay with me forever?"

She smiled, her eyes sparkling with mischief. "Depends."

"On?"

"Whether you can deliver on your early promise."

Anton laughed, knowing he had fallen hard, head over heels in love. "Oh, I plan to. You love me?"

He saw the answer swimming in her eyes long before her words answered him. "All of you."

"Then I have a challenge for you."

One delicate brow rose. "Oh?"

"Let's see if you can manage to stand on those heels when you come."

His fangs pierced the tender flesh of her neck with a soft pop. No blood ever tasted so delicious as the warm fluid passing over his tongue, filling him and making him whole. He savored her sweetness and gathered her close. It didn't take but thirty seconds before he had to wrap his forearm about her waist to steady her on those five-inch, fuck-me heels as he made good on his promise.

## ABOUT THE AUTHOR

A daydreamer at heart, Patricia A. Rasey, resides in her native town in Northwest Ohio with her husband, Mark, and her two lovable Cavalier King Charles Spaniels, Todd and Buckeye. A graduate of Long Ridge Writer's School, Patricia has seen publication of some her short stories in magazines as well as several of her novels.

When not behind her computer, you can find Patricia working, reading, watching movies or MMA. She also enjoys spending her free time at the river camping and boating with her husband and two sons. Ms. Rasey is currently a third degree Black Belt in American Freestyle Karate.

Printed in Great Britain
by Amazon